Veronica Henry has worked as a scriptwriter for *The Archers*, *Heartbeat* and *Holby City* amongst many others. Veronica lives with her husband and three sons in North Devon. Visit her website at www.veronicahenry.co.uk or follow her on Twitter @veronica_henry

By Veronica Henry

Wild Oats
An Eligible Bachelor
Love on the Rocks
Marriage and Other Games
The Beach Hut
The Birthday Party
The Long Weekend

THE HONEYCOTE NOVELS
Honeycote
Making Hay
Just a Family Affair

2515

P.

Please return or renew this item by its due date to
avoid fines. You can renew items on loan
by phone or internet:

023 9281 9311

www.portsmouth.gov.uk

Portsmouth
CITY COUNCIL
Library Service

An Orion paperback

First published in Great Britain in 2010
by Orion Books Ltd
Orion House, 5 Upper St Martin's Lane,
London WC2H 9EA

An Hachette UK company

A CIP catalogue record for this book is available
from the British Library.

Typeset at The Spartan Press Ltd,
Lymington, Hants

Printed and bound in Great Britain by
Clays Ltd, St Ives plc

The Orion Publishing Group's policy is to use papers that
are natural, renewable and recyclable products and
made from wood grown in sustainable forests. The logging
and manufacturing processes are expected to conform to
the environmental regulations of the country of origin.

www.orionbooks.co.uk

To my beach boys

FOR SALE

A rare opportunity to purchase a beach hut on the spectacular Everdene Sands, North Devon.

'The Shack' has been in the same family for fifty years, and was the first to be built on this renowned stretch of golden coastline.

'The Shack' benefits from a rare licence to be occupied ten months of the year, as well as lighting, electricity and running water.

20′ × 20′, it has four bunks, a small kitchen and spacious living area, veranda with stunning views

Offers invited

Contact the owner, Mrs Jane Milton,
or the estate office

1

THE SHACK

A light breeze ruffled the steel-blue ocean. The sun, growing ever bolder as the season progressed, was determined not to be intimidated by the clouds that had hovered earlier. They had rather reluctantly drifted away an hour ago, threatening to be back as they left, like playground bullies, but in the meantime the beach was bathed in light and warmth. The chill gradually came off the sands. Lundy Island sat squat and determined on the horizon, looking as if it might cast off any moment and float its way across the Atlantic.

Roy Mason emerged from his shed at the head of the beach, hands curled round the second mug of tea of the day. The first had been just before he left his tiny stone cottage high up in one of the winding streets that made up the village of Everdene. If he could have had a pound for every time someone stuck a note through his door asking if he wanted to sell, he would have been able to afford one of the new-build split-level homes that were being built on the top road. The developer's sign proudly boasted that all of phase one had been sold. There might be a housing slump in the rest of the country, but not here. Not when the air smelled sweeter than any fabric conditioner, the surrounding hills were soft and rolling and studded with the fluffiest white sheep, and the view took your breath away. Roy had never tired of it, in all his years. Not that he'd ever seen much else. His mug, by dint of a large red heart, might proclaim that he loved New York, but he'd never been, and nor did he want to go. His daughter had brought it back when she'd been Christmas shopping. Roy didn't begrudge her the experience, but he didn't want to share it.

He drained the last of the sugary tea, put down the mug and collected up his tools. Proper tools, with wooden handles that had moulded themselves to fit his hands over the years, smooth and solid beneath his fingers, not like the lightweight plastic efforts they sold now that snapped and bent and buckled as soon as you put them to task. It was all about cost-cutting these days. Shaving down the margins. There was no pride.

To Roy's mind, there was no point in doing something unless you gave it your best. He never cut corners. He did things properly, the old-fashioned way. Someone had sent a flyer round once, undercutting his prices, and a few of the owners had been tempted. The lad might have been cut-rate, but he was also cack-handed and ham-fisted. Roy had watched him trying to hang a new door. It was comical. He felt sorry for him, he was only trying to make a living, but he hadn't a bloody clue. In the end, he'd given up, gone off up country, and Roy had picked up with the old customers where he'd left off, no hard feelings, nothing said. He wasn't one to bear a grudge.

He'd been the unofficial caretaker for the beach huts

4

since they first went up. His father had built them for the estate, and Roy had been his gofer, the fetcher and carrier. Twelve to start with, but they had gone like hot cakes, and gradually the line grew until it had doubled, then tripled, until it reached as far as the line of rocks that created a natural stopping point. And now he was kept on by most of the owners, to do maintenance and repairs, to check for damage and break-ins over the winter.

Some owners were tight and only paid for their hut to be repainted once every three or four years. A false economy. The wind and rain that swept through over the winter, sand-blasting the wooden slats, was unforgiving; the wood needed protection. Some owners kept their huts plain; others saw it as an excuse to express their personality and chose garish colours that somehow worked in the seaside setting, a fairground riot of reds and greens and pinks and oranges. Some of them had their own names: 'Oysters'; 'Atlantic View'; 'Valhalla'. Nothing sparklingly original, but it added to the sense that this was a community, that each hut was a home from home.

Roy loved the lack of logic, the crazy mismatched line that marched down the length of the beach. He knew each one of them, their idiosyncrasies, their histories, who had owned them over the years. Each time one of them was sold, he was unsurprised by the astronomical prices they fetched. It was the same all over the country, if you were to believe the Sunday supplements, and these huts were a cut above the rest, being big enough to sleep in if you didn't mind bunk-beds and a howling wind. They were still pretty basic, but there was electricity and running water, and at night the fronts twinkled with fairy lights. Despite the lack of luxury, people still flocked to buy them. There was a waiting list in the estate office. All Roy hoped when a hut changed hands was that the new incumbents would treat their hut with respect and obey the unwritten rules of the beach.

He had applied the last lick of paint, oiled the last lock, replaced the last piece of flapping roof felt. The huts were pristine, ready for the season to begin. Soon the beach would be alive with the special sounds of summer. The shouts and squeals of children frolicking in the surf. The thwack of tennis balls against cricket bats. The smell of burning charcoal and roasting meat. The thrum of the coastguard's helicopter as it passed by on its patrol, swooping low over the sands and then shooting up into the sky, off to the next cove.

He spent the morning fixing a new price list to the side of his shed. Roy still worked for the estate as well, maintaining the huts they owned and organising their letting, and renting out windbreaks and deckchairs. At night, he took people out fishing for sea bass. It satisfied the inner Hemingway in them, mostly the men. There was something about fishing that bonded men. Women never took to it in the same way – they were always slightly mystified by the attraction, if they ever ventured out. He could see they were bored. They would much rather buy their bass from the converted ice-cream van that drove along the coast road every evening, selling lobster and crab.

His mobile rang in the pocket of his shorts. Another reason for the popularity of this beach – a good phone signal for all those BlackBerry-toting career people who needed to keep in touch with the office. Roy didn't see the point. It wasn't a holiday, if your employers could keep tabs on you, or if you could keep tabs on yours. But that seemed to be the way of the world.

It was Jane Milton. Her warm voice danced down the line and his stomach gave a little squeeze of pleasure. He liked Jane. She always paid her bill on time, never expected things to be done yesterday. She spoke to him as an equal, not like some of the buggers.

'Roy. It's Jane. I'm in London with a friend at the moment – how's the weather down there?'

'Set fair for the week, I should say.' He had no idea if it was. The weather here had a mind of its own. But that was what she wanted to hear, so that was what he told her.

'Marvellous. I'll be back down this afternoon. The rabble won't be arriving until the weekend, so I'll get a couple of days' peace and quiet. Many people down yet?'

'Just the regulars.'

He could see a few hardy surfers in the water, which still had an icy chill. It took till September to warm up.

'Good.'

He heard a slight tension in her voice.

'Everything all right?'

She sighed.

'This is going to be the last summer, Roy. I've hung on as long as I can, given the circumstances, but I'm going to have to sell.'

His eyes picked out the Milton hut. A tasteful light blue, with a veranda. He didn't reply for a moment, as was his way. Roy was thoughtful, never felt the need to respond immediately. He liked to take his time. He

7

remembered her telling him she hadn't got a bean to live on. That she was selling her house. *Downsizing*, she'd called it, but she pronounced the word with as much distaste as if she was saying *dogging*. If she was selling the hut too, then things must be really bad.

'I'm sorry to hear that.' Roy spoke eventually. 'You'll have no shortage of buyers, if that's any consolation. I get people asking me all the time if there's any for sale.'

'Well, I'm not going to sell to any old person. And definitely not that dreadful man who badgers me every summer. He can go to the bottom of the list.'

Roy chuckled. He knew the bloke. The one who phoned him up imperiously asking him to fill the fridge with stuff from Tesco, expected him to pump up his children's inflatable dinghies. He was a caretaker, not a bloody butler. He didn't mind doing that sort of stuff for anyone else, mind. It was just the way the bloke *asked*. Of course he would want the Miltons' hut. He was an Alpha male, he only wanted the best.

'I'll open the hut up for you. Give it an airing.'

'See you later, for a cup of tea.'

Jane was resolutely cheerful. She had only wavered for a moment. He had heard the catch in her voice, the hint of anger at having been left in such a terrible financial mess when her husband had keeled over on the platform at Paddington. The hut had been hers, left to her by her mother. Graham Milton hadn't been able to take *that* with him when he shuffled off this mortal coil.

Roy had been disgusted when Jane told him the details. It was a disgrace, to leave your wife in poverty like that. There had been no pensions, no life insurance, no cash, and a huge mortgage on their Georgian rectory to pay off and no endowment to cover it. Graham Milton might have been a financial advisor, but he obviously didn't heed his own advice. He probably thought he was being clever, cashing in all their assets, making investments that he thought were going to make him rich quick. Only the gamble had backfired. Instead of coming clean, he had desperately tried to plug the gaps, but got himself deeper and deeper into debt. It was the stress of keeping it all quiet that had killed him, everyone agreed. And poor Jane, totally oblivious until the solicitor and the accountant had broken the news to her, widowed and penniless overnight.

For all Graham Milton's airs and graces – and he'd had a few, not like his wife – he wasn't a gentleman, not in Roy's book.

He hung up. The call had unsettled him. He wasn't usually sentimental, but Jane Milton selling up was like the end of an era. She had the plum hut, the best pitch at the top of the beach, the first one to be built. People would be falling over themselves to buy that one. He could imagine the article in the *Telegraph* already: *on the market for the first time in fifty years* . . .

He remembered clearly the day she'd arrived. She'd been Jane Lowe then, of course. She'd fluttered over the beach in her polka-dot dress, her legs long and bare, her brother and sister scampering behind. He knew as soon as he set eyes on her that a girl like her would never take a boy like him seriously. He'd left school at fourteen, didn't play tennis, his parents didn't even own their own house, let alone have money left over to buy a beach hut.

Roy told himself to not even try. He didn't want to set

9

himself up for humiliation. She was bound to have a boyfriend already, called Gregory, or Martin, who would turn up in a Triumph Spitfire and cricket flannels to whisk her off for gin and tonics at the golf club. All Roy had was a bike. He could hardly stick her on the crossbar and pedal her down to the local pub.

There had been one summer, the summer they were both seventeen, when they'd started to get quite close. He'd been selling ice creams, and she used to come and talk to him in the kiosk, because he had a wireless. They'd listen to the latest hits, discussing their merits, and sometimes she would dance, and he'd long to have the nerve to dance along with her, but he was far too self-conscious. Not like Jane, who didn't care what anyone thought, swaying and twirling and clicking her fingers. Once, she'd grabbed his hand and tried to make him dance too, and he thought he might die, of a combination of embarrassment and the thrill of her touching him.

'Loosen up, Roy,' she laughed at him. 'Dancing's good for you. It's wonderful!'

Thank God another customer had arrived at that moment, and he tore himself away and busied himself serving a 99, concentrating as the stream of sweet ice cream oozed its way into the cone until he cut it off with a practised flick of the wrist. And then Jane's mother had waved from the hut, indicating lunch was ready, and Jane had skittered off, dancing her way across the sands.

His chance had gone.

And then she'd got that job, disappearing up to the house on the cliff. After that, he'd never really seen her, except for that one night, the night he couldn't really think about even now without a huge twinge of regret, an overwhelming longing for what might have been, even though it could never have been. Not in a million years. And then she was gone, up to London, until years later she came back as Mrs Milton, by which time it was far, far too late, of course, because by then he was married to Marie.

Roy sighed. Even now, if he narrowed his eyes a little bit, to block out the telephone mast on the hill in the distance, and pretended it was the Beatles on the radio instead of Take That, nothing much had changed. The horizon never altered, the sea was the same, he could still be there . . .

The Lowe children were sick with excitement when their father bought the first hut on Everdene beach. They had been watching them go up for the past six months, whenever their parents brought them to the beach at the weekends or in the holidays. When their father had presented them with a big key, with a brown label attached emblazoned with the number one, they had been puzzled. Then Robert had screamed, 'A hut! He's bought a hut!' and they had raced over the sand to be the first, all arriving at once, crowding round the door.

Inside it was as snug and well equipped as a gypsy caravan. Two sets of bunk beds – Robert and Elsie would have to go toe-to-toe, because there were five of them altogether, with Mum and Dad and Jane having one each. Dear little cupboards and a Calor gas stove. Deck-chairs were neatly stacked in one corner. There was a shelf, with hooks to hang cups, and rails to hang wet towels. A perfect little home from home. They were to stay there all summer, with their father travelling down at weekends.

It wasn't long before they couldn't remember life without it. The water was their natural habitat. They spent most of the spring, all of the summer and some of the autumn diving in and out of the waves, scrambling over the rocks and bounding over the dunes, armed with fishing nets, buckets, spades, sandwiches. Now they would have somewhere to store all their treasures, somewhere to huddle if it rained, somewhere to dry themselves off and hang their wet towels. And their mother could sit inside all day, doing whatever it was she did – fussing, organising, cooking, writing letters.

Three years on, however, and the eldest Lowe, Jane, was not so enamoured. Where once she would have pounded along the beach, her pale yellow hair streaming behind her, now she was bored absolutely rigid. A summer spent on the beach with her tiresome younger siblings? She might as well be dead. She sat in one of the striped deckchairs, flicking idly through magazines, knowing full well that if she actually got up and joined in she would feel far, far better, but something inside refused to let her and so she remained stationary, day after day, with the stubbornness of an adolescent.

She could still be in London, having fun. Maybe most people had gone home for the summer vac, but not all. It wouldn't be bloody dead, like this place. She thought longingly of the smoky little clubs and cosy pubs where she'd been spending her evenings. Of course, she wasn't supposed to leave the college at night, but she and Sandra had found a way of getting out and getting back in again without being noticed. And it wasn't why her parents were forking out all that money. They wanted her to come out with tip-top typing and shorthand skills so she could have a career. How very enlightened of them. Jane didn't want a career. She wanted a good time.

Typically, she had spent seven months at Miss Grimshire's before she had discovered the real delights of London nightlife. And the final two months, before she left with her certificate (merit and 140 words per minute, despite burning the candle at both ends), had passed in a flash and suddenly she was back in Everdene, leaving her new self behind, a party-loving creature who wasn't yet fully formed. She wanted bright lights and action and clothes and music and laughter . . .

Finding herself in this total backwater with no hope of any social life whatsoever had plunged her into gloom. Well, there was a social life, but it involved rounders on the beach or burnt sausages – not drinking brandy and ginger in a tiny club with music throbbing through your body.

And so she was sulking. Her mother was not best pleased. Her mother was incensed. She wouldn't stop banging on about her daughter's new-found lassitude. Prue Lowe didn't believe in sulking, or lolling, or dozing, or festering – all the things Jane felt inclined to do. Prue was an up-and-at-it sort of person, a doer, an organiser, and she never knew when to leave well alone.

'You can't just sit in that deckchair moping all holidays,' she chided her eldest daughter. 'Go and get some exercise. Have a walk along the beach.'

Jane just rolled her eyes and went back to her magazine. She'd read it four times already, but the chances of getting anything up to date in the general shop in

Everdene were pretty remote. She was all right if she wanted knitting patterns and foolproof recipes for a sausage plait, but not if she wanted to know what she should be wearing this autumn.

Not that she had any money to buy the clothes she salivated over.

The closest she got to having fun was sitting with Roy Mason in the kiosk where he sold ice cream, listening to the radio. She made him turn it up when one of her favourites came on. She tried to get him to dance, but he jumped away from her as if he'd been branded whenever she touched him. Boys in London didn't jump away from her, far from it. Maybe she just wasn't Roy's type? He seemed very keen on Marie, whose mother ran the café at the end of the promenade. Marie worked in there too, and sometimes she came down to the beach with a bacon sandwich for Roy, and Jane made herself scarce. Two's company, after all.

The third time Marie had found Jane with Roy, she cornered Jane in the post office.

'You keep away from him,' she warned, an accusatory finger pointing in Jane's face.

'Hey,' replied Jane, holding up her hands to indicate her innocence. 'We've only been talking.'

Marie shot her a look of pure venom. Jane kept away from Roy after that, not because she was afraid of Marie, but because she didn't want to cause trouble for Roy. He was nice. He was far too good-looking for Marie, with his dark hair and brown skin and kind eyes. He didn't know he was good-looking. You could tell that by the way he carried himself. Not cocky and arrogant like some of the boys she'd met, who thought they were God's gift when they weren't, far from it. Maybe the city did that to you, made you more confident than you should be. It had certainly made her more confident.

As the days dragged on, Jane could tell her mother was running out of patience. Prue wasn't tolerant of people who didn't fit into her idea of how things should be. Jane was spoiling her fantasy of a happy seaside family holiday. She clearly expected her daughter to be gung-ho, and take part in the same activities as her younger brother and sister. If Prue had her way Jane would be scrambling over the rocks in her Start-rite sandals, squealing every time she spotted a crab, tucking with gusto into the selection of sandwiches Prue provided for lunch – fish-paste, egg or Marmite.

Jane certainly didn't begrudge her siblings the experience, but it didn't mean she wanted to take part. And it wasn't as if she wanted to sit here, full of torpor, her very being crying out for something, *anything* to happen, though she didn't know quite what. It was the slowest agony, and she wasn't entirely sure of the cure, but she was pretty sure she wasn't going to find it on Everdene beach. She couldn't explain it to her mother, who obviously expected her to stay the same age for ever. Carefree, childlike, innocent.

It was ironic, therefore, that Prue organised the very thing that made sure Jane would never be innocent again.

It was a Thursday morning, and by eleven o'clock the sun was burning bright in the sky. Jane was uncomfortably hot, and was taking refuge in the cool shade of the hut. She was contemplating walking into the village and calling Sandra from the telephone box, to find out if she was having as dull and miserable a time as she was. Maybe she could ask her to come and stay? They wouldn't be able to get up to much, but at least they could gossip and giggle together. Debate the merits of the boys they had met. She'd ask her mother if she could invite her – Sandra could come down by train, Daddy wouldn't mind motoring over to the station to collect her . . .

'Darling!'

Jane started, her eyes flying open. She'd been on the verge of drifting off. Her mother was standing over her.

'You will not believe what I've arranged!'

She had a smile on her face Jane knew of old. A mixture of self-satisfaction and determination, which meant Prue was pleased with whatever she had done, and whoever she had done it on behalf of had jolly well better be pleased as well. Jane's heart sank. If it was golf lessons, she would absolutely refuse. Her mother had been muttering about organising something for her at the club. Jane thought she would rather die.

'I've got you a job.'

Jane stared at her. This wasn't what she'd expected.

'There was a card pinned up in the post office. *Competent typist wanted.*'

Jane breathed out slowly. It could have been worse. Much, much worse.

Her mother was still looking excited. There must be more. She leaned forward.

'Terence Shaw,' she pronounced.

Jane gazed at her, quite blank.

'Terence Shaw!' repeated her mother. 'The novelist!'

Jane frowned and shook her head.

'I've never heard of him.'

Prue gave a little tut of impatience and Jane felt aggrieved. Her mother was no great intellectual – Jane couldn't remember the last time she'd seen her reading a book – so why the scorn?

'You must have. He's . . . infamous. Sells bucket-loads of books, apparently. Rich as Croesus. Which is why he can afford one of those . . .'

Prue waved her hand vaguely towards the houses further down the beach, on the top of the cliff. There were only half a dozen of them, built in the nineteen thirties, sprawling Art Deco houses with flat roofs and curved fronts, set in their own grounds. They each had a *Great Gatsby* smugness, with their spectacular views and private tennis courts.

'He wants someone to type his latest novel. Six hours a day.' Prue paused dramatically before divulging the next nugget of information. 'Six pounds a week!'

Jane sat up. Now she was definitely interested! Six pounds a week? Her mind raced back to the magazines she'd been perusing – what would she be able to afford if she was earning that kind of money?

'He'd like you to start this afternoon. Two o'clock.' Her mother was ushering her up out of her seat. 'Come on, come on – you need to get yourself tidied up. You can't start a job looking like that, with your hair all over the place.'

'But he hasn't even met me yet,' Jane protested, getting up nevertheless. 'How does he know he wants me?'

'Darling, I told him you'd been trained by Miss Grimshire. And that you'd got a distinction—'

'Merit. I only got a merit,' Jane corrected her. Her mother was prone to exaggeration.

Prue flapped away her objection.

'He's hardly going to be spoilt for choice for typists down here. He seemed quite happy. In fact, he said as long as you were quiet and kept yourself to yourself . . .'

Jane was already at the sink, washing the dust and sand from her hands and face, doing rapid calculations. By the end of the summer she should have over thirty pounds left to take up to London when she went to look for a job. There certainly wasn't going to be anything to spend it on down here. Thirty pounds! What heaven, what bliss!

Half an hour later, with her mother's grudging approval as to her appearance, she walked halfway down the beach, and then took the steep path up through the dunes that led to the back road which served the houses where Mr Shaw lived. The marram grass slapped at her legs as she walked, and the sand insinuated its way into her sandals. She took them off and emptied them out before she walked up the drive. She wondered what he would be like to work for. She imagined a little old man with spectacles and a woolly jumper, a little bit absent-minded, but essentially quite kind. She would have to bring him tea, which he would forget to drink. And eventually she would tidy his office for him, thereby transforming his life, and he would be awfully grateful. Miss Grimshire talked a lot about how to manage your employer. It was best if you went about organising them without them noticing you were doing it. An efficient secretary could make her own and her boss's life so much easier, if she knew the little tricks.

She had arrived at the front door. There wasn't a bell that she could see, so she rapped her knuckles as hard as she could on the wood. There was no answer, so she tried again.

And again.

Jane reckoned that after three knocks either there was nobody in or the person inside didn't want to answer, and so she turned to go, relieved but at the same time not entirely thrilled at the prospect of going to sit on the beach again for another day. At least a tedious typing job would have given her money—

The door was jerked open.

'What?' came a bark.

Jane turned to see a wild-haired, bare torso-ed man. He was over six foot and as brown as a berry, wearing a pair of baggy khaki shorts, nothing on his feet. He had dark curls that were swept back off his face, and eyes that looked as if they had been burnt into his face with a branding iron – dark, deep-set.

He didn't look pleased to see her. She felt tempted just to run and avoid any sort of confrontation, but he could probably catch up with her in two strides.

'Hello,' said Jane brightly. 'I'm Jane Lowe.'

He looked at her with annoyance.

'Who?'

'Your typist?' She corrected herself. 'The typist.' She wasn't his typist, exclusively. 'My mother spoke to you.'

'Oh yes.' He still looked annoyed, but he stood to one side to let her in.

'Were you not expecting me?'

He gave a small sigh of annoyance and made a dismissive gesture with his hand.

'I suppose so.'

Jane felt as if she was a huge inconvenience, like someone who had come to read the meter. She followed him into the house, through a cool dark hallway and into the living room.

She had seen the house so often from the outside. They walked past it whenever they went to the best rock pools at the far end of the beach – it loomed rather menacingly over the sands, the signs at the bottom of the garden warning 'Private Property – Keep Out' in red letters. It was strange, now being inside. The living room was vast, the floor made from polished wood, and the entire wall overlooking the sea was made of windows. She was used to seeing the sea from the hut, of course, but from here the view seemed even more spectacular, winking and glittering for miles.

'Whatever you do, please don't say what a wonderful view,' he warned her. 'It's been said once or twice before.'

'I wasn't going to,' she retorted. 'I see it every day. I'm sick of the sight of it, if you must know.'

He looked at her, and she thought she detected the hint of a smile on his rather cruel lips.

There was a large desk in front of the windows, smothered in paper and books. And empty mugs and glasses, as well as a bottle of brandy. An ashtray overflowed with cigarettes, some half-smoked, perched on an open dictionary. Jane itched to whisk the mess away and make everything tidy, but somehow she didn't think Mr Shaw would take to interference kindly, just yet. Miss Grimshire had explained that it often took time to lick an employer into shape. She suspected Mr Shaw would take longer than most.

'I was going to wait till I went back to London to have it typed up,' Mr Shaw was explaining, 'but my editor wants the manuscript sooner than I thought. Are you fast?'

Jane nodded.

'And accurate?'

Again, she nodded.

'Good.' He scooped up a bundle of papers. 'Follow me.'

She followed him obediently out of the room, disappointed that she wouldn't be working in there. Instead, he led her up the staircase and down a corridor into what had been a bedroom but was now a study. Apart from one small window that looked over the front of the house, the walls were lined with more books than Jane had ever seen outside a library. There was a small table with a typewriter and a stack of fresh paper.

'I've put you here because I can't stand any noise. Keep the door shut. If you want a drink or something to eat, just help yourself from the kitchen, but don't bother me.'

He dropped the papers on the desk and gave her a nod.

'Ten till four, I told your mother. I can't have anyone in the house for longer than that. The important thing is not to interrupt me. On pain of death.'

He looked at her, his eyes boring into her. She managed a smile.

'Of course not.'

He gave a curt nod and left the room.

Jane raised her eyebrows. He certainly wasn't what she had expected. Much, much younger than the crusty old Mr Shaw she had imagined, probably in his mid-thirties, she thought. And incredibly rude. In fact, she suspected he might have been a tiny bit drunk – she thought she had caught the smell of brandy as he left. Well, she would certainly do her best to keep out of his way. She didn't need to be spoken to like that by anyone.

She sat down tentatively at her new desk. It wobbled slightly. She looked at the pages of manuscript he had given her. Black slanted writing swirled over the paper in an indecipherable tangle, interspersed with angry crossings-out and arrows and asterisks.

Halesowen, she read, *was the sort of town that made you want to slit your wrists. Unless you had the misfortune to be born there, in which case you didn't know any better. But if by some cruel twist of fate you ended up there, having enjoyed the pleasure of some other part of our sceptr'd isle, eventually you would start to look longingly at the blue road map on the inside of your arm, wondering just how much it was going to hurt.*

On a stifling summer's evening, Anita Palmer was asking herself just that.

Jane made a face. Where on earth was Halesowen, she wondered? And was that where he was from? He had a slight accent, a twang she couldn't place, but then Jane wasn't strong on accents – most of the people she came into contact with spoke just as she did, unless they were staff.

She shrugged, and put a piece of paper into the typewriter, turned it until it was exactly so, then carefully began to type.

An hour later she felt filled with frustration and a slight sense of panic. His hieroglyphics were so hard to decipher, it had taken her this long to type a single page, and even then by the time she had reached the end she realised she had left out a line. She gave a little cry of annoyance and crumpled the paper in her hand, then inserted a fresh piece, starting again at the beginning. She felt slightly panicky. At this rate she would never get to the end.

Before she knew it, it was four o'clock. She had managed to produce three pages of typing. She wasn't sure what to do, whether to leave without saying goodbye, or to tell him she was going.

In the end, she decided she would show him what she had done. When she walked into the living room, he was leaning back in his chair, his hands hooked behind his head, staring out of the window. He turned to her, and although he didn't smile, he didn't snarl either as she proffered her efforts of the afternoon.

'Will you want to check it?' she asked.

He took it without looking and put it down on his desk.

'I'll read over everything you've done each night. If there's any corrections you can do them first thing, before you carry on. That's how I used to do it with the previous typist.'

The Previous Typist? Didn't the poor girl have a name?

'Fine,' said Jane. 'I expect I'll get faster. It takes a bit of getting used to, your writing.'

He gave a little nod, as if in agreement, then turned

away from her, back to his work. She left the room. As soon as she got out of the front door, she breathed a sigh of relief. She felt as if she had been holding her breath all afternoon.

Just think about the money, she told herself. Just think about all the dresses you can buy. And she kicked her shoes off and ran, all the way down the path and down the dunes, getting faster and faster until she reached the beach.

The next day she had a good look around the room she was working in before she started.

There were rows and rows of his books. Hardbacks, in pale colours. Some in English – she counted eight different titles. And all the others in every other language you could think of. Some she could discern – French, Italian, German – but some she couldn't, though she suspected some were Scandinavian, and some in Chinese and Japanese. She leafed through them in wonder, thinking how fantastic it must be for someone in another country to want to read what you had written. She read the reviews on the flyleaves. He was certainly highly thought of, if they were to be believed.

She hadn't really taken in what she was typing the day before, but he had left her work on the table, with just a couple of alterations, and she read it through again. This time she took in the narrative. It seemed to be about a middle-aged woman, the Anita Palmer of the first paragraph, a well-to-do but bored housewife to whom nothing much seemed to happen. She wondered how on earth he knew so much about middle-aged women – the details he had included seemed accurate, what she was wearing, what she was cooking. And he seemed to understand what was going on in her head. The fact that she was bored. Screamingly bored. And that she was irritated by her husband. Jane had seen her own mother react in the same way to her father.

As she began typing the next chapter, the point of view changed to a young lad who worked in Mr Palmer's factory. Entirely different to the woman, but they both shared a certain disillusion with life. Boredom. They both seemed to be asking themselves the question, 'Is this it?'

His language was spare, the dialogue sparse, but somehow the words seemed to draw a very vivid picture of the world he was creating. She found herself totally drawn in, wondering about the fates of the characters. Her fingers moved faster and faster over the typewriter as she raced to the next chapter.

It wasn't what she expected him to write at all. She'd expected something manly and thriller-ish, involving espionage and murder and the Iron Curtain, something she wouldn't understand. Certainly not something that she would be interested in. And not something so . . . emotional. The characters were both so unhappy; they both felt so trapped. She found herself longing to know what happened next.

From Terence Shaw she heard nothing.

By one o'clock she was starving. She crept into the kitchen and picked a dusty glass off a shelf, then ran the tap. It came out more forcefully than she expected, spattering back up at her and drenching her blouse. She gave a cry of annoyance and stepped back, then stepped forward again to try and turn off the tap.

Terence Shaw was standing behind her.

'I suppose you're hungry.'

He said it as if it was a huge liberty, to dare to need food.

Jane bit her lip.

He strode over to a small fridge, yanked the door open and pulled out a plate. On it was the remains of a large pork pie. He rummaged about and produced a handful of tomatoes.

'Come on, then,' he said to her, and she followed him obediently, through the palatial living room and out of the French windows onto the terrace outside. There were a couple of old chairs and a rickety table. He put the plate down and went back inside, returning with a bottle of wine and two glasses.

'I don't think I should . . .'

'Why not?'

'I won't be able to concentrate.'

'Rubbish. A good Chablis focuses the mind wonderfully.'

He poured a substantial amount of straw-coloured liquid into a glass and pushed it towards her. Jane sipped it tentatively; Terence Shaw took a slug of his and smacked his lips in satisfaction.

'Delicious.'

'Mmm.' She didn't like to say that to her mind it was sour. She liked her drinks as sweet as possible.

'So. Tell me about Jane.'

He stuck his long legs out, picked up a hunk of pork pie, and stared at her.

'Um. There's not much to say, really. I've . . . just left secretarial school. In London.'

'So, you're hoping to get a job working for a company

26

director, share a flat with some nice "gels" in Kensington, then meet the man of your dreams and get married?'

He was mocking her. She supposed his prediction wasn't so very far away from what would probably happen, but did he have to sneer? But try as she might, she couldn't think of a retort. And the really infuriating thing was, now he had so ably predicted her future, it sounded so dreary, so unexciting. For an awful moment, she thought she was going to cry. Not because he had been cruel, but because it seemed unfair that she was so *obvious*.

She screwed up her eyes in the bright sun and looked at the sea while she considered her reply. She couldn't see the huts, they were too far down the beach, tucked under the dunes out of sight, but she imagined her family sitting having egg sandwiches, and for a minute she wished she was with them. Feeling safe, and not being interrogated.

'Well,' she managed eventually, 'I'm not so very sure what else a girl like me is supposed to do. I'm not awfully good at anything. And I'm not very brave. So yes, you're probably right.'

He had the grace to look a little shamefaced. Her reply was so disconsolate.

'In that case,' he said, 'we'll have to see about making you a little more adventurous.'

The look he gave her made her feel warm. Or was it the sun combined with the wine, which she found she had drunk even though she'd initially found it unpalatable. 'Do you read?'

She felt embarrassed by his question, because she didn't, not really. The last thing she had got through was

27

Forever Amber, because everyone else at the college had been reading it, the tattered copy passing from hand to hand. But she didn't think the misadventures of a restoration hussy were what Mr Shaw would consider literature, judging by what was on his shelves.

'Everybody reads, don't they?' she replied, evading the question rather neatly.

'You'd be surprised.' He refilled his glass. 'I sometimes think if more people took the time to read *proper* books, there would be fewer problems in the world.'

No, thought Jane, *Forever Amber* wouldn't be in that category. Terence Shaw wouldn't consider it proper on any level.

When she came to go back to her little room, her head was swimming slightly, but she was glad her new employer seemed to have thawed, and wasn't quite as curt as he had seemed initially. She was surprised to find herself picking up his manuscript eagerly. Anita Palmer had just met the young lad from chapter two, Joe Munden. Jane had a feeling she knew what might happen next.

She stopped typing with a start when Terence Shaw came in.

'It's five o'clock,' he told her, and she wasn't sure if he was annoyed she had outstayed her welcome or impressed by her conscientiousness.

'I'm sorry,' she stammered. 'I wanted to find out what happened . . .'

The smile he gave her lit up his face, in fact the entire room.

'That's good,' he told her. 'That's . . . good.'

He plonked a book on the table. *Lady Chatterley's*

Lover. Jane's cheeks flushed pink. She'd heard about it – who hadn't?

'See what you think of this.'

And he walked out. Tentatively, she picked up the book, expecting it to be hot. The papers were still full of the court case.

She couldn't take it back to the beach hut. Her mother would flip if she saw her reading it. Actually, blow her mother. She was the one who had organised the job. And Jane couldn't help it if her employer had forced the book upon her.

Anyway, she could slip another cover on it. She looked at the bookshelves and selected another volume of the same size, removing the dust cover, her heart thumping.

As she left, she realised it was Friday. Was he expecting her over the weekend?

'Mr Shaw?' she asked tentatively. 'Do you want me over the weekend?'

He leant back in his chair, smoking his cigarette thoughtfully.

'No such thing as time off for a writer, when they're in full flow,' he informed her. 'But you needn't worry, I suppose. See you first thing Monday.'

'Thank you.'

'And it's Terence. Mr Shaw makes me sound like a . . . schoolmaster. Or a magistrate.'

He shot her a dazzling smile. He looked entirely different when he smiled.

Jane just nodded. She couldn't imagine having the nerve to call him Terence, but she didn't say so. She'd just have to avoid calling him anything for the time being.

*

She spent most of Saturday trying to read *Lady Chatterley*, lying on a scratchy car rug on the sand. She was careful to make sure her mother didn't cotton on to what she was reading. She found it a struggle, it was terribly wordy, but she was determined to persevere. Something inside her wanted if not to impress Terence Shaw, then at least to prove to him that she wasn't just a silly little girl with no thought for anything other than boys and dresses.

Even if that's what she had been up until now.

By teatime she found lying in the sun concentrating had made her head throb. Against her better judgement she agreed to take part in a rounders match with some of the other children on the beach, and was surprised to find she enjoyed it.

'You see,' said her mother triumphantly. 'You just needed something to do.'

Maybe, thought Jane, and found herself glancing along the beach to Terence's house, wondering how many more words he had managed to scrawl out over the weekend.

On Monday morning she scurried along the beach and up the cliff path.

'I don't think he writes as well as you,' she told Terence of D.H. Lawrence, solemnly, and was flustered when he laughed long and hard, and patted her on the shoulder.

'Thank you,' he managed eventually, and she wasn't sure what he found quite so hilarious. It was true. Lawrence waffled on, while Terence got straight to the point – he made you feel exactly what the characters were feeling, even if he did occasionally use words she'd never heard of. She was slightly unsettled by his reaction, but felt that she had pleased him. And it was with eagerness that she picked up his manuscript. She was far more intrigued by Anita Palmer's plight than Constance Chatterley's.

She was gradually getting used to his scrawls, and transcribed them more swiftly. When she came upon words she didn't know, she pulled down the dictionary from the shelf and looked them up. She had never given any real consideration to words before, and she was amazed to find there were words for feelings she had never pinpointed or identified in her short life. She found herself regretting not paying more attention at school, but none of the teachers had ever made her want to read, or increase her vocabulary. Jane had been a user of adjectives like 'nice' and 'good' and 'fun'. Whereas now, in the space of one morning, she had discovered 'ebullient', 'coruscating', and 'eviscerated'. Not that she was likely to use any of them on a daily basis, but it was interesting. She felt . . . stimulated.

Her fingers galloped on. Sometimes Terence invited her to share lunch, and sometimes he didn't. Gradually she found herself relaxing in his company. His bark was definitely worse than his bite. She found the courage to tidy his desk – she had to do it every morning, but he didn't seem to mind when she whisked away the empty mugs and glasses – he seemed to drink an awful lot – and emptied the ashtray.

One afternoon he came into her room to find her with her head in her arms, sobbing. He looked alarmed.

'What is it?' he asked.

'It's chapter nine,' she sobbed in reply. 'I don't believe

31

she'd do it. She loves him more than anything else in the world. And she wants a baby more than anything in the world.'

Anita Palmer and Joe Munden had embarked upon an affair, with inevitable consequences.

'She wouldn't get rid of it,' Jane insisted through her tears. 'You've got to change it.'

Terence pulled her to him and stroked her hair while she sobbed.

'Oh Jane,' he sighed. 'I can't change it. I can't change it because that's what happened.'

She pulled away, staring at him as the realisation dawned on her.

'It's you!' she exclaimed. 'You're Joe!'

He nodded.

''Fraid so.' He looked away, his eyes screwed up slightly. Was he trying not to cry?

'That's awful,' she whispered. 'That's terrible. Where . . . where is she now?'

He shrugged. His expression was bleak.

Without thinking, she threw her arms around him.

It wasn't really him she was hugging, it was Joe. The young, barely formed young man whose whole future had come crashing in on him, whose world had been turned upside down by a woman who should have known better. But Terence seemed to take great comfort from her embrace.

'Oh, Jane . . .' There was a crack in his voice. 'Jane . . .'

He pulled her face up to meet his. She could see his tears through her own. There was a long moment while they gazed at each other, and then . . . he kissed her.

Jane felt as if she was falling. Every nerve ending in her body crackled; a sensation like the faintest sea breeze skittered over her skin from head to toe. Nothing whatsoever told her to resist. There was no hesitation, no question. It was as meant to be as when Joe met Anita. She remembered reading the words and marvelling at their power. And being envious of their experience. And now here she was, feeling the same thrill, as Terence picked her up and carried her down the corridor through into his bedroom, dropping her gently onto the bed. She lay there, eyes wide, her breathing shallow.

'We don't have to do this . . .'

'Yes, we do,' she breathed, and with an unexpected bravery pulled him down to her. She wanted to be part of this man, this man who had felt so much, suffered so much, this man who had made her think for the first time in her silly, superficial life.

He unbuttoned her dress carefully, kissing each bit of her as it was exposed – her collarbone, her shoulder, the back of her neck, her breast – oh God, she never knew that was what it was going to be like. She shivered as he continued his exploration, unable to believe what was happening, thrilling at the sensation of his lips on her skin.

'I've never—' she managed to gasp.

'Sshh,' he replied. 'I know.'

He calmed her, stroking her with firm, confident hands. She sank back into the comfort of the mattress as his fingers brushed the inside of her thighs. Instinctively she pushed herself towards him – she wanted to feel his touch, something inside was screaming out for contact. She'd never felt an urge as strong as this before – she'd

33

experienced mild flutterings and pinpricks of pleasure when she'd danced with boys in London. Never this overwhelming, almost desperate *need* . . .

When he finally touched her she gave a little gasp of shock, and then relaxed. It was alien to her, to have someone touch her there, but it felt so right, so delicious, and she didn't feel self-conscious, not at all. He stroked her for what seemed like hours, and she purred with the pleasure of it, something immense building up inside, a sweet pain piercing her, drilling right into her core.

Suddenly he stopped. She opened her eyes in indignation, but he rolled on top of her, spreading her legs so he could push himself inside her. And that felt even better, as if she was being totally possessed. She thrust at him to recapture the sensations, and he moved with her, and back it came, the pulsing, melting whirlpool . . .

Her legs tightened round him as her first orgasm crashed through her.

They lay for what seemed like hours, their arms wrapped around each other, not speaking. Occasionally he brushed his lips against her, as if to reassure her, but they were both in their own world, filled with wonder. She breathed in the smell of him, felt his sweat on her skin, unable to believe how relaxed she felt, lying naked next to him.

Eventually he peeled himself away and she suddenly felt cold, as stark reality seeped into the room. What now? Did she just go back to her typing? Or would he expect her to leave?

'We're going to have such fun, you and me,' he whispered, and she felt a smile spread over her face and her uncertainty vanish.

Somehow she knew it wasn't going to be easy, but she was ready for it. She was totally entranced. Spellbound. By his talent, by his wisdom, by the knowledge he instilled in her and the feelings he had awoken. She was totally in his thrall.

When she came to work each day, she never knew what mood he was going to be in or how he was going to treat her. Sometimes he barely acknowledged her existence, and she might as well not have been there, in which case she went upstairs and carried on with her typing, happy to wait until he thawed. Sometimes he greeted her effusively and just wanted to talk. Other times he grabbed her, kissed her, pulled her down onto the floor. And he could switch himself off as quickly as he turned himself on. Blowing hot and cold was an understatement. He went from wintry, Arctic disregard, when his eyes barely seemed to see her, to the blazing heat of ardent passion, when all that seemed to matter was her.

It was funny, but the uncertainty heightened everything for her, somehow. Of course she was disconsolate if she went back to her family in the evening having barely exchanged a word with him, but it made it all the more exciting when she became the centre of his universe the next day.

She dreamt of becoming his muse. She dreamt of articles in the paper, about him declaring that he couldn't write a word unless she was near him, how she inspired him. She dreamt of a house in London, with a yellow drawing room, and dinner parties, with her drifting in wearing the latest creations from the latest fashion house.

Mr and Mrs Shaw. Jane Shaw. Terence and Jane Shaw, synonymous with glittering social gatherings and the very latest of everything. She would carry on typing out his work – he wouldn't let anyone else near his masterpieces. She was his right-hand woman, his talisman, the one he couldn't live without.

And a baby! There would be a baby. Or maybe three. She dreamt of dear little babies that would fill the gaping hole left inside him by whoever the real Anita was. He had never recovered from the loss, that much she knew, but at least she could help him heal it a little bit. What would they be like, she wondered, her babies? A bit dense, like her? Or geniuses, like him? He would be for ever grateful to her, for giving him his dearest wish. And they would come down here, to Everdene, and he would build them the most magnificent sand-castles, round which he would weave the most wonderful stories . . .

She never put any pressure on him. She never asked him about their future. She was far too sensible for that. But when he looked at her after they made love, when he smiled deep into her, and brushed his lips against hers, she knew that he needed her.

She marvelled at how life had turned out. There she'd been on the beach, longing for glamour and nightlife and London, and the answer was there all along. The key to her happiness was only half a mile away, and it had been her mother who had found it.

Prue was very smug about her transformation.

'You just needed something to keep you busy,' she told Jane. 'The devil makes work for idle hands.'

Jane smothered a smile when she thought of some of the things her hands had done over the past few weeks. Her mother would be horrified. And yet she would have to come clean eventually. When the time came for Terence to take her back to London. It wouldn't happen until he had finished the book. She knew he could see no further into the future than that, and she wasn't going to distract him. Patience was all she needed.

In the meantime, she painstakingly typed out the words that were flowing from him faster and faster as he reached the climax. It was a masterpiece. She knew that. She didn't need him to tell her. She was desperate to know the outcome, totally absorbed in the fates of the characters, swept along by their respective journeys, experiencing their joy and their despair. No one could fail to be riveted. As each chapter unfolded, she felt more and more proud.

The day came when he delivered to her the last five pages. His eyes were feverishly bright as he brandished them, and she jumped up and hugged him. He pulled her to him and started kissing her, but for once she dragged herself away.

'No. I want to finish typing. I want to find out what happens. Go away. I'll call you when I've finished.'

He went back down the stairs, grumbling. She laughed to herself, smoothing out the pages, inserting a fresh piece of paper for the home stretch.

She was very nearly at the end when she heard a car in the drive.

She looked out of the window. A Mini had pulled up at the front of the house. Bright yellow. And out of it jumped the most beautiful woman Jane had ever seen, in the shortest dress she had ever seen, with white knee-length boots, the absolute height of fashion. She could see her eyelashes from here, framing huge brown eyes in a pale face. She was holding a bottle of champagne.

Jane could tell by the smile on her face exactly what she was here for.

She drew away from the window, feeling her stomach curdle. She could never, in a million years, compete with a woman like that.

She heard her knocking at the door.

And the door open.

'Surprise!' A peal of laughter floated up the stairs. 'Darling, you did it! Well done. You are a genius.'

Jane bit her lip, looked down at the typewriter and typed *The End*.

Ten minutes later, she went into the living room.

The woman had unzipped her boots and was lying on the sofa, sipping a drink. She was even more ravishing up close. Jane could smell her perfume. It had changed the whole atmosphere in the house.

She waved gaily at Jane.

'Darling, hello! I'm Barbara. Grumpy Guts is in the kitchen. Have a glass of champagne . . .'

She jumped up and went to pour Jane a glass.

'No, thank you. I'm fine—'

'Come on. You deserve a medal, putting up with him all this time. Have you had to type the whole thing out? You are clever. His writing is appalling. I couldn't do it.'

'No. I need to get back. Thank you . . .'

She backed out of the living room and up the stairs. Tears blinded her as she gathered up her things. What a little ninny she'd been. Of course he had a girlfriend. Or wife – perhaps this was his wife? How could she possibly have thought she was the centre of Terence Shaw's universe? In those few terrible moments all her dreams gathered together and floated out of the window, laughing at her as they drifted off across the ocean.

She patted the neatly typed manuscript into shape. She collected up all the handwritten pages and put them into order – she had kept them in case he had ever wanted to refer to them. She opened the door. Terence had gone back into the living room. She could hear their voices clearly – Barbara's languid, husky drawl, Terence's rich, low rumble.

'You haven't been making love to that creature, have you? She looks miserable as sin.'

'Christ, no.' Terence's response was lazy, laconic. 'Mousy little thing. I like something with a bit of spirit.'

Barbara's chuckle indicated that she had just that. And the ensuing silence indicated that the conversation was over and they were indulging in more important things.

Jane stood in her office, fists clenched, heart thumping, her cheeks red.

Something with a bit more spirit?

Before she had a chance to have a second thought, she swept up all the papers off the desk and grabbed her handbag. She marched down the stairs and into the kitchen, where she lifted the lid of the wood-burner that heated the water. The handwritten pages went in first. The flames inside made short work of the paper, and she watched in satisfaction as every last scrap was devoured and turned to ash.

Then it was the turn of the manuscript.

As she held the pages of her labour in her hand, she felt tears well up. At that moment she was swept away by fury, by the injustice, but she knew that once the anger had subsided, the real pain would kick in. This revenge would do nothing to anaesthetise her. There would be no respite . . .

Before she went, she left the title page on the lid of the wood-burner, just to make sure he understood what she had done.

He came to find her a few days later, of course. She saw him hovering further down the beach, his hands in his pockets. She wasn't afraid of confrontation. She went to meet him, and they walked down the beach together, out of earshot of anyone in the huts.

She couldn't read his expression. It was neither cold, nor angry. His voice was calm.

'You've destroyed a year's work.'

She tilted her chin and met his eye, shrugging.

'You've ruined my life.'

'Is this about Barbara?'

'You never told me about her.'

'I never made you any promises.'

Her mouth twisted. She wanted to cry, but she was determined to smile. Of course he hadn't made her any promises. She'd made it all up for herself, the fairy-tale ending.

'I suppose I just *assumed* I meant something. How idiotic of me.'

He hesitated for a moment. He looked pained, as if he was about to say something momentous. Then he sighed.

'I'm sorry.' He didn't clarify quite what for. Breaking her heart? Using her? Being caught out? Losing his work? He held her by the shoulders. He looked deep into her eyes. 'I'm sorry, Janey.'

He let his hands drop, then turned and walked away, back towards that steep path she had taken so many times over the past few weeks, her heart thudding with the excitement of seeing him. His steps were taut with tension. She looked up towards the house, and saw Barbara waving at him from the balcony.

She knew no one would ever make her feel the way he had. Ever again. She had tasted it, the gut-wrenching emotion that drives all humans, that sets them apart from animals. The emotion that fuelled his writing. The emotion he had felt with his heroine, Anita Palmer, and that he would never feel again. Which was why he could pick up and put down the likes of her and Barbara, toy with them, use them to his own ends.

She went back into the cool of the hut. Her parents were dozing on the beach, Robert and Elsie were mucking about in the shallows. She picked up her handbag and looked inside.

It was all there, bar the title page she had left on the burner. She drew it out carefully, two hundred and forty-two pages. How much of it would he be able to remember? How long would it take him to write it again? Would he bother?

She hoped he spent nights writhing in agony over what he had lost. She hoped it tortured him. She hoped that he desperately tried to recall the plot, the descriptive passages, the wonderful dialogue that had reduced her to tears, but that it would elude him, taunting him. She hoped that he felt just one fifth, one tenth of the agony she had been feeling.

Maybe that way he would learn his lesson.

At the end of the summer, her mother arranged a party for the beach-hut owners. They had all got to know each other over the holiday. Friendships had been formed, the children made up little gangs, depending on their ages. Everyone who had anything to do with the beach was invited; the couple who ran the post office, Roy and his family.

Her father constructed a big fire, so they could cook sausages and roast marshmallows. Everyone contributed something to eat. The Ship Aground provided kegs of beer for the men, and there was a deathly punch for the rest of the grown-ups, with bits of fruit floating round in it.

Jane drank four glasses. She had got used to drinking wine with Terence, and so had developed a head for drink. The fifth tipped her over the edge, gave her a devil-may-care courage.

As the sun descended towards the sea, a shining gold disc surrounded by pink, she took Roy by the hand and drew him round behind the huts. As darkness descended they stood close to each other.

'Hold me,' she instructed and he did, sliding his arms rather awkwardly round her, then pulling her to him. She shut her eyes and put her lips to his. He responded eagerly, pulling her in even tighter.

She felt nothing. He kissed her, and she felt nothing. Terence had only had to look at her and she felt torrential passion well up inside her. Kissing Roy was perfectly pleasant. She didn't feel disgusted or revolted. But it was nothing special. It didn't make her want to die for him. It didn't make her head spin or her legs feel as if they were going to give way underneath. It was like . . . eating an apple. As everyday as that.

She pulled away from him. She couldn't use him like this. Roy was far too nice to be an experiment. He deserved better. Someone who could feel, for a start.

'I'm sorry,' she whispered.

'What is it?' he asked, concerned.

She shook her head and walked away. The sun had disappeared entirely, and the chill night air clamped itself around her. She could sense him watching her, sense his disappointment, and his bewilderment.

She slipped into the beach hut, scrambled up to the top bunk, and pulled the blankets over her. Sleep had become the only true escape. She shut her eyes and waited for it to wash over her, so she could be free from all the thoughts jumbled up in her head, made even more confused by the punch.

When her parents finally came back in with Robert and Elsie, they found her fast asleep.

The following week, she bought a daily newspaper in the post office and applied for three jobs in London. She received interviews for two of them by return of post. She took the train up to Paddington, and by the end of the day she had been offered a job as personal assistant to the managing director of a car showroom in Mayfair. Eight pounds a week.

She found the manuscript when she was clearing out the house to sell.

It made her heart jump. It skittered crazily in her chest, even more than it had when the police had knocked at her door and told her about Graham.

She sat down to read it, the black letters on the yellowing pages as familiar as if she had typed them only yesterday. She felt she could almost have recited the whole book from start to finish, even though she had buried it in the recesses of her mind all these years. Fifty years.

If Terence Shaw had left her with anything more than a hole where her soul should have been, it was a love of books. Reading had got her through her miserable, love-less marriage to a man she had thought was decent and honourable enough to do as a companion, but he had turned out to be far from that. Reading and children had got her through it – she had poured her love into them, a different love from the one she had been denied, but a meaningful and satisfying love nevertheless.

Summers had been the best. Her mother had left her the beach hut, and she had taken the children down there for the whole of July and August, with Graham coming down there if and when he felt like it. It didn't much bother her if he appeared or not, although she preferred not. And there she read, voraciously, while the children played. Bags full of books she had borrowed from the library or friends, bought from second-hand shops, ordered as a result of reviews she had read. She devoured the Booker shortlist every year. Ten years ago she had started a book club, which was still flourishing, and the other women were always astonished by the depth and breadth of what she had read over the years. She wasn't a book snob – she loved a Danielle Steele as much as a Dickens, a Jilly Cooper as much as a J. M. Coetzee.

They filled the hole in her soul.

And so, as she reread the manuscript, she knew she was qualified to judge it.

It was a masterpiece. It was an effortless, coruscating – she remembered the day she'd learnt that word – piece of writing that would speak to anyone who read it. It was timeless, universal, as relevant to her now as it had been when she had first read it.

She set the last page back down. She felt ready. It would be wrong to deprive the world of this work any longer. Fifty years was enough. She'd had her revenge. Now Graham was dead, she was ready to move onto the next phase of her life. The last phase. She wanted peace. After all, she was old. Her body no longer raged in its quest to relive those feelings she'd once had. However long she had left, she wanted it to be calm, gracious and dignified. While she still had the manuscript, the silent feud would rage on.

It was surprisingly easy to contact him. A website, a publicist, an email, a phone call from his people to arrange lunch. At a private members' club in Soho – a dark blue door down a little alleyway. She rang the buzzer and gave her name over the intercom, then announced herself again when she reached the reception desk. A girl with shining long hair and a tartan dress made her sign the register, then led her through a maze of corridors to a small room. It was painted in the same dark blue as the door, lined with books, and had an assortment of small sofas and chairs arranged around coffee tables.

He was sitting in a corner. She was astonished at how small he was. Where once he had towered over nearly everyone, now he was tiny, a shrunken little being.

His eyes were the same. Hooded, burnt into his face. Only now the shadows underneath were a sickly yellow.

She ordered a drink from the girl and sat down in the chair opposite him.

'Jane.'

For years she had imagined this moment. Him speaking her name.

It left her cold.

She put the manuscript down on the table between them.

He stared at it for a full minute before he spoke. He reached out and touched it, flicked through the pages. He didn't need to count them to know they were all there. He raised his eyes up to hers, the eyes she had once drowned in. The ones she had dreamt of so many times during her life.

And he laughed.

She gazed at him coldly. He wasn't going to diminish her gesture.

'You have no idea what you did to me, have you?' she demanded. 'I was so completely in love with you. I never

46

loved anyone again. And I don't suppose you ever gave me another thought.'

'Of course I did,' he said, and his vehemence surprised her. 'You have no idea how I felt, do you?'

'No,' she replied. 'How could I? You never told me.'

He reached out a clawed hand and pulled his glass towards him, staring down into it ruminatively.

'You had a lucky escape, you know.' He swirled the liquid round, and Jane heard the ice clink. 'I never made anyone happy. I've never been able to. Not least myself.' He drank deep. 'I'm a silly, weak, foolish, selfish old man. What the youth of today would call a waste of space.'

'Yes,' said Jane. 'I know.'

And suddenly, she did know. He was right. He would never have made her happy. Not in a million years. She would just have been a stepping stone to his next liaison, the next woman who fed his rotten, narcissistic ego.

'It's your best book,' she told him. 'I've read them all.'

'You're right,' he admitted. 'I didn't want to write again, after losing that. I did, of course. Only way I knew to earn a crust.'

Crust? He was a multi-millionaire, she knew that. The nation had an appetite for the rather trite action thrillers he had taken to. The sort of books she had thought he would write in the first place. They were superficial. Dishonest. They sold by the shed-load, piled up in supermarkets and airport bookstores, candy that rotted your brain.

'Were you . . . happy?' he asked her.

'No.' Her answer was direct. He took a breath in, and

then began to cough. The fit was interminable. It racked his body, pain flitting across his face with each spasm, as if he was being knifed. By the end he slumped back in his chair, exhausted.

'Can I get you something?' Jane asked gently, but he shook his head.

He was incredibly still. For a moment she wondered if he was dead. But she could see the rise and fall of his chest, and he seemed to be sleeping sweetly. She didn't want to disturb him. Besides, she had nothing left to say. It had all been said.

She found the girl behind the reception desk and tried to pay for her half of the bill, but the girl was firm. Mr Shaw wouldn't hear of it, she was sure. Jane wasn't going to spend any time arguing. She wasn't going to feel guilty about him buying her a gin and tonic. He owed her a great deal more than that. He owed her her whole life.

She walked back out into the streets of Soho. The light was strangely bright after the tenebrous atmosphere in the club. It was inappropriate. It didn't suit her sombre mood at all. She hailed a cab and jumped inside, grateful to be shielded from the sunlight. She was glad when she finally reached Paddington, the familiar hubbub of the station where you could be somebody and yet nobody, just another person on their way to somewhere else.

She sat down in the train carriage and shut her eyes while the rest of the passengers came on board and jostled for seats, shoving their packages and laptop bags onto the insufficient luggage racks. Around her she could hear people calling home, reporting back as to when their train would get in, what time they would be home for dinner. There was no one for her to call. There'd be no one waiting for her at the station, no one to lean over and give her a kiss while she told them what she had been up to. No one who'd been out to buy ingredients for supper. She'd be going back to a taxi and an empty fridge. She should have bought something from M&S at the station. A little bubble of resentment rose up inside her, and she pushed it away.

She wasn't going to think about it. She wasn't going to wonder what life she might have had if she had never met him. The happiness she might have been allowed to feel. She was going to pick up the pieces of what was left of her life, and make the most of it. Between Terence and Graham, they had managed to destroy her. But she had her children and her grandchildren, and they hadn't managed to destroy her love for them. This was going to be her summer.

Eventually she reached the station and found a taxi, which put her down at the top of Everdene beach. She climbed out, weary from her journey but as ever exhilarated by the view and the sea air. She filled her lungs and stepped out across the sands until she reached the hut.

Inside it was reassuringly familiar. It had hardly changed since the day her father had bought it. There were new curtains at the window – nautical blue and white – and a new cooker and fridge. It smelt the same, slightly damp, slightly tangy. There were the same board games and paperbacks, the same chipped mugs and plates.

The fridge door was shut and she went to open it, worried that mould would have built up inside. She was surprised to find it was on, and inside she found milk, cheese, eggs and bacon. Further investigation revealed a loaf of bread, a box of tea and a packet of chocolate digestives in the cupboard.

It could only have been Roy. He was the only one with a key.

She felt a flicker of warmth leap up inside her, just as if she had held a match to the pilot light on the little cooker. How wonderful to be thought of.

As she unpacked her things, she looked forward to the weeks ahead. The little hut would be cramped, filled with a succession of her offspring and their offspring, a complicated timetable of comings and goings that depended on work, school, university, exam results, holidays abroad, social engagements. She wouldn't bother trying to keep up, she never did. She took each day as it came. Catered for whoever was there. Fitted in round their madcap plans.

They would all be there for this weekend, for the opening. And she'd have to tell them. It would break her heart, if she let it. There was nothing she could do. She couldn't afford to keep it going. And she knew none of them would be able to buy it from her – they had too many financial commitments between them already. Anyway, it was probably best to make a clean break. She would give each of them a little money from the sale, to put towards a holiday. Small consolation, but it was the best she could do, given the circumstances.

She sat down later that evening to draft an advert. She'd get her grandson Harry to do it on his laptop and get it printed out in the town nearby. She wouldn't need to market it hard – a copy through each of the other beach-hut doors, a few pinned up in the village. Word would get round, offers would come in.

By the end of the summer, the deal would be done . . .

2
SEASHELLS

It was astonishing how easy it was to lie.

Only, strictly speaking, she wasn't lying. She really was going down to Everdene to kit out the beach hut for the summer. She really was going to stop at IKEA in Bristol and stock up on melamine mugs with spots on, and new rugs, and a coffee table and a big bag of tea lights and some lanterns and a couple of bean-bag chairs. And then scrub out the hut until it gleamed, rearrange the furniture, put up some new pictures, make up the bunks with fresh linen – all for the first set of holiday-makers who were due to arrive the week after. It was two days' work at least.

So she wasn't actually lying. Only by omission. Although every time she thought about it she went hot under the arms and panicked. Her hand hovered over her mobile incessantly. She could cancel any time, she knew that. It was up to her. She was in control of the situation.

The problem was she wasn't in control of herself.

Incipient infidelity was a curious thing. It made her feel as if she was walking on air one minute, then as if she had the weight of the world on her shoulders the next. She would be skipping around the aisles in Sainsbury's with a silly grin on her face, *singing* to herself, for heaven's sake, only to go home and bury her head in her arms for half an hour, completely paralysed, unable to speak, think, operate on any level. Oh, the agony and the ecstasy. Pandora's box wasn't quite open yet, but she definitely had her fingers on the lid, ready to prise it off.

How had this happened to her? Sarah wasn't the sort of person to be unfaithful, although she suspected no one was until they found themselves on the brink of it. No one went into marriage thinking, 'It's OK, I can sleep with whoever I like when I get bored. No biggie.' It just happened.

The obvious answer was that it was a mid-life crisis. She was, after all, thirty-six. Technically mid-life, if you still went by three score years and ten. Her children were eight and six, which meant life was far, far easier than it had been – they were at school, they didn't need so much mollycoddling, they could get themselves ready for bed, do their own teeth, wipe their own bottoms. So she had more time on her hands – she was no longer in that fug of lack of sleep, car seats and push-chairs and potties, everything slightly crusted in dried food, biscuit crumbs everywhere. Life had a routine, a pleasant, manageable routine, and she was organised enough to keep on top of most things – she wasn't an anal control freak, but neither was there full-scale panic on a regular basis. She remembered spellings and swimming kit and home-made cookies for the school coffee morning most of the time, and didn't go into meltdown if something was forgotten.

So yes, maybe she did have too much time on her hands.

As for her and Ian, if challenged, she would have said they were still *basically* quite happy. She remembered when they had first got together, the tiny little house they had bought in Harbourne, a fashionable area of Birmingham with a warren of streets full of aspirational couples just like them. They had done it up themselves, spending the weekends sanding floorboards and stripping skirting boards, revealing all the original features but giving it a modern twist with Sarah's paint effects, so that when they eventually came to sell it, when the two girls came along and they finally couldn't squeeze another thing inside its four walls, they got what seemed a ridiculously high price for a two-bedroomed terrace.

It had been Ian who had insisted they move to Hagley, a 'village' on the outskirts of the city, insisting that the schools were better, that the girls needed fresh air and access to the countryside. The move coincided with him joining a big corporate firm in Birmingham, a totally different kettle of fish from the family-run outfit he had been working for. Sarah wasn't sure if it was the change of house or the change of job that had altered him, but after the move Ian seemed to have a different set of values.

He seemed very preoccupied by things that didn't matter a jot to Sarah – what cars they were driving, where they went on holiday, what they wore, where they ate out, who they socialised with. When she confronted him about it, he asked what was wrong with him wanting the best for them? And she supposed there was nothing wrong, as such, but he didn't need to be so *obsessed*. She'd been quite happy with her old Micra, but he had insisted on chopping it in for a shiny new Golf, even though it meant taking out a loan. And he'd bought her a private number plate for her birthday, which was absolutely the last thing on earth she had wanted. She wanted to be anonymous when she was out driving. She didn't want people to watch her while she hashed up parallel parking on the high street. He had watched in satisfied smug pleasure as she had opened it, and she had to feign gratitude, even though she would have far preferred . . . well, anything, quite frankly.

And Ian always had a plan these days, a scheme, a scam, usually something that had been planted in his head by one of the partners at work. Sarah had questioned these plans at first, but always glazed over when he got the figures out. The first had been to purchase a flat in the rather ugly new block that had been built at the end of their road, to let out.

'The figures add up,' he told her. 'If we buy it on an interest-only basis, the rent we get will cover the repayments. It'll wash its face, easy.'

Wash its face? Where did he get these expressions? Sarah couldn't argue with him – she didn't have a clue about interest rates or APRs – and so suddenly they were the owners of a four-bedroomed house *and* a flat. Then another one, which he had been tipped off was going cheap. Then another.

'It's good for the girls,' he assured her. 'Even if we don't benefit, it's a legacy for them.'

Sarah couldn't help feeling that the whole exercise was to make Ian feel as if he was one of the gang. She hated it when they were out and he talked about their 'property portfolio'. It made her cringe.

He wasn't like that all the time, thank goodness. Just enough to put her teeth slightly on edge. Like they did when he pulled on his Armani jeans – since when had Levis not been good enough? And when he polished his BMW at the weekend – what on earth was wrong with a bit of dirt?

And sometimes he looked at her critically when they were going out. He had suggested once or twice that she smarten herself up a bit, and she had been outraged. Did he want her to be all fake tan and blond highlights, like the rest of the wives in their coterie? They had no sense of expression. She might not be smart, but she knew how to dress as an individual. She wasn't going to put on their uniform of designer jeans and sparkly tops and six-inch heels. She was quite happy in her little dresses and vintage cardigans and biker boots, her hair piled into a messy topknot. She certainly wasn't going to change to make him feel as if they belonged.

Once he had looked at her hands. There was paint under her nails, which were short and ragged, and the skin was chapped from white spirit and wiping them on rags.

'Why don't you get your nails done?' he asked, and she realised he wanted her to have hands like the other women, soft and pampered, with their false nails, square-ended with white tips. The very idea made her shudder. They had hands like porn stars, hands that were made for rubbing themselves suggestively over a man's chest in a meaningless gesture.

And anyway, the people they mixed with didn't put

her under any pressure to don their uniform. The women always cooed over what she wore, admiring her bravery. 'You're so arty,' they sighed, 'so *boho*.'

'I'm just *me*,' she would reply, though she wanted to retort that she wasn't a sheep. She didn't put her name down for a designer handbag at the local boutique, she bid for one on eBay or found something in a charity shop.

She could tell Ian disapproved, but he hadn't always. He'd once loved her for her kookiness. He'd been proud of the fact she was an artist. He'd shown everyone the fairy mural she had done for the girls' bedroom in Harbourne. He'd loved that she decorated their Christmas presents with potato prints and shells she'd sprayed silver. Now he seemed embarrassed. He wanted to buy everything in Selfridges and have it gift-wrapped, all shiny paper and sharp edges. If he had his way, he'd book her an appointment with a personal shopper and have her made over from top to toe, until she looked like a clone. A fully paid-up member of the Terracotta Army, as she privately dubbed them, on account of their permanent spray tans.

In fact, the only thing she had done lately that he had approved of was buy the beach hut. It had been her idea. She had seen the For Sale sign when they were having a day at the seaside in Everdene two years ago. She had 'done the maths'. If they used it for two weeks of the year, and rented it out for the rest, it would 'wash its face'. Not least because they wouldn't have to fork out for a fortnight in Portugal or Antigua or wherever the hot destination of the moment was. The girls far preferred mucking about on the beach and going for fish and chips to shacking up at some chichi hotel. And Sarah hated, *hated*, flying.

Ian hadn't been sure at first. Largely, she suspected, because it hadn't been his idea, but in the end he hadn't been able to argue with the figures. And now Sarah was secretly gleeful that it was the only one of their properties which, if it hadn't gone up in price, was certainly holding it. And they had no trouble renting it out, whereas one of their flats had been empty for nearly four months, which had eaten into their reserve fund.

Which was why she was heading to Everdene to get ready for the season.

And Oliver Bishop.

They met at a drinks party. A drinks party at a grand house in Race Course Lane – rather mystifyingly named, because as far as Sarah could see there was no race course, but it was the poshest address locally and Ian had been thrilled to be asked to the Johnsons, who were top dog in the area.

By ten o'clock, everyone was half cut and was either in the massive conservatory ('Amdega!' Ian told her in an awed tone) or the adjoining kitchen ('Smallbone!' The same tone), Sarah had gone back into the garden to have a cigarette. A roll-up. It was a habit she had never broken, an art-school affectation that made her something of a social pariah. Anyone else with any common sense had stopped smoking years ago, usually when they got pregnant. But Sarah enjoyed her illicit roll-ups. Only one or two a day, hardly worth bothering to stop. It was her little rebellion. The thing that was hers and no one else's.

A figure stepped out of the back door. She hoped it wasn't Ian coming to tell her off. She wasn't going to shrink into the shadows. She drew on her roll-up, defiant.

It wasn't Ian. It was one of the other guests.

'Thank God,' he said. 'Another smoker.' And lit up a Camel with a Zippo.

He looked about twelve. Tufty, sticky-up hair. Ceaselessly roaming eyes that slid from her eyes to her cleavage to her bottom then back to her mouth without apology. A demonically charming smile. He even smelt dangerous – a musky cologne that made Sarah's endorphins stand to attention at once. He had trouble written all over him.

He sucked in the smoke as if it held the elixir of life.

'Goodness,' she commented. 'You look as if you needed that.'

'After talking to that lot? Yapping on about where they're going skiing?' He threw his eyes up to heaven in a gesture that was slightly camp, but there was no doubting his sexuality. She looked at him with interest. Did he feel the same way she did, bored to death with the conversations? Listening to them compare the merits of the Trois Vallées versus Austria. Debating how they were going to get there – by car or air or snow train. The women spent hours discussing ski boots and salopettes and what colour was in this year. Sarah couldn't care less, as long as she was warm and dry. She had worn the same outfit four years running, and there was still plenty of wear in it. Nobody had actually said anything but she could tell they all noticed.

Personally, she wasn't bothered about going skiing – the girls enjoyed it for about two days and then got exhausted, and she was never going to be a daredevil on the slopes – but Ian had looked utterly panic-stricken when she had suggested giving it a miss this year. Then she'd asked if they could go on their own and he had been irritated by the suggestion. The social life was a big part of the holiday for him. Sarah would have liked to snuggle up in their own chalet, happy to spend the evening in front of the fire with a glass of wine and a good book, but no – they all had to troop out to what-ever restaurant was in vogue and boast about their bravery on the piste.

'Do you ski?' she asked Oliver tentatively.

'Yes, but I don't spend three months talking about it beforehand.' He gave her an impish grin, then adopted a mock pompous voice. '*We always go to St Anton. Bloody marvellous – can't beat it. Take the same chalet every year . . .*'

Sarah snorted into her wine glass.

'So,' he said. 'Tell me about yourself. No – hang on a minute. Let me guess.'

He put his head to one side and studied her. Then put out his hand.

'Messy hair.' He touched one of the strands of dark copper that framed her face. 'Interesting jewellery.' He set one of her long beaded earrings swinging with the tip of his finger. 'Not too much make-up. Just enough . . .'

The back of his knuckle hovered by her bare cheek.

Sarah realised she was standing stock-still, holding her breath.

'I'd say something arty.'

She nodded.

'I'm an illustrator.'

He spread his hands and gave a modest nod as if acknowledging to himself how clever he was. 'So – what do you illustrate?'

'Well, anything. Brochures, packaging. And I've done a couple of children's books.'

'Wow. I'm impressed.'

'Don't be. It's not exactly *The Very Hungry Caterpillar*.'

He looked bemused.

'Best-selling children's book of all time?' She looked at him archly. 'I take it you don't have kids?'

'I do,' he replied. 'But I'm not usually at home for story-time. I'm away a lot.'

For some reason this made her blush.

'Well, that's a shame. It's one of life's greatest pleasures, reading to your kids.' She sounded so prim. She wasn't prim. Why was she coming over like a school-teacher all of a sudden?

'Mmm-hmm.' He was looking at her, nodding earnestly, but with a smile. He was teasing her. She felt warm again. Inside her heart was lolloping along at a slightly faster rate than usual.

'And what about me?' he asked. 'What do you think I do?'

Sarah rolled her eyes. He was making this into a game, and she wasn't sure she wanted to play. But she went along with it. She scrutinised him. His hair was messy too, but the sort of messy that comes from an expensive haircut, not just unkempt, like hers. His jeans were faded, he had on black baseball boots, his shirt was untucked, white but with square mother-of-pearl buttons that meant it was expensive. Nice watch – square copper face, roman numerals, dark brown crocodile-skin strap. Definitely Watches of Switzerland, not Ratners.

Wealthy. Maverick. Slightly rebellious. Not a corporate man.

'Something to do with the web?' she guessed. 'Or PR?'

He shook his head.

'Not even warm.'

'Dentist? Car salesman? Chef?' Her guesses were random now.

He frowned.

'You're not even trying.'

'But I've got no idea. You could be anything!'

'I'm a barrister.'

'You're kidding?' Her eyes widened in surprise. 'You don't look like one.'

'You mean I'm not a corpulent, red-faced buffoon?' He laughed, showing perfect white teeth. Naturally perfect, not cosmetically enhanced. 'So is your husband here?'

'Yeah.' Sarah's heart sank. For some reason, she didn't want to point Ian out.

'Is he an artist too?'

'No. He's a chartered accountant.' She made a face. 'What about your wife?'

She saw a flicker of something before he answered.

'Divorce lawyer.'

'Ouch.'

'Buyer beware.' He gave a rueful smile. 'You probably saw her in there. She's the life and soul of the party. Big networker, my wife. Always on the lookout for potential clients.'

Sarah wrinkled her nose.

'That's awful.'

'That's business.'

They smoked in companionable silence for a moment. Sarah felt a little unnerved. In that short exchange she felt a sense of camaraderie with this stranger. She realised she didn't even know his name.

'I'm Sarah, by the way,' she said.

'Oliver. Oliver Bishop. But you can call me Ollie.'

They shook hands. When she went to take her hand away, he held onto it. He looked at her thoughtfully.

'What?'

'You look as if you need waking up.'

'Waking up?'

'You look as if you're on autopilot. As if you're not . . . really being you.'

She frowned. How could he know that? That's exactly how she felt, as if she was going through the motions. As if all her feelings had been neatly packed away because she had no use for them at the moment. Not all her feelings, perhaps. She loved her children, passionately.

And she still loved Ian. But not with that deep-rooted passion that made you want to sing out loud. She loved him . . . like a brother, she supposed. Maybe that was the same for everyone after a certain amount of time. Her friends certainly complained about having sex with their husbands. Groaned wearily about having to spend any time with them. Positively rejoiced if they went away on business, as they could have the house to themselves and watch *Desperate Housewives* without—

'We should have lunch.'

She jumped out of her reverie.

'Lunch?'

'Don't look like that. People do it all the time.'

'But why? Why would we have lunch? Or do you mean all four of us?'

He laughed heartily at this and Sarah felt indignant.

'I'm sorry, I'm not the sort of person who thinks it's normal to have lunch with another woman's husband.' She knew she sounded frosty and uptight. When really she wanted to get her diary out and make a date straight away.

'It's perfectly normal, if he's discussing artwork with her.'

'Artwork? You're a barrister. Why would you need artwork?'

'I have other interests. I've got shares in a vineyard in France. I'd like you to design a label.' He was utterly convincing. Tying her up in knots. Presumably using the tactics he employed in court. 'What's your mobile number?'

Looking back on it now, this was the moment at which her life had changed. She should have refused to give it to him.

Instead, she told him, and he gravely punched it into his phone, then dialled.

She felt her phone go in the pocket of her jeans. The vibration drilled right down into the core of her. But she just smiled and put her cigarette out on the garden wall, hoping he wouldn't notice her hand shaking.

'I better go back inside. Circulate.'

He grimaced and mimed putting a gun to his head.

'Good luck.'

Inside, she scanned the guests until she picked out the woman who must be his wife. She was stunning. Amazonian, wearing a paisley silk halter-neck dress that left nothing to the imagination but wasn't remotely tarty.

'We're going to St Moritz,' she was declaring. 'Ollie's been there ever since he was tiny. He won't go anywhere else. We stay at the Badrutt.'

Sarah could just imagine him, gliding carelessly down the most treacherous of black runs, sauntering into the hotel afterwards, pushing back his hair, greeting the doorman, confident but casual.

What on earth had he taken her number for? She wasn't in his league. He was bored, probably. He'd look at his phone tomorrow and wonder whose number it was, then delete it. She went over to the table, where several half-empty bottles of champagne were going flat, and poured herself a glass.

Ian came over to her. He looked a bit drunk, but happy. He thrived at social occasions like this.

'Hey, babe.' Babe? Babe?! 'The Johnsons have asked if we want to go to Cheltenham with them.'

Sarah looked puzzled.

'Why?'

'Racing,' he hissed, looking round to make sure no one else had heard her ignorant question. 'They've got a box. You'll have to dress up.'

'Dog-racing? Ferret-racing?'

'Oh, for God's sake . . .'

Sarah shrugged.

'Sure.' There was no point in protesting. They were obviously going, and that was that.

'There's no need to be churlish. It costs a fortune to hire a box. You should be flattered.'

'I'm flattered. I'm . . . very flattered.' He looked at her doubtfully. 'Really.'

She drank two more glasses of champagne to get her through the rest of the evening. Twice she caught Oliver's eye but avoided talking to him. She couldn't cope in public with the way he made her feel. In the short space of time since they had met, he had made her ask herself too many questions.

He caught up with her just as they were leaving. She was coming out of the master bedroom where her coat had been on the bed. There was just the two of them in the corridor.

'We're going now,' she said, flustered.

'Oh,' he replied. 'Well, that's a shame. It was nice meeting you.'

He leaned in towards her. She turned her cheek, ready for the usual air-kiss, but he put a finger on her jaw and brought her mouth round until it was nearly touching his and brushed his lips, fleetingly, along the length of hers. Nothing invasive. Then he shut his eyes and rested his forehead against hers. She breathed in the smell of him, the clean shampoo, the musky cologne, the cigarettes. He gave a tiny sigh of longing. Then pulled away reluctantly.

He was playing her. Of course he was. If he'd pounced on her and shoved his tongue down her throat, she would have pulled away in revulsion. It was so subtle, so very nearly almost nothing, that she was screaming inside for more.

He walked backwards, holding her gaze for a couple of

moments before wiggling his fingers in a gesture of farewell.

'See you. Sarah.'

Oh my God.

Don't fall for it. Don't fall for it, Sarah. He's a bloody barrister. He's used to putting on an act. Convincing people. Taking them in. He's a walking cliché – rehearsed, practised, word perfect. And don't kid yourself you're the first. If you were watching the movie, you'd scream at the television: 'Don't do it!'

It was no good. She switched off the voice in her head and touched the phone in her pocket with a smile.

He made her feel feminine.

Interesting.

Mysterious.

And as horny as hell . . .

When she got home, she pulled out her phone. His number was there under 'missed call'. She sat fully dressed on the loo seat in the bathroom, staring at it, agonising for ages. Should she add him to her directory? Or leave him out, so if he did send a suggestive text and Ian happened to find it she could deny all knowledge? Should she put him unashamedly under Oliver Bishop? Or file him under Plumber or Garage Man, or even Olivia? So that if he rang at an inopportune moment she could ignore it?

In the end she put him under Bishop. He wouldn't phone. After all, she realised, as the champagne she had drunk evaporated, she had just been a mild distraction for him at a boring party. Nothing more.

*

He phoned nine days later. Perfectly, cleverly timed. Just when she had given up hope of ever hearing from him, but before the memory of the effect he'd had on her faded. So that when she saw his name come up, her heart leapt in unison with something further down in her loins and her pulse tripled. A thousand questions crowded her mind – what did he want, what should she do, where did they go from here? Questions that could only be answered if she answered.

She grabbed the phone. Should she answer it knowingly, thereby admitting she had programmed his number into her phone? Or with curt efficiency?

'Sarah Palmer?' She spoke her name with a slight query, as if she was no longer quite sure that was indeed who she was.

'Sarah Palmer.' He spoke her name with a teasing wonder and reverence.

Something delicious slithered its way down her spine.

'Yes?' She tried to sound officious, but she couldn't keep the smile out of her voice.

'I was wondering about that lunch.'

There was no point in carrying on the pretence that she didn't know who this was.

'Lunch,' she mused. 'I don't know. I'll have to see if I can . . . fit you in.'

'Well, *I'm* free tomorrow. I'll be at the Stag's Head at one. If you fancy it.'

'I'll . . . um, see if I can move my schedule around.' She paused. 'It was . . . wine labels you wanted to discuss, right?'

He laughed a dieselly, treacly laugh.

'Wine labels. Whatever.'

The Stag's Head was an uber-upmarket gastro pub that brought a hint of Tuscany to leafy Warwickshire, all creamy walls and rustic tables and expensive cars in the car park. The sort of place where a year-old Golf with a private plate went totally unnoticed. Sarah wore faded jeans, boots and a sloppy grey sweater. As if she had been working all morning and had just slapped on some lipstick to nip out for a working lunch.

But sexy. Damn sexy, she knew that, because the sweater slid seductively at will off her shoulder, and she had a grey silk bra underneath. And her hair was tousled, as if she had just rolled out of bed. And her dangly silver earrings, like corkscrews, brushed against her neck as she moved. And the sweep of grey eye-liner on her top lids made her eyes smokily seductive. Sarah knew all this, because she was an artist, and an artist was trained to observe, and judge what effect a stimulus had on its audience.

He was already in there. He'd ordered wine – Gavi de Gavi, potently rich and creamy – and a platter of antipasti which was waiting on the table: olives, Parma ham, figs, buffalo mozzarella, chargrilled artichokes, as well as hunks of artisanal bread and a bowl of peppery green oil with a slick of balsamic vinegar. She slid into the chair opposite him and put her bag down.

'Hi.'

He poured two inches of wine into an enormous glass by way of reply, and pushed it over to her.

'I'm surprised you came.'

'I need work as much as the next girl.' She widened her eyes, slightly sickened by her kittenish behaviour.

He picked up his glass with a smirk.

She sipped at her wine, unable to stop herself smiling.

To her surprise, he didn't embark on suggestive banter. They talked. Properly. Like adults. About any number of things. Her work, his work. A celebrity's misguided remarks in that morning's paper. The food – delicious, they both agreed. Whether the Stag's Head was as good as its sister pub in a nearby village. The stress of children's homework – he never got involved, Sarah did. Anyone eavesdropping would not have suspected a thing.

Until the zabaglione arrived. Just one portion, for her, in a tall glass, with a single long-handled spoon.

His eyes never left her face as she ate. And she tried desperately not to make it suggestive. No licking the drops of sweet cream from her lips, no symbolic insertion of the spoon into her half-open mouth. No offering him a taste. Yet her eyes never left his face either, and underneath the table their legs were entwined.

'Well,' he said as she put down her spoon. 'What now?'

'I've never . . .'

'I know.'

'How do you know?'

'Because you're so deliciously artless. And so obviously terrified. But so completely unable to stop yourself.'

'I haven't done anything yet. And I might not.'

'That's what they all say,' he replied, and she threw the mint crisp that had come with her espresso at him.

He was infuriatingly arrogant, and so sure of himself. Every tiny scrap of common sense that Sarah possessed told her to walk away, to thank him for a nice lunch and walk away.

'I'm not going to a hotel,' she told him.

'Of course not. It's tacky. Premeditated. And it leaves a paper trail.'

'So speaks the expert.'

'Married to a divorce lawyer.'

Her stomach did a loop-the-loop. This was dangerous territory. Which was, presumably, what made it so enticing. She'd read about the adrenalin, the dopamine, the serotonin – the crack-cocaine high of an affair. And if this feeling was anything to go by, she wanted more.

'I've got a beach hut,' she murmured. 'In Everdene.'

He raised an eyebrow.

'How very Swallows and Amazons.'

There was nothing Swallows and Amazons about what she had in mind.

'We rent it out. I'll be going down there soon, to get it ready for the season.'

'What a coincidence. I'm away then too.'

She frowned.

'I haven't told you when.'

He smiled.

'I know.'

And now, here she was, surrounded by IKEA bags, feeling simultaneously sick and elated.

For the millionth time, she asked herself what she was doing. It wasn't as if she and Ian were desperately unhappy. He wasn't a wife-beating bully, or a heavy drinker, or a gambler. It wasn't as if their sex life had dwindled to

71

nothing – if statistics were anything to go by, they were doing pretty well.

It was more that she was so tired of feeling that she wasn't the person her husband wanted her to be. And that there was someone out there who seemed perfectly enchanted by who she was. And to feel enchanting was incredibly seductive. Added to that was the sense that she knew Oliver so well – they'd talked on the phone countless times since their lunch, and although there was continual flirting and innuendo there was also a genuine connection. He was bright and funny and interested in what she was doing – she couldn't remember the last time Ian had so much as asked what she was working on. He viewed her work as little more than a hobby, something to keep her in baubles, which she thoroughly resented as actually she hauled in quite a bit when you added it up.

None of that entitled her to have an affair, of course. And she knew that Oliver was a womanising love rat. He'd told her as much. He was entirely unashamed of his conquests.

'It's just how I am,' he told her, and she should have walked away there and then. But the fizzing and the elation and the frisson when his name came up on her phone were just too powerful.

As seven o'clock approached, she sat on the step of the beach hut. It had been a glorious May afternoon, and as the sun began its downward journey, she watched the sky turn a luminous pink, a sight that on any other day would have had her pulling out her watercolours and trying to recreate it on paper. Instead, she was wrestling with her conscience, thinking of all the times she and Ian had sat here with a bottle of beer or a glass of wine once the girls were tucked up and thought how lucky they were.

And now she was going to besmirch their sanctuary with her smutty little assignation. The hut didn't deserve to be a witness to her infidelity. It was a happy place, a safe place, that had brought them and the girls so much pleasure. How could she even think about asking Oliver here? She was selfish, selfish and disgusting. Not to mention quite likely to get caught. OK, it was still quiet, no one had come down yet for the season, but there was every chance that one of the other owners would pop down just as she had. Or that Roy, who looked after things when they weren't there, might wander along to say hello. What on earth would he think, finding her here with another man? He was so lovely, Roy. He had a sort of strength and wisdom to him, with his hazel eyes and his calm, gentle voice with just a hint of a burr. But he didn't miss anything. He was constantly observing, as people who live by the sea often are – they have to be aware of their surroundings to survive. What would he think if he saw her here with her lover? Would he keep her secret?

Sarah shuddered at the thought. Imagining herself momentarily through Roy's eyes brought her to her senses. She couldn't go through with this – she absolutely couldn't. She'd let Oliver come in for a glass of wine, tell him she'd lured him here under false pretences, and if he was half a gentleman he would go . . .

And then she saw him, at the top of the beach. He was just passing the first hut. Her insides leapt involuntarily as she watched him walk over the sand. He had his shoes in one hand, a bottle in the other. Was it too late to run, she wondered? She could slip behind the huts, run along the back to the car park, jump into her car and flee for home. She'd be home by ten. She'd tell Ian she missed him. She could slip into bed with him, tickle his neck like she used to, he would roll over towards her with a smile. If sex was what she wanted, she could have it. No problem.

Her heart was thumping as she stepped back inside the hut. It was almost in her throat as she picked up her car keys, her handbag. Her legs felt as if they could barely carry her. Run, Sarah, run.

But if she ran, she'd never know. And she would never have the courage to orchestrate this situation again. She wanted to breathe the same air he was breathing, to touch his skin. It was a physical yearning that totally overrode any logic in her head. Like the rabid desire for chocolate two days into a diet. No matter how sternly she told herself no, she always gave in. She put her hand on the handle, hesitating.

She couldn't resist temptation. She never had been able to.

She put her bag down, dropped her keys on the table. Her cheeks were burning. She had ten seconds to muster up the courage to tell him this was wrong, that she had to go, that he couldn't stay.

'Hey.'

She shut her eyes before she turned to look at him in the doorway. She could smell him. Sense him. His very presence in the hut changed the way the air felt on her skin. As soon as she saw him, she felt her soul shifting deep inside her.

'Hi.'

What a ridiculous thing to say.

His eyes were roaming around the hut, taking it all in – the duck-egg blue woodwork, the ticking curtains, the abstract unframed canvases.

'This is pretty nice.' He walked in further, absorbing his surroundings, clearly impressed. 'Is this where you bring all your lovers?'

'God, no. Of course not. I've never brought anyone here. I told you . . .'

'Oh yes. I remember. You've never been *unfaithful*.'

He put an ironic emphasis on the word. He was mocking her. She felt riled.

'What's so wrong with that?'

'Nothing. Nothing. It makes it all the more . . .'

'What?' He infuriated her. She remembered that now. How he made her feel so unsophisticated when he teased her. Like a naive little schoolgirl. She was standing with her hands by her sides, no idea what to do. She didn't want him to look at her immaculate interior design taste. She wanted him to grab her. She wanted him to be unable to contain himself, to consume her. She wanted him to feel like she did. Effervescent and out of control.

A drink. That would calm her down.

'Do you want a glass of wine?'

'Sounds lovely.'

She was struggling with the cork when he came and stood behind her. Her hands were shaking and her mouth was dry as she stretched up to take two glasses from the cupboard. She bent her head to pour the wine carefully.

He kissed her on the neck.

She gave a gasp. Liquid honey slid down inside her, settling in the pit of her stomach. She shut her eyes, swallowed, as he rested his hands on her waist. She turned, clutching the glasses as if they were weapons.

'Here.' She held one out to him.

He chuckled.

'I feel like a fox,' he told her, 'with a tiny frightened rabbit.'

'I am frightened. I've never done this. I told you. I don't know the rules.'

'The rules are,' he took the glass out of her hand and put it next to his on the side, 'there are no rules. We can do what we like. No one knows we're here.'

And he pushed her up against the wall and kissed her.

Sarah woke at five the next morning. She'd had, by her estimation, about one hour and forty minutes of rather disturbed sleep. She longed to pull the covers back over her, snuggle into Oliver and drift off again, but her mind was racing. She slipped out of bed, pulled on her jeans and a jumper. The kitchen was piled high with the detritus of the midnight feast they'd had. She'd made crab linguine, dicing garlic and chilli and flat-leaf parsley while he watched. Wild animal sex gave you an appetite like nothing else.

Sarah ignored the mess and crept through the door.

Outside the world was a pale grey. The air was cold and damp but she inhaled it sharply into her lungs. Her eyes were stinging, her head muzzy, every muscle in her body ached. She hugged her arms around herself, for comfort as much as warmth, and walked down towards the water as it inched its silver way along the shore.

Last night had been incredible. They'd had fighty, bitey, can't-keep-your-hands-off-each-other sex. Teasing, laughing, playful sex. And, most heartbreaking and inexplicable of all, tender can't-take-your-eyes-off-each-other sex, which had made her cry.

'Why are you crying?' he'd asked, bewildered.

'Because it's so wrong,' she'd sobbed. 'Because it's so right, but it's so wrong.'

'It's not wrong,' he tried to assure her, but of course it was.

And now, as she looked out at the horizon, where a reluctant sun was starting to nudge its way tentatively into the next hemisphere, she prayed for the strength to stop straight away. She'd go back to the hut, wake Oliver up, tell him he had to go and that was the end of it. She shivered as the dawn breeze danced round her, wishing it was yesterday, wishing she had found the courage then to put a stop to the madness.

She sat on the bed next to him.

'Oliver.'

He opened his eyes sleepily and smiled. He put out a hand to touch hers.

'My God, you're like a block of ice.' He lifted the duvet. 'Come in here. I'll warm you up.'

'No.'

'Come on.'

He sat up, wrapped his arms round her and pulled her back down with him, wrapping the covers over her. Frozen to the marrow by the early-morning mist, she craved warmth. Just five minutes, five minutes, and then he would have to go.

He did have to go. Eventually. After they had spent another crazy hour exploring every inch of each other's bodies, because despite her protests, despite every intention that she would resist any overture, her clothes had magicked themselves off her in seconds. And early-morning, cold-light-of-day sex was even more intimate than late-night, slightly drunken sex.

She'd started to tell him this couldn't go on, that this was a one-off, but he put a finger to her lips.

'Don't be a cliché,' he told her, laughing, and she gasped with indignation. She lay under the covers watching him get dressed, completely poleaxed by all the emotions she was feeling, unable to put them into any order. She couldn't just let him walk away without making it clear, absolutely clear, that this wasn't her thing, she wasn't an adulteress, she was basically a happily married woman—

'Bye,' he said, swooping down to deliver an almost paternal kiss to her brow, and then he was gone. Her mouth was still open with unspoken words when the door shut behind him.

Then she was alone. Shivering uncontrollably under the duvet. She thought she might be in shock. She looked at the clock over the sink in the kitchen area. It was still only seven o'clock.

She slept fitfully till nine, when she dragged herself out of bed and started to tackle the mess, flinging crab shells and empty bottles into a black bin-liner. Normally she would sort everything carefully for recycling, but she couldn't be bothered. It was all she could do not to throw herself back onto the bed and howl. But she had no sympathy for herself.

You've made your own bed, girl.

It was OK. It was just a one-off. Everyone was allowed one mistake. She would bury it, move on. She wouldn't see him ever again. She'd delete him from her phone. Even better – block him. She wasn't sure how to do that, but she'd figure it out. It was unlikely she'd bump into him in the near future. He knew the Johnsons, but they didn't have that many friends in common, he and his wife lived in Warwickshire, she lived in Worcestershire. Another county entirely. She'd find another project to take her mind off him. She had several more ideas for children's books – her publisher was always badgering her for more. She'd get on with it. In fact, she had a brilliant idea for a seaside book – a whole series based on a friendship between three mermaids who were also vampires, aimed at the teenage market.

She tried desperately to focus on her idea as she worked. It was a great visual – mermaid vampires with long black hair, tattoos, red lips. She could see it taking off, becoming the next big thing. A movie, maybe. Fame, fortune, a sequel . . .

And then she picked up the pillow he had slept on and breathed in his scent. She sat on the bed, falling backwards with a groan. Who the hell was she trying to kid? She lay there, reliving every kiss, every touch, every orgasm. How could she live without that again? When would she see him again?

She didn't want an affair, she reminded herself. She'd had a taste of sin, and that was enough. She didn't think her system could cope. The anticipation, the guilt, the panic, the regret, the longing, the wonder of it all – and that was before you even took into account the physical rollercoaster.

Eventually she curled up into a ball and drifted off. Maybe if she wasn't so tired, she could deal with the maelstrom raging inside her. Yes, she'd definitely feel better if she got some sleep . . .

She was woken by her phone. She jumped up, startled. Her first thought was that it might be Oliver. She desperately wanted to hear his voice, hear him say what an amazing night they had shared.

Vanity. That's what an affair was about. Vanity and the need for reassurance.

She grabbed the phone from the draining board. IAN flashed up on the screen. She swallowed her disappointment. She put the phone down without answering. She couldn't face speaking to him. He would know. He'd be able to tell by the tone of her voice. And she didn't trust herself not to cry, to break down completely and confess all.

So she left it.

When the phone finally stopped ringing, Sarah thought she might be sick. She ran outside the hut, bent double, retching into the sand. Whoever said adultery was glamorous?

Eventually her retching subsided. She remained bent over, her hands on her knees, breathing in deeply to keep down the rising panic and the nausea.

'You OK?'

Shit. It was Roy. He was ambling along with a box of

tools, obviously on his way to repair one of the other huts.

'Fine. I . . . had some crab last night. I'm not sure it agreed with me.'

She stood up, pushing her hair back from her forehead.

Roy gave a sympathetic chuckle.

'Crustacean's revenge, eh?'

She nodded, gesturing weakly at the hut. 'I'm just . . . getting ready for the first lot of guests.'

'We're set for a good summer.'

'Let's hope so, after last year. I'm surprised we've had any bookings at all, after all that rain.'

'People love the seaside. They always will.' He lifted his toolbox. 'Anyway, I must get on. I hope you feel better. Flat lemonade. That's what I recommend.'

Sarah slumped back down onto the steps and watched him go. Her stomach felt stronger, but she was drenched in sweat. The sea was a good half-mile out, but that's what she needed. Total immersion, so she could wash away her sins.

Half an hour later, Sarah lay on her back looking up at the sky as the waves nudged her back in to shore, feeling the salty brine wash every last cell of Oliver's DNA from her body. She wished she could lie here for ever, like some ineffectual sea creature, and never have to face the consequences of what she had done. There was no escaping it. She had to look at her life, her marriage, her state of mind and figure out what had gone wrong.

There was nothing as painful as shame and regret. She had no one to blame but herself. She certainly couldn't point the finger at Oliver. He had just been the catalyst. At no point had he forced her into anything against her will. No, she was entirely culpable.

Eventually she became completely waterlogged. She could feel the tips of her fingers wrinkling. She stood up and waded back into the shore, her lips dry and cracked. She had a terrible thirst. Not surprising, given the amount she had drunk, and the physical activity, and the heat of the sun beating down on her.

She looked along the beach and her heart stopped. She could see Ian, walking determinedly towards her, a girl in each hand. They were in their home clothes. What on earth had happened? Hadn't they gone to school? Had he taken the day off to surprise her? What if he'd come down the night before, and had walked in on her and Oliver? Her blood ran cold at the thought. Or what . . . what if someone had cottoned on, and had phoned to tell him what was going on? Surely Ian wouldn't bring the girls with him to confront her?

She couldn't read his expression as he arrived, and anyway, the girls were leaping all over her, squealing with excitement at this unexpected trip.

'What are you doing here?' she asked, trying her best to look pleased, and not guilty in any way.

'I can't talk at the moment. Wait until the girls are tucked up in bed.'

He seemed subdued. A little grim. Sarah's heart was leaping frantically in her chest, as if it was looking for the quickest way out.

'Did you take them out of school?'

'I picked them up early. They were chuffed to bits.' He

smiled, but the smile didn't seem to meet his eyes. There was definitely something wrong.

'Well, I haven't got enough food in to do supper . . . We better get fish and chips.' Shit. What if he looked in the bin? Two crab shells, the empty bottles. And she was pretty sure the wine glasses were still on the draining board. She'd left them there to dry. 'In fact, why don't you go and get them and I'll . . .' What? Tidy away all the evidence of my infidelity? 'Just finish up my jobs. You can leave the girls here . . .'

Thank goodness he agreed. As he made his way back up the beach to head for the chip shop, Sarah shot back inside, leaving Meg and Amy to play in the sand. She sniffed the air – did it smell of sex? Oliver's distinctive cologne? His cigarettes, which were so much stronger than her roll-ups? Would she have time to change the sheets? She was glad she had brought two spare sets from IKEA. She couldn't, absolutely couldn't, face the prospect of sleeping with Ian in the same linen that was soaked with the sweat of their – well, lovemaking wasn't the right word. She whipped the duvet off, wrenched the sheet from underneath, pulled off the pillow cases, all the while looking wildly round for any other evidence. She tugged the rubbish bag out of the bin and tied it up – Ian would have no reason to look inside, she could make an excuse to take it up to the big bins in the recycling centre later, arguing she didn't want the hut to smell of fish and chips.

Adultery was certainly testing her ingenuity. Although for all she knew, she was wasting her time, and had already been caught. Her stomach was on spin cycle, as was her head. She lit two of the scented candles she had bought, put away the glasses and cutlery. Emptied the cafetière – she hadn't drunk coffee since she'd had the girls, only tea, so Ian would undoubtedly wonder who she had made it for. Her skin was crawling with prickly paranoia.

Ian was in the doorway, holding a bag of fish and chips aloft.

She smiled. There was absolutely no way she was going to be able to face food.

'Lovely. We don't need plates, do we?'

They ate on a rug on the sand at the front of the hut. Sarah forced down as much as she could, swallowing each chip with difficulty, picking at the snow-white flakes of cod in their golden batter. Meg and Amy provided enough chatter for them to seem like a happy family. Anyone passing by would have felt their heart melt at the idyllic scene.

Afterwards, Sarah jumped up and gathered up the wrappers, pushing them into the bin-bag and tying it into the tightest knot possible.

'I'll take this up to the recycling—'

'No. I'll go. You put the girls to bed.'

'No, I—'

'I'll take it.' His tone was firm. Not to be argued with. And to protest would arouse suspicion. Sarah relented.

She watched as her husband carried the bagful of evidence across the beach, praying he wouldn't find some reason to open it. She could find an excuse for most of it. Probably. But not the condoms. She imagined the irrefutable evidence nestling amongst the detritus. Shame released its bile into the chips in her stomach, and for the second time that day she thought she was going to be sick.

Half an hour later, when the girls were fast asleep, Sarah brought them each a mug of hot tea and they sat out on the steamer chairs she had bought at vast expense the summer before. The night air was chill, but they had on jeans and fleeces. She knew they couldn't skirt around whatever it was that had brought him down any longer. And if she had been found out – well, she would have to face the consequences.

'So,' she curled her hands around her mug. It was almost too hot, but the discomfort took her mind off what was to come. 'This is all a bit unexpected. What brought you down here?'

She tried to smile. He looked at her. There was a terrible expression on his face.

'I'm going to give it to you straight, Sarah.'

She could taste fear. It was almost choking her. She held her breath.

'I've been made redundant.'

She sat stock-still for a moment. She felt sweet, sweet relief zing through her veins. It was almost exhilarating. Then the import of what he was saying filtered through. She let her breath out again slowly as she considered what to say.

Shit.

Redundancy was certainly something they'd talked about – everyone had to face up to the possibility in the current climate – but Ian had told her time and again that his partners had reassured him his job was safe. With his track record he was indispensable.

Apparently not. And without his income, they were fucked. They had a huge mortgage, car loans, the house cost a fortune to run.

'How . . . why? I thought . . . ?'

'It's pretty much last in, first out.'

'Oh God.'

'Yep. Oh God. And they're not being over-generous with the pay-off either.'

'Well . . . will you be able to pick up a job with one of their competitors? You said you kept being approached . . .'

'When times were good, yes. But not now. And no one wants the person who's been chucked out on their ear.' He looked so small and helpless. 'Shit, Sarah. I'm so sorry.'

'Sorry? What do you mean? It's not your fault.'

'Of course it is. I'm supposed to be the provider, aren't I?'

'Yes, but you might get something else. You don't know till you've tried.'

'I have tried.'

She looked confused.

'I knew about this weeks ago. I've been trying to find something else. I hoped I could come to you and say . . . here's the bad news, but there's good news too. But there isn't.' He paused. 'There's only bad news.'

He put his head in his hands. She put a tentative hand out to stroke his back, not sure if he wanted physical reassurance.

'Hey. It's not the end of the world.' He looked up. The bleakness in his face told her that it *was* the end of his world. And of course, it was. Loss of face, loss of status, loss of income. Everything that had become so important to him. She ploughed on, injecting as much optimism into her voice as she could. 'We can downsize. We don't need such a big house, or two swanky cars. We can sell one of the flats. Or this . . .'

'No.' His tone was sharp. 'Not this. This is the only place I don't feel . . .'

He trailed off, looking awkward.

'What?'

'I don't feel the pressure.'

'Really?' Sarah was intrigued. She didn't realise he felt like that here. She always thought he would prefer to be somewhere else, somewhere glamorous, somewhere he could boast about at the next dinner party.

'Nothing matters here, does it? You can be yourself. No one judges you. Or expects you to perform. Or checks out what you've got.' He looked out to sea gloomily. 'The thing is, Sarah, I know I've been a total knob for the past couple of years. Trying to . . . be one of them. Trying to keep up. I know you hated it, all the showing off and the splashing the cash. But I thought it was the only way to get on. See and be seen and all that.' He turned to her with a rueful grin. 'And I'm sorry. You must have thought what a tosser half the time. And you'd be right, because it's all come to nothing . . .'

Sarah's mind was racing. Maybe this redundancy was a good thing. Maybe this was the crisis that was going to save them. For now she was seeing a glimpse of the Ian she had fallen in love with.

'It hasn't come to nothing,' she contradicted him. 'We've still got each other. And we're not on skid row yet. Let's look at this as an opportunity. A chance to

87

check back in with each other and work out what we really want.'

'But I don't know what I want! I think about the future and all I can see is a big blank. I'm terrified, Sar.'

She reached over and stroked his arm reassuringly.

'Listen. Count your blessings. We're healthy. We've got two gorgeous girls. We're in positive equity. And I've got work – I can easily build up what I'm doing. I get loads of enquiries I have to turn down because I haven't got time, but maybe if you're around to help—'

'Be a house husband, you mean?'

'No! I'd never expect you to do that. But you could help me get a bit more organised. Do me a business plan, do the book-keeping, help me with marketing . . .'

She trailed off. He didn't look impressed with the idea. She felt stung. OK, so she wasn't Philip Green or Alan Sugar, but if he really was out on his ear then surely he should be keen to help. It was in both their interests.

Bloody male ego. She was going to have to tread carefully.

'OK,' she went on. 'Maybe I should work all that out for myself.'

'I can't just go from the boardroom to the kitchen table, Sarah.'

She wanted to punch him. Why the hell not?

'Have we got anything to drink?' he asked.

'Um – I don't think so.'

'I'm sure I saw a bottle in the fridge.'

The Chablis that Oliver had brought. They hadn't got round to drinking that. Sarah jumped up, suddenly panicking that there would be a sticker from some upmarket Warwickshire wine-merchant stuck on the side.

'Oh yes – left over from last summer. I'll go and get it.'

She was pulling out the cork when the phone went in the pocket of her fleece. She nearly jumped out of her skin. She fumbled, pulled it out. Oliver. She should have felt a thrill, but instead she felt dread. Everything was happening too quickly. It was all closing in on her. If she was going to survive, something had to give.

She flicked her eyes towards the door. Ian was still sitting outside. He wouldn't be able to hear. She answered the call, speaking quickly before she could change her mind.

'Listen, Oliver. I'm really sorry. I can't do this. Ian's just been made redundant. We're in total crisis mode. Please – don't ring me. I can't cope. I really can't.'

To her horror, she thought she was going to cry. This was her sacrifice. Wasn't that always the way? Wasn't it the woman who always had to give in and make compromises? Because no way was she going to be able to cope with redundancy *and* adultery. And it wasn't as if Oliver was going to offer her some wonderful alternative. They weren't going to go running off into the sunset together. So he had to go.

'OK.' His reply was calm and measured. She desperately wanted the reassurance of his arms around her. 'You've got my number. Call if you want me. Any time.'

She swallowed. It would be so easy to make another assignation. The easiest thing in the world. But it would make everything else so complicated.

'Thank you,' she whispered, and hung up the phone.

Hot tears blinded her as she pulled the wine glasses out of the cupboard, the same glasses she and her lover had used the night before. She poured out the Chablis – premier cru, she noticed. What else? They'd better enjoy it. There wasn't going to be much premier cru in the immediate future.

She took the glasses outside, handed one to Ian, then sat down. He took a sip.

'Nice,' he commented, and Sarah thought how horrified he would be if he knew its provenance. She raised her own glass to her lips. She'd done the right thing, she knew she had. Now, it was just a question of working out a way forward.

Vampire mermaids, she thought. Vampmaids? Mervamps? She'd write a proposal out as soon as they got home, send it off to her agent. Then she'd go back through all the queries she'd had over the past couple of months, chase them up, see if she could resurrect some work. And she'd finally get round to building herself a website, get some business cards printed . . .

She looked over at Ian. He was leaning back in his chair, eyes closed. My God, she realised – he was actually asleep. He was snoring. Dead to the world. Totally fucking oblivious.

Just when, she wondered, just when, exactly, had his problem become *her* problem . . . ?

She fingered the phone in her pocket thoughtfully. She could call Oliver back, tell him she did want to meet after all. In five minutes she could have their next assignation lined up and Ian would be totally oblivious. Just like he was to their predicament, seemingly. She didn't, of course. She sat and finished her wine, mulling over ideas in her head, 'doing the maths', working things out.

And all the while she was strangely comforted by the thought that, if she ever wanted to, she could.

3

BLUE LAGOON

Sea Breeze. Blue Lagoon. Sex on the Beach.

Maybe Everdene wasn't the greatest place on earth to come and dry out after all. The sea looked like one big mirage – God's own cocktail, with the early-evening sun hanging red as a maraschino cherry. She was salivating at the sight of it as the six o'clock longing kicked in.

Not that she usually made it to six o'clock. Fiona's personal yardarm had long ago zoomed backwards to . . . oh, one o'clock if she was lucky. But usually twelve. Never earlier than that, she was proud to say, because she liked to spend the mornings sober and get the tasks that made it seem as if she was in control of her life out of the way. Paperwork, shopping, phone calls, hair appointments.

Not that she was ever *entirely* sober. When you tanked back over two bottles of wine a day, it was never out of your system. But by midday, reality was usually starting to kick in, and she was ready to don the golden cloak. And it never failed her. It wrapped her in its softness and shushed her troubled mind.

Though there were many people who could ask, quite fairly, why troubled?

Yes, indeed, Fiona. Why troubled? A million-pound house in SW19, an amiable husband who earned pots of money, two gorgeous, bright, funny children. And OK, maybe not a figure to die for (you might as well imbibe liquid Mars Bars as Pinot Grigio), but no one could ever deny that Fiona McClintock was enchantingly pretty, with her golden curls and china-blue eyes, and actually, curves and cleavage were far more attractive than the toned, honed gym-bunny look sported by most women in Wimbledon Village. Fiona was made for the DVF wrap dress, and she had a row of them in her wardrobe for her fabulous, fabulous social life.

So yep, on paper she had it all. Except maybe a career, and she'd never really wanted one of those. She had always wanted to be a full-time mother, and she didn't see why she should have to defend that decision. So she didn't. And most people, on meeting her, realised there was no point in confronting her with some post-feminist inquisition. She was clearly popped on this earth to worry about not much more than flower-arranging and canapés and what to choose from the Boden catalogue.

And she was busy busy busy. She was the undisputed queen of the social scene, for ever organising drinks, dinner parties, soirées, 'girls'' lunches. Hallowe'en, Bonfire Night, Valentine's Day – she rarely passed up an opportunity for a social function. Anything, quite frankly, that enabled her to slug back her ration in the company of others, so she wouldn't feel like the dependent drinker that she knew deep down she was.

She knew she hadn't fooled anybody, not really. She knew they spoke about her behind her back, that there were raised eyebrows and knowing nudges. But nobody had the balls to come out and say it.

'Fiona. You're an alcoholic. And you need help.'

And so she just carried blithely on. It wasn't as if she couldn't function. She worked hard to make sure she never forgot anything, that the children looked immaculate, that the house was perfect, that she was the best turned-out mother in the playground. On paper, she was the epitome of respectability. The headmaster phoned her to discuss playground politics (she was chairman of the PTA, and her first action had been to introduce wine to the dreary never-ending meetings – everyone agreed that it made the hideous back-biting and sniping bearable). The vicar never missed her post-carol service mulled wine and mince pies (she was in charge of the church's annual shoe-box-to-war-torn-country collection). She was on the tennis club committee (although she was usually too half-cut to pick up a racket, she was ace at organising their social events), two charity committees, she was a member of a book club. You couldn't accuse Fiona of having time on her hands.

When the wake-up call came, it was a shock to her, but nobody else.

By the time the school run came, Fiona would usually have drunk three large glasses of wine. Using the maths of the delusional, she calculated that one and a half of those would be out of her system by then, going by one unit an hour, and the remaining glass and a half was – well, only a glass and a half. Not over the limit in anyone's book. She honestly believed herself when she told herself she was all right to drive. After all, she was a responsible

94

parent, a loving mother. She wasn't going to put her own children's life at risk, or jeopardise anyone else's.

The twisted wreck that had once been her Porsche Cayenne said otherwise. And thank God she had been on her way to school, not on her way back, so the children weren't in the car. It happened in the middle of Wimbledon Village. Right outside Daylesford Organics. She sat in the police car waiting to be breathalysed and watched practically everyone she knew drive past her car and clock it, their heads snapping round in astonishment. Although actually, none of them was astonished. They all agreed it was only a matter of time.

It hadn't even been her fault. She had swerved to avoid someone who had stepped out from the pavement, only then they had thought better of it and stepped back but by then it was too late – Fiona was on course for the lamp-post.

The noise had been the strangest thing. A crumping sound, very loud, but without the reverberation you always heard on the television. She hadn't panicked at first. She told herself it was going to be fine, no one was hurt, the car was insured. It was only when the breathalyser went red, and the policeman looked at her gravely and told her she was going to be arrested because she was nearly twice over the legal limit that she felt the first claws of panic.

Tim collected her from the station, after first collecting the children from aftercare. He showed no concern for her well-being after the accident, or her ordeal at the station. He was cold, measured, which was more frightening than if he had been incandescent. They faced each other across the granite-topped island in the kitchen, Fiona thinking that really this probably wasn't the time to dive into the fridge and pull out a bottle, but never had she wanted a drink more. Her head was throbbing, muzzy from the stress and the shock. She couldn't think straight. She really didn't want to talk about what had happened, but Tim was pointing at her, jabbing a finger in a manner that was uncharacteristic. He was usually so mild-mannered and easy-going.

'You're going to have to do some serious thinking to get us out of this mess,' he was proclaiming.

'I know. But we should get a courtesy car on the insurance. And I can always arrange for the girls to get a lift—'

He looked at her in disbelief.

'I'm not talking about lift-shares. I'm talking about your fucking problem.'

Fiona flinched. Tim hardly ever swore. She tried to smile, shaking her head to show she didn't understand.

'Problem . . . ?'

'For heaven's sake, Fiona. I've tried to rein you in. Time and again. Screwing the lid back on the bottle so you can't drain it dry every night. Keeping us out all day on a Saturday to put off the point at which you get the corkscrew out. Steering the waiters away from you at a cocktail party. It's embarrassing, Fiona. Whenever we go out somewhere, you're completely blotto by nine o'clock—'

'Who isn't?' She felt rightfully indignant. He was talking as if all their friends were card-carrying members of some temperance society.

'Most people aren't. Most people are relaxed, not

almost incapable of speech, bouncing off the walls. Crashing out at the dinner table, for Christ's sake—'

'Once! And I was tired!'

'You were unconscious! You'd drunk yourself into oblivion. Like you do every night.'

He stared at her. She didn't know where to look. She tried to smooth down her hair, look as if she was in control.

'OK. So maybe I've been drinking a bit too much. It's just a habit. I can deal with it. It's just a question of cutting down—'

'Cutting down?' Tim's voice oozed pure vitriol. 'To what? Just the one bottle a day?' Fiona looked wary. 'You think I don't know? You think I believe that half-bottle of white wine you get out of the fridge every night is the same one you put back the night before? I know it's a fresh one, that you've guzzled the rest in between . . .'

She drew herself up to meet his accusing glare, ready to defend herself.

'So why don't you say anything, if you know so much?'

'Fiona, I do. I have and I do. You don't want to listen. You don't want to know. And frankly, I don't understand why.' He threw up his hands to indicate their surroundings. He looked helpless. 'You've got everything . . .'

She looked at the floor.

'I know.'

'So what's the problem? Are you so unhappy? Do you not like being married to me?'

'No, I'm not unhappy . . .'

'Then what?'

Her tears were falling thick and fast now.

'I don't know. Maybe I do need . . . help. Professional help.'

'You don't think I'm going to fork out for you to go to The Priory, do you?' he snarled. 'You just need to get a grip.'

'I will. I will . . .' She could feel snot starting to bubble out of her nose. He looked at her in disgust as she wiped it away with the back of her hand.

'In fact, just get out. I don't think I can even bear you in the same house at the moment.'

'You're kicking me out?'

'We've both got some thinking to do.'

'What about the children?'

'What about the children? I'll take them to school, as you obviously can't. And I'm perfectly capable of cooking them supper. Just leave a list of their weekend commitments—'

'You're serious.'

'Never more so.'

'Where do I go?'

'I don't know. But I suggest somewhere without a mini-bar, or a compliant friend.'

Fiona felt herself crumpling. She flicked a glance at the fridge.

Tim looked at her, a sardonic grin twisting his mouth.

'Glass of dry white wine, dear?'

Suddenly she felt angry. It was all very well him being so judgemental after the event, but if he'd realised she had such a problem, why hadn't he done anything about it?

She drew herself up, mustering as much dignity as she could.

'OK. If that's the way you want it. I'll go down to Everdene for a few days. See if I can . . . work it all out.'

'Please do, Fiona. Because quite frankly, I can't see a way forward the way things are.'

Tim and his brothers shared the hut at Everdene between them. They'd bought it ten years ago, in an attempt to recreate for their own children the idyllic summers they had spent on the beach. Only it had become a source of friction, none of them being able to agree on when they should be allowed to use it, or how much money should be spent on maintaining it. Fiona knew it had lain empty and unloved all winter, but they would all be fighting come the warm weather and the school holidays. In the meantime, it was hers for the taking. The ideal refuge for a woman who needed to take stock of her life.

She caught the train down to Everdene the next morning. Tim took the children to school, leaving her to take a taxi to the station having flung a few things into a suitcase. He showed no sign of backtracking on what he had said the night before. If anything he was more thin-lipped and ungiving. She'd hugged the kids, told them she had to go away for a short while, and they had been heartbreakingly understanding, if a little puzzled. Fiona never went away from home.

Nor could she remember the last time she'd been on any sort of public transport. She sat on the train watching people file past her on their way to the buffet car, coming back with paper bags that belched out the scent of toasted bacon buns. They would sell wine in the buffet. Of course they would. Unbelievably, it had been nearly twenty-four hours since her last drink. She looked around her, at the teenage girl frantically texting with a half-smile on her lips, the businesswoman pecking at her laptop, the man on the phone to his hapless estate agent, giving him a rollicking and not caring who heard. None of them was gasping for a drink.

She couldn't fall at the first fence. She had to at least arrive at her destination sober. She could do this, of course she could. She sat and flicked through the magazine she had bought at the station, and found herself pleasantly distracted by the articles and the fashion, picking out dresses and shoes for herself.

An hour and a half later, she struggled off the train and out onto the station forecourt and into a taxi.

'Everdene Beach, please.'

She thought about asking the driver to stop at Marks and Spencer. She needed food, after all, a few nice nibbles to keep body and soul together over the next few days. But deep down, she knew if she went into M&S she would head straight for the wine section, pop herself in a couple of bottles. It was better to avoid temptation.

As the taxi rumbled over the cobbles of the station forecourt and pulled out onto the road that led to Everdene, she put her head back and shut her eyes wearily. She couldn't run away from it for ever. She had to look into the black hole. It was the black hole she tried to keep filling, but that always came unplugged and emptied itself, leaving her with a gaping jagged rawness inside.

Her childhood home had been a silent, joyless place, its windows blind with closed curtains, low-watt bulbs throwing sinister shadows. Her mother didn't like light. It triggered her headaches. So the three of them, Fiona and her mother and father, moved through a crepuscular twilit world, Fiona always blinking when she came out of the front door into what she thought of as the real world.

Her father did his best to keep things together. On top of his already stressful job as a civil engineer, he tried to run the house, keep an eye on Fiona's progress at school and monitor his wife's mental health – a test of his nerves as much as hers. Whenever he left the house, he felt a sense of dread. He could never be sure what he was going to come back to. Euphoria, with every item of her wardrobe scattered around the bedroom, music blasting, make-up smeared all over her face. Or despair, which meant an ominous silence, a vacant stare. He never knew which was worse.

Food was simply a fuel, a necessity, never a source of pleasure or enjoyment. At eleven, Fiona took over the catering, unable to bear the unpalatable and unimaginative stodge her father served up. Her repertoire wasn't terribly gourmet, but at least her macaroni cheese had proper cheddar in it, not just a packet sauce that tasted of sick. Neither of her parents was particularly interested in what she cooked, but at least she could take a modicum of pleasure from what she ate if she made it herself.

Her mother was beautiful, with large sad eyes and a dark bob that always seemed to be perfect although Fiona had never known her go to the hairdresser. She was tall, with painfully thin arms and legs, her knobbly wrists sticking out of the end of the jumpers she wrapped herself in, because she felt the cold terribly. She drifted around the house aimlessly, usually silent, sometimes watching television, mostly sleeping. Although sometimes she would come into Fiona's bedroom and interrogate her about her life, words spilling out of her in a chaotic jumble. Then she would clap her hand over her mouth as if she was trying to shove the words back in where they had come from. Fiona preferred it when she was silent. Silence she could handle.

Her desperate father tried to make it all up to her. Every now and then he would drive her to London, dropping her off at the big Top Shop in Oxford Circus, telling her she could have whatever she wanted. He would turn up an hour or two later with his cheque book, never quibbling at the amount she had spent. Her friends were green with envy, but she would have swapped all the shoes and dresses in the world for just one day of normality, when the air wasn't thick with portent.

The third time her mother tried to kill herself, her father decided enough was enough and sent Fiona to boarding school. She was fourteen.

'It's no life for you, stuck here. It's too much responsibility. You should be with girls your own age, having fun, listening to records, putting on make-up.'

The school he chose wasn't a particularly posh or grand one. Fiona was a willing student, but not particularly able. Information seemed to trickle out of her head, as if it could find no reason to stay in there, so she was spectacularly bad at exams. Ambleside wasn't bothered about exam results, just an ability to pay, and was therefore stuffed with girls whose parents were clearly happy to pay anything to get them off their hands.

It should have been hard arriving as a new girl into a school with friendships that had been long established, but Fiona settled in surprisingly easily. Despite her troubled home life, she was a sunny-natured, confident girl, and she quickly found herself popular. In fact, her arrival rather upset the status quo.

Her year had long been ruled by Tracey Pike. Tracey, it was generally agreed, was as common as muck, but her father was very, very rich. And what she lacked in intellectual prowess she made up for in charisma. She was loud-mouthed and large-breasted, with a cloud of black curls and a low boredom threshold. She ruled the fifth year with a rod of iron, dictating what everyone should wear, what they should listen to, who was in and who was out, playing people off against each other.

Fiona quickly worked out that she needed Tracey as an ally in order to survive. She didn't fear her in the least – what on earth could Tracey do to hurt her? By facing up to her she got Tracey onside. Soon she was able to dissuade Tracey from her more extreme ideas and ill-disguised bullying. This gave Fiona an almost heroic status amongst the other girls, who had suffered Tracey's tyranny for years. Frankly, after a manic-depressive mother, Tracey was a piece of cake, though Fiona suspected that Tracey was simply biding her time, awaiting the opportune moment to overthrow the pretender to her throne. She didn't trust her one bit.

The showdown came one Saturday afternoon. The problem with Ambleside was there was nothing to do at the weekends. A relentless drizzle was falling, leaving a school full of pupils sluggish and dopey with boredom.

A group of girls made toast on the landing outside the dormitory. Eating was their only distraction. They huddled round the toaster with a loaf of sliced white bread, waiting impatiently. A slab of butter stolen from the kitchen gradually became studded with crumbs.

'Bet you can't walk from one end of the banister to the other,' Tracey said to Lindsay, a thickset creature who had often been at the mercy of her cruel tongue.

Lindsay looked trapped. If she bottled out she would look like the loser that Tracey had always taken her for. If she took the challenge, this was the ideal opportunity for her to prove herself. Her eyes darted from one onlooker to the next, desperately hoping for someone to tell Tracey not to be ridiculous. They were on the fourth floor. If you looked over the banister you could see down four flights of stone steps to the reception hall below.

'It's only about eight foot. Just like walking on the balance beam in the gym.'

Tracey was smirking. She was out for blood today. They'd lost at netball, of which she was captain, and the evening stretched ahead of them with nothing to do. Watching Lindsay squirm was her idea of entertainment.

'Leave it, Tracey.' Fiona stuck her knife in the Marmite and began to spread it.

'No,' said Lindsay. 'I'll do it.'

There was a horrified silence.

'You don't have to,' said Fiona, taking a bite of her toast.

'Course she doesn't,' said Tracey. 'She'll just prove she's a spineless wimp.'

'I can do it,' Lindsay insisted. 'Like you say, it's only like the balance beam. How hard can it be?'

Several pairs of eyes surveyed her doubtfully. Lindsay

was no gymnast. She was hardly light on her feet, had no sense of balance.

Fiona put her toast down and stepped forward.

'I'll do it first, if you like,' she offered. 'Prove it's easy.'

She recognised the delicacy of the situation. If she pulled rank and told Tracey to back off, Lindsay was going to come out of it badly. This was her chance to prove herself once and for all, and get some respect. But Fiona wanted to show her a bit of solidarity. If she took the fear out of the dare, then maybe Lindsay could manage it without mishap.

She could feel Tracey's eyes on her as she scrambled onto the banister. Tracey knew the power axis had subtly shifted towards Fiona, and that everyone was praying Lindsay would prove herself.

Fiona knew she could do it. She used the wall to steady herself while she adjusted her balance. She looked firmly ahead to the newel post at the end. Barely seven feet. Of course, it was harder than the balance beam in the gym, because the banister wasn't flat, but slightly domed, and the wood was more slippery, slick with furniture polish.

She held her arms out and walked, slowly, deliberately. When she got to the end she leant down and one of the other girls held her hands so she could jump.

'There,' said Tracey triumphantly to Lindsay. 'Easy. Your turn now.'

The rest of the girls looked at each other awkwardly. It was all very well Fiona doing it, but Lindsay was a different matter. They watched as she assessed her challenge.

She clambered on using a chair. She clung onto the wall longer than Fiona had, edging her feet round.

Scarcely anyone breathed. Fiona began to chew on her thumbnail. It had been easy, she couldn't deny that, but if Lindsay did lose her balance she wouldn't have a chance. She cast a glance at Tracey, whose eyes were gleaming with relish. She was enjoying every second of Lindsay's discomfort. What turned someone into such a sadist?

Lindsay began to walk. No one spoke as she planted one slightly pudgy foot in front of the other, arms stretched out. For a moment she seemed as graceful as Fiona had been, sure and confident.

Halfway across, she hesitated. There was a collective gasp as she began to sway. Lindsay shut her eyes for a moment, then opened them and carried on, but she seemed to have lost her nerve. Her eyes grew wide as her panic built. She was three-quarters of the way across. Fiona could sense her terror. Instinctively, she put her hand out so Lindsay could grab it, so she could help her down.

'No!' Lindsay flinched away from her, not wanting her help, wanting to prove she could rise to the challenge. And in that moment, she lost her balance completely. One moment she was there, the next she was falling. All that could be heard was the sound of her body hitting the railings.

There was a moment of silence while all the girls looked at each other then rushed to look over the banisters. Four floors down Lindsay's figure looked tiny and still. One girl began to scream. Another bolted for the head of the stairs, about to run for help, but Tracey blocked her path and looked over at Fiona.

'You killed her,' she said. 'You got up there and

showed her it could be done. She couldn't back down after that. And if you hadn't put your hand out, she'd never have fallen. You killed her.'

Fiona stepped back.

'No,' she said. 'It was your dare.'

Tracey looked round at the rest of the girls, who were frozen in fear.

'None of you stopped her, did you? You were all happy to watch.'

The realisation that they were all to blame, that they were all complicit, swept through the assembled girls. Two began to weep.

'It's OK,' Tracey assured them, taking control. 'We say we found her up there. We say we tried to stop her, but she wouldn't come down. If we all stick to our story, then none of us gets into trouble.'

She looked from one to another, her eyes boring into each individual. They all nodded. No one dared disagree. They were all too frightened of an investigation, and of being blamed. It would be all too easy for Tracey to point the finger. She was more than capable of implicating someone else to save her own skin.

From the ground floor, the sound of hysteria rose up through the stairwell.

The school did their best to cover up what they billed as a tragic accident. They held a simple but beautiful memorial service in the chapel, and Tracey, as the leading light of the speech and drama department, read a poem that left no one dry-eyed. The incident was never mentioned again amongst those who had been party to it.

And now Fiona wondered just how many of them

thought back to it, and how often. She had never stopped blaming herself. She should have stepped in straight away and put a stop to the dare. She should never have tried to help Lindsay to stand up to Tracey. And she shouldn't have unnerved her by holding out her hand. She was culpable three times over. The memory haunted her day and night – the vision of Lindsay's poor body being battered by the railings on the way down, the hard, cold stone of the floor at the bottom. She could never share her guilt with anyone, but eventually she learnt to live with it. It was her punishment, her penance, and she would have to bear it for the rest of her life.

It was when she had her own children, however, that it became too much to bear. Now she fully understood the impact Lindsay's death must have had on those who loved her, the terrible, awful grief of a parent who had lost a child. The horror built up inside her, and she lived in constant fear that somebody, one day, would do the same to one of her children. That justice would be done for Lindsay.

Over time, she began to realise that drink made it better. That a little glass of something dulled the pain, blotted out the gnawing rat-bite of her conscience. It was a wonderful solution. So, so easy. She worked out the perfect amount to keep the memories at bay, a blissful state of semi-oblivion.

Of course, she couldn't control the dose for ever. Sometimes it took more to blot things out. And sometimes she wanted complete oblivion, angry that she was forced to live her life like this, resentful that she was living a lie, so she drank herself into a stupor. It was so hard, keeping the secret.

She wasn't going to do it any more. As she unlocked the key to the hut, she looked around her. She wanted to come to this beach with her kids and enjoy its simple pleasures. She didn't want to be held hostage by a bottle of wine. Time and again she had sat in her deckchair watching the children play, wondering if anyone would notice if she hoicked a bottle out of the cool-box. She longed to be free of the tyranny, and sit there making sandcastles, not noticing what the time was or even being aware that it had passed. She wanted to be happy.

She knew how to track down Tracey Pike. She had followed her progress carefully since leaving school, via an elaborate combination of the old school newsletter and Friends Reunited. Tracey wasn't the type to keep quiet about her achievements. She was a hugely successful businesswoman, with three flashy boutiques in North London. Fiona had their numbers in her diary. When she phoned the second one and asked for Tracey, she was told to hold the line.

'Tracey Pike.' Her harsh tones sent a shiver down Fiona's spine.

'Tracey. It's Fiona.' There was a silence. She knew she didn't have to elaborate or explain. Tracey knew exactly who she was, and why she was phoning. 'We need to talk.'

'Right.' Fiona could sense the tension from two hundred miles. 'I'll come to you. Where are you?' She obviously didn't want Fiona anywhere near her perfect lifestyle. She didn't want a skeleton tumbling out of the closet where she kept her designer dresses.

Fiona told her.

'I'll drive down tomorrow,' Tracey told her crisply, and hung up.

She arrived at midday, dressed for St Tropez, not Everdene, in cropped denim jeans and towering espadrilles, a huge pair of Givenchy sunglasses holding back her hair, which had clearly undergone some drastic chemical process to make it straight. Her breasts were even larger than Fiona remembered. Her face was considerably less heavy of feature. Someone skilful had been at her with the knife.

She embraced Fiona like a long-lost friend rather than something rather nasty that had come out of the woodwork. That was Tracey's way, to lull you into a false sense of security. Fiona's stomach turned over, at the memory, the fear of what was to come, and the revulsion of her overpowering perfume. She knew she must look terrible by comparison, with her hair scraped back and no make-up, drawn with the effort of not drinking. Her head was pounding. She thought her body had probably gone into shock.

It was all she could do not to suggest they decamp to the pub.

Tracey didn't bother with any niceties about how lovely the beach hut was. She lit a cigarette without asking if it was all right.

'So,' she blew out a plume of smoke. 'What's the score?'

'I can't keep quiet any more,' Fiona told her. 'I need to tell the truth.'

Tracey looked quizzical.

'Why?' she asked. 'It's not going to bring her back.'

'I can't stand the guilt any longer. I'm not worried about ruining my life, but I'm ruining other people's. My husband's, my kids'.' She took in a deep breath. 'I'm an alcoholic, Tracey. I drink to forget. Every day I drink to wipe out the memory. Oh, I can function OK. Pillar of society, me. But I know everyone knows, and they know I know, and I know they know I know . . .'

She trailed off, exhausted. It was the first time she had said those words. *I'm an alcoholic*. And she was still here.

Tracey shrugged. Luckily, Fiona hadn't expected sympathy.

'We all deal with things differently, don't we? I'm a workaholic. It's all I do. Everything in my life is to do with my business. I don't have a family.' She gave a wintry smile. 'This is the first day off I've had for six months. And that includes weekends. My staff are mystified. They know something must be up for me to be off. Either that or they think I'm away having something fixed.' She stared at Fiona. Her eyes were still small. No surgeon could fix that. 'So what difference do you think a confession's going to make?'

Fiona steeled herself. She was going to have to be firm, because she knew Tracey would talk her out of it.

'We killed Lindsay because we were too busy trying to prove to everyone who was in control. It was our bloody egos that put her up on that banister. And I can't live with it any more. I need it out in the open, so I can deal with my guilt. So I can help the people I love, and who hopefully love me, understand why I am like I am.'

Tracey lit another cigarette. Fiona could see that although she was playing it cool, she was rattled.

'I don't see the point in dredging it all up. It'll be a

nightmare. The press'll be all over it like a rash. It's a great story. Bullying schoolgirls send pupil plummeting to her death and keep it quiet for twenty years? Then there'll be the court case. If you didn't drink before, you will after.'

Fiona shut her eyes.

'And what about Lindsay's family? How do you think they are going to feel, knowing we were toying with her just to prove who was top dog? That's not exactly going to bring them any comfort, is it? You can't pile misery onto someone else just to make yourself feel better.'

Fiona could feel tears welling up. She looked out towards the beach. A mother was walking along the sands with her toddler. He was determined not to hold her hand, plodding along stolidly. She remembered her two when they were that age. Just about . . . God, what wouldn't she give to have those years all over again and do it properly.

'So what do I do?' She turned to Tracey pleadingly. 'I can't keep it quiet any longer. I can't walk around with this terrible secret for the rest of my life.'

Tracey pulled her card out of her bag.

'Go and see this bloke. He sorted my head out. He knows all about it. He'll help you . . .'

Fiona looked at the card. Tracey Pike's shrink? Is that what her life had come to? She must be desperate.

She *was* desperate. Her whole body ached with longing. Not for absolution. Just a bloody drink. She could keep the secret for all eternity if she drank. But she didn't want to drink any more. She wanted to be a normal person. A happy person.

Maybe it was a curse. Maybe she was destined never to

be happy, like her mother. She couldn't bear the thought of her children thinking back on their childhood the way she did hers, their mother figure a black spectre who hung over the house, draining it of any chance of joy. She wanted to take them swimming in the sea without fear of drowning. She wanted to have a conversation with them without repeating herself, without the maniacal, forced laughter that made them stare back at her, wide-eyed. She wanted to decorate the Christmas tree with a clear mind, not through a fug of mulled wine.

She just wanted to be a normal mummy. Was that too much to ask? She gave a heavy sigh.

'Look,' said Tracey. 'You're just using it as an excuse. It's a habit. You've piled all the reasons you're unhappy with your life onto what happened that afternoon. Get over it, Fiona. Move on. I guarantee if you start blabbing now, after all this time, it'll cause more grief than you can imagine.'

She wanted Tracey out of here. It was a mistake. But she had thought it only fair to tell her. She might have been the instigator of the crime, but Fiona had aided and abetted. Now Tracey was taking over, as only Tracey could. And Fiona couldn't argue with her. Everything she said made sense. A simple confession wasn't going to turn her into someone who bounced out of bed with a smile on her face. There was a lot more work to do than that.

'You're right,' she said wearily. 'Of course you're right.'

Tracey nodded, satisfied. She picked up her bag, slung the chain handles over her shoulder. She wasn't going to hang around. She was a busy woman. She walked over to the door, then turned.

'I hope you work it out,' she said softly. 'You have a lot to live for.'

For a moment, Fiona saw a glimpse of vulnerability. For all her chutzpah, she realised, Tracey was hiding behind a façade. She wondered what had gone on in her life to make her the way she was. She'd probably never find out. She lifted her hand in a gesture of farewell. There was no air-kissing this time, no meaningless hug. Just two women who wanted to get away from each other as quickly as possible.

After Tracey had gone, Fiona flung open the double doors of the beach hut to get rid of the toxic smell of her perfume and cigarettes. She sat on the top step, thinking about what she had said. It was always my way or the highway with Tracey – had she done her usual trick, of brainwashing her with her quicksilver tongue? Or was she right? Fiona didn't know what to think any more. But as she looked out to sea, she felt a tiny trickle of optimism. If Tracey had done one thing, it was to make her realise how lucky she was. To have a husband and children who loved her, despite everything. At least, she thought they did. Tracey had no one. She had 'single' written all over her. And although she was obviously very successful, it seemed a hollow victory.

She thought she would phone Tim and see how they were all getting on. Perhaps she would suggest he bring the children down tomorrow – they could spend the weekend at the hut. The weather looked as if it was going to be nice. She would go to the shop and make up a big picnic – they could walk along the coast path to their favourite beach, the one they called the 'secret beach', because it was quite a hike to get there and most of the tourists couldn't be bothered to make the effort, so they usually had it to themselves. She'd go and buy a wetsuit, go bodyboarding with the children. They were always desperate for her to go bodyboarding with them.

She grabbed her phoned and dialled Tim's number, euphoric with excitement at her plan. He answered curtly on the second ring.

'Hello?'

'It's me. I wondered . . . how you were getting on.'

'Fine.'

'How are the children?'

'Fine.'

Fiona hesitated. She hadn't expected quite such monosyllabic hostility. Wasn't he going to ask how she was? She wasn't sure whether to tell him she hadn't had a drink since she'd crashed the car. She wasn't sure it sounded like such an achievement.

'I . . . wondered if you fancied coming down here tomorrow? With the children? It's beautiful. And the forecast's good . . .'

'What?' He sounded incredulous, as if she'd suggested a private jet to Dubai.

'Why not? Daisy can miss ballet for once, and I don't think Will's in a match.'

'Fiona, I don't think you get it.' She was chilled by the tone in his voice. 'We can't carry on playing Happy Families like this. You obviously have no idea what effect you have on the rest of us. How your behaviour has impacted on us. Do you know how much easier it is without you around? Just two days has made me realise that. The children are more relaxed. I can relax . . .'

Her heart fluttered with fear.

'What are you saying? You don't want me back?'

'Not for the time being, no. I think we need some time out. Maybe you should get a flat.'

Her knees were trembling. She sat down on the step, her mouth dry.

'You don't understand. I'm doing so well. I can handle this. I haven't had a drink since I left, Tim. I can do this.'

'Yeah. Until the next party. Or the next crisis.'

Why was he being so harsh? Surely he should be supportive?

'Is that what you really think?'

'I'm only going by experience.'

A horrible thought struck her.

'You can't stop me seeing the children.'

'No. But I think we should leave it at least a week before you come back. We've all got some serious thinking to do.'

A huge lump rose in her throat. She leant her head against the door jamb, too weak to protest. Too weak even to respond.

'Fiona?'

She put her finger on the red button to end the call.

She sat on the step, staring out at the sea. No matter what happened in everyone's lives, the tide still turned. In and out it came, like clockwork, never letting anyone get in its way. The sea didn't care what happened to her and neither, it seemed, did anybody else. She looked at her toes. The bright pink polish was starting to chip on her nails. Usually she would have been to the nail bar today. She was always immaculately turned out – nails, hair, make-up – because it was so much easier to pretend you were in control if you looked the part.

She needn't bother any more. She might as well let herself go completely. She didn't have to pretend. She could reveal her true self. A total bloody mess. The world could see her for what she was.

She stood up. If everyone was going to treat her like an alcoholic, then she would behave like one. She glanced at her watch and was surprised to see it was nearly six. Perfect. She'd wander over to the Ship Aground, the pub in the middle of Everdene where the surfers all hung out. She would go and get completely, utterly rat-arsed. Tim, Lindsay, Tracey – none of them could get her then.

Half an hour later, she was sitting at the long bar that ran the length of the Ship Aground. It might not be high season but it was already half full, with locals and people who had come down early for the weekend to take advantage of the fine weather that was forecast. The pub did a roaring trade all year round, because they served great food but didn't charge an arm and a leg for it, and because the atmosphere was so relaxed. Big screens on the wall showed surfing videos, scrubbed pine refectory tables with benches were mixed in amongst giant shabby-chic sofas. There was a band playing tonight – three boys with ponytails and black jeans fiddled about with drum kits and mic stands. The Urge, they were called, and Fiona gave a rueful smile. She couldn't remember the last time she'd had an urge. Drinking certainly dampened your ardour. In fact, she couldn't remember the last time she and Tim had made love. That was terrible. Men needed sex as much as they needed food and drink. She put her hand to her mouth, desperately trying to recollect. Before Christmas? Definitely before Christmas. Oh my God. How was he managing? Maybe he was getting it from somewhere else? Maybe that was why he was throwing her out? Maybe he had another woman tucked away somewhere, and this was all a convenient excuse?

The barman brought over a tall glass with vodka, ice and lime, and a bottle of tonic. She picked it up and poured it in slowly, anticipating the relief it was going to bring her. As she raised the glass to her lips she thought no, Tim wouldn't be unfaithful. He wasn't the type. The truth was he just didn't fancy her any more. Perhaps not physically – she hadn't changed all that much in appearance – but he'd lost all respect, all affection. Theirs wasn't an equal partnership. He soldiered on, trying to keep it all together, while she tottered around living for the moment she could get her next fix.

Like right now. She drank deep, savouring the prickle of the quinine as it coated her throat, relishing the kick of the vodka which would hit her nervous system as soon as she swallowed it. Faster than wine, which was a more subtle descent into fuzziness. Vodka was hardcore; vodka was for people who didn't pretend, and she wasn't any more.

She indicated to the barman to bring her another. He raised an eyebrow as he brought it over.

'Drowning your sorrows?' he asked.

'Nope,' she replied. 'I'm celebrating.' She waggled the glass at him. 'Celebrating the fact I can do what I like from now on. I don't have to make excuses any more. My name is Fiona, I'm an alcoholic and I don't give a toss.'

She threw back her drink. The barman looked at her, mildly alarmed.

'Another?' he guessed.

'You got it,' she grinned.

He shrugged as he took her empty glass away to refill it. It wasn't his job to judge. If he judged everyone who drank too much in this place, he'd be out of a job.

By eight o'clock, Fiona felt wonderful. She had ordered a plate of nachos, smothered in salsa and guacamole and melted cheese, and washed them down with another three vodkas. The band were tuning up, the bar was heaving, full of people waiting for the weekend to start. There was a real party atmosphere, and she felt happy. Wimbledon seemed a million miles away, Tracey's visit a million years ago, the crash even longer.

Oh yes. This was why she drank. Oh yes.

She smiled as a group of lads on a stag night bustled in. They were all dressed as fairies. Underneath their tutus they were fit and toned, which made their costumes even more ridiculous. Broad shoulders sported silver wings, and they all had on blond wigs.

One of them tapped her on the head with his star-tipped wand.

'I shall grant you just one wish,' he warbled, and she laughed.

'Vodka and tonic, then,' she replied, and he looked around warily.

'I'm not going to get walloped by an angry husband?' he asked.

'No,' she assured him. 'I'm on my own.'

'OK,' he grinned, and she saw he had lovely eyes. Greeny-grey, with long lashes. She felt glad she'd changed and put on some make-up. She probably had ten years on him, but she didn't look too bad.

The band struck up the opening chords of 'Satisfaction'. There was a rousing cheer, and people pushed their way to the stage area and started dancing. The fairy punched the air in appreciation and started singing along tunelessly.

The barman handed Fiona her replenished drink.

'I know it's none of my business, but you have had quite a bit, you know,' he warned her. 'You'll feel like shit tomorrow.'

'You're right,' she said happily, raising her glass to him. 'It's none of your business.'

By ten o'clock, Fiona had been officially adopted by the stags and Liam, who turned out to be the best man, had taken her firmly under his fairy wing.

'Tonight's my responsibility,' he confided. 'It's Dan's stag night. It's up to me to make sure nothing goes wrong.' He looked over at the groom, concerned. He was deep in conversation with a brunette, riveted by her plunging neckline. 'That's the chief bridesmaid. She's seriously got the hots for him. I've got to make sure nothing happens, or I'm a dead man.'

'Leave him to it,' Fiona told him airily. 'He's big enough to look after himself. Let him enjoy his last night of freedom. It's all going to be downhill from here anyway.'

He looked at her askance. She was feeling woozy by now, even drunker than usual.

'Oh dear,' he said. 'Problems?'

'My *husband* says I've got a problem,' she confided.

'Just because I had a bit of a prang in my car. Well, I wrote it off, actually – but only because some idiot walked out into the street. I mean, what was I supposed to do? Run them over, or bash into the lamp-post?'

She was very close to him. He looked at her, then stroked her hair consolingly. He was, she guessed, as drunk as she was.

'Never mind,' he said, and she suspected he hadn't really listened to what she had said, just surmised that she needed reassurance.

'Thank you,' she said, nuzzling into him. He put his arm round her and gave her a squeeze. She looked up and he bent his head, kissing her. Just the briefest of kisses, but on the mouth.

'You're gorgeous,' he said, and she felt warm inside. It was, she realised, a long time since anyone had been nice to her.

Someone came over with a tray full of flaming sambucas. They pressed one on Fiona, who knocked it back to rousing cheers. Then another. Then another. She slid off her seat.

'Must go to the loo,' she slurred.

She weaved her way through the crowds to the toilets, every now and then having to grab onto someone to steady herself, but they didn't seem to mind. Everyone in here was happy. She was happy.

She flopped onto the loo seat and rested her head against the wall of the cubicle. Bloody Tim. Who the hell was he to judge her?

It took her quite some time to wriggle out of her jeans for a wee and then get them done back up again, but she managed it. She peered in the speckled mirror over the sink, fluffing up her hair with her fingers, then went to get her lipstick out of her bag. Shit, she'd left her bag in the bar. Never mind – this wasn't the sort of place people nicked your stuff. It wasn't London.

She went back out to find it. It was on the floor where she'd left it, thank God. She bent down to pick it up, lost her balance.

Liam reached out an arm and she took it gratefully.

'I think I should . . . go home,' she told him.

'Do you live far?'

'I've got one of the beach huts. On the . . . beach.' She gestured outside vaguely.

'Very nice.'

Her head was really spinning now. She held on to his arm more tightly.

'You want me to walk you back?' he asked.

She nodded. She barely heard the accompanying cheers and wolf whistles from his mates as they walked out together.

'Don't listen to them,' Liam smiled at her. 'They're just jealous. Come on. Let's get you back.'

They walked past the groom, who was sitting on a chair with the brunette astride him. Liam pointed a warning finger at him, and he just shrugged sheepishly.

'Last night of freedom,' Fiona reminded Liam. 'Don't spoil his fun.'

The walk back to the hut seemed endless. The sand was hard to walk over, especially when you'd had too much to drink, so Fiona kicked off her shoes. The sand was freezing. She arrived at the door, fished about in her handbag.

'Thanks,' she said, smiling up at Liam.

'Aren't you going to let me come in?'

'Well . . .' She was startled. It hadn't occurred to her that he might want to come in, but of course he did. Why else had he walked her back? Not just to be a gentleman.

'Come on. Let me have a look. I've always wanted to see what these places were like. See how the other half lives.'

'They're nothing special.'

'They should be. There's one for sale up the top. Over a hundred grand they want for it. For a bloody shed!'

Fiona felt guilty. She'd always rather taken the hut for granted, but she supposed they were lucky. It was a special place. She stood to one side and let him through. She flicked on the lights, illuminating the interior. He closed the door behind her and pulled her to him.

'Come here,' he said softly, and she realised he had absolutely no interest in looking at the hut at all. What an idiot. She should have just slipped out of the Ship Aground without saying goodbye. She was too drunk to remonstrate, too drunk to argue. He began to kiss her.

It was nice. It was really, really nice. To have someone holding her, and stroking her hair, and kissing her. She melted into him, almost purring.

'Let me get out of this stupid costume,' he mumbled, and she began to laugh. What a ridiculous situation, a woman of her age snogging a man in a fairy outfit . . .

She woke up frozen to the marrow. The door of the beach hut was flapping open. Her hip bones felt bruised. Her mouth felt bruised. She was naked.

Oh my God, she thought. I've been raped.

She tried to track her thoughts back. She remembered Tracey, her conversation with Tim, going to the Ship Aground . . . On the floor was a piece of tinsel. She remembered it, wrapped around a tousled blond head. Liam? Liam.

Then she remembered laughing, wrapping the tinsel round him. Afterwards, when they were lying on the bed . . .

Rape? Of course it wasn't rape. She had taken him willingly back to the hut. There were a million witnesses. She had kissed him, she'd wanted him to love her. It had felt good, to hear him tell her how wonderful she was. To lie in someone's arms, laughing. Not to have someone looking at you with distaste, their eyes cold, turning their back on you in bed.

She sat up, shivering violently, the horror of what she had done hitting her. She had got so drunk she had gone out and pulled a man. Then slept with him. She felt hot with shame. She got to her feet. She needed to brush her teeth. She scrubbed and scrubbed, washing away all traces of his saliva. It was five o'clock in the morning.

She sat in a chair with a duvet wrapped around her and watched the dawn break. She needed help. She needed a priest. She needed bloody exterminating. What use was she to anyone? She was a terrible wife, an even worse mother. They'd all be better off without her.

Would it never go away? Were the events of that afternoon going to hound her into an early grave? Or was there a way out? She wasn't a bad person. She truly wasn't. She never thought ill of anyone, or did them any deliberate harm. She didn't deserve this never-ending punishment.

She wiped away a tear with the back of her hand, but they kept falling thick and fast until she was sobbing. Eventually she couldn't cry any more. She put her hands to her face, breathing deeply to calm herself.

This was, she realised, rock bottom. In the space of a week she had written off her car, slept with a stranger, probably lost her husband, and possibly her children too. She couldn't sink any lower. She had had everything, and now she was looking at a future so bleak she didn't know what to do next. Where did she go from here? She certainly couldn't stay in the hut – the other brothers would be queuing up to use it before long. Where would she live? What would she live on? Tim had mentioned a flat. How did she go about getting one? Would he pay for it? He'd probably consider it money well spent, just to see the back of her.

And then it occurred to her. He was her husband. He had to take some responsibility for the state of their marriage. It was all very well laying the blame at her feet, but he had just stood by and let the car crash, literal and metaphorical, happen. He had to help her.

But first she had to ask for it.

He must have spent years wondering what he'd done to deserve a drunk for a wife. How could he know the reason, when she'd never told him?

If she told him, he had to help her. Wasn't that what marriage was about? For better, for worse? And you couldn't get much worse than what she had done. It was her only hope. If he told her to go to the police, then so be it. Never mind Tracey. This wasn't about Tracey – she could look after herself. This was about Fiona salvaging what she could from the wreckage.

She sat back for a moment, debating the wisdom of her decision. What did she have to lose? He couldn't, after all, think any less of her than he did at the moment. She got to her feet slowly. She felt almost as if she was in a trance. She could see a silver thread of hope. She had to hold onto it.

She rummaged for her phone, pulled it out, dialled home. It was only half six, but she didn't care.

He answered on the third ring. He sounded alert, concerned.

'Hello?'

She closed her eyes. For a moment she was looking down over the banisters again, down on that little body that lay so still. Maybe, just maybe, with a bit of help, the next time she looked the body wouldn't be there.

'Tim? It's me. I need your help. I need to tell you something. I just . . . need you to listen . . .'

4

OCEAN VIEW

Well, hoo-bloody-rah and amen to that, thought Chrissie Milton when she heard the news. She felt like kicking off her shoes and running across the sand waving her arms in the air. She didn't, of course. She assumed a serious air and murmured commiserations. Honestly, anyone would have thought someone *else* had died, the way everyone was going on. At the end of the day, it was just a bloody beach hut. A glorified shed you'd only pay five hundred quid for in B&Q, quite frankly. OK, so there was the view – everyone always banged on about the view – but it wasn't worth over a hundred grand, not of anyone's money. And definitely not hers.

It was the first Milton gathering of the summer. Jane's birthday, the annual bash that kicked off the Everdene season, when all the clan gathered, wherever they were, and celebrated with a champagne picnic on the beach followed by dinner at Martine's, Everdene's finest, and only, French restaurant. Today's celebration was the first family gathering since that dreadful funeral, when the truth had come out about the mess Jane's husband had left her in. Chrissie was the only one who hadn't been surprised. You only had to look at Graham Milton to know he was playing both ends against the middle and wasn't clever enough to pull it off. Chrissie had had his card marked from day one, which was why he'd never liked her. Well, one of the reasons. Not that she gave a stuff what he thought. And it certainly didn't matter now he was six foot under.

There were thirteen of them on the beach altogether. Jane and her three sons, David, Philip and Adrian. Chrissie, who was David's wife, and the fragrant Serena, who was Philip's. And the six grandchildren, from eighteen-year-old Harry to dear little Spike, who was just six. After they'd all gathered round and toasted Jane's birthday, she made the announcement about having to sell The Shack.

'It breaks my heart to do it,' she told them. 'The Shack has been the glue that has held this family together over the years. But needs must . . .'

Chrissie rolled her eyes. Glue? The hut had been the scene of more arguments than she cared to remember. The Miltons couldn't get together without some sort of a drama or crisis. There was always an imagined slight or injustice to set the cat amongst the pigeons. Graham Milton had been an out-and-out bully, playing his sons off against each other and openly enjoying the resulting chaos. And Jane spoilt them all to death, with no idea that she was constantly pandering to their whims. Between the two of them they controlled every decision their sons made. Chrissie thought it was totally unhealthy. What sort of a man let his parents dictate to him like that? It accounted for most of the friction between her and David. She mocked him for referring to his parents so incessantly. She loved her own parents, but she didn't feel the need for their approval or their input at every turn. She was an independent woman with her own mind, which was now becoming an issue, because the balance of power had altered dramatically between them.

Chrissie had always been a bright spark. Not academically – not at all, she had barely scraped five GCSEs – but she could talk the talk, spot an opportunity at fifty paces, add up a row of figures in her head and charm the pants off anyone. As soon as she left school she went into sales. She could sell anything from vacuum-cleaner bags to diamond rings – it didn't matter what it was, she had the patter. She made good money and she spent it – on a nice flat, a nippy motor, sexy clothes and hot holidays. She worked hard and she played hard.

She was playing very hard indeed when she met David at the races. The Hennessy Gold Cup at Newbury. She was in a private box, courtesy of the company she was working for – a day out, no expense spared, for all the sales team who had outstripped their targets. Chrissie was in her element, in a tight-fitting bright pink jacket and skirt and towering heels, drinking champagne on someone's else's account, living the high life. David was in the adjoining box, the guest of a wealthy client of his boss. They met on the balcony, watching the favourite romp home, only a dark blue rope separating them.

She thought he was the most beautiful man she had ever seen. And he was – tall, with dark hair that fell into his green eyes and a sprinkling of freckles that made him look cute, but not effete. They sat on the balcony sharing a bottle of champagne, then another, and then he had kissed her over the rope. The biting November wind made her shiver, and he wrapped his cashmere overcoat around her, pulling her into him and she felt, for the first time in her life, cared for. Until then she had been Miss Independent, scorning every attempt at chivalry – not that much chivalry came her way, in her world – but somehow David was different. Of course, she knew he was in a class above her. You only had to look at the sober, tweedy suits of the crowd he was with, their careless confidence and their cut-glass accents, whereas her crew were flashy, loud-mouthed, didn't really know how to behave, waving fistfuls of cash around and drinking straight out of their bottles of Veuve Clicquot.

They went straight from the races to dinner. He phoned ahead and booked a table at The Vineyard, a stunning hotel just outside Newbury. Stylish, discreet, the walls were smothered in breathtaking original art, the food was sublime, the wine superlative, but David and Chrissie could have been in Burger King for all the notice they took of their surroundings. They couldn't keep their eyes off each other. It was a natural progression for him to see if there was a room available.

She saw the look of horror on Graham Milton's face when David brought her home for the first time to meet his parents. Yet with typical bourgeois middle-class hypocrisy, he couldn't keep his eyes off her breasts. Just how long would you last, she wondered to herself, if you put your cock between my tits? Two bloody seconds. She deliberately dropped cream on her cleavage while she was eating her sweet – or pud, as Jane called it. She looked her future father-in-law straight in the eye and slowly, deliberately, wiped it off and licked her finger. She would have put her life savings on him having a massive erection under the white linen tablecloth.

She wasn't going to let Graham Milton let her feel inferior. She was brassy, she knew that. Her bright blond hair was shamelessly dyed, she wore clothes that were too tight, skirts that were too short, heels that were too high, exposed too much of her chest. She drank too much, she was loud, she was opinionated, she swore, she smoked. But she knew how to live. She knew the difference between right and wrong. And she was a success. More of a success than David, though she would never have pointed it out. David was a yes-man. He worked for a friend of his father; he was a salaried hack who had got as far as he was ever going to go and seemed happy to accept that. Whereas Chrissie wanted the earth, the moon and the stars – but she wasn't going to pretend to be someone else to get it.

No matter how hard the Miltons tried to make her feel uncomfortable, presumably so she would leave their son alone and go and find another victim, Chrissie stuck to her roots and her guns. And when David proposed, and they set the wedding date, she was able to celebrate in true style just who she was, and there was nothing the snooty Miltons could do about it. She went out of her way to make the wedding as far from what they wanted as possible; conspicuous consumption all done in the worst possible taste, from the ceiling full of helium balloons and the DJ playing 'The Macarena', to six miniature bridesmaids in gold satin and a stretch limo. Of course she could have chosen a country-house hotel, had the poached salmon and a single matron of honour in a tasteful dress, but if she had gone down that road it was *her* relatives who would have been made to feel uncomfortable, and she was buggered if that was going to happen.

From day one, it was an unspoken war between her and the Milton-in-laws, as she called them. She certainly couldn't call on David to defend her, not openly. He basically wanted a nice time, and not too much responsibility, and no confrontation. He was spineless, she soon realised. He didn't have the power of his own convictions. Chrissie wanted a nice time, too, but she realised that it didn't just fall into your lap like it had his. Her dad hadn't called in a favour from a friend because she'd muffed her exams and couldn't get into university. She'd fought her own battles from day one.

She had her babies three in row – Jack, Emma and Hannah – and it was while she was still on maternity leave that she had the light-bulb moment which was hopefully going to give them the life they both aspired to. Chrissie was ambitious, but she knew that motherhood and sales were mutually exclusive. If you were on a sales team, the hours were punishing, and the paperwork that had to be done in the evening was even more punishing, so while she was at home with the babies she looked around for a solution. It wasn't long before she spotted a launderette for sale in the local paper. She shot round there immediately, the youngest two in a double buggy and Jack tagging along behind, taking a pile of dirty washing as cover, and watched the comings and goings. It was run down, half the machines were out of order; it was grimy and soulless. But it had potential as a little goldmine.

She went to the bank, produced a deposit from her own savings and negotiated a loan on the basis of a business plan she bashed out on the home computer. Then she contacted the owner of the launderette and offered him a laughable price, cash, no questions asked. Instinct told her he was in a tight financial spot, and she was right. Two months later she had the keys.

She turned it round in an instant. Bright blue and white paint, new machines, music in the background, comfy chairs, a drinks machine. By the end of the year, the launderette was in profit and she was scouring the papers for suitable premises for the next one. Then she expanded into dry-cleaning – more upmarket, but equally profitable. She was the Queen of Clean. And even though it was hard work keeping on top of all of it, she was her own boss, and every penny she made went into her own pocket. She made a quiet fortune. She was making twice as much in a year as David. Not that she ever shoved it down his throat or flashed it around. She treated the family to a luxury BMW estate and herself to a zippy little Audi TT, then reinvested the rest in two more properties. She kept the extent of her success very quiet, because she knew what the Miltons were like. They loved to speculate and ruminate, and somehow her success would be used against her, another source of disapproval, as if it wasn't ladylike for a woman to make money. And she didn't want to demean David – she still loved him, for his easy grace and charm, his obliging nature, his skills as a father. Even if they didn't always see eye to eye – occasionally the imbalance got to him, and he would lash out, but their rows didn't last long. Deep down he worshipped her, loved her for all the reasons the rest of the Miltons looked down on her, and that made her love him all the more. But an imbalanced marriage is always a difficult one.

It would be very interesting, she thought, to see how the family would treat her now that Graham was no longer around to spearhead the anti-Chrissie campaign. And now that it was obvious she was the only one with any cash floating around – she might not gloat about it, but they all knew she was minted. She smirked slightly into her champagne, then told herself off. It wasn't nice to revel in other people's misfortune, but she wouldn't be so gleeful if they hadn't all taken their lead from Graham.

After the birthday tea, Chrissie and David went back to Ocean View, the bed and breakfast the family used when there wasn't enough room for everyone in the hut. They were going to have a lie-down before they got changed and met the others for dinner.

David was visibly shaken by his mother's news.

'Well,' he said. 'It's quite clear what we've got to do.'

'Is it?' asked Chrissie warily.

He spread out his hands to indicate how obvious the solution was.

'We're going to have to raise the money to buy it. We can't let it slip out of the family. We were the first people to have a hut on this beach. It's our legacy.'

'And how do you propose we raise the money?' asked Chrissie. 'Your mother's asking for offers over a hundred and twenty grand. We can't just stick that on the mortgage. It's big enough as it is.'

David looked at her. She shook her head at him.

'Your salary won't cover it, David. We're at four times already. We'd be mad to go any higher, even if they'd give it to us. Which they probably won't. Don't you read the papers?'

He looked away for a moment, then cleared his throat awkwardly.

'I was thinking . . . as it's an emergency . . . you could . . . sell one of the launderettes?'

Chrissie put her hands up. She feigned surprise, although secretly she had been wondering just how long it would take him to pluck up the courage to ask.

'Oh no. Oh no no no no no.'

'Why not? It's a good investment – these huts keep their value, even in a recession—'

'That's not the point. The point is the launderettes are only valuable as a package. They're all propping each other up. It's a deck of cards. Take one out of the equation and you put the whole lot in jeopardy. '

'I don't see how.'

Chrissie bit her tongue. Of course he didn't. That's why he wasn't a businessman but a mere employee in someone else's company.

'It's our family duty,' he carried on.

'Rubbish,' replied Chrissie crisply. 'Our duty is to our kids, and if I'm going to sell one of the launderettes to fund a holiday home, it'll be in Spain or Cyprus or Majorca – somewhere we can go all year round. Not the bloody freezing west coast of England.'

'But the kids love it here.'

'The kids would love it anywhere there's water and other kids to play with. It's not a tragedy, David, it's a fact of life.'

He stared at her.

'You really are a hard-nosed bitch, aren't you?'

She shrugged.

'If that means I'm not sentimental, then yeah.'

David was trembling with emotion.

'Is that really how little you value this family?'

She took in a deep breath. Maybe it was time to voice some home truths.

'I value them about as much as they value me,' she answered. 'Don't you think that's fair?'

She saw him roll his eyes.

'You've always had a chip on your shoulder about not being good enough.'

'Actually, no, I haven't.' She felt a surge of anger. She didn't want to get into this – when she'd watched Graham's coffin disappear into the ground, she'd hoped for a fresh start. But it seemed his prejudice lived on, and she bloody well wasn't going to keep her lip buttoned any longer. 'I've always thought I was good enough for you. It was your ignorant pig of a father who decided the moment he set eyes on me that I wasn't good enough, and he made damn sure I knew it until the day they put him in that bloody coffin. And the rest of you took your lead from him. Sneering, smirking, nudging each other—'

'I don't know what you're talking about.'

'You all think you value good manners so highly, but between you, you're the rudest bunch of people I have ever met. I was brought up to make people feel welcome, make them feel good about themselves. But you and your family have done their best to make me feel an outsider. I'm not a *Milton* – because I didn't have my own silver napkin ring at home, I didn't go to a posh school—'

'You see?' he broke in. 'Chippy.'

'I am not fucking chippy!' She picked up a shoe and threw it at him. He sat up in alarm, blinking.

'Jesus, Chrissie.'

'You make me so *angry*—'

'Well, you've just proved it, haven't you? If you were well brought up, you wouldn't scream like a fishwife and throw your shoe at me.'

Chrissie drew herself up with all the dignity she could muster.

'At least if I die,' she managed to say, 'I won't leave you in the financial shit. What kind of a man leaves his wife penniless? A total loser. And, I can assure you, no gentleman.'

She was going to go too far. She could feel it. She looked up at the ceiling, prayed for the strength to stop there, to keep her mouth shut. By now David had rolled off the bed and was getting to his feet, looking upset. She'd gone too far already.

'How dare you speak about my father like that? Have you no respect?'

Chrissie narrowed her eyes.

'Actually, no, I don't. I never did, and I certainly don't now he's dead. I'm not going to pretend.'

'In that case, maybe we should just get a divorce. If that's honestly how you feel.'

David always trotted this out when he felt threatened and undermined. He didn't mean it. It was just her cue to tell him how much she loved him. Today she wasn't going to play.

'Try that, and I'll run those launderettes into the ground before you can say knife. And half of nothing is precisely nothing.'

David looked completely shell-shocked and for a moment Chrissie felt ashamed. He looked like a little boy lost. About fifteen years old. As if his whole world had fallen apart. She shouldn't have shouted at him like that, but years of being marginalised had made her feel indignant. Why shouldn't she be able to voice how she felt?

Because she was the one who was in the position of strength, that was why. The Miltons had only marginalised her because they felt threatened. She might hold her knife like a pen – well, not any more – but she had what they all wanted. The ability to make something of herself, to take risks.

Chrissie walked across the room and ran her fingers over her husband's chest. He might be a bit of a loser on the business front, but he was still sexy. Sometimes she wanted to tell him just to shut up and look nice.

'Move on, David,' she murmured. 'That's how life works. You can't cling onto things.'

'You don't understand, do you? What it means to lose something that's been in your family.'

'Maybe I don't, no. The only thing *I'm* going to get left is a couple of racing pigeons and a shelf full of Lladro—'

'That hut is part of our heritage. It's in our blood. It should be handed down to generation after generation of Miltons . . .'

Chrissie stared up at the ceiling.

'David?'

'Yes?'

'Get over it.'

She turned away. She slid out of her robe and squirted

a handful of body cream into her hand then started to work it into her skin.

'Anyway, if you love it down here so much, you can always hire one.'

David glared at her.

'You really, really don't get it, do you?'

She stood in front of him, her magnificent breasts glistening with recently applied lotion.

'David. It's time for a new beginning. Goodbye Everdene, hello the rest of the world. Now for fuck's sake get dressed for dinner.'

David flopped onto the bed with a groan and buried his face in the pillow. Chrissie pulled a dress out of her suitcase and shook it out. He wasn't going to make her feel guilty. Every summer they were held to ransom by the bloody beach hut. She didn't have an issue with the next generation enjoying it. They were all great kids, they all mucked in together, and she didn't begrudge the cousins time together, not for a second. But David and his brothers were completely dysfunctional. Competitive, argumentative, jealous, always homing in on each other's anxieties. Graham had seemed to thrive on it, almost seemed to goad them, while Jane ran around trying to placate everyone but at the same time desperately not being seen to take sides. Chrissie refused to get involved. Occasionally she was tempted to pull the pin and throw in a hand grenade and wait for the explosion, but she didn't want to descend to their level. Instead she drank wine, read books, surfed on her laptop, made phone calls to her friends, painted her nails, but the whole set-up made her feel slightly ill.

It was definitely time for a new start.

*

The Miltons totally dominated the tiny French restaurant at the foot of the hill that led out of Everdene. They'd had a huge long table: all the kids sat at one end and devoured Martine's legendary roast chicken and *frites* while the adults went for the *à la carte*. The food was good – honest, well-cooked bistro fare and despite, or more probably because of, Graham's absence, the mood was convivial, helped along by plenty of Kir Royales.

After *tarte au chocolat*, Chrissie went outside onto the terrace for a cigarette, and wasn't surprised when Philip joined her with a Cohiba. They sat on a bench next to the patio heater put there for the smokers – being French, Martine understood the need.

Philip was drunk. Four Kir Royales, the lion's share of the red wine, and a hefty Calvados he was cupping in his right hand. Chrissie was more than relaxed, but hadn't tipped over into the danger zone.

'Well,' said Philip, blowing out a plume of richly scented cigar smoke. 'Bit of a blow, Mum's announcement.'

'It's not really surprising, is it? Given the shit your father left her in. Makes total sense to get rid of it.' Chrissie knew she was being brisk, but she had to make her feelings clear from the start.

Philip turned to look at her. He wore a smile that was more of a smirk – he could never smile without seeming patronising, because he genuinely did think he was better than most people. If David had got the looks, then Philip got the brains. He'd been to Oxford, and now he was a professor of English at a university in the Midlands. Lots of kudos, lots of people licking his arse, but not a lot of money. Especially not once you'd taken school fees out of the equation. Philip and Serena didn't believe in state education. They believed in giving their children the best possible start in life, so the two of them went to a horribly expensive private school. Chrissie couldn't understand how they could rationalise the expense, which took up at least half of Philip's salary. She was sure Harry, their eldest, would have got into medical school wherever he had been educated.

Philip was swirling his Calvados round in his glass now, obviously gearing up for a change of tack.

'You know I've always admired you, Chrissie.'

'Well, you've hidden it well.'

'We're both winners, you and me. We've got a lot in common.'

'Have we?'

'Drive. Ambition. A need to accomplish.'

'Possibly,' Chrissie conceded, although in Philip's case his drive was all about feeding his ego. She could imagine him swanning about the campus, fantasising about his students falling in love with him, preening himself in the mirror before every tutorial to make sure his tie was tied just loosely enough, his hair was just tousled enough, to ensure maximum adoration.

'Come on. You can't say you don't feel a connection.' He put his cigar in his right hand, the hand that was holding his glass, then reached out and touched her waist.

'Er, no, I don't, Phil. There's no love lost between us. Never has been.' She knew he hated being called Phil.

'Yes, but it's just a cover, isn't it?'

141

He was stroking her hips, edging his hand up towards her breasts.

'Touch my tits, and it might be the last thing you do.'

He gave a little moue and moved his hand away. He put his head to one side and looked into her eyes.

'What are we going to do?'

'About what?'

'If Mum sells the hut, we won't be seeing each other. I don't know if I can live with that, Chrissie. Our little summers together keep me going.'

'I thought you and Serena were very happy?'

He flicked the ash off his cigar.

'Oh, we poddle along on the surface. But there's no passion.' He gave her a look that was supposed to be searing. 'In fact, I can't remember the last time we had sex.'

'God, how awful. And you a red-blooded male. That must be a terrible trial. Unless you have . . . other arrangements?'

Again that irritating smile. Then he moved in closer and slid his arm around her.

'I could certainly *make* other arrangements.'

Chrissie wriggled out of his grasp with an exasperated sigh. She wasn't going to slap him. He didn't merit that much attention.

'Phil – why don't you drop the pretence and just come straight out with it? You want me to buy the hut.'

To his credit, he didn't miss a beat.

'You know it's the only decent thing to do. None of us mere mortals can afford it.' He smouldered at her again.

'And maybe you and I could come down here alone one weekend. Necessary maintenance.'

'Is that what you call it?' Chrissie couldn't help smiling. God, he was arrogant beyond belief. 'Sorry, but all my cash is tied up. I couldn't buy it even if I wanted to.'

He scowled. He was clearly trying to figure out if she was lying. Chrissie stubbed out her cigarette. She wasn't going to stay around to listen to any more of his lecherous nonsense. What an unbelievably deluded twat. Had that been a gamble on his part, or was he really vain enough to think she fancied him?

Serena approached her the next morning on the beach. They were sitting outside the hut on the deckchairs, surrounded by magazines and bottles of suntan lotion, keeping half an eye on the children. Except for Spike, who was Adrian's responsibility, they were all old enough to roam the beach on their own and not have their parents hovering over them, but Chrissie always liked to have her three in her eye-line.

It was a dazzling day, a clear blue sky, the surf high enough for bodyboarding but not alarming, a gentle breeze. Serena stretched her legs, wiggled her toes and sighed.

'I'm going to miss this place.'

'We all are,' Chrissie agreed. 'But we should think ourselves lucky that we had it at all.'

'It seems such a shame, just to let it go like that.'

'Jane will do well out of it. Look at it that way.'

Serena was studying her nails. Chrissie could see her brain ticking away under her blond fringe, wondering how to play it.

'I was thinking . . . maybe we should club together, all of us? Keep it in the family.'

Chrissie tried hard not to show her irritation – what was this obsession with the family? She put on a puzzled expression. She was going to make Serena work hard for this.

'How would that work, exactly?'

'Well – split it between the three boys. It would only be forty thousand each. That's not so hard to find.'

'Well, it definitely would be for Adrian. And we're certainly stretched on our mortgage. I don't know about you two . . .'

Serena's baby-blue eyes clouded over.

'But I thought . . . I thought . . . you were quite well off?' She looked down, her cheeks high with colour. 'I was thinking . . . perhaps we could borrow the money . . . from you?'

Chrissie surveyed her sister-in-law. She felt sorry for her, chained to Philip. She didn't think Serena had much of a life. She was pretty much just there to serve her husband, the great academic. He clearly hadn't married Serena for her brains, but her soft, kittenish beauty. He didn't want an equal, he wanted someone he could control, so he could please himself. And Serena was a willing enough servant, as far as Chrissie could make out. If Philip said jump, she asked how high? Not a dissimilar relationship to Jane and Graham, she mused. The bully and the doormat.

'Look, Serena. I don't know where everyone's got this idea that I'm loaded. I own a couple of launderettes. A hundred and twenty thousand is a lot of pound coins. I'm sorry, but I can't afford to bankroll this one—'

'We'd pay you back! With interest.'

Chrissie shook her head.

'Apart from anything, I don't *want* to invest forty thousand pounds in this hut.'

'But we've always had such happy times here.'

Chrissie looked at her quizzically. What made Serena happy, she wondered? Probably having her husband here, by the sea, where she knew he couldn't shag his students. What a miserable existence. Chrissie, however, was not responsible for the state of Serena's marriage. She picked up her magazine.

'Sorry,' she said, giving no further explanation. She didn't have to explain anything to her sister-in-law.

Adrian was a different matter entirely.

On the second night of the birthday weekend, the middle generation all piled up to Tallulah's nightclub while Jane looked after the children. Tallulah's had been in Everdene since the dawn of time. It was dark and seedy, with sticky floors and the loudest, most brilliant music. The resident DJ seemed to have the knack of exactly judging his audience's mood – every track was a surprise, a gem, a memory. None of the Miltons ever went to a nightclub any other time of the year, but this had become a tradition. They let their hair down and danced the night away. The Milton men were all surprisingly good dancers, exhibitionist Chrissie was often told she should have been a pole-dancer, and given enough to drink Serena got into the groove in a dreamy, detached sort of a way. They ruled the dance floor between them, swapping partners, swapping styles, finding an energy that eluded them on a daily basis. They would all suffer the next day, but they needn't do anything but doze on the beach.

As Chrissie swirled under the mirror ball, she had just the tiniest pang of regret that this would be the last time they did this. Careful, she told herself, you're getting sentimental.

Adrian touched her on the elbow and indicated he was going outside. For a spliff, she guessed. None of the others touched the stuff but she didn't mind it from time to time, so she went out to be companionable. They stood in a little courtyard at the back of the club, listening to the pound of the bass through the walls.

'I guess this is the last time we'll all come here,' she remarked, drawing hard on the joint and enjoying the fuzziness it gave her. Adrian took it back off her with a sigh.

'I feel like such a fucking loser,' he told her. 'The Shack's the closest thing Spike's got to a family home. And I can't do anything about it.'

Chrissie frowned.

'What about your place? Isn't that home? And Donna's?'

'They're not homes. They're houses. Spike lives for coming here in the summer with all his cousins. He has a shit time most of the year, you know. Donna's . . . a nightmare. Not just to me.'

Donna was Adrian's ex-girlfriend, and Spike's mother. She'd got pregnant by Adrian six years ago, just before they split up, and had almost refused to let Adrian have anything to do with the little boy whatsoever. She was a monster, highly strung, self-centred, manipulative, unreliable . . . Chrissie had only met her once and loathed her on sight. She moved the goalposts constantly and used Spike as a weapon to get what she wanted from Adrian – mostly money. But as Adrian didn't have much, she threw tantrums and made empty threats, mostly involving emigrating to Australia, and every time she did this Adrian was gutted, despairing.

He was, however, his own worst enemy. If David got the looks and Philip the brains, then Adrian got the talent. He was a breathtakingly gifted cabinetmaker, could coax the most exquisite pieces of furniture out of the most unassuming piece of wood, yet he couldn't motivate or organise himself to run a business. Instead, he took work as a jobbing carpenter, and even though his workmanship was far beyond that of a normal chippie, he usually ended up getting sacked as he frequently failed to turn up on the job. He had no sense of urgency, didn't seem to understand that when people took him on they expected things finished in a reasonable time frame. As a result, he was as poor as a church mouse, which didn't seem to bother him because he wasn't a material person. But having a small child meant he at least had to provide a roof over Spike's head, when he was allowed access. In the end, Chrissie knew, Jane and Graham had bought him a tiny flat, something which had caused much ill-feeling amongst the others at the time.

His mother's announcement had shocked him, however. It almost seemed to galvanise him.

'I'm going to have to seriously get my shit together,' he told Chrissie. 'I can't let The Shack go, for Spike's sake. He adores all his cousins. They're like his brothers and sisters. He lives for the summer, so he can spend time with them. If this place goes, then that's it for him.'

'So what are you going to do?'

'Take out a mortgage on the flat, I guess,' he said. 'Mum and Dad bought it outright, when they were financially secure. I've got enough equity.'

'But what about the repayments?' asked Chrissie, ever practical. 'You've got to meet the payments. And you don't have a regular salary.'

'Well, I'll have to get one.' Adrian fiddled with the black leather and silver bangle on his wrist. 'All this has made me realise, Spike's the only one that matters in all this. Mum'll be all right. You lot will be all right. You've all got each other. Without The Shack, Donna calls all the shots. She's happy for him to be here all summer while she pisses it up with her mates. But I can't keep him cooped up in the flat.'

Chrissie leant back against the cool of the wall. Her head was slightly woozy, pleasantly so. Adrian's words had touched her. His determination to do well by his son had touched her even more. His bony, angular face and his deep-set eyes had looked so intense. She hadn't really looked at the situation from the point of view of Spike. Adrian was right. His cousins were like his brothers and sisters. He trailed quite happily in their wake all summer, and they looked after him without complaint, for he was a game little boy who never moaned.

How could she condemn Spike to summers with his awful mother, or stuck in Adrian's flat like a battery chicken? He needed sunshine, sand, freedom, fresh air, laughter.

'Look,' she said. 'There's a chance I might be able to swing something. Serena suggested we buy it between us. Maybe I could work something out . . .'

Adrian looked at her, surprised.

'I didn't mean . . .'

'I know you didn't.'

He put his arms around her. They were very close. They touched foreheads.

'You're amazing. You know that?' he told her.

'Don't say that. I haven't done anything yet.'

But she felt a little glow inside, a sense that perhaps she was going to do something good, and change someone's life for the better. Spike was all of their responsibility, because Adrian was . . . well, Adrian.

They stumbled back into the club arm in arm, slightly stoned, the music a shock to their system. Chrissie indicated that she was going to get a drink, and disentangled herself from Adrian's arm. At the bar, she turned to see if anyone else wanted a drink. And what she saw made her heart skip a beat.

Through the seething mass of bodies, Adrian gave a discreet thumbs-up sign to Serena. Serena gave him one of her kitten smiles in return. Chrissie felt a knife through her heart as she watched them move through the crowds towards each other.

Jesus, how could she not have noticed it? She could see the body language now! Butter-wouldn't-melt Serena and little-boy-lost Adrian. She watched as they took each other by the hand and made their way to the dance floor, their eye contact a little too lingering for brother- and sister-in-law, their fingers laced a little too tightly.

Chrissie felt sick. She staggered her way to the toilets, a heaving mêlée of young girls swapping lipsticks and God knows what else. She pushed to the front of the queue and grabbed the first cubicle to come free, to squawks of indignation.

She wasn't actually sick, but she stood with her head between her legs, deep breathing. Bastard. She had felt genuine concern for Adrian. He'd made a total fool of her. She'd bought his sob story, believed his determination. She wondered how they had planned to approach her, if it had been Serena's idea to play the Spike card. Everyone knew she had a soft spot for the little boy. How could you not? He was innocence itself. How long had they been having an affair, she wondered? What was their long-term plan? Was Serena going to leave Philip? She wouldn't blame her.

My God, she realised. The Milton men were just like their father. She pushed back the distasteful memory. She brought it out as seldom as she could, but it was always there in the back of her mind. Graham Milton pushing himself on her in the beach hut late one evening, when the others had all gone star-spotting – there was a meteor shower. His whisky breath, his hot hands on her breasts, his insistence that no one would have to know, that it was all right, that she needn't feel guilty . . . She had never told anyone, not Jane, not David. They could continue to worship the slimy old goat for as long as they liked, but she knew if she said anything she would end up being the guilty party, the one who had been parading around in a bikini, the one who had been giving the come-on.

Like father, like sons. Though not David, she hoped. He had his faults, but she had never suspected him of infidelity. She wasn't being naive, he just wasn't that type. Besides, he wouldn't get a better time in bed with anyone else. She was pretty sure of that.

She felt shaken, though. Her judgement had let her down. Chrissie prided herself on her ability to suss people out, and she'd got it badly wrong with Adrian and Serena. She felt betrayed, too. They were happy to use her. They'd clearly discussed it in quite cold-blooded terms.

Chrissie didn't let anyone use her. She wouldn't let anyone trick her into buying The Shack. If she did end up putting in an offer, it would be her legacy, for Jack and Emma and Hannah, and the rest of the Miltons could bloody well wait until the end of time for an invitation.

She put on a slick of red lipstick and shook out her hair. She adjusted her dress so another inch of her cleavage showed. She smiled, her eyes glittering, and then she walked out of the toilets and back into the club, straight onto the dance floor and into her husband's arms.

'You ever double-cross me,' she whispered to him. 'You ever two-time me or fuck me over, and you are finished.'

He looked at her, startled, then laughed.

'You've been at the wacky baccy with Adrian,' he said. 'You're being paranoid.'

He wrapped his arms round her and pulled her to him. The music curled itself about them. She put her head on his shoulder, wondering if she could trust him, wondering if that rogue Milton gene was inside him too.

Across the dance floor, she saw Adrian and Serena slip out of the door. At the bar, Philip was watching her, lazily, his eyes narrowed.

She shivered.

'Just because you're paranoid,' she thought, 'doesn't mean they're not out to get you.'

Frankly, the sooner The Shack was sold, the better.

5

SANDCASTLES

Janet watched in pride as her son drew out the foundations of his castle carefully in the sand. He had the exact measurements written on a piece of paper. He had all the tools he needed by his side. He had several hours before the tide came back in for his trial run. And three more days to run through it again. Three more days until the competition.

Her heart constricted slightly when she thought about it. The competition was the highlight of Alan's year. He spent months preparing, experimenting with different designs, then practising. If anyone deserved to win, it was Alan. And of course, for the past three years, he had. The look on his face as he clutched the trophy to his chest made it all worth while, but Janet always worried this was the year he would lose. As soon as they arrived at the beach hut, she became tormented with doubts, almost crippled with the fear of his dejection if the trophy was handed over to someone else. And it could happen. The Everdene Sandcastle Competition was becoming bigger and bigger, the prize money was considerable. People were coming from all over the country to take part. Businesses were sponsoring competitors to put their logos on the front of their castles. The local news team were coming this year to film it; there were rumours of a whole programme being made. There were food stalls, drink stalls, entertainment, glamorous girls distributing leaflets. What had started as a bit of fun on the beach had become big business. Like anything good in this country, it had sold out. Gone commercial.

Janet's hands gripped the rail of the veranda as she watched her son coming back up the beach with two large buckets of water. Water was as essential as sand in the building of a castle. It was the moisture that held the construction together. She watched as he poured his cargo carefully over his plot and mixed it in to get the perfect texture. It was a science as much as an art.

Of all the epithets thrown at Alan's condition over the years, simple was the one his mother liked most. Simple meant easy. Simple meant straightforward. And to Janet, that was exactly what he was. There were plenty of other words that had been used. Not all of them euphemistic. Backward. Not all there. Retard. Two sandwiches short of a picnic. Challenging.

Special needs, they would have called him now, of course.

Not that she had ever really had a proper diagnosis. They blamed lack of oxygen at birth. She had known something was wrong when she was in labour. Call it a mother's instinct. The pain had been unnatural; she could sense the baby inside her belly writhing in discomfort. The midwife had told her sharply not to be so stupid when she described her fears. Childbirth was supposed to hurt.

Now, of course, they would have had him on a monitor. They would have known the cord was wrapped around his neck. They would have known her baby was in distress, and they would have taken the appropriate action, instead of leaving her for hours, sick with dread, until she had finally delivered him.

Her beautiful, wonderful, damaged baby.

They hadn't known anything was wrong at the time. On the surface, he looked perfect. But gradually, as he failed to develop as fast as his peers, a picture emerged, and the difficult delivery had become the scapegoat. By then, Janet adored her son more than any other mother had ever loved a child.

Not once did she bemoan her situation. She seemed to accept quite happily that it was her lot to look after him. He was slow to potty train, slow to speak, slow to learn how to use a knife and fork, but Janet never got frustrated. She had the patience of a saint with Alan, and he always got there in the end, which made her all the more proud of his achievements.

Unfortunately, her husband wasn't as enamoured. He had no patience with the little boy, and would shout at him when he was slow to react, or got things wrong. Janet caught him looking at his son with contempt and loathing once too often. Eventually she told him to go. They would be better off without him. Alan didn't need someone breathing down his neck and belittling him. He needed love and encouragement, not ill-concealed scorn. Her husband didn't need telling twice.

For the past thirty years, it had been just the two of them. Of course it was hard. She was a single mother with a disabled child. Her husband, once he had gone, didn't see it his duty to make any contribution towards his offspring and she certainly didn't demand it. She could manage. She *would* manage. She devoted herself to Alan entirely, and woe betide anyone who suggested she might need a break. Why would she need a break from the person who was her reason for living?

When he was in his early twenties, the social services put pressure on her to let Alan go into sheltered accommodation. They insisted it would do him good to have a bit of independence. They were confident he would be able to manage. But Janet refused. He belonged with her. She was there to look after him. She didn't want any respite. The thought of waking up without Alan in the house filled her with dread. What on earth would she do without him? The snotty social worker dared to suggest she was being selfish, that she didn't have Alan's interests at heart. Didn't have his interests at heart? She had devoted her whole life to him. Bloody social workers – they weren't happy unless they were interfering and making you feel bad about yourself. She soon sent her away with a flea in her ear.

Then there had been what she had come to think of as the Rachel fiasco. That had given her a terrible scare. Alan attended a centre three afternoons a week. She had come to collect him early, because she needed to pick up a prescription from the surgery on the way home. She had found him holding hands with a woman, sitting on the bench in the garden. Appalled, she had grilled the people who ran the centre and found out the truth. Alan and Rachel had been 'close' for weeks. The staff didn't see what the problem was. They thought it was sweet.

Janet thought it was dangerous. It upset the status quo.

It upset the balance of Alan's life, to bring in a third party. Besides, what if this Rachel was just toying with his affections and ended up breaking his heart? Worse, what if they got too close and . . . It was an instinct, after all, to mate, wasn't it? It would be a disaster.

Janet had to nip it in the bud. She quickly made arrangements for Alan to attend another centre, in another town. It meant a bit more travelling, but it didn't matter. He was confused at first, but he soon settled in. She didn't worry that he might ever find his way to the old centre. Alan didn't understand the bus timetable, and had a hopeless sense of direction. He'd never be able to find his way back to Rachel, and Janet was super-vigilant to make sure he didn't transfer his affections to anyone else.

It was soon after the Rachel fiasco that he had discovered sand sculpture. He'd seen it on the telly, and he wanted a go. He'd always been good at art. He was five when she realised he had a talent. The pictures he drew even at that young age were vivid and accurate. And so she fed his talent over the years, spending all her extra money on materials for him, marvelling at how this part of his brain had obviously remained intact. She went to the Early Learning Centre and bought him a big blue plastic sandpit, then filled it with sacks of pristine sand. And he began to sculpt. Simple things at first – a horse's head, a turtle. Then more complicated – a sphinx, a dragon, a minotaur. She was delighted that he had found a new passion, and hoped that it helped dim any memories of Rachel that he might be harbouring. He had mentioned her once or twice, but the sand sculpting seemed the perfect distraction. He wasn't really a people person, Alan. He was a doer.

Someone had told Janet about the annual sandcastle competition at Everdene. She had saved hard for months to scrape together enough money for them to go. A beach hut seemed like the perfect place for them to stay, and so she rented one for a week. He would be able to practise on the sand right outside their door. And she didn't like hotels or bed and breakfasts. They never did things properly, the way she would. They went there on the bus, Alan excitedly clutching his sketches, his case filled with the tools he would need.

He hadn't won the first year. It had all been a bit strange and new, and he had been nervous. But they'd had a wonderful time. The sun shone down on them, and Janet had enjoyed being a bit lackadaisical. They'd thrown out their routine. She didn't have to do any housework, not really. Or proper cooking. They'd made the most of the chip shop, and the pasty shop, and the kiosk on the front that sold crab sandwiches and little paper cups of cockles. They'd even gone for scampi at the Ship Aground, sitting outside on one of the tables that overlooked the beach. Oh, and cream tea at the big hotel on the front. It didn't matter that they'd gone a bit over budget. She'd just have to do without for a couple of weeks – not get her magazine, or have her hair done. They both agreed at the end of the week to come back next year.

The second year he had been better prepared and more confident in his surroundings, and had the victor's flag stuck by the front of his drawbridge. Janet had taken a picture and had it blown up to put over the fireplace in the lounge, along with the trophy that sat on the mantel-piece. It still made her heart burst with pride. He'd won the two years running after that as well.

Janet's biggest fear was that somehow the judges would decide it would be fair if the prize went to someone else this year. She had heard a few grumblings the year before about it being a fix, but how on earth could it be a fix? She certainly had no influence over anyone. It was judged purely on merit. But still she felt uneasy. She had no idea how Alan would react if he didn't win. Maybe they shouldn't have come back. Maybe they should have quit while he was ahead. Was she wrong to expose him to it again, getting his hopes up?

Her misgivings faded once they arrived at the hut and settled in. After four years it had become a home from home, and they had their rituals. Janet unpacked their belongings and rewashed all the cups, plates and cutlery provided in the hut – you never knew if the previous person had done a proper job – while Alan went to find the perfect pitch for his practice runs. Over the next couple of days, he acquired quite an audience – teams of young boys eager to help, to run down to the sea with buckets. He was incredibly patient, showing them the meticulous care needed to construct the perfect sculpture, how you started from the top down, how you could use a drinking straw to blow out the more intricate pieces of carving. And at the end of the day, he let them destroy his creation before the tide came in to do it for him. Janet always felt sad to watch the fruits of his labour crushed underfoot, but he never seemed to mind. A sandcastle wasn't for keeps, he told her.

The day of the competition finally arrived, gloriously

sunny. There seemed to be more competitors than ever this year, and Janet felt butterflies as she wandered up and down the different plots, expertly assessing their potential, eyeing up the tools they had brought with them. There were lots of families who didn't have a hope, who were presumably just in it for the fun – the dads taking it very seriously, while the kids hopped up and down with impatience, waving their spades. By the end of her tour, she estimated about five serious contenders who were consulting elaborate sketches, and who had a look of determination in their eyes.

Alan was quite happy in the middle of his plot. Having practised three times on site he had it down to a fine art, and was busy laying out the foundations. There was a couple next to him not taking it at all seriously – a pair of teenagers messing about, pouring sand down each other's backs. At one point the girl squealed and ran away backwards, not looking where she was going and nearly crashing into Alan's plot. Janet clenched her fists, but the girl realised what she had done, apologised to Alan prettily, so Janet relaxed.

There was nothing she could do now. It was all in the lap of the gods. She just had to make sure Alan had enough suncream on, and drank plenty of fluids – he'd got badly burnt the year before last, as she had underestimated the strength of the midday sun. And she'd bring him regular snacks. She had a pile of sandwiches made up in the hut, and some fruit, and at some point she'd go and buy him an ice cream.

There was a party atmosphere building up. The competition had grown and grown in popularity, to the point where the local radio station sent down a DJ to whip up the spectators into a frenzy of anticipation. The bass of the music boomed out across the beach; seagulls swooped overhead cawing at the invasion, their beady eyes sweeping the beach for scraps of food. The television crew wandered up and down, stopping to interview each competitor. When they came to Alan, Janet shot out from the beach hut and came to supervise. In the end, she felt it was best if she spoke for Alan.

'He's always been a wonderful artist,' she explained to the world at large. 'And the Sandcastle Competition is the highlight of his year.'

'I believe he's held the trophy for the past three years?'

'We're quite confident,' smiled Janet. 'He's been working on this design for months. Every detail is historically accurate.'

'Definitely a work of art,' commented the interviewer.

A work of genius, thought Janet privately, but it wasn't really her place to say so. It never ceased to amaze her, how he could construct something so wonderful out of a few million grains of sand. His fingers swooped, scooped, patted and caressed, coaxing the sand into shape. His minions were on hand, pointing out areas of potential weakness. Eventually Neptune's castle emerged, proud and glorious, the great god himself presiding over his domicile, trident aloft.

The teenagers next to him were taking a break, slugging back beer, wiping the sweat from their brows. The girl was in a bikini top and cut-off shorts, her long copper curls scooped up in an untidy pile on top of her head. For a moment, Janet had a glimpse back to another girl – a carefree sixteen-year-old with romantic hopes and dreams. She shook away the memory. She wouldn't swap what she had, if she had her time over again, she told herself. She walked over to the nearest ice-cream van and bought Alan a Magnum. White was his favourite. She was rewarded with a smile, but he barely had time to pause and eat it. When he was engrossed, nothing would distract him.

The mid-afternoon sun beat down relentlessly. Scantily clad girls moved amongst the contestants and the audience handing out bottles of water. Chart-topping hits pounded out, the DJ getting more and more hysterical as the moment of judgement approached. The judge was some sort of local celebrity – a singer with a boy-band, with gelled-back hair and mirrored sunglasses, who had spent most of the afternoon signing his name on young girls' arms, to many squeals of excitement. Janet watched carefully as he moved his way amongst the entries, wondering what his criteria were for judging. Did he have any idea about artistic merit, or technical skill? He was accompanied by the organisers of the competition – a couple of bigwigs from the local council, she guessed – and a representative from the building company that were sponsoring the competition. Everywhere they went they were shadowed by the television crew, eager to capture every moment.

Gradually they whittled their choices down to about five. Janet watched, eagle-eyed, as they moved between them, conferring amongst themselves. Alan was still in the running. Of course he was. There was no doubt that his castle was the most superior. It was only a matter of time. He didn't seem remotely perturbed by the outcome. He was busy chatting to people who came to talk to him about his work, smiling away, quite oblivious.

It was down to the last three. Alan and his Neptune's castle. The teenagers next to him, whose work was now evident as Sleeping Beauty's castle, smothered in briars and roses. And a crop-headed man and his long-haired mate who had built a reconstruction of Portmeirion. Janet thought her heart was going to burst out of her chest. She couldn't bear the suspense. The DJ wasn't helping.

'We're going to have a winner any minute. The judges are in dispute, apparently. They can't agree . . .'

How could they not agree? It was blatantly obvious who was the winner. The skill, the craft, the detail, it was all there. Janet supposed they had to tease it out, like all the reality television shows. They had to milk it for the cameras. Everything was a charade these days.

When she saw the judge finally come to rest by the young couple, and stick the flag that denoted first prize into their turret, she thought she was going to be sick. She couldn't read the expression on Alan's face, or even be sure he understood. The couple were hugging each other, the girl with her wild red mane, the boy with his dark hair swept back. Lucky, healthy, privileged kids to whom this was just a joke, a novelty, something to laugh over in the pub tonight. Not the reward for a year's hard work. She felt a sour taste in her mouth. Disappointment. Resentment. The television crew were muscling in, poking their microphones towards the couple. The girl shimmered and sparkled, her eyes lighting up as she expressed her delight at winning.

Of course they had gone for her. It was going to be on television. They wanted someone who looked good, who could articulate her feelings, who would be the perfect spokeswoman for the cynical money-making machine the contest had become. They didn't want a middle-aged man with learning difficulties who would struggle to communicate his feelings, even though he had overcome more obstacles to achieve this than the winning couple would ever experience in their combined life-times.

She watched as Alan and his team of helpers leapt up and down on his handiwork in their ritual destruction. Next door, the winning castle stood proudly, the victor's flag fluttering in the breeze. Janet felt an overwhelming urge to go and stamp it down herself, crushing each of the towers with her foot, kicking in the drawbridge, but she knew that would be bad form. Instead, she went and put the kettle on for a cup of tea.

One thing was certain. She couldn't go through it all again – the build-up, the anticipation, the tension, the disappointment.

They wouldn't come back next year.

6

BEACHCOMBERS

When, exactly, had the Ginger Ninja turned into a Titian temptress?

The last time Harry Milton saw Florence Carr, she was a spotty, frizzy-haired skinny little thing, youngest daughter of the family three huts down whom everyone tried to avoid because they were total trainspotters. And now? Now she was quite simply stunning. The ginger frizz had morphed into copper ringlets, her eyes were green flecked with gold, the Everdene sun had kissed her skin palest bronze.

She took his breath away.

Harry had groaned when his grandmother had told him the Carrs had invited them down for a barbecue.

'Oh no,' he protested. 'The Boring Family. They are so massively uncool.'

The Carrs looked like something out of the nineteen fifties, with their badly knitted jumpers, cagoules and thick-rimmed glasses. Nerds, the lot of them. They were always striding about with binoculars, or one of those laminated maps on a piece of string round their necks.

'We've got to go, darling,' his grandmother chided

him. 'Mr Carr's been giving me lots of professional advice. Gratis. Accepting their invitation graciously is the least I can do. So please come. Just for me.'

Harry concurred, good-naturedly, because he knew his grandmother had been put through the wringer and had been left in a terrible mess after his grandfather died. That was why she was having to sell the hut. Harry couldn't believe this would be his last summer at Everdene. He'd been here every year since he was born, with his brothers and sisters and cousins and uncles and aunts, all of them coming and going in a steady stream. Sometimes his grandmother was left with all her grandchildren, while the middle generation went on with their jobs safe in the knowledge their offspring were having the time of their lives. They all squashed in somehow. There was no privacy, of course, which became difficult as they got older, but actually they didn't care.

For the past few days it had been just him and Jane, and it had been rather nice. After all, she wasn't like normal grandmothers. She didn't fuss and cluck, or disapprove. She was very laid-back, had her finger on the pulse of what was happening in the world. 'Groovy Granny', they sometimes called her for a joke. And she was generous. She always knew when to slip you fifty quid on the quiet, and she'd paid for him to have driving lessons the year before. Now she was strapped for cash, of course. Harry didn't understand quite what had happened – how could his grandfather have left her in such a mess, when he was supposed to be a financial adviser?

Anyway, Harry knew it was kind of Mr Carr to give her advice – he was some sort of hotshot accountant – so of course he agreed to come to the barbecue. He hadn't bothered to make much of an effort to dress up, because the Carrs were the least fashion-conscious family on the planet – Mr Carr wore socks under his sandals, and the boys always had on shorts that were either embarrassingly small or ridiculously large, and Mrs Carr looked as if she got all her clothes from a charity shop.

So when Florence emerged from the depths of their hut with a tray of meat for the barbecue, looking beyond cool in cut-off denim shorts, a White Stripes T-shirt and gladiator sandals, Harry nearly dropped his beer.

'Hi.' She flashed him a smile, revealing perfect teeth and a dimple. He tried not to stare as he took in the snake tattoo on her perfectly flat, brown stomach, the armful of silver bracelets, the tongue ring – bloody hell, Florence Carr with a *tongue* ring? She was a total babe.

'Florence is off to Cambridge,' her mother was saying proudly. 'To do law. She wants to be a barrister.'

'I'm having a year off, though,' Florence added. 'I'm going to South America.'

They both looked at Harry expectantly. He struggled to find his tongue. The tongue he hadn't had the bottle to get pierced, even though he wanted to.

'I'm off to Bristol. To do medicine.'

'Cool,' said Florence. 'You having a gap year?'

'No,' replied Harry. 'It's such a long course. I didn't want to be a pensioner when I came out.'

Everyone laughed, and he took a swig of beer. He felt a bit strange. He wished he was wearing something a bit edgier than a pair of combat shorts and a Jack Wills sweatshirt. And bloody Crocs, for God's sake. One of the great things about Everdene was it didn't matter what you looked like, you just dressed for comfort, and even if everyone looked like a knob in Crocs they still wore them and it didn't matter.

Florence tossed her mane of hair back over her shoulders and took a slug of beer from her bottle.

'It's open mic night at the Ship Aground later,' she told Harry. 'If you fancy going.'

'Sure,' he said, and felt his heart beat faster.

This was really weird.

He never fell for girls. They fell for him. If he saw someone he took a liking to, he crooked his finger and they came running. Girls with glossy hair and long, coltish legs who smelt expensive. Yet he had never been left almost speechless by someone. He wasn't sure it was a feeling he liked. Was this love at first sight? And what was he supposed to do about it? He didn't even know if she had a boyfriend, if some uber-cool bloke in skinny jeans and a Kurt Cobain haircut was going to rock up any minute and claim her for his own.

His eyes barely left her throughout the barbecue. She was confident, unselfconscious, gregarious. She took charge of the cooking – Harry remembered from past experience that the Carrs could massacre a simple sausage; they were either raw or overcooked – but Florence had marinated chicken pieces in honey and ginger, and made a couscous salad which her parents eyed with suspicion, slick with olive oil and flecked with finely chopped flat-leaf parsley.

'Jamie Oliver,' she told everyone, and it was, as Harry had suspected it would be, delicious.

For dessert, she sliced open bananas still in their skins, drizzling them with rum and pushing in squares of chocolate. Then she wrapped them in foil and put them on the dying embers of the barbecue. The Carrs just seemed to accept that this phoenix had risen from their midst. They took their instruction from her meekly.

Harry watched her eat her banana. She was sitting cross-legged on the picnic rug, her hair tumbling round her shoulders, excavating the chocolatey goo with a plastic spoon, licking up every last drop of sweetness. He felt a ravening hunger deep inside. He wanted to kiss away the sticky confection from her lips, devour her. The feeling alarmed him. It was so powerful. Visceral.

He started as she looked up at him, smiling. She knew.

'Shall we go, then?' she asked him, tossing her paper plate into a nearby bin-bag. 'I don't suppose the wrinklies will mind.'

Wild horses couldn't have stopped him.

Harry loved the Ship Aground. He'd had his first illegal drink there at thirteen, his first kiss at fourteen, and his sixteenth birthday party. He'd worked there three summers in a row, collecting glasses. He knew all the staff. They were almost like family. Yet he never tired of it. It was filled with the local hardcore, and the perennial surfers, but kept itself fresh with the constant ebb and flow of summer tourists who fell for its charms.

It was bursting at the seams tonight as he walked in with Florence. He pushed through the crowds, nodding and waving at acquaintances, until they reached the bar, where he ordered them both drinks. The open-mic night was in full swing. People came up to do their turn, some clearly talented, others incapable of even holding a tune. They found a seat, unbelievably – two stools in a corner round an upturned barrel – and had to sit very close to

hear each other. They talked about music, about Glaston-
bury (she'd been, he hadn't), and the best gig they'd ever
been to (Red Hot Chili Peppers him, Beyoncé her). And
as an Alanis Morisette wannabe walked off the stage,
Florence put down her glass.

'Right,' she said. 'I'm going to have a go.'

He jumped up and followed her, fascinated as she took
the stage, conferred briefly with the drummer and guitarist, and stepped up to the mic. He had never met anyone
so self-assured. There wasn't a moment's hesitation or a
flicker of nerves. She smiled at the audience. There was a
ripple of applause at the opening chords. Harry recognised
it as Joan Armatrading, one of his mother's favourites, one
she subjected them to in the car when they were young,
along with Fleetwood Mac and Genesis, before they took
control of the CD player.

Then, almost in a whisper, Florence began to sing
'Love and Affection'. As she murmured the lyrics her eyes
momentarily locked with his.

For a moment he could barely breathe. Was this a
message, or was she just playing with him? Something
cold yet hot slithered into his blood, his heart, the
marrow of his bones. This wasn't just want. This was
need.

He didn't take his eyes off her as she went in on
herself, transported to another place, swept away by the
lyrics. The rest of the audience was as transfixed as he
was. He might think she was singing this for him, but
everyone was under her spell. And as the song built, she
held a rapport with the guitarist and drummer, their eyes
meeting, sharing smiles, even though they had only met
five minutes ago, and Harry felt a burning envy. Music

did that, it gave people a bond, an instant connection. His fingers were tightly gripped round his glass, his knuckles white with tension and jealousy.

As the song finished, she gave a little self-deprecating curtsey, then jumped off the stage to rapturous applause. When Harry tried to tell her how brilliant she was she shrugged it off with a laugh.

'You were amazing.'

'Not really.'

'Are you in a band?'

'God, no. I couldn't stand all those egos. Or all those tedious rehearsals.'

'You should be. You've got such talent.'

She rolled her eyes.

'Not really. I'm just copying. I couldn't write a song of my own.'

'Have you tried?'

'I don't want to.'

He was in awe, nevertheless. At someone who could get up on stage and perform like that, yet think nothing of it.

He'd never met anyone before who was more blessed than he was. It was sometimes very dull being the golden boy, the boy who couldn't fail, because there was almost nothing to strive for. Doors opened easily, people fell over backwards to do your bidding. It was like eating too much chocolate. You could have too much of a good thing. Life had no edge, no bite, when you were damn near perfect. Harry was head boy, captain of cricket, lead in every school play, president of the debating society. And he'd always had any girl he wanted. It wasn't that he hadn't enjoyed their company, but none of the relationships he'd had so far felt nourishing. They were . . . merely pleasant. They didn't make him come alive inside, they didn't make his soul sing. Florence was the first girl he had met who had sparked something inside him. And he hadn't a clue how to handle it.

By eleven o'clock they were quite drunk. He'd been buying her shots all night. Drunkenness suited her – she didn't go all floppy and giggly like a lot of girls. She became even more self-assured. Glittery and dangerous. It only made him want her all the more.

In his vodka haze, he remembered one rule. A rule he'd never had to bring into play before. If you really wanted a girl, you didn't show it. You had to play it cool. At half past eleven, with a monumental effort of will, he told her he was going home.

'I've got some stuff to deal with,' he said vaguely.

She looked disconcerted.

'Bor-ing,' she told him.

'I know,' he smiled. 'Sorry.' And he walked away.

Don't look back, he told himself. Don't look back.

It worked. The next morning she came up to his hut and knocked on the door. He couldn't believe the thrill he felt when he saw her red hair through the glass. The ferment in his blood when she smiled and asked if he wanted to go surfing.

'Sure,' he replied, as casually as he could.

'Did you get your "stuff" done?' She raised her eyebrows archly, looking for a clue.

'Yeah.' What he'd actually done was lie for hours in his bunk in a slightly drunken torment, wondering how to play things next.

'Hi, Mrs Milton.' Florence flashed Harry's grandmother a dazzling smile as she came back from the shop with a pint of milk.

Jane smiled back at the pair of them.

'We're going surfing – if that's OK,' Harry told her. 'You'll be all right?'

'Course.' Jane pointed to a pile of paper waiting for her on the table. 'I've got a heap of paperwork to deal with. It seems to be never-ending.'

'Oh yeah,' said Florence. 'Dad was saying you're going to have to sell the hut. What a bummer.'

Harry winced. He knew Jane didn't much like discussing it. But she didn't seem to mind Florence's forthrightness.

'Yes,' she said drily. 'It's a real bummer. But that's life. Nothing good lasts for ever.'

'Doesn't it?' Florence wrinkled her nose. 'Why not?'

Why not indeed? thought Harry. This summer, for instance. He hoped that was going to last for ever.

They spent all day together at the bottom end of the beach where the seasoned surfers hung out. The waves were higher here and the grockles couldn't be bothered to walk down this far, so there weren't any obese families stuffing their faces with chips and stubbing their cigarettes out in the sand.

Florence was good at surfing – of course – but in the end Harry had more stamina. She lay on her towel watching him, until eventually he had to admit defeat. People thought surfing was just about standing on your board, but actually it was knackering – paddling out against the tide, using your upper body strength to stand up just at the right moment, then keeping your balance before wiping out.

There was nothing better than surfing exhaustion – it was an all-over tiredness, a combination of physical effort and being at the mercy of the elements: the sun, the water and the wind. Afterwards they lay side by side on the beach, then Florence rummaged in her bag and produced ham sandwiches and chocolate fridge cake that her mother had made. Later, they made their way back up the beach at the languorous pace of the truly relaxed, windswept and sun-kissed. As they reached the Carrs' hut, Harry prayed she would want to come out again that evening.

'Meet you for a drink later?' he asked. 'I've got to have supper with my grandmother. She's had a bit of a shit time lately.'

'Hey, you don't have to explain,' said Florence. 'See you in the Ship about ten?'

Harry and Jane ate mushroom omelettes with salad and French bread at a little bistro table outside the hut. They agreed this was the best time of day, when the majority of people had gone home but the diehards were still enjoying the waves and the sand. Dogs ran round in ecstatic circles, kites fluttered in the evening breeze, plumes of smoke gave away people having barbecues.

'You seem to be getting on well with Florence,' commented Jane. 'Considering you all used to go out of your way to avoid her like the plague.'

Harry grinned ruefully.

'I don't think it's the same person. I think they

swapped her. I think some other family's got the Ginger Ninja.'

'She's certainly grown up,' said Jane. 'But be careful . . .'

'Be careful?' Harry frowned. 'What do you mean?'

Jane took a sip of her wine and decided she'd said too much. It was just a feeling she had. Feminine intuition. A sense that Florence was enjoying being admired by Harry, because you'd have to be blind not to see his infatuation. And she felt very protective of her grandson. A grandmother wasn't supposed to have favourites, but how could Harry not be her favourite, with his easy charm and affectionate nature? He'd stayed on this week specially to keep her company, because he was worried about her. Not many eighteen-year-old boys would worry about their grandmother like that.

She wasn't going to voice her concern, though.

'Oh, just ignore me,' she told him. 'I suppose I'm feeling a bit . . .'

She waved a hand in the air to indicate a general lack of oneness with the world. He reached over and touched her arm.

'You'll be OK,' he assured her. 'We'll all look after you.'

Jane didn't want to be looked after. She didn't want to rely on her family for anything more than wonderful moments like this. She didn't want to be a burden. She wanted to be a pleasure that could be picked up and put down, dictated to by nothing more than the seasons – Christmas, Easter, birthdays, the summer. She felt a little burst of anger again at her predicament. Bloody Graham, she thought for the millionth time. Spoiling everything like this for everyone.

She smiled over at Harry. He was obviously anxious to go and meet Florence again, but was too polite to say so.

'Off you go,' she said. 'I'll wash up.'

As she watched him go, she said a little prayer for his heart. Such a fragile thing, that organ that ruled your physical being.

Tonight was just dancing at the Ship. No bands, just a DJ blasting out funk and disco from the seventies. Florence looked like an angel in a floaty white dress spattered with white sequins that set off her tan. It was hot and they both drank too much, becoming woozy from booze and the day's exertion. They held onto each other as the DJ slowed the music down. Harry recognised Barry White. Another of his mother's blasts from the past. But you couldn't argue with it. You couldn't dance to it with another person and not want to get closer to them. The gravelly voice and the relentlessly throbbing beat took you over. Their eyes were locked. He went to kiss her but she shook her head, pulling him through the sweating hordes and out of the door, leading him back down to the beach, down behind the huts where it was dark, and sheltered from the wind, and no one could see you.

Now she was kissing him. He was touching her golden skin with his fingertips. Weaving his fingers through that mass of curls. She tasted wonderful – sweet but salty. She ran her tongue ring over his top lip and he shivered. He slipped his hands under the flimsy cotton of her dress, ran his hands up her body until he felt her breasts.

She arched her back and pushed them into his palms, welcoming his touch. Her nipples were hard.

He was hard.

'Fuck me, Harry,' she whispered hoarsely in his ear.

Normally, he wouldn't need telling twice. But he didn't want it to be like this. A seedy shag up against the back of a beach hut? This was his first true love, a woman he was in awe of. A woman he revered. He wanted to undress her slowly on a bed, feast his eyes on her beauty, make proper love to her, make it a night she would never forget.

'I don't want to do it here,' he told her.

'Come on,' she goaded him, tugging at his belt with one hand and feeling his cock with her other. He groaned. This was the most exquisite torture.

With a mighty effort of will, he pulled away.

'Call me weird,' he said, 'but I'd rather do it somewhere . . . comfortable. I'm not really into al fresco sex.'

She pulled away from him, frowning. He sensed a sudden change in her mood. A sulkiness.

'It's not that I don't want to . . .'

'You *don't* want to.' She smiled, but her eyes narrowed. 'If you don't fancy me, just say.'

'Fancy you? Of course I fancy you. Florence, I . . .'

He couldn't say it. He couldn't say he loved her. He'd sound such an idiot. He'd barely known her twenty-four hours. Well, he'd known her for years, strictly speaking, but not *this* Florence, this bewitching creature that had him losing sleep, his appetite, his bloody mind . . .

'Fine.' She started adjusting her clothing, covering herself back up. That electric skin, those softly firm breasts.

'Listen,' he said urgently. 'Tomorrow . . .'

She put her hands on her hips.

'Tomorrow's the sandcastle competition.' Clearly, in her mind, a sandcastle competition and a lovers' tryst were mutually exclusive. 'You are going to help me, aren't you?'

'Of course . . .'

Any excuse to spend more time with her.

'Good. I'll see you in the morning.'

She walked away from him, back towards her hut, her head held high and her shoulders back, clearly still smarting from his reluctance. If she only knew.

He went to bed that night in despair. He could smell her on him, the scent of burnt oranges. He didn't think he would sleep, but he did, and when he did, he had troubled, mixed-up dreams filled with her face, her voice, her very essence. He woke at four o'clock with a shout, and was appalled to find tears on his face. He thought he might be going mad.

The next day he woke with resolve. He got dressed quickly and walked up the beach and into the village to the tourist office. He knew they kept a list of hotels and guest houses that had vacancies, because his family often referred friends there when they came down to stay. The helpful assistant printed him out a list. He quickly dismissed the top three establishments as too old-fashioned and fuddy-duddy, but the fourth, a bed and breakfast called Beachcombers, described itself as 'fresh and funky, a romantic getaway with a luxury edge – wi-fi, white linen and breathtaking views'.

He walked along the esplanade until he found it –

an old Edwardian villa on the front that had been given a total makeover, with seagrass flooring, ice-cream-coloured walls and unframed canvases. The owner was a willowy surfer-chick with a friendly smile who didn't look at him askance when he asked to see the room they had available.

It was small but perfect, painted in turquoise and white, with a tiny little balcony framed by voile curtains. Harry's heart thumped as he booked it.

'Just for one night,' he told the owner. 'It's a surprise for my girlfriend.'

'We can arrange champagne. And fresh flowers. And chocolates.'

Why not? thought Harry.

'All three, please,' he grinned, imagining dropping rose petals one by one onto her bare skin and pushing truffles into her mouth.

At quarter past eleven, Florence came to find him.

'Come on,' she said. 'The competition starts at midday. We mustn't be late.'

The sandcastle competition had become an annual ritual for anyone who spent the summer at Everdene. The Miltons always entered, with whichever part of their family was present, though they never won. It had become bigger and bigger over the years – Harry could remember when it was just a few dads and kids with buckets and spades, but now it caused chaos in Everdene, with emergency car parks set up in farmers' fields to cope with the extra visitors.

They quickly found their pitch, and Florence unpacked her day's supplies. Harry got the feeling that winning was important to Florence – she was eyeing up the competition with a fervour he didn't feel.

'That weird guy over there has won for the past three years,' she told him, pointing to a bloke on the neighbouring pitch who was obviously not quite the full ticket. 'I'm going to beat him if it kills me.'

Harry privately thought a sandcastle competition wasn't really worth dying for, but he didn't say so.

'And look,' she nudged him, pointing. 'There's Marky Burns. He's judging.'

He saw a gleam in her eye that he didn't like, a gleam that set a shiver of unease shooting through his belly. Marky Burns was the closest thing Everdene had to a local celebrity, a member of a boy-band which had notched up three number ones two years ago. Marky was striding round with a news crew in his wake, looking self-important and, Harry thought, rather a twat. But who was he to judge?

All day he followed Florence's instructions, running down to the sea for buckets of water to wet the sand and get the right consistency. She'd designed a Sleeping Beauty castle, smothered in roses and briars, and it was quite spectacular. Yet Harry couldn't help feeling uneasy. She kept checking the progress of the man next door, who was building Neptune's castle – a definite contender. Harry got the feeling Florence would go and stamp on his work-in-progress given half the chance.

'Isn't it just supposed to be a bit of fun?' he asked her at one point, and earnt himself a steely glare.

At three o'clock the whistle went and all the competitors stopped, grateful for respite, and the judging began. The time went agonisingly slowly, as Marky

Burns and the other judges wandered from pitch to pitch, comparing notes. The local DJ wound everyone up and played hideously cheesy beach songs, together with messages from the competition sponsors.

'It's all got a bit over the top, don't you think?' he asked Florence, but she wasn't paying attention. She was tracking the judges' progress, assessing how much time they had spent analysing each entry. Harry wasn't sure whether to pray for them to win, in which case he could whisk her away to celebrate, or to lose, in which case he could whisk her away to make it up to her. Was a woman more compliant in the throes of triumph or despair? He couldn't be sure. Nevertheless, the decision was out of his hands. But he smiled to himself as he thought about the little turquoise bedroom that waited for them, and the champagne that would be chilling.

When the judges came to their pitch, Harry stood to one side and let Florence do the talking. He noticed how she addressed Marky Burns over the others, flicking her hair over her shoulder and widening her eyes as she described the concept behind her work.

'I wanted to do something feminine,' she explained. 'Sandcastles are often so masculine, with harsh lines. I wanted to do something soft and curvaceous, something that you want to caress. Something . . . womanly.'

The other judges nodded earnestly. As they turned away, Florence caught Marky Burns's eye and winked. He smirked back at her. Her message was pretty clear. Harry felt sick. No one else had seen it but him. He looked down at the sand. He might as well just walk away now. But then Florence came up and put her arms round him. She smelt of suntan lotion, and the free ice cream that had been given to them by one of the sponsors. It made him giddy.

'Hey. You've been brilliant. Thank you. And if we win, the champagne's on me.'

She squeezed him tight. He felt mollified. Maybe her flirtation had been all about the winning and nothing else. He hoped so, but he wasn't entirely confident. This was a whole new feeling for Harry. He had never felt insecure about a girl before. He'd never felt his stomach burn with panic that the object of his affections was looking elsewhere. He'd never felt his heart lurch with fear. He'd never wanted to stab another man in the back, like he wanted to stab Marky Burns with his stupid mirrored sunglasses and his stupid raffia cowboy hat.

Florence grabbed his hand excitedly.

'They've made up their minds. Look, they're heading for us.'

They watched as the judges walked slowly towards them, holding the victor's flag.

'It could still be the bloke next door,' said Harry. 'It's between him and us.'

'He won't win. No way,' Florence assured him, and she was right.

As Marky Burns plunged the flagpole into the turret of their castle, a thunderous applause struck up, accompanied by cheers and whistles. Harry turned to Florence, ready to give her a congratulatory hug, but she already had her arms around Marky's neck. The cameras were going crazy, the news crew were zooming in. She was whispering in his ear; he had his hands on her ribs, just under her breasts.

Harry turned away, a bitter taste in his mouth. And as

he looked over, he saw the man from the neighbouring plot look disconsolately down at his castle. Only for a moment, but it was enough to make Harry feel a twinge of guilt. By rights, this man should have won. It was clear it was a close-run thing between the two of them, but Florence had managed to tip the balance in her favour by using her wiles. He felt rather ill. A woman came over to the man, taking him by the hand like a small child. Presumably it was his mother; presumably the man was a bit simple. It was wrong. What Florence had done was wrong.

The next moment he found himself knocked flying as Florence hugged him tight.

'We won, Harry!' He could feel her heart beating through the thinness of his T-shirt. 'I couldn't have done it without you.'

She kissed him on the mouth, and in that moment, all his misgivings floated away. So what if she'd flirted with the judge? That was life, wasn't it? He felt a wonderful warmth zing through his veins and his head go light as she pulled him forward by the hand to face the cameras.

'This is Harry,' she told them. 'We've been friends for absolutely years. And I couldn't have done it without him.'

He wanted to take her to the room straight away. He told her he had a surprise, but she wouldn't have it.

'Everyone's piling up to the Ship,' she told him. 'And there's going to be free booze.'

By everyone, it was clear she meant Marky Burns and his entourage. And the free booze didn't seem to extend to Harry. Just Florence, who was drinking Smirnoff Ice as if it was going out of fashion. And holding court to her newly captive audience. Harry stuck it out until he could bear it no longer. Until he saw Marky pin Florence to the wall, one of his long legs in between hers, his hip pushed suggestively up against her pelvis. She was looking up at him, laughing, curling her long hair round her fingers.

She was nothing but a star-fucker. If you could call Marky Burns a star. Which Harry didn't. He was a has-been from a second-rate boy-band. If he'd been an international superstar, Harry might have understood Florence's embarrassingly sycophantic behaviour, but he was hard pushed even to remember the name of the band Marky had been in.

The problem was it didn't make him want her any less.

The room suddenly seemed to close in on him. Too much sun, too much booze. He pushed his way outside, gasping for fresh air. The sound of the bar receded behind him as the door shut. He felt a breeze on his face and thought of the little blue bedroom, waiting, puzzled, the champagne going flat, the roses wilting, the chocolates melting.

He was still holding his bottle of Smirnoff Ice. In a fit of rage, he threw it against the stone wall that separated the front of the pub from the road. As it shattered into pieces he felt shock. He'd never done anything like that in his life. It went against everything, his upbringing, his moral code. Part of him told him to go inside and find a broom to sweep it up before someone was hurt, but he was too drunk. Too drunk and too afraid that if he went back inside he might go and punch Marky Burns right in the middle of his face.

He had to go home. He headed for the beach. Every time the door of the pub opened, he heard music and laughter, taunting him. He imagined Florence kissing Marky Burns. He should be kissing her, right now.

He reached the door of the hut. His grandmother was still up, watching television on the tiny portable. He stumbled in.

'Darling, are you OK?' She looked up, concerned.

'Too much sun,' he mumbled.

She stood up. 'Let me get you some water . . .'

'I'm fine. I just need . . . bed.'

He pushed past her, knowing he was being rude. But if he didn't, he would either be sick, or cry, or both. He flopped into his bunk, just managing to kick off his shoes, and pulled the covers over his head. He was going to feel like death in the morning.

Death didn't come close. He wasn't sure which hurt more, his head or his heart. Being out in the sun all afternoon always gave him sunstroke, he should have remembered that. He rolled over and went back to sleep.

At eleven o'clock, he woke to find his grandmother placing a cool hand on his forehead. She was holding a large glass of water in the other.

'Darling, I'm not going to ask too much. But you were in a bit of a state last night.'

She held out two tablets and the water. He sat up and swallowed them gratefully, hoping against hope that he hadn't said anything awful to upset her.

'I wasn't . . . rude, was I?'

Jane laughed. 'No. Not at all.' She looked at him shrewdly. 'Florence?'

He just shut his eyes and groaned in reply.

'Tell me to mind my own business, if you want to. But on the other hand, if you want a shoulder to cry on.'

She was so amazing, his grandmother. She always understood just what you were feeling, and knew just what to say.

'I didn't realise it could be so hard,' he told her. 'And the weird thing is, I don't even like her that much. I mean, she's a show-off. And shallow. And totally me me me. I can see that.'

'Anyone can see that,' replied Jane, then told herself Harry wouldn't want her to judge Florence, just his state of mind. 'But she's a very attractive girl. I can understand why you've fallen for her. Totally.'

Harry finished his water and lay back on his pillow.

'Thanks, Gran,' he managed, and shut his eyes. His head was pounding. 'I don't know what to do. Suddenly it's as if . . . she's the only thing that matters in my life. How can that be? I mean, I barely know her. Not this Florence, anyway. It's crazy . . .'

'That's love for you,' Jane told him. 'Irrational. Obsessional. Uncontrollable. Destructive.'

Harry opened his eyes again. He looked at his grandmother with interest. She was speaking from the heart. And with an uncharacteristic bitterness.

'You're not talking about Grandpa, are you?' he asked. 'You're not talking about what he did to you?'

'No,' she replied. 'I'm not. What he did was despicable, but it hasn't hurt me inside. I was long beyond that by the time he died.'

She reached out and took his hand.

'I want to tell you a story, Harry. About something

186

that happened to me when I was about your age. Because I don't want you to go through what I went through. I don't want you to waste more than a minute of your precious life on someone who doesn't matter. You are worth so much more than that.'

And so she told him the story she had never shared with anyone before. The story of a young girl and an older man, and a relationship that was never meant to be. And how she had spent her life longing for what might have been, never allowing herself to be happy with someone else, making the wrong choice and probably making other people unhappy into the bargain. If Graham hadn't made her happy perhaps it was because deep down he knew he was second best, and no one likes being second best.

'I know it's not going to make it any easier right this second,' Jane finished, 'but think of this as a cautionary tale. No matter how wonderful you might think Florence is now, no matter how happy you think she might make you, don't let her rule your life.'

Harry managed to sit up.

'That's such a terrible story,' he said, stricken. 'I had no idea.'

'Well, of course you didn't, darling. By the time you came along, I was the world's leading expert at pretending I was happy. And to tell you the truth, I *was* happy by then. I don't know that I was a terribly good mother, but being a grandmother is wonderful. You children have all brought me more joy than anyone deserves, so altogether I'm very lucky.'

She bent down and hugged him.

'Listen, lecture over. You don't want to listen to an old

woman banging on. If I were you I'd go back to sleep. I'll make you some lunch when you wake up.' She gave him a quick kiss. 'Sleep tight. But think about what I've told you.'

Harry watched her go from his bunk. He was in awe. What an amazing story. He'd always admired his grandmother, but he never knew she was harbouring such a torrid secret. He felt desperately sad that she had been so unhappy all her life. And as he drifted off to sleep, he realised that the only way he could make her tragedy less . . . well, tragic, was by learning from her mistake.

Fuck Florence, he thought, then laughed ruefully. He hadn't had the pleasure.

Jane went back into the living area and sat down in her pale green Lloyd Loom chair. It was agonising, seeing someone you love in pain, knowing there was nothing you could do to take it away. She would gladly have taken his suffering for herself. She knew only too well the gnawing feeling Harry would have inside him, how he would be torturing himself with the possibility that things might change, one moment filled with optimism then the next plunged into gloom. But of course she couldn't. He had to suffer himself. She reminded herself that it was the ability to hurt like this that makes us human, that he would come back stronger in the long run.

She sighed, and reached down for her handbag. The letter had arrived three days before, forwarded from her solicitor to the post office in Everdene. She had recognised the writing on the cream bonded envelope immediately – how could she not, after all those hours of deciphering his assertive scrawl? Even half a century on her heart had leapt into her mouth at the sight of it. How often had she dreamt of a letter from him, a letter begging for forgiveness, a letter declaring he couldn't live without her? Of course it had never come.

She smoothed out the paper again. She'd already read it a dozen times.

My dear Jane

Thank you so much for returning Exorcising Demons *to me. I don't know what finally prompted you to do so, and I certainly didn't deserve to have it back.*

I admired your actions that day more than I can tell you. When I saw the flyleaf on the stove, my feelings were so mixed – total horror, of course, but an absolute thrill that you had such spirit and had executed such a just punishment. I longed to run after you, steal you away from your family, make you mine for ever more, but it wouldn't have been right. You were so young, so bright – you didn't deserve a life sentence with the selfish, self-indulgent monster I had become, and I got much worse, I can tell you. Although sometimes I wonder if you would have mellowed me, been my salvation in some way. I don't think so – the rot had well and truly set in by the time I met you.

Time and again over the years I was tempted to pick up my pen and write to you. I always searched the streets of London when I was out, hoping for a glimpse of your beautiful, laughing face, perhaps in a café or disappearing into the Tube. When I walked past shop windows I would pick out dresses for you, when I went to a restaurant I would imagine what you would choose to eat if you were with me. The longing never left me, not really. I told myself that if fate ever did deliver you to me again, then we were meant to be, and I would claim you back. But fate never did.

Part of me was tempted to throw the manuscript on the fire as you had, but as you know I am a coward, a man who has never had the strength of his own convictions. My publishers, needless to say, are delighted. They had long given up hope of getting something lucid out of me in my old age. You may have read in the press that they are rushing out a special edition for the autumn – unbelievably there are legions of people out there eager to lap up whatever I care to write.

I know the story of where the manuscript has been and how it was returned to me would have the press salivating, but I have a shred of decency left in me and wouldn't wish to exploit you any more than I already have. So it shall remain my secret – our secret.

Thank you again, my dear Jane. You are, and always were, a far better person than me, and I hope you found the happiness I imagined for us with someone else.

Terence

She put down the letter. Tears stung her eyelids, and she wept again, quietly, for the girl who had wasted her life, for the true love she had never found. She stuffed the letter back in the envelope and put it in her handbag, astonished that the pain could have lasted so many years, could still eviscerate her. She didn't know whether the fact he had longed for her all that time made it better or worse. Of course, it could have been written for effect – Terence Shaw was more than capable of spinning a pretty tale, dropping empty words onto a page to salve his conscience, recasting himself as the hero of the tale.

Oh well, she decided. At least she had been able to share the experience with her grandson, and perhaps spare him the same pain she had suffered. Although she suspected not. Words of wisdom were all very well, but they couldn't force you to make your head rule your heart. Love, no matter which way it came upon you, was usually painful in the end.

There was a knock on the door. Hastily she brushed what was left of her tears away. She could see through the glass that it was Roy, and she hurried to answer.

He looked a little bashful.

'I've got more sea bass than I know what to do with,' he told her. 'My freezer's full to bursting. I wondered . . . if you would like to help me out?' He paused, then gave a shy smile. 'Come for supper, I mean.'

Jane couldn't help looking surprised. She and Roy had always been friends, but it had never been any more than sharing a cup of coffee. She felt a rush of pleasure at his invitation.

'I'd love to.'

'Tonight? Eight o'clockish?'

'Fantastic.'

He raised a hand in a salute of farewell and made his way back up the beach. Jane watched him disappear into the crowds, past the ice-cream kiosk – the very same one Roy used to work in. If she cast her mind back, she could smell the sweet vanilla, feel the warmth of the sun, hear the tunes on the wireless. She felt as if she could step back into yesterday.

What if she'd kissed him in the kiosk, like she had

known he wanted her to, in between customers? What if the kiss had been as sweet as the ice cream they were selling, making her heart pound? He would have inoculated her against Terence Shaw. She would have shown no interest in her employer. She would have been eager to finish her day's work and rush back to her new-found love. A sweet, innocent, rite-of-passage love, a relationship that was entirely appropriate.

Of course, it would never have come to anything. Even then, Jane had wanted more than Roy would have had to offer, and would have left him at the end of the summer. But at least she would have emerged unscathed, bright-eyed and optimistic after a summer romance. Not bruised and damaged, internally scarred.

She sat back down on her chair. She felt incredibly weary. Burrowing about in the past was draining.

She woke to find Harry shaking her shoulder anxiously.

'Gran? Are you OK?'

'I'm fine. I'm fine – I must have just dropped off.' She looked up at the clock on the wall. It was a quarter past four.

'I'm going for supper with Roy.'

Harry looked at her, grinning, one of his dark eyebrows raised.

'Yeah?'

Jane walked over to the sink to pour herself a glass of water. She could feel her cheeks flushing slightly.

'So what are you going to wear on your hot date?'

'It's not a hot date,' she protested. 'He's overrun with sea bass.'

'Uh-huh.' Harry was enjoying teasing her. 'He could have just put it in the freezer.'

'His freezer's full.'

'Of course it is.' He came and put an arm round her shoulder, squeezed her. She loved that he wasn't afraid to show affection, her wonderful grandson. 'You'll have a great time. Roy's a dude.'

Dude was the ultimate accolade in Harry's world.

Jane reached up, brushed the dark hair out of his eyes. If the course of her life had been different, she would never have known this wonderful boy. She wouldn't have swapped him for the earth, moon and stars.

'You OK?' she asked gently.

'I will be,' he told her. 'Time the great healer and all that.'

They hugged, and she looked at the clock. Did she have time to go into town and get something new to wear for this evening? Nothing spectacular, but maybe a new sweater. Or some earrings. She felt a tiny tingle in her tummy and laughed. Pre-date nerves at her age? How ridiculous . . .

Later that evening, Harry stood in the doorway of the hut with a restorative can of Coke. He forced himself not to look to see if Florence was around. Instead, he watched his grandmother make her way up the beach. She had looked wonderful tonight, with a white fitted T-shirt and cropped jeans and her sequinned flip-flops, a dark blue linen cardigan slung round her shoulders. Her eyes were smiling, properly smiling, for the first time this holiday. And although he was empty inside, Harry felt a little shoot of hope. She had been brimming with sparkle and optimism, and if she could feel that, after everything she had been through, and everything she had told him, well, maybe, just maybe, so could he. Not yet, not today, but one day. Maybe soon.

7
DRIFTWOOD

Marisa Miller arrived at the Everdene Sands Hotel with one good suitcase and a smile for all the staff.

They all adored Mrs Miller. The doorman stood to attention, instead of wondering when he could nip off for a cigarette. The receptionist sat up straight and forgot her nagging period pains. And the manager came hurrying out of his office, where he had been agonising over his debts at the bookmaker, wondering how he had ever got himself into this mess, and greeted her with an outstretched hand and a wide smile.

Steven wished fervently that all the hotel's guests were as charming as Mrs Miller. His life would be so much easier. And he wished he could offer her the service she deserved. He was ashamed that costs had been slashed recently at the hotel, thanks to the economic climate. The bath towels weren't as thick and plentiful as when she last stayed. The number of staff had been cut, and they didn't offer an evening turndown any more. Once, the rooms would have been discreetly tidied, the pillows plumped, the curtains drawn, the soft bedside lamps lit.

Now, when a guest came back to his room of an evening, it was just how it had been left.

Steven had told the staff in advance that Mrs Miller was to be looked after properly. He knew she was coming, because she had written to him to tell him so. It was, she told him, six months since her husband had died, and she felt strong enough to return to the place where they had always had their annual holiday. The manager felt privileged, and he wanted to make sure that Mrs Miller didn't regret her decision. It wasn't often he took pride in his work these days. There was hardly any point, because you rarely got thanks. People were so swift to complain – they found fault with anything and everything in the hopes of getting a refund – so why bother going the extra mile? He hated himself for becoming so cynical. When he had trained as a manager, it was all about the customer. Now it was all about saving money.

For Mrs Miller, he was determined to make an exception. She would have the best. Extra-fluffy towels. Chocolates on her pillow. He had arranged for fresh flowers in her room. And he had reserved one of the hotel's beach huts for her exclusive use. The hotel owned two for the use of guests, who could hire them on a daily basis. Mrs Miller was to have one for the whole week at no extra charge. She had, after all, been coming here for over thirty years. Stephen didn't care if it caused a stink.

His outstretched hand was ignored. Instead, he found himself kissed on both cheeks, her skin cool on his.

'Steven. How lovely to see you.'

He breathed in her scent. Jicky by Guerlain. He knew, because there was always a bottle on her dressing table. Not that he was a stalker, but the scent had haunted him since the day he had first met her and he wanted to know what it was. Women these days smelt so harsh and cloying. Mrs Miller left a lingering trace of lavender and vanilla that intrigued rather than assaulted you. Stephen had wondered about buying some for his wife, but she had left him before he had a chance to track down where to buy it. It wouldn't have suited her anyway.

In the meantime, he braced himself to give his condolences.

'Mrs Miller, I am so sorry about your husband. On behalf of the hotel, may I express our sorrow at your loss . . .'

He'd picked this expression up off *CSI Miami*. He hoped it didn't sound insincere.

Mrs Miller took one of his hands in hers and smiled.

'Thank you, Steven. Though, you know, it was for the best in the end. It was no life for him.'

He nodded. He knew about the stroke too, because she had written to him last year to cancel their stay and explain why they wouldn't be coming. Life was so bloody cruel. In all his years as a hotel manager, he had never seen a couple so obviously still in love as Mr and Mrs Miller. A lot of husbands and wives who came here looked as if they would cheerfully push each other off the highest balcony. But the Millers knew how to keep the romance alive, even at the age of – what? He didn't know, but they must be in their seventies. Yet they had more verve than most people half their age.

He picked up her suitcase and took the key from the receptionist.

'Let me take you up to your room.'

She smiled graciously with no protest and followed him to the lift. Inside, he breathed in her scent again.

Maybe one day he would meet someone he could buy it for . . .

Marisa Miller had been born plain Mary Bennett, but when, at the age of nine, she determined on a career in ballet, she changed her Christian name in anticipation of a more glamorous life. Her single-mindedness, together with a supportive dance teacher, meant she landed herself a place at a leading ballet school at eleven, despite her parents' misgivings that it would be a hard life. Marisa was certainly a talented dancer, but that wouldn't be sufficient to succeed in a world that was renowned for being tough and competitive. Nevertheless, she found the drive and dedication needed. Ballet was her whole world. Her focus was unnerving, even to teachers who were used to girls with naked ambition. So it was very hard for them, when Marisa was seventeen, to take her to one side and tell her she wasn't going to cut it. Not as a prima ballerina – and she would accept nothing less. She wasn't the sort of girl to languish in the corps de ballet. No one could put their finger on it, as was often the case, but somehow she didn't have that extra something. She was graceful, beautiful, technically correct – yet everyone who studied her agreed she was never going to be a Margot Fonteyn. And so it was gently suggested that she should find another career path.

She took it stoically. To look at her, you would never think her world had been taken away. From that day, she never had anything to do with the ballet again. She took a job as a secretary in a small auction house off Bond

Street. She knew that something would come along to change her life, and in the meantime, she spent her wages on buying the very best clothes she could afford. She had a sharp eye for quality and a nose for a bargain, and she never looked anything other than immaculate. She went to the most expensive hairdresser, bought exquisite silk underwear and stockings, the softest leather shoes. She wore simple but eye-catching jewellery – none of it real, of course, but the class she radiated made even the cheapest string of pearls take on a lustre. And although she was discreet, not flashy, in her choice of dress, she knew she was noticed. She could feel eyes follow her wherever she went. Men where intrigued, women envious.

Marisa was always ready.

The first time she set eyes on Ludo Miller, she knew he was the one. She had begun the habit of going to lunchtime concerts – the ballet had given her a deep love of classical music, and she often slipped into the cool of a church or a concert hall for a stolen hour. And she liked to watch the people, watch them be transported by the music, taken on their own journey away from their cares for a short space of time.

Ludo Miller was the conductor. The string quartet was playing Puccini's *Crisantemi*, lesser known than most of his operas – a tragically moving piece he had allegedly written in one night on hearing of the death of the Duke of Savoy. Ludo was wearing black – a black shirt and immaculately cut black trousers. His eyes were dark, his hair thick and slightly dishevelled, and his demeanour was intensely serious. He had no awareness of his audience, only the music. She could see him pulling the emotion from the strings of the players, making each note more exquisitely mournful than the last, until it nearly broke your heart. By the end, she had tears pouring down her face. No one had ever moved her like that. And although you could argue it was Puccini, not Ludo Miller, that aroused the emotion, she knew a lesser conductor would have made the piece quite forgettable.

As the last of the applause died away and the audience began to leave their seats, Marisa knew she didn't have long. She made her way up the aisle to where Ludo was folding away his music. She positioned herself in front of him, so he would have to look her in the eye.

'That was exceptional,' she told him.

'Thank you.' He bowed his head in a gesture of appreciation, and went to pick up his baton.

He was used to praise and admiration. She would have to do something else to capture his attention.

'I'd . . . like to take you out to dinner.'

His head jerked up. She smiled at the surprise in his eyes. That had certainly done the trick. Women never made the first move, not in those days. Her invitation was audacious.

He didn't speak. He seemed quite nonplussed. She carried on smoothly, as if it was the most natural thing in the world for a twenty-two-year-old girl to ask a man at least five years her senior out for dinner.

'I know a very good restaurant near here. Would you join me this evening?'

He surveyed her up and down, still not saying a word. She felt herself grow deliciously warm under his scrutiny, as his eyes travelled over her collarbone, her neck, her hairline, and then met hers. Their gazes locked, and there was a moment when the earth stood still on its axis, momentarily halted by the momentousness of their joint realisation that this was a point of no return.

'Thank you,' he replied, and for the first time she saw him smile. 'That would be delightful.'

She walked back to work, her head dizzy, her blood several degrees warmer. She asked her boss if she could leave two hours early and he agreed quite readily – she was the most conscientious employee he had ever had, so he was happy to indulge her. She went to Fenwick, and bought a lavender linen dress, a new lipstick and a bottle of Jicky by Guerlain. Smell, she knew, was one of the most powerful of the senses. And if this was her only chance with Ludo Miller, she wanted to leave no stone unturned.

Of course, he was entranced. They barely ate, although the food was excellent. There was no polite, stilted conversation – they shared immediately their hopes and dreams, their passions, their secrets . . . And in the leafy square outside the restaurant, they kissed for the first time. The moon shone down on them, drenching them in its beams, a silvery cocoon that might never let them go.

They led a charmed life together. She left her job at the auction room soon after they met and became not so much his personal assistant as his manager. He had, until then, been scarcely able to manage his affairs, being virtually incapable of running a diary, being on time or remembering a commitment unless he had someone breathing down his neck. Sometimes it was a miracle he turned up to his concerts at all. His mind was on a higher plane. He thought of nothing but music; the mundane passed him by on its way somewhere else. Marisa, by contrast, thought of everything, from the taxi at the airport to take him to the concert hall to the tube of his favourite toothpaste in his sponge bag.

Being organised like this meant that Ludo could commit himself to twice, three times as much. His charisma and flair made him a popular choice with both audiences and the orchestras he conducted. He always found something in the music that other people had missed, and he enabled his musicians to find that extra something too. He became a minor celebrity, a heart-throb in a world that didn't really deal in heart-throbs. He was one of the few classical personalities to be recognised by the general public, as he had done more for popularising classical music than any of his contemporaries. His passion was infectious. He was an engaging and witty chat-show guest. And instantly recognisable, in his trademark black clothing, which as his popularity increased was supplied by Armani, some said free of charge, as he was the perfect ambassador.

And Marisa felt fulfilled. She might not have been able to live her own dream, but she was instrumental in making sure Ludo fulfilled his potential. She became almost as well known as he was, as his constant companion, with her timeless chic. People often spoke of the chemistry they had as a couple. Perfect opposites, brilliantly matched. Her poise and organisation, his flamboyant chaos. It was as if they inhabited their own little world that no one else could enter. They only had eyes for each other. They need only exchange a glance and it was as if an entire conversation had taken place in the blink of an eye. It was unnerving. But it didn't make them any less popular.

Of course, Ludo could be difficult, when he wasn't oozing charm for the cameras. Other wives often asked Marisa how she put up with him. He was scatterbrained, unreliable, volatile. Rude, so rude – he never suffered fools gladly, and would speak his mind in public. Awkward silences after acerbic comments thrown across dinner tables were commonplace. Marisa never flinched with embarrassment as some wives might. To her, Ludo's opinions were sacrosanct. She just smiled, like the indulgent mother of a naughty child. Marisa wouldn't have had him any other way. Besides, he was a genius, and geniuses, as we all know, are allowed to behave as they like.

Initially she escorted him wherever he went, to ease his passage, but when the babies started arriving – one, two, three, four, in quick succession – it became impractical. And so she ran the centre of operations from a large office in their house on the outskirts of Oxford, and let him loose on the world without a chaperone but with a neatly typed list of everything he needed to know.

He had no shortage of female admirers. Of course not. Any woman who saw him conduct knew that he was hot-blooded. Marisa guessed that when he went on tour there was probably any number of knocks on his hotel room door. She shut her mind as to whether he ever answered those knocks. As long as none of them mattered to him, as long as these women were disposable, she accepted that he had to make love while he was away just as he had to eat and drink. After all, he always came home to her.

Their two-week holiday every summer was an

immovable ritual. They could have holidayed anywhere in the world, from Antigua to Zanzibar, as the guests of the most illustrious hosts, but they loved the old-fashioned Englishness of the beach at Everdene, the fresh air, the endless horizon. And for that fortnight, they forgot all about music and aeroplanes and schedules and just enjoyed themselves. They took the same beach hut every year, and Ludo devoted himself to entertaining his wife and four children, scrambling over rocks, crabbing, flying kites, cremating sausages in the home-made barbecue he made out of a metal bucket. They were never happier, and always returned to the mêlée of the real world refreshed and safe in the knowledge that Everdene would be just the same next year.

As Marisa and Ludo grew older, and the children stopped coming with them, they continued the tradition, although they took to staying at the Everdene Sands Hotel. This afforded them a little more comfort, but they still spent their days in the beach hut, reading novels, listening to music and sipping chilled white wine.

As he approached seventy, it seemed impossible that Ludo would retire. He still had the vigour of a man half his age. His mind was even more questing, his interpretation of the most obtuse pieces of music even more brilliant. His mop of black hair became streaked with grey, making him look even more distinguished. He was awarded an OBE. He wrote his autobiography – or rather, Marisa wrote it; Ludo would never remember the details – and it was a bestseller. He had a Sunday morning radio show on a commercial classical music station. Ludo Miller's star continued to dazzle.

And then tragedy struck, after a concert in Toronto.

Ludo collapsed, the victim of a massive stroke. He was flown back home, sent to the best specialist in London, but the prognosis was grim. There was little hope of him recovering. He was virtually paralysed, and the doctors were not optimistic. He could do nothing for himself, couldn't speak or communicate. In one moment their charmed life together had been eradicated; the bursting of one small blood vessel turned them upside down, inside out and back to front.

There was no question of Ludo coming home, once the hospital had established there was nothing more they could do. There was no way Marisa would be able to look after him herself. He needed twenty-four-hour care. She spent weeks researching care homes, but nowhere seemed good enough. Most of them were grand old houses that had been converted, houses that deserved better. It seemed these days only extortionate nursing fees could keep a house of any magnitude running. In the end she chose a purpose-built home with clean lines and state-of-the-art facilities. Yet its walls still reeked of sadness and desperation. Probably the sadness and desperation of the relatives who came to visit. The patients were largely unaware of their plights, quite possibly because they were tranquillised to keep them docile, existing in a twilight world of routine that ground on relentlessly until such time as fate intervened to release them. Marisa never met anyone's eye when she went to visit. She didn't want to take on board anyone else's misery.

She visited every day, although it destroyed her. Watching Ludo being fed was the most traumatic experience, as a nurse shovelled what was effectively baby food into his mouth. Some instinct made him chew, though half of it was dribbled out again. Marisa felt repulsed. She could never bring herself to feed him. She thought it would be the ultimate humiliation.

The agony was that no one could tell her what was going on in his mind; whether his thoughts were completely lucid, but trapped. Was he shouting at her from inside to release him from his torture? Or was he perfectly happy, existing in some kind of haze? Was he still thinking of music? Were there miraculous combinations of notes swirling around his brain that he was trying to impose order upon? If his mind was intact, how on earth did he get through the day? Did you train yourself, eventually, to look forward to the arrival of the eleven o'clock custard cream? Shrink your world down into the trivial in order not to go screaming mad? Or was he screaming mad?

Every now and then a random word came out, but it seemed entirely disconnected to anything. She never knew how long it took him to summon up the energy to speak. When he had said 'ticket', what on earth had it referred to? Something that was bothering him at the time, or something that had happened years ago? Or had the twisted alleyways in his mind simply produced that word instead of another?

Until the day he had said, quite lucidly and clearly, 'No more'. And then repeated it. In a tone that was so positive, so firm, that she couldn't ignore it, or misinterpret his meaning.

It had torn at her heart. How could she play God? It wasn't just the moral implications, it was the practical ones. She knew that Ludo would have had no compunction about her putting him out of his misery. She could almost hear him saying, 'For Christ's sake, just put a pillow over my head and be done with it.' But it wasn't as easy as that.

She'd read up on euthanasia. Endlessly. Where once her reading matter had been nothing more stretching than Barbara Vine or Joanna Trollope, now it was a moral maze that always left her feeling queasy. Of course, there was a place in Switzerland you could go to. Assisted dying, they called it. Dying with dignity. Yet the thought of a fatal dose in an anonymous apartment in Zurich made her shudder – and that was before she even considered the difficulty of getting someone virtually immobile on a plane. She couldn't do it without help and who could she ask for help? Certainly not her children. She had never discussed the conundrum with any of them. They were concerned for their father, of course, but they had their own lives to lead. This was her problem, and it was her duty to find the right ending for her beloved.

Yet how could she? The problem was she had hope. Ludo had always been so strong, such a fighter, and she believed in him utterly. She was convinced that he was doing his utmost to make all those neural pathways repair themselves, and that one day he would open his eyes, smile at her and speak her name. How could she make a plan when she had convinced herself of that eventuality? That was the only way she was able to survive. Believing.

She spent a year in turmoil. Trying to find an answer. And nothing gave her solace. The local vicar tried to help, but his words, his kindness, gave her no comfort. Even music provided no escape. She was only reminded of better times, happier times. In the end, she could only endure silence. The house that had once rung with music, debate, children's voices, laughter, the chink of wine glasses, was as quiet as the grave.

Then one day, when she arrived at the home, the matron came hurrying out to intercept her. She knew immediately. It was another massive stroke. This time it had done its job properly. Their purgatory was over. Marisa sank down into the nearest chair and wept. Not tears of grief – she had wept enough of those already – but tears of relief that the decision had been taken out of her hands. She no longer had to spend the days searching for an answer and the nights sleepless with anxiety, or the few hours where sleep deigned to come upon her tortured by dreams sprinkled with grim reapers and harbingers of doom and vials of colourless liquid that bring oblivion . . .

And now, here she was, six months later, opening her case upon the very bed where she and Ludo had spent some of their happiest hours. They had always been at their most content in Everdene. They were always able to relax and unwind after a hectic schedule of summer music festivals and concerts. They would look back over what had happened in the past year, and then look to the future, decide what changes to make, what fresh challenges to set. It was a time to breathe and recharge, a time away from the telephone and the computer.

She threw open the window and breathed in the ozone. Her room overlooked the beach, and she could hear the reassuring pound of the surf. Sunlight twinkled on the waves, throwing off a metallic glitter. She longed for the feeling of sand between her toes, the cool of the water on her ankles. She felt if not happy, then at least at home.

It had been the right decision to come here. And now she had to get ready. She felt surprisingly calm. There were no tears. She ran a deep bath, pouring her own deliciously scented oil into the water, and washed away the dust and mire of the journey, then slipped into a white robe. She dialled room service, and ordered a meal. She was quite exacting, but the kitchen were compliant. They would, they assured her, do their best. They'd had their instructions.

Then she dressed, did her hair and her make-up. How many millions of times had she been through this ritual? Her look had barely changed since her twenties. The immaculate chignon at the nape of her neck. The sweep of dark eye-liner over her lids. The barely-there gloss that added a shimmer to her lips. The squirt of Jicky to her lips and cleavage. The silk underwear. The Balmain dress cut on the bias. The Chanel ballet pumps.

There was a knock on the door. She answered it to find a young waiter with her supper trolley. He wheeled it in and wished her 'bon appétit'. She smiled her thanks, and pressed a five pound note into his hand. He thanked her effusively and left, and for a moment she debated the wisdom of her decision. Human contact always made her falter . . .

The meal was perfect. It was an imitation of the first meal she and Ludo had shared. A steak, well cooked, just as she liked it, and new potatoes and green beans. And a slice of peach pavlova to follow. And with it, a bottle of

209

Chassagne Montrachet – Ludo's favourite. She was surprised to be hungry.

When she had finished, she pushed the trolley outside the door for it to be taken away, and set about tidying the bedroom. She packed her travelling clothes back in her case, cosmetics and perfume and hairbrush. She took out a beach bag and checked inside that it had everything she wanted, then put it to one side and zipped up her case.

Then she tidied up the bathroom, hanging up all the towels. She smoothed down the bed, even though it was immaculate. She couldn't bear to leave it in a mess.

She stood and looked at herself in the mirror. She had a critical eye when it came to her appearance, but she gave herself an approving nod. Then she picked up the bottle of wine and put it in her bag with a wine glass, and left the bedroom.

As she walked through the foyer, Steven came hurrying towards her, concern on his face.

'Mrs Miller, was your dinner to your satisfaction? Is there anything we can get you? A liqueur, perhaps, on the terrace? It's still warm – we have patio heaters.'

She touched his arm in a gesture of gratitude.

'Thank you, Steven. I just want some fresh air. I'll never sleep otherwise. I thought I'd go down to the beach hut . . .'

He hurried behind the reception desk and found her the key. He let her go without demur. He was good at his job. He knew when to push, and when to concede.

As she took the key, Marisa looked at him.

'I just want to thank you for everything.'

He gave a shrug.

'It's my pleasure.'

'No, honestly. This hotel has given me . . . us, a great deal of pleasure over the years. I'm very grateful.'

And she went. As she left, Steven watched after her, frowning slightly. She had seemed overly insistent in her thanks. Something didn't quite ring true.

The walk along the front of the huts to the one the hotel owned was longer than Marisa remembered, and walking over the sand was arduous. In the end, she kicked off her shoes and carried them. The sand was cool beneath her toes. She hoped no one would recognise her. They'd made friends here over the years. Not friends you kept up with necessarily, but people you greeted with enthusiasm when you saw them again. She didn't want company tonight.

She reached the hut finally, and struggled with the lock for a few moments before the door finally swung open. She flicked on the light. It was so familiar. The blue and white striped deckchairs. The way it smelt, slightly damp. The memories took her breath away. She put down her bag, her hands trembling, as all the years of happiness washed over her. At the time, she'd had no idea what the future held.

She opened the beach bag and drew out a small portable CD player. She plugged it into the wall. She opened one of the deckchairs and placed it in the doorway, then sat down. The susurration of the sea and the cool night air soothed her. The moon glowed silver, just as it had that night in the square, when they had shared their first kiss.

She took out the bottle of Chassagne Montrachet, and poured herself a glass. Then she took out her tablets.

She'd been saving them, ever since the doctor had prescribed them. She told him she couldn't sleep, after Ludo died, and why would he not have believed her? Then she pretended she had lost the bottle, left them on the bedside table when visiting a friend, and she'd been given a repeat prescription.

It would be so easy . . .

She pressed the start button. Puccini's *Crisantemi* drifted out of the speakers. The piece he had been conducting when she first set eyes upon him. That was how he was going to be when she met him again. The brilliant young maestro. And she would be the elegant, poised young woman who had dared to ask him out to dinner. The perfect couple.

She took a few more sips of wine, savouring its richness. She relished the cold night air on her cheeks. She revelled in the exquisite notes of the music. There was still beauty, even though he had gone. She could still feel.

She put down her glass and went to her bag, extracting one last item. Then she began to walk towards the water. The tide was a long way out. The dry sand became wet and cold, smooth beneath her ballerina feet. She walked without looking back, Puccini trailing after her on the breeze.

Steven decided to go and check on Mrs Miller's room before he went off duty. He didn't trust the chambermaids to do their job properly. They were all too eager to go rushing off to the pub. He slipped into the room with his master key. It was immaculate, and he felt a tiny bit of remorse that he had underestimated his staff. The pillows were plump and stood to attention, there were fresh towels. Then he paused. It was a little too immaculate. There were no belongings scattered anywhere. Usually there would be some clothing in evidence, toiletries on the dressing table, a book on the bedside. But there was nothing. Just Mrs Miller's suitcase, resting on the stand.

He checked the bathroom, and the bedroom again. Everything seemed to be put away. He stood over the case, hesitated for a moment, then snapped it open. Everything was in there, neatly packed.

He looked out of the window at the beach in the near distance, and felt unease prickling at his neck. What did this mean? She had packed everything away, gone down to the beach . . .

He closed the case again, snapping the locks shut, then hurried out of the room, down the stairs – the lift took too long – and out of the revolving door, casting a glance at the clock on his way out. A quarter past ten. Surely she would be back by now? With the best will in the world it would be chilly on the beach at this time.

He scuttled along the sand, realising it had been years since he had set foot here. Like living in New York and never seeing the Empire State Building. He passed along the line of huts, head down. Some people were still outside, enjoying the night air, smoking the last cigarette of the day. Others were inside, and he could see their shadowy figures through the glass, eating, drinking wine, reading a novel, playing cards.

He arrived at the hut at last. The door was wide open, the lights blazing. A mournful piece of music was playing on a portable CD player. A bottle of wine, nearly empty, sat on the table – he recognised it as one they served in the restaurant. He saw a medicine bottle on the table next to the glass and his blood ran cold. He picked it up. Shook it. There was a reassuring rattle and he felt a sweet momentary relief, but he was still concerned.

He turned to look at the sea. Everything was in shades of dark blue and grey, edged with silver. The tide was as far out as it could go, and it was difficult to see, but he could just make out a figure, standing still at the water's edge.

He swallowed, uncertain as to how to proceed. Should he intervene? What would be worse, to interrupt someone's privacy, or to wake up tomorrow and discover the worst, realise that you should have stepped in? As he pondered his dilemma, the music came to an end, then went back to the start. It stirred something deep within him, brought tears to his eyes. He had never felt emotions like this for another human. His life so far had been dull, prosaic, without passion or true meaning. He determined he would do something to change that, as soon as he could. He didn't know what, exactly, but surely he deserved something better than the humdrum, the workaday, the monotonous . . .

But he didn't have time to wallow. He set out across the beach, huddling himself against the late-evening breeze. When he was ten feet away from the shore, he halted.

She was standing barefoot in the shallow waters. In her hands, there was a small container. She was staring over the horizon, the navy sky above her peppered with silver shot. The faintest trace of music could still be heard. And in that moment, Steven realised what it was she had come here to do. He stood still, silent with respect. Even from here he could feel her love as she carried out the final task, the act that represented the end of a perfect marriage, at least on this earth.

Eventually she turned to walk back up the beach, carrying the urn, now empty. As she passed Steven, she smiled.

'It's where he would have wanted to be,' she told him.

The ashes glittered on the surface of the water as the waves carried Ludo Miller gently out to sea.

8
SURF'S UP

It was always a given that Dan and Kirsty would get married at Everdene. After all, they'd met on Everdene beach; they spent every free weekend they could down here, jumping in the car on a Friday night and driving hell for leather down the motorway. They were the archetypal surfer dude and chick, with their almost matching tousled blond hair – hers *slightly* longer than his – their year-round golden tans, their lean strong limbs. The wedding was going to be held at the Everdene Sands Hotel, and when Jenna discovered the hotel owned a pair of beach huts it had seemed only natural to use one for the honeymoon night. So here she was, as the wedding day dawned pink and hopeful, putting the finishing touches to a setting that was already perfect.

As chief bridesmaid, she'd had plenty of practice making things perfect. After all, this was the fifth time she had been given the honour. She supposed she should feel lucky she had so many friends who valued her so highly, but now it was getting beyond a joke. If she heard anyone else say, 'Always the bridesmaid, never the bride', she wouldn't be responsible for her actions.

Jenna had long faced up to the fact that she wasn't the sort of girl men fell in love with. Not like Kirsty. Kirsty was the reason why Tiffany made diamond rings, why Bollinger made champagne, a girl who'd had more than her fair share of proposals. She'd certainly had Jenna's share.

It wasn't that men didn't like Jenna. They adored her. They flocked round her. They gawped down her cleavage, fondled her arse, dragged her into bed. They just didn't ask her to marry them. Ever.

Where, she wondered, was she going wrong? She was bright, solvent, attractive, gregarious. She didn't think she was particularly needy or demanding. What could she change about herself to make her a potential bride? What was it about Kirsty that meant she had been spoilt for choice, and was now heading up the aisle with her chosen one? Jenna supposed there was an element of mystery to Kirsty – she was cool, slightly aloof, didn't over-share – while Jenna, by contrast, was open and extrovert, but she was never going to change. Did she deserve to be punished just because she was happy to tell a story against herself and make everyone laugh, because she was always the first on the dance floor with her arms in the air, because she liked a drink or six?

She sighed. Today wasn't the day to dwell on it. She had to finish things off in here, go and get ready herself, then make sure Kirsty was organised. Which she would be. Nothing ever went wrong for Kirsty. She had, Jenna decided, a charmed life. Everything unfolded in front of her like a fairytale. Like today. It was going to be a dream wedding.

She took a last glance around the beach hut. The bed

was low to the floor, a froth of white linen, piled high with lace-edged pillows and scattered with rose petals. An ice bucket sat next to it, flanked by two long-stemmed glasses. Fairy lights were strung from the rafters, scented candles waited to be lit. Jenna would come back later, just as the bride and groom were about to leave the reception, to light the candles, put the champagne on ice, turn on the music . . .

She took the disc she'd burned earlier out of her handbag and slid it into the CD player. It had taken her ages to compile, a labour of love trawling through the internet and her own music collection, but she thought it was the ultimate honeymoon soundtrack. She pressed play to make sure it worked.

Al Green began to sing. 'Let's Stay Together'.

Jenna looked around the hut. She'd forgotten nothing. It was the ideal place for the happy couple to begin their life together. Dan and Kirsty. Soon to be Mr and Mrs Harper. She imagined Kirsty, slight and beautiful, being carried over the threshold, then laid gently in the middle of the bed, Dan looking down at her adoringly . . .

A huge bubble of something rose up inside her and grabbed her by the throat. Jealousy? Resentment? Despair? Panic? She felt it choking her. It was completely overwhelming, a tsunami of bitterness. She was powerless in its path. Shit – this wasn't supposed to happen. She was supposed to be good old Jenna, the perfect matron of honour with a smile on her face, even though inside her heart was breaking.

She couldn't take it any more.

She sank to the floor and began to cry.

*

Dan Harper and his best man Liam were down at the bottom end of the beach, catching the best of the early-morning waves. They were both passionate about surfing, and it seemed the natural thing to do on the morning of Dan's wedding. It was invigorating, mind-clearing, and the best way to address pre-match nerves. How could they worry about the forthcoming nuptials when they were doing battle with the sea, utilising every muscle in their body, feeling the exhilaration as they rode in towards the shore? They whooped and hollered with the adrenalin.

They were best mates, buddies since the day they'd both arrived at senior school, bonding over their love of sports and Pearl Jam and pretty girls. They'd shared pretty much every rite of passage – first drink, first cigarette, first hangover, first car crash – and discussed every life-changing decision they'd had to make ad infinitum ever since. They shared their darkest secrets and their deepest fears. Today was going to be strange. Today was going to alter the status quo, because someone else would become more important in Dan's life, but they were cool about it. They'd still be friends. Always.

Finally, after forty-five minutes – they had promised half an hour, but the conditions were so perfect it seemed wrong to stop – they dragged their boards out of the water and walked back up the beach. Just enough time to get back to the hotel, shower, change into their wedding regalia and slip down to the terrace bar for a sneaky sharpener.

Liam slung his arm round his friend's shoulder.

'Hey, buddy. No last-minute cold feet?'

'No way.' Dan shook his wet blond hair out of his

eyes, laughing. 'This is it, mate. It's weird – you never think you're going to be ready to settle down to married life, but suddenly it feels like the right thing to do.'

'So this time next year the pitter-patter of tiny feet?'

'Maybe. So get yourself ready. You'll be godfather.'

Liam grimaced.

'Can I handle the responsibility?'

'Course you can.' Dan nudged his mate in the ribs. 'And anyway, it's your turn next. You need to get on with it.'

'Yep,' agreed Liam. 'Only I just haven't met the right girl yet. How do you know . . . ?'

'You just do.' Dan grinned, nodding his head towards three girls in bikinis coming down the beach past them, their arms filled with beach bags and towels and paraphernalia, ready for a day in the sun. 'How about one of these?'

The girls giggled and nudged each other as they passed Dan and Liam. One turned back just as Liam did, and their eyes locked for a moment.

'Damn,' he said. 'Yet again my responsibilities get in the way of my libido.'

'Hey, feel free. I can get someone else to hand me the rings. It's not that hard.'

'No way.' Liam slung his arm around his friend's shoulder again. 'There's plenty more where she came from.'

They came out of the slipway at the top of the beach, onto the little road that led through the village and up to the hotel. As they passed the Ship Aground, neither of them commented on Dan's recent stag night. It was history, one of those nights where stuff happens that doesn't get mentioned again. What goes on tour, stays on tour, that was the unwritten code, and they both stuck to it rigidly.

They turned into the gate that led to the lawns in front of the hotel.

'OK, buddy,' said Liam. 'Meet you on the terrace in half an hour and I'll buy you a brandy.'

'Make that a double,' grinned Dan as they walked in through the hotel entrance, two mates who'd shared years of friendship, one of them about to embark on the next of life's adventures.

Kirsty Inglis gazed at her reflection in the mirror, searching for any blemish, any tiny imperfection.

Her dress was a simple column of sheer white chiffon, the spaghetti straps showing off her tan. Her blond hair had been curled into long, loose ringlets that fell just past her shoulders. She wore a silver necklace with a shell that nestled in her collarbone. On her feet she wore Havaiana flip-flops encrusted with Swarovski crystals. Her fingers and toes were painted in the palest oyster pink. She looked part mermaid, part beach babe, part fairy-tale bride.

Happy that she was as close to perfect as she could be, she finally allowed herself a smile of approval, then picked up a glass of the champagne that the hotel had sent up to her room and took a sip. She had insisted on getting ready by herself. Kirsty didn't want a phalanx of hangers-on fussing over her. She'd delegated what she couldn't do to the professionals – the manicurist and hairdresser had been and gone as quickly as they could first thing – but she'd dressed herself and done her own make-up. And now she was ready, with over an hour to spare. Her chief bridesmaid, Jenna, was supposed to be coming up to share a glass of champagne with her, but Jenna was late. She always was. And in some ways, Kirsty didn't mind. She wanted a bit of time on her own to prepare. Jenna would only wind her up, make her nervous – she wouldn't mean to, but Jenna was like an overwound clockwork toy, and it was contagious. Just the thought of her gave Kirsty the jitters . . .

She took in a deep breath to calm the fluttering in her stomach, unable to believe that this afternoon she would be Mrs Daniel Harper. Obviously she would be keeping her maiden name for professional purposes – she hadn't spent the last ten years building up a reputation as a personal trainer and nutritionist only to throw it all away – but otherwise she wanted to take her husband's name. She wanted them to be a proper couple, especially when they went on to have a baby. Which they would very soon, she hoped. She was ready. She was thirty-two – not old to be a first-time mother by today's standards. Ideally they would fit in a boy and a girl before she was thirty-five, the age your body clock started to go into decline. Kirsty always had everything planned. She didn't leave much to chance.

She breathed in again. She had started the day with a yoga session on the beach, way before anyone else had stirred. As the sun came up she'd laid her mat on the cool sand and worked her way through her poses. She never missed a day, and as a result she was lean and graceful. Afterwards she had gone for a swim, plunging into the ice-blue waves, carving through them with strong, sure strokes. She was back at the hotel by half past seven, relaxed and invigorated, ready for a breakfast of fresh fruit, yoghurt and mint tea. There was no sign of anyone else in the wedding party yet, but it didn't surprise or bother her. She was used to being the only one who was an early riser, and she was quite content with her own company.

She closed her eyes and wondered if her parents were on schedule – she hadn't heard from them yet. They were driving down from Hampshire this morning; she had offered to put them up the night before, but they didn't like to be away from home for too long because of the dogs, and they had decided they would prefer to stay over on the wedding night. Kirsty imagined them getting ready, her mother fussing over her outfit, her father offering repeated reassurance that went unheard. Kirsty smiled to herself. Her parents' marriage had been strong and predictable. They had, as far as she knew, never wavered. Kirsty hoped her marriage to Dan would be as steadfast – though perhaps not quite so . . . well, dull. She wanted more than gardening and springer spaniels.

She breathed in again, ready to let her mind take her away to a calmer place, when there was a knock at the door. She jumped up and ran across the room to open it, suddenly eager for a distraction. Outside in the corridor stood Jenna. She looked dishevelled, distressed – and she was still in her jeans. Kirsty was puzzled. She should be ready by now.

'Jenna? What's the matter?'

Jenna stared at her, her eyes wide. Her face was blotchy. She'd obviously been crying.

'I can't do it!' she declared. 'I can't go on living the lie any longer.'

And she burst into noisy sobs.

Kirsty smiled to herself. Jenna loved a bit of drama. She stood to one side to let her friend in.

'Come on in, then. Spill the beans. What have you done now?' Her tone was slightly teasing. Anything could have happened – a flirtation with the night porter, a skirmish with the waiter at breakfast.

Jenna pushed her way past Kirsty and sat down on the bed. She put her face in her hands for a moment, then looked up. She spoke in a whisper. Kirsty had to bend down to catch what she was saying.

'I've been going over and over it in my mind, and I can't not tell you. I can't let you go down the aisle without you knowing the truth. It's up to you to decide what to do.'

The semblance of a frown furrowed Kirsty's smooth brow. Jenna was making this even more convoluted than usual.

'Jenna – what are you talking about?'

Jenna's eyes filled up with tears. 'I slept with Dan on his stag night.'

Kirsty blinked. Once. Twice. She thought perhaps she hadn't heard right.

'Sorry?'

'I don't know how it happened. One minute we were having a laugh in the Ship Aground. The next minute he was trying to kiss me. And . . . I don't know . . . it just came to a head . . . I was drunk. We were drunk . . .'

Kirsty stood in the middle of the room. She put a hand to her head, trying to take in what Jenna had just told her.

'Why are you telling me this now?' she demanded.

'Why didn't you tell me before? Or not tell me at all . . . ? It's the morning of my wedding, Jenna.'

'I wasn't going to tell you. But I don't know – it just seemed wrong, letting you walk down the aisle without you knowing the truth. I didn't want you marrying a lie . . .' Jenna tried to wipe away her tears, but they kept falling thick and fast.

Kirsty walked over to the window and looked out. In the distance, the sea was glittering in the mid-morning sun, a cloudless sky above. It was the weather she had been praying for; the weather she had gambled everything on.

Her perfect day.

'What were you doing there on his stag night, anyway?' she asked. 'It was for the boys, surely? You didn't tell me you'd gone.'

'Liam asked me to come down. To sort stuff out. He wanted to check out the hotel, make some arrangements.'

Kirsty was staring into the middle distance, as if she wasn't listening. Then she turned, and looked straight into Jenna's eyes.

'To be honest, it doesn't surprise me. I know what you're like. Dan got drunk, and you propositioned him.'

'No—'

'Admit it, Jenna. You've always wanted him for yourself. I've seen the texts you send him. He doesn't bother wiping them off because he hasn't got a guilty conscience.'

Jenna looked down, miserable, unable to defend herself as Kirsty railed on.

'You're pathetic, you know that? The only way you can get the man you want is by getting him so out of his tree he doesn't have an option.' She shrugged. 'I guess it's what stag nights are all about. Getting your unfinished business out of the way before you start on your new life. That's all you were to him, Jenna. A bit of unfinished business.'

There was a momentary silence. Kirsty bit her lip to stop herself from breaking down. She couldn't afford to cry – not at this stage of the game. She had to keep it together.

Jenna stood up with as much dignity as she could gather.

'He wasn't *that* drunk, I can assure you,' she spat back. 'And I'll tell you something else. He deserves better than you. He deserves better than some ice maiden who's got her whole life mapped out in front of her. You're not capable of emotion. Look at you – even now, you're in complete control. I don't think you've even got a heart.'

If only she knew, thought Kirsty. If only she knew how much it was taking her to retain her composure, when inside she was petrified.

'Yes, I have,' she replied quietly. 'I've been betrayed by the two people closest to me in the world. But shrieking and wailing isn't going to help. It's not going to mean it never happened.'

She walked over to the bottle of champagne and poured a glass. Her hands were shaking. She managed to steady them before she handed it to Jenna.

'Drink that. Then go and get yourself ready.'

Jenna looked at her in amazement.

'You're going ahead with it?'

Kirsty nodded.

226

'You're hardly a threat, are you? After all, who's the bridesmaid – and who's the bride?'

And with that she swept out of the room.

Jenna bent double, her head in her hands, hot tears trickling through her fingers. She had never known pain like it.

What had she done? And why? What kind of person dropped that bombshell on her best friend? Why had she done the one thing guaranteed potentially to destroy three lives? She curled herself up into a ball on the bed, a low guttural moan coming from deep inside, wondering just where she would rewind to if she could – this morning, the stag night, the day she first set eyes on Dan Harper . . . ?

Kirsty strode down the corridor, her head high. She pulled her mobile out of the bag she'd grabbed as she left the room, scrolled through her numbers, dialled. He answered on the first ring.

'Liam, it's Kirsty.'

'Hey, beautiful—'

'I need to speak to you,' she interjected swiftly. 'Now. Meet me on the slipway in five minutes.'

And she hung up, punching the button on the lift at the end of the corridor. By some miracle the doors opened with a ting straight away and she got inside. Two other guests smiled – everyone loves a bride, after all – but she didn't smile back. It was almost as if she didn't register them at all.

Liam put down his coffee cup. He didn't like the tone in Kirsty's voice. He sensed trouble. He supposed everything had gone rather too well up to now. He and Dan had been chilling on the terrace, enjoying a pot of coffee and a sneaky cognac before the ceremony began, two friends seemingly without a care in the world. But they were ignoring the elephant in the room – what John Irving called 'the undertoad'. Liam had a nasty feeling the undertoad had got out and was now hopping around, slimy and warty, looking for trouble.

'Hey,' he said to Dan. 'Got something I've got to do. See you in a while.'

Dan looked up at him and nodded. He looked pretty laid-back for a guy who was about to get married, but then nothing really fazed Dan. He was a cool customer. He looked amazing too, in his charcoal-grey linen suit with the white shirt untucked underneath, and his trademark snakeskin boots which were worn with just enough irony to save him from looking like a tosser.

Liam walked out of the hotel, across the road and along the grassy dunes that led to the slipway. He could see Kirsty sitting on the wall. Passers-by were giving her glances – not surprisingly. She looked stunning, shimmering in the sunlight. Almost like a mirage. If you shut your eyes and opened them again, she would be gone.

'Hey.' He sat on the wall next to her. 'What's the problem?'

She raised her eyebrows and tilted her head to one side. 'Like you don't know?'

'No . . .'

'Dan and Jenna?'

Liam pressed his lips together. Shit. He thought as much. Who had spilled the beans? Had one of the other stags blabbed to his girlfriend, who'd decided to tell Kirsty the truth? Or had—

'My bridesmaid has just informed me that she slept with my husband-to-be on his stag night.' Kirsty's voice was calm. 'I'm not sure where I go from here, Liam. We've got a hundred and fifty guests arriving in the next half-hour. I'm supposed to be meeting my parents in ten minutes. The timing isn't great. And I'm not one for a drama. I don't want to make a scene.'

This was true. Kirsty wasn't a drama queen. Not like bloody Jenna. Why the hell couldn't she have kept her mouth shut? What kind of girl dropped a bombshell like that on her best friend when she was about to go up the aisle? An unhappy one, he supposed. A jealous, green-eyed, slightly unhinged, slightly embittered thirty-something party animal with high hemlines and low morals. A girl who felt threatened by her friend's perfection, a girl who was disgruntled with her lot in life . . .

Now, however, was not the time to question Jenna's motives. Now was the time for some serious damage limitation. As best man, it was up to him to make sure his best mate's bride made it up the aisle.

'Kirsty – we were absolutely hammered. None of us had a clue what we were doing. If Dan and Jenna ended up shagging, I don't suppose he can even remember. I'm not saying it was right, Kirst. And maybe I should have done more to stop it. But it didn't mean anything.'

Kirsty sighed.

'You know what? I know that.'

'It was just—'

'Please don't say it was just a shag. We are talking

229

about my best friend and my fiancé. Two people who are supposed to love me, not betray me.'

Liam cursed inwardly. He could see the whole scenario unfolding now in his mind's eye. He could see the determination in Jenna's eyes, the way she had homed in on Dan, scarcely leaving his side all evening. Her hand on his arm, then her arm round his neck, then her mouth on his, her sitting on his lap. Liam had been preoccupied, had chosen to turn a blind eye, although there was no doubt where the evening was heading. Jenna's message was loud and clear and Dan – Dan had enjoyed the attention. Jenna was very good at making men feel good. He wasn't excusing Dan, not for a second, but he had probably thought, in his drunken state, what the hell? One last night of freedom.

Dan had been filled with guilt the next day, there was no doubt about that. He'd been very quiet during their round of golf, presumably wallowing in an agony of remorse, compounded by a wicked hangover. Liam wouldn't have swapped places with him for the world, but part of him felt responsible. Maybe as best man he should have organised a game of paintball, instead of a debauched evening of Olympic drinking which could only lead to trouble. But Liam hadn't known Jenna was going to turn up. She said it was a coincidence, that she'd come down for the weekend with some friends, but looking back now Liam hadn't seen any evidence of them.

He looked at Kirsty. He knew that whatever he said would have a massive impact on what happened next. He didn't have long to decide how to play it.

He liked Kirsty. He really did. But he knew she was a

perfectionist. He knew she liked things her way, and expected everyone around her to step up to the mark. He knew that nine times out of ten Dan would step up to that mark, but he obviously had a weak spot. Would that weak spot be his ultimate downfall? Was he cut out for a lifetime of dancing to Kirsty's tune? Or should he, in the light of what had happened, bail out now? Maybe Dan would be better off with someone like Jenna, someone more laid-back who wouldn't make so many demands?

No, thought Liam. No couple was perfectly matched. Everyone had to make changes and compromise. Dan needed someone like Kirsty, to tame his wilder side, to coax him into the next phase of his life. A Jenna would bring him down with her. He wouldn't move on. He would be stuck in his jack-the-lad twenties for ever.

And Kirsty, for all her demands, was a good person. She deserved the handsome, charming Dan, whom she would mould into a loving husband and father. They would make a wonderful couple, and wonderful parents. This was a blip. A very badly timed blip, he had to admit, but he was confident he could talk Kirsty round, if only because he genuinely believed what he was about to say.

'Kirsty,' began Liam in a reassuring tone. 'Dan adores you. If I thought he didn't, I'd tell you right now, and save you the agony of finding out later. It's up to you now, Kirst – but if you choose to walk away because of a stupid one-night stand, it'll be a bloody tragedy. You guys were made for each other.'

He held her by the shoulders.

'I know Jenna meant nothing to him. I did the same thing myself. I picked up a woman in the bar and slept with her. It was a crazy night. Champagne, tequila shots, sambuca – that's no excuse, I know. But please – don't ruin your life and Dan's because of a moment's madness.' He gazed into her eyes and smiled imploringly. 'He's going to be a wonderful husband. He wants me to be godfather to your first kid. I've got it all lined up – a first-edition Harry Potter. I want to be there at the font in a year or so . . .'

He trailed off. What the hell more could he say?

There was a single tear glittering like a diamond on Kirsty's cheek. She lifted a finger and wiped it away, then looked at her watch.

'I'd better go and find my parents,' she said. 'I was supposed to be meeting them ten minutes ago. They'll be freaking out.'

'So . . . what's happening?'

'I need to think, Liam. I need to weigh it all up.'

She slid off the wall and walked away. Liam watched her go, his heart pounding, the metallic taste of guilt in his mouth. Had he done all he could to rectify the situation? The situation he could have averted, let's face it, if he hadn't been so self-obsessed that night. If he hadn't been caught up in the thrall of that woman, he would have had his wits about him and sent Jenna packing with a flea in her ear. But he had been entranced.

He didn't like thinking back on his own behaviour even now. He'd found the woman attractive, very attract-ive. She was posh, pretty, obviously well off – and flirtatious. How could he resist? But she was also drunk and vulnerable. He should absolutely have known better. If he'd been a gentleman, he'd have walked her back to her beach hut and left her.

When he had got up to leave as dawn broke, she had

opened her eyes. The stare she had given him was so blank, like a china doll gazing into the middle distance, glassy, sightless. He'd wanted to ask her name, but it seemed so crass. He was still drunk when he left her, but not so drunk his conscience didn't needle him on the way back to the campsite. He'd crawled into the huge tent he was sharing with the other blokes, stuffed himself into his sleeping bag and slept till midday, when he was forced to get up and play a round of golf.

The memory of her had haunted him ever since. He hadn't stopped wondering what had happened to her, what she had remembered when she had woken up, whether she regretted sleeping with him. There had been no way for him to contact her. They hadn't exchanged numbers.

Then, when he and Dan had come down the day before for the wedding, he had seen her. It wasn't so surprising – she had told him that she spent a lot of the summer in Everdene with her family. She was in the Spar shop, two small children with her, perfectly turned out, the little girl in a pink spotty sundress, the boy in surfing shorts and a long-sleeved T-shirt. She had looked perfect too, the ultimate yummy mummy with her blond hair in a ponytail and her Calvin Klein sunglasses on her head.

He wanted to say something to her, wanted to make sure she was all right, but he didn't dare. He didn't want to break the bubble she was in, the three of them poring over the open freezer, each child allowed to choose an ice cream. She'd looked up and seen him standing at the end of the queue with his shopping basket, and she'd blinked slowly. She had given him a tiny, tentative smile, then looked away. He understood. She'd recognised him, but didn't want anything to do with him. It made him feel grubby. And even more ashamed.

He should never have had sex with her. He should have talked to her, about whatever it was that was troubling her, because he could sense she was a woman in crisis. But some visceral urge had taken them both over. He reminded himself that she hadn't protested at all. She had wound her arms around his neck and pushed herself against him willingly enough. There had been no mixed signals.

Yet he had come away knowing it was wrong. It still didn't sit easily with him. He hadn't really drunk much since, wary of what he might turn into – a chauvinistic player who treated women like objects. And he hadn't been able to get her out of his mind; it kept wandering to those china-doll eyes. What had made someone who seemed so perfect on the surface so unhappy?

It had been a crazy night. And not just for him. He dragged himself back to the problem in hand as he made his way to the hotel. Bloody Jenna. What was she thinking of? He was going to kill her. He was going to bloody kill her.

Dan wondered where the hell Liam had got to. They were supposed to be heading down to the ballroom any minute, where the civil ceremony was going to take place, to meet the registrar and make sure everything was in order. At this rate they were going to be late, and he didn't want anything to go wrong. He wanted the day to be perfect. Not for himself – he wasn't all that bothered, he'd have been happy with a few mates at the register office – but for Kirsty, who had been working hard for months to get everything just right. He knew how important every detail was to her, from the fresh pomegranate juice and prosecco down to the last white-chocolate profiterole. Dan was determined nothing was going to spoil it, and was irritated with Liam for disappearing at the eleventh hour. He wondered who it had been on the phone, and what had been so important? He felt a little bit of disquiet gnawing at him. It was nearly one o'clock. Liam should definitely have been back by now. What if . . . ?

Don't be stupid, he told himself. Jenna wouldn't say anything. But he could feel his palms sweat slightly, and a prickle of unease make its way down his spine and into the pit of his stomach. He hadn't seen Jenna since the stag night. She hadn't contacted him since, thank God. At first he had worried that she might go all *Fatal Attraction* on him, start bombarding him with even more texts and phone calls than usual, but she had fortunately been very discreet. He hadn't heard a squeak.

Why the hell had he done it? If he thought about it too much, he made himself feel sick. Jenna had made it so easy. Nuzzling up to him, whispering in his ear, winding herself around him.

'Just once,' she told him. 'Because you know you want to. And it's much better to do it now than when you're a married man. Get it out of your system.'

And in his drunken state, he had succumbed to her suggestion, because he and Jenna had always got on, and he couldn't deny he found her attractive, even though she was so very different from Kirsty. Maybe that had been the attraction? A base curiosity, a last-minute need to check out what was on offer and make sure he'd made the right choice.

Not that he could remember much about it. He dimly recalled staggering out of the Ship with her, and staggering up the hill to the campsite. It was only when he woke the next day and found her next to him that he realised what he'd done. He'd got rid of her pretty sharpish, but her scent had clung to him for hours afterwards, even though he had scrubbed and scrubbed himself in the shower. Of course, he really only had himself to blame. Jenna might have laid a trap for him, but if he'd been any sort of a man he could have side-stepped it, instead of throwing himself straight in.

It was OK, he told himself. In just over an hour's time, he would be a married man. Jenna would know better than to remind him of what they had done. She was Kirsty's best friend, after all.

Although what kind of best friend slept with her friend's fiancé?

Dan thought about ordering another cognac. He pulled out his phone and looked at the time. Ten minutes to kick-off. Where the hell was Liam?

'Just pack up your things and I'll get you a taxi from reception.' Liam was grabbing stuff from round the room and shoving it all back into Jenna's open suitcase. Jenna was lying in the middle of the bed, staring up at the ceiling. 'What the hell were you thinking of, Jenna?'

'I love him,' replied Jenna simply. 'I didn't realise till this morning, but I love him, Liam.'

Liam stopped in the middle of folding up Jenna's bridesmaid's dress.

'So does Kirsty, I think you'll find,' he replied drily.

'I loved him from the day I first met him. When we all came down here for the weekend – do you remember? Seven years ago.'

Liam didn't. They'd been down here so many times, he couldn't remember specific occasions. He and Dan were at the core of the gang, and it grew and shrank and grew again, reorganising itself into different ramifications – friends from uni, friends from work, friends from the gym, football, people they'd met on other holidays, friends of friends. He couldn't remember how or why Jenna had been grafted on, but she'd been a stalwart. And then Dan had brought along Kirsty, who he'd met at a friend's housewarming. She was the girl in the flat upstairs. And today, most of the people in the gang were here, arriving in the car park, dressed in the finery that was a far cry from their usual Everdene uniform of jeans and board shorts and halter-neck tops. Ready for the happy union of their founder member and his bride.

'It's not fair.' Jenna didn't think she could cry any more, but here they were – more tears, squeezing themselves out of her eyelids, which were now so puffy as to make her almost unrecognisable.

'You know what? Life isn't. But it doesn't mean you can trample over people, just because things haven't gone your way. What has Kirsty ever done to hurt you?'

'Kirsty's got everything.' Jenna remained stubbornly unrepentant. 'If she doesn't marry Dan, they'll be queuing round the block within nanoseconds. She'd be spoilt for choice.'

'But Dan's her choice.'

Jenna zipped up her case and stood up.

'Do you think she'll still marry him?'

Liam picked up her case. He was going to escort her out the back way, in the service lift and out by the laundry, so she wouldn't bump into any guests.

'I hope so,' he answered.

Jenna's lip trembled for a moment, but there were, at last, no more tears.

She pulled the CD out of her handbag.

'You'll have to sort the hut out for me. Put that on the CD player. And light the candles. And don't forget the champagne . . .'

She gave a final little hiccup of grief. Liam relented for a moment, and wrapped his arms round her.

'It's OK, Jenna,' he told her. 'It'll be OK.'

She gave him a weary smile.

'Yeah. I'll get over it. Good old Jenna. Always the bridesmaid . . .'

Kirsty was with her parents in a little private drawing room on the first floor of the hotel. She didn't want any of the guests to see her as they arrived, so the receptionist had tucked them away in here, a room from another age, set aside for writing letters or curling up with a book. Kirsty smiled her thanks as the waiter put down a tray of coffee things on a table and looked at the two of them on the sofa opposite her, grateful for their presence, their solidity.

Thank goodness they'd got here without any mishap. Her father's driving was increasingly perilous these days, and her mother was a dreadful map-reader. She'd thought about buying them a sat nav, but she knew it would stay in its box, something to be terrified of, not something to be embraced. They were in their early sixties – she'd been a late and only child – but they seemed so much older. Put her father next to Mick Jagger or Ronnie Wood and there would be no comparison.

Her mother pushed the plate of shortbread over to her.

'Eat that, darling. The sugar will do you good. You need energy to get through the day. Heaven knows when you'll get a chance to sit down again.'

Kirsty picked up the biscuit absent-mindedly. It was easier to capitulate than protest. Her mind was whirling. What was she supposed to do? She couldn't, absolutely couldn't, confide in them, her dear parents who were obviously so excited about her big day. They would be horrified, and there would be no question of her over-looking Dan's misdemeanour once the truth was out. Her father would confront him immediately, defend his daughter's honour. Her mother would sob whilst trying to console her. They would be unconditionally sup-portive. They would whisk her back home, put her to bed in her old bedroom. Kirsty could imagine the end-less cups of tea, the inquisitive noses of the dogs, the claustrophobia, the hopelessness.

But she had to make up her mind. Did she make the ultimate melodramatic gesture and walk out, here and now? Wasting several thousand pounds that had been invested in the wedding, not to mention the honeymoon in Bali they had booked? It would mean going right back to square one, to being single, and all the difficulties that entailed. She'd be no spring chicken this time round, and it was tough finding Mister Right out there.

On the other hand, did she just overlook Dan's crime?

There was no time to confront him now; the ceremony was due to start in less than a quarter of an hour.

'Darling,' her mother was saying. 'Are you all right? You look pale.'

'Leave her be,' her father interjected. 'She's bound to be nervous.'

'Perhaps she needs some fresh air . . .'

'I'm fine.' Kirsty smiled brightly and put the short-bread down, hoping her mother wouldn't notice. 'I'm going to pop up to my room and finish getting ready. Dad, I'll meet you back down here at ten to. Then we can go down to the ballroom. Mum – will you be OK to find yourself a seat? Liam will have saved you one . . .'

She could picture it all in her head. Dan and Liam and the ushers, directing people to their places, handing out orders of service. The ballroom, with its crystal chandelier, the gold chairs, the white scented flowers she had chosen . . . She closed her eyes to fight back tears as her mother hugged her, unfamiliar in a coral jacket and matching skirt that was a total contrast to her usual slacks and jumpers.

'You look gorgeous, Mum,' Kirsty told her, not sure if the lump in her throat was pride at her wonderful parents, who she knew would be there for her whatever she decided, or the emotional fallout from Jenna's bombshell.

She fled the room. She would go up in the service lift – she didn't want to risk meeting anyone in the main lift. In the quiet of her room, she'd be able to make up her mind what to do.

*

There was a stony silence as Liam rode down in the lift with Jenna, her bag at their feet. He wanted to see her into the taxi, make sure she didn't cause any more trouble. He was already late – he should be in the ballroom right now, with Dan. Dan would be doing his nut.

Ting. The lift was stopping on the third floor. Shit, thought Liam as the door opened slowly. They didn't have time for this.

Outside the lift was Kirsty.

The three of them stared at each other for a moment. The doors were about to shut again. Liam pressed the button to keep them open.

Kirsty stepped backwards instinctively. Then Jenna stepped forward.

'I need to talk to you.'

'Jenna!' Liam grabbed her by the shoulder. 'Don't you think you've said enough?'

'There's something else—'

'Please . . .' Kirsty put her hands up in defence. 'I don't want to hear any more.'

She turned to go, distressed, but Jenna put a hand on her shoulder.

'Kirsty. Listen. Everything I said . . . it was all a total lie.'

Kirsty stopped in her tracks and turned. Liam kept his finger on the button. Jenna stepped forward.

'I . . . didn't sleep with Dan.' She looked defiant, but her voice was shaky, her eyes bright with unshed tears. 'I admit I went back with him to his tent. I would have slept with him. I can't pretend I wouldn't. But he passed out. He'd had so much to drink he crashed straight away.

241

When he woke up the next morning, I let him think . . .
we'd done it. He couldn't remember a thing from about
ten o'clock, so he believed me. He was totally gutted. He
went outside the tent and threw up. Then he chucked me
out. Told me he never wanted to talk about it again, that
it hadn't happened. He was furious, with himself and me.
It made me feel really good, I can tell you. That someone
could be so disgusted they'd slept with me . . .'

She pressed her lips together and blinked hard.

'I pretended to myself that we did have sex. I wanted
to think just for a moment that he'd wanted me. And
then I wanted to spoil it for you, because . . . he didn't
want me. He pushed me away.'

Liam and Kirsty looked at each other over Jenna's
head.

'He loves you,' she told Kirsty. 'And he wouldn't look
at another woman. Yeah, he let me kiss him. Sit on his
lap. But he was only humouring me. I was kissing him.
He wasn't kissing me back. He was just going along with
it to be polite. He didn't want to cause a scene in the
Ship. And he only let me go back to the campsite because
I didn't have anywhere else to stay. He said I could crash
in his tent.'

She wiped away the tears that were falling again.

'Dan wasn't guilty of anything, Kirsty. It was all me.
And I'm sorry.'

There was silence. Then Kirsty gave a little smile and a
nod of understanding.

'Thank you,' she said finally. And then she held out
her arms and gave Jenna a hug. She could, after all, afford
to be magnanimous. Then she let her go and turned
away.

Liam took his finger off the button and let the lift doors close.

The erstwhile bridesmaid and the best man rode down to the ground floor, as the bride ran up the stairs to her bedroom to fetch her bouquet.

The Everdene Sands Hotel was welcoming its guests, wrapping them in its four walls, listening as they ooh-ed and aah-ed in delight at its perfection as they walked down the cool, white corridors to the ballroom. Here the French windows were flung open, leading out onto the verdant lawns, beyond which the sea was laid out in an expanse of silver and turquoise. Gradually, the guests began to settle. As they sat down the noise level fell but the anticipation rose. The air was sweet with the scent of white roses and sea air, and a pianist played soft, tinkly jazz.

Kirsty stood by the closed doors of the ballroom with her father, her arm hooked in his. Her heart was thumping. This was it, the moment every girl dreams of. It had come so close to not happening. For a second she wondered where Jenna was, whether she would come back yet again to spoil the fairytale, but she banished her from her mind. Jenna was history.

The wedding organiser threw open the doors with a smile. Kirsty looked through them and down the length of white carpet to the end. And there she saw her husband-to-be. And he turned, and she saw a light in his eyes that was honest and true. Her heart leapt with joy.

She began to walk.

There was a pale moon hanging in the sky, an entourage of stars clustered around it, as Dan Harper carried his bride across the damp sand. Her ringlets hung loose, her shoes had long been abandoned, and she was laughing as they arrived at the door of the beach hut.

'I thought we were just going for a walk,' she protested, as he struggled to put the key in the lock without putting her down.

'Surprise,' he told her.

The door swung open, and he carried her effortlessly over the threshold.

'Oh my God,' she breathed in awe, as she looked around the room. Hundreds of candles flickered. Music played softly. Champagne chilled in a bucket; there was a platter piled high with cupcakes and fruit. There was a huge pink heart painted on the wall, with an arrow through it. D at the top, K at the bottom.

Dan laid Kirsty gently on the bed. It was like falling into swansdown. She stretched her arms above her head and sighed at the perfection of it all.

'Dan . . . this is wonderful. This is so special. It means everything to me.'

He came and lay down beside her.

'It was Jenna's idea,' he told her.

Kirsty rolled onto her side and looked into her husband's eyes. He lifted a hand and stroked her hair.

'Liam told me everything. About what she said to you. I'm so sorry . . .'

'I don't understand,' said Kirsty. 'How can she think of doing something so wonderful, like this? And then . . . try and spoil everything?'

He put a finger to her lips.

'Shhh,' he ordered. 'Not tonight. Nothing is going to spoil tonight.'

He pulled her to him, and she slid her hands underneath his jacket, working it loose from his shoulders. As she began to unbutton his shirt he took her face in his hands. The two of them lay, bathed in the glow of the candles, and their lips met.

A hundred miles away, a heartbroken girl let herself into a dark, empty flat.

9

MAKING WAVES

What kind of a man did that? What kind of a man waited until the woman he professed to love was forty-one, and had started taking her folic acid supplements, before telling her it was all over, he had got a research post in Italy, and he had no intention of taking her with him? Not that she would have necessarily gone if he'd given her the choice, because she had her own career, but she would have liked to have been given the option.

But there was no option. Eight years eradicated in the blink of an eye. And the pain of realising that the man you had hoped would be the father of your child wasn't the person you thought he was. That he was selfish, deceitful and arrogant. And cruel. Almost inhumanely cruel. In the event, Helena was grateful that she hadn't got pregnant by Neal, because she wouldn't have wanted a child of hers to inherit the capacity to hurt someone even half as much as she had been hurt.

She had watched him pack his things up in their flat, and had been astonished by the cold and calculating manner in which he had divided up everything they had bought jointly. In the end, she told him to take the lot. What was the point in having three espresso cups each? He might as well have the whole set in his Florentine apartment: she couldn't remember the last time they'd used them anyway. Who made posh coffee at home when you had Starbucks? Besides, she was grateful for a clean slate. She would go and buy everything new, as part of the therapeutic process. It wasn't as if she couldn't afford it.

Which was, she suspected, where the problem lay. Her success, her status, her prestige. His male ego simply couldn't take it. She was a cardiothoracic consultant at a big hospital in Bristol. He was an artist, with a chaotic studio he shared with another load of artists in the backstreets of Totterdown. OK, so maybe producing enormous canvases smothered in thick oil in seventeen shades of grey wasn't on a par with giving someone the gift of life several times a day, but Helena had never thought any less of Neal because of it. The world needed art and culture as much as it needed life-saving surgery. It would be a bleak and empty place without it.

Whatever the reason for his flit, she hadn't been able to talk him out of it. She had raged, she had wept, she had tried to assume a calm and reasonable tone and discuss it like an adult, but he was adamant. He barely gave her a reason: it seemed he didn't want to justify his decision with a rational explanation, just a blanket statement that it was for the best.

On his last night, she had tried to seduce him. He was always putty in her hands in bed. Maybe, just maybe, she would get pregnant, although she knew it was a little too early on in her cycle. They hadn't officially tried yet – she had only been off the pill three months, she had wanted time to let the supplements kick in before conceiving. But he had resisted her advances. Never, ever in their entire relationship had he turned down sex. It broke her completely. Her staff would have been astonished to see the mighty Helena Dickinson – goddess, role model, ruler of the CT ward with a rod of iron – on her knees, sobbing like a baby, begging him to think again.

What on earth had she done to deserve it? It wasn't as if he'd found out she'd been banging the director of the health trust, or selling the organs of dead patients for profit. Their relationship had been symbiotic. Passionate. Fun. Fulfilling. Easy, for heaven's sake. They rarely argued over trivial matters – though they did engage in heated debate about things that were important to them.

Was it because she was too old? She was aware of the age gap. She was a woman – of course she was. Although Helena came across as sexy, confident, sure of herself, there were still times when she looked in the mirror and wondered where that fresh-faced medical student had gone. She bought ridiculously expensive creams to keep the wrinkles at bay. She exercised religiously to stop middle-aged spread. She had the grey in her hair covered professionally and regularly. As a result, to the casual observer she looked no older than Neal's thirty-seven, but maybe he saw the cracks. Maybe he'd had a glimpse into the near future and didn't like what he saw.

She didn't want to think this was the reason. She would go mad if she did. No one knew this, but Helena's appearance was her Achilles heel – surprisingly superficial for one who had achieved so much. She hid her insecurity well, because it didn't really suit the image she had constructed for herself, but nevertheless she watched herself like a hawk for signs of deterioration, and addressed them with whatever weapon she could find, although she had yet to resort to surgery.

Instead, she told herself it was Neal's fear of how a baby would affect their relationship that had made him bolt. His inability to be mature enough to face fatherhood, because Neal was effectively a child himself. Although they had discussed it at length, and reached the decision to try for a baby together, he must have had some objection that he couldn't voice. It wasn't uncommon for a man to get cold feet about recreating. Helena had been through the experience with enough of her colleagues to know that they came round in the end and became doting fathers. Try as she might, she couldn't get Neal to admit that this was the problem.

'Then what is it?' she pleaded.

'I don't know. I can't explain. But it's not you. It's me.'

Great. The most frustrating platitude of all time. Of course it was her.

Nevertheless, Helena didn't miss a beat. She drove him to the airport, bought him a copy of *Status Anxiety* by Alain de Botton from the bookshop, kissed him, watched him disappear through the gate in his battered corduroy jacket and jeans, his dark curls touching the collar, and tried not to imagine who would be the next person to run her fingers through them. She sobbed all the way back in the car, then stopped at John Lewis and bought a new set of hideously expensive bed linen, china, glasses, a teak salad bowl with matching servers, a food mixer, a massive chenille floor rug – totally schizophrenic retail therapy, and so much that she had to arrange to have it delivered the next day, but it might all replace the lack of Neal in the atmosphere. By the time she got home she was calm. She poured herself a glass of champagne and sank onto the sofa to decide what she was going to do next.

If she sat quietly enough, she was sure she could hear her body clock ticking, like the crocodile in *Peter Pan*. Of course, she only had herself to blame for leaving it so late. It was her bloody ambition, her drive to succeed, her desperate need to get to the top. All the time she had been working all the hours God sent and scrambling up the career ladder she had ignored the little voice inside that had told her to stop, take a break, get things into perspective and think about what she wanted as a woman rather than a doctor. And when she had finally listened to that voice, her partner of eight years had let her down.

Helena Dickinson had run out of time.

Just over a month later, she was sitting in the sunshine on the balcony of a beach hut at Everdene Sands, her feet up on the railing, taking in the magnificent view. It wasn't the sparkling sea that interested her so much as the people in it, the black blobs that were lurking behind the wave line ready to catch a ride into shore. She smiled as she wondered if one of these would be the suitable candidate, the one she would choose.

It was, she knew, a daring, audacious, madcap, slightly crazy plan, and one she hadn't shared with anyone else, because anyone with a scrap of common sense would have talked her out of it. But Helena had thought through her options, viewing the issue from all sides and giving it as much care and consideration as she did the treatment of any of her patients. She weighed up the pros and cons, the ethics, the risks, the alternatives. She was known on the ward as a bit of a maverick, the consultant who would take the risky option, the one who was prepared to be experimental, and she was simply following this through from her professional to her private life. And to her, the plan made perfect sense.

She wanted someone to father a child. Quickly. There was no time to embark on a relationship – it could take weeks, months, even years to reach the stage where she and a partner would agree on procreation. And she'd thought and thought about it but she just didn't fancy the idea of a donor. She wanted some sort of human contact with the father of her baby and besides, although she knew the ethics of the donation industry were pretty watertight, she still couldn't be sure that whatever characteristics she requested weren't overlooked, or that someone else's wish-list might be mixed up with hers, or that one of the lab technicians might be having an off day and might think 'That one will do', lobbing an unsuitable match into the Petri dish.

So she was going to pick up a stranger. Sleep with them. Anonymously, so that if she did become pregnant and have their child, they would never know. After all, this was a journey she was quite prepared to travel alone. Helena had always been independent, and she certainly wasn't scared of being a single mother. She earned a good salary, there was an excellent crèche at the hospital, and at least that way she would get her own way over all the usual dilemmas, from whether to give the MMR jabs onwards. In fact, she thought being a single parent was far easier than trying to negotiate your relationship through sleepless nights and projectile vomiting. She'd seen even the most solid of partnerships buckle under the strain.

Of course, it wasn't ideal, but her situation wasn't ideal. Ideal would have been Neal sticking round long enough for her at least to conceive, even if he had then done a bunk. Helena was used to weighing things up quickly and making an informed decision, and this one had been easier than a lot of the decisions she had to make on behalf of her patients, because at least she knew her own mind and wasn't second-guessing what someone might want, or what was the best thing to do for them.

The only slight guilt she felt was on behalf of whoever she chose as the potential father. Would it be wrong to keep from them the fact they had a child? She overcame this by assuring herself that they would never know. Her mother had been fond of saying, 'What the eye don't see, the heart don't grieve over', and Helena wasn't going to deprive herself of the opportunity to have a child just because of the sensibilities of someone who wouldn't have a clue anyway.

And so, having overcome all the moral issues in her own mind, there only remained the practical question of where to find a donor. The hospital was out of the question. Tempting though it was to select a medical student or a registrar, it was too close to home. The chances of having to work with the father of her child in the future were too high. Besides, Helena knew enough about genetics to know that you didn't breed like with like. She didn't want her child to be highly strung and overbred. More than anything, given the job she was in, she wanted it to be physically strong.

Hitting on Everdene as her hunting ground had been inspired. She'd been there frequently when she was a registrar at the hospital in Exeter, more years ago than she cared to remember. She remembered it as a happy, positive place where the sun always seemed to shine, and, she recalled with a grin, it was populated with any number of hunky surfers. And surfers were usually fit, intrepid, with a sense of adventure. They might not be rocket scientists but their philosophy of life was usually a positive one, and their qualities set off her more cerebral attributes. A surfer, Helena decided, would be the perfect sire.

And so here she was, in the beach hut she had rented for a week to coincide with her most fertile period. She felt relaxed as soon as she arrived. The atmosphere was so laid-back, in total contrast to the atmosphere of the hospital where every second of her day was timetabled. Here she could eat when she liked, sleep when she liked, read what she liked – her time was her own and no one else's. It didn't belong to a fellow consultant, or an anxious patient, or an over-conscientious nurse, or the infinite paperwork that went with the job. Helena was practised at teaching herself to switch off, and she knew that if she wanted to conceive it was of the utmost importance not to be uptight and tense.

You couldn't be tense here. She looked out at the perfect curve of the beach, the pale green of the burrows behind it and the darker green of the hills behind them.

The sea, which changed every moment, unfurling every shade of blue (she tried not to think of Neal and his painter's eye when she looked at it). The lightest breeze danced on her skin. The sun caressed her with a gentle warmth. She stretched out with a sensual languor and reached down to the platter of mango, pineapple and melon she had cut for herself.

She wasn't going to think too hard about what she was about to do. It was like any physical challenge: the more you intellectualised it, the more you saw the potential hazards and the less likely you were to do it. Like abseiling, or skiing, or diving off the top board, she wasn't going to look down, she was just going to jump.

Besides, just driving through the tiny village and down to the car park that served the beach huts had convinced her she was doing the right thing. Everywhere she looked there were broad-shouldered, toned, fit young men, boards under their arms, striding out towards the waves. OK, so not all of them were prime specimens, but there were plenty to choose from.

She waited until the sun started to drift downwards towards the sea before making her move. She remembered the sunsets here as being spectacular, and tonight's was no exception, washing the sky in extraordinary pinks and oranges and golds that didn't seem real. Once again she was sharply reminded of Neal – no matter how strict she was with herself he still sneaked back into her mind uninvited, and she had to harden her heart, reminding herself of the cruelly trenchant position he had taken.

The sun was just kissing the horizon, a gilded ball of salmon pink, as she got herself ready. She pulled on a pair of faded boot-cut jeans with high black ankle boots, then added a belt with a big silver buckle and a tight white T-shirt. Her breasts were still pert, aided and abetted by an uplifting Aubade bra, her legs were long, her waist narrow. She didn't look like a CT consultant, more like the wife of some seventies rock icon, with her choppy blond bob and glacial blue eyes. There was no full-length mirror in the hut she had rented, so she had to hope for the best, but she was fairly confident of her ability to attract the opposite sex.

She picked up her bag and headed out of the door, breathing in the now cool night air. She negotiated her way in her high heels across the sand – silly, really, but the extra height made her legs seem endless, and she needed all the weapons she could get. Outside the Ship Aground she paused for a moment, her stomach fluttering slightly. No one who looked at her would be able to guess her mission.

'Come on, Helena,' she told herself. 'Go for it.'

She had no choice, for the alternative was to face a childless future, which she knew she didn't want.

Inside, the babble of voices hit her. The Ship was heaving, as it always was. At this time of night, there was still a slight division between the family area, where parents half-heartedly tried to force food down their by now overtired children, the touristy section and the bar, where the diehard locals hung out around the pool table. Later, when the parents had taken their offspring home and food stopped being served and enough drink had been downed, these edges would blur and the rabble would become homogeneous.

Helena looked over to the eating area and tried to imagine herself there in a year or so, pushing potato wedges into a reluctant mouth, dabbing at a tiny chin with a paper napkin, pulling a protesting body out of its high chair. It seemed an impossible future. But why not? She knew she would feel a strong pull to bring her child back to the place of its conception, and Everdene was ideal for family holidays.

Which meant she should probably avoid a local if she could.

She ordered a glass of white wine and soda from the bar. She was trying to avoid alcohol as part of her pre-conception regime, but she really couldn't do this stone-cold sober. It wasn't as if she was going to tank down a flotilla of alcopops and risk foetal alcohol syndrome. One or two wouldn't hurt. She ran her gaze through the crowds, weighing up the potential. She knew that when she saw him, she would know.

In the end, she found him outside. The heat inside was stifling, the noise was becoming too much to bear, and Helena was finding it hard not to make it obvious she was on her own. She'd been approached several times. Not in a bad way, most people were just being friendly, but it did bring home to her the risky madness of her plan. So she went outside for some fresh air to clear her head, and to look at the night sky, which was bright and clear. Maybe she would find some guidance amongst the stars.

He was leaning against the stone wall that separated the pub from the road, nursing what looked like a Scotch or a brandy. He too was gazing at the sky.

'You reckon the answer's out there?' She kept her tone light and friendly.

He turned, with a lopsided, quizzical smile.

'I doubt it.'

She came and stood next to him, leant her forearms on the rough stone. From here she could appraise him more thoroughly. He was tall – six foot, she estimated – and well proportioned. Hair in a fashionably scruffy cut that would need attention in a couple of weeks but was looking its best right now. Logo-less black T-shirt that revealed well-defined but not overdeveloped biceps, one of which had a Celtic band tattooed on it. The faintest drift of some aftershave she didn't recognise but approved of – slightly citrussy. Not public school but not a chav either, which was what Helena felt most comfortable with. She couldn't bear arrogance, but she liked a man who could choose wine from the wine-list without going into meltdown. This guy looked affluent but not flashy – confident, attractive.

'Do you come here often?' she joked. She was going to have to resort to clichés to speed up the process.

'As often as I can,' he replied. 'What's not to like?'

'I know.' She took another sip of her drink. 'It's a while since I've been, but it seemed like the perfect place to get some down time. I've had a bit of a tough time in the past few weeks.'

She flicked a glance over to him to judge his reaction. Was he silently willing her to fuck off so he could carry on with his stargazing?

But he seemed quite happy to chat.

'Me too,' he admitted. 'I've just been best man at my mate's wedding. It all went a bit . . . tits up.'

'Weddings can be a nightmare.' Helena had never had

to suffer her own, but she'd been to plenty and had seen the stress and the fallout.

'This was beyond a nightmare.'

'Did the bride and groom make it up the aisle?'

'By the skin of their teeth.' He turned to look at her, and as he smiled, she could see he had laughing eyes. Conspirator's eyes. She felt her pulse increase a little. 'It was all OK in the end. When they left for the airport this morning they couldn't keep their hands off each other. I couldn't face going back to work, so I've taken a few days off to recover from the trauma.'

He rubbed a hand over his face and ruffled his hair. Helena could see he had felt the strain – despite his tan, he looked tired.

'What do you do?'

He gave a small grimace. 'Well – I was going to be a professional footballer. Tried out for some of the second-division teams but . . . knee injury. The old cruciate ligament.'

'Like Gordon Ramsay?'

'Kind of,' he replied. 'Except I'm not a Michelin-starred chef. I'm a physiotherapist. I thought if my injury was going to stop me doing what I really wanted, then at least I could help others with theirs.'

'Seems like a good plan.'

'And actually, now I'm glad. My life's my own. I've got a great client list. I earn a good living, but if I want to block some time out of my diary I can.' He gestured towards the sea. 'I spend as much time as I can here. I can't play football or ski any more, but at least I can surf.'

'It's supposed to be addictive.'

'Have you never tried?'

'Do you know what – I've been here loads of times, but I've never actually had a go.'

'You totally should. You'd love it.'

His eyes shone with the passion of one obsessed with his hobby. Helena grinned impishly.

'I just need a good teacher.'

She saw the shutters come down almost straight away, and realised she was going too fast, too soon.

'What about you?' he asked, changing the subject. 'What do you do?'

She decided to pitch her status slightly lower. He didn't look the type to be intimidated – in fact, he might consider it a challenge – but the less he knew about her, the less complicated it would be.

'I'm a rep. For a drug company. Spend most of my time on the road.'

'Bribing consultants to use your products?'

'Shamelessly. Using every trick in the book.'

She met his eyes, laughing, knowing that she was both lying and flirting. She quite enjoyed it. He held up his empty glass.

'Fancy another?'

It was so tempting. She'd already had one, but part of her wanted to let her hair down and enjoy her alter ego. But she had to be careful. She wanted to keep her wits about her.

She'd have one more. She could sip it slowly.

'Go on then. White wine and soda. Thank you. I'm Helena, by the way.'

'Liam . . .'

He took her glass and she watched him walk back

inside with an appraising eye. So far, so good. A physio was a good job – to get a reputation you had to be dedicated and conscientious. He had great dress sense, good manners, he seemed to have a sense of humour. She only had her gut to go on to make sure he wasn't a psychopath. And she trusted her gut. She had to, in her job.

She looked up at the star-studded sky, trying not to remember that it was the very same sky Neal would be looking up at in Florence. She wondered if he already had a replacement for her. They would be standing arm in arm, reckless after a bottle or two of potent Italian red, gazing at the navy-blue velvet . . .

Stop it. She was looking forwards, not backwards. She wasn't going to spend another moment thinking about someone who'd wasted eight years of her life. Helena burrowed in her bag quickly for her Lancôme Juicy Tube, swiped it over her mouth, pressed her lips together so it wouldn't be obvious, then ran her fingers through her hair. Focus, she told herself. Focus.

At the bar, Liam waited patiently for the barman, wondering why the hell he had asked whoever-she-was if she wanted a drink. Helena, that was her name. He had broken his resolution already. Well, not completely, but there was no denying he was embroiled in a conversation with an attractive woman who was clearly free and available and giving out signals. He'd fallen into the trap.

Had he learnt nothing from the past few weeks? The stag night fiasco had shaken him to the core. Both his own sordid one-night stand, and the five-act drama that was Dan's. He still didn't know what to believe, Jenna's hastily revised version of events or her original story. Nor did he want the details. All he was glad of was that Dan and Kirsty had left for their honeymoon quite happy. But it could so easily have gone another way. One night of laddish behaviour in the Ship could have ended in the whole wedding being called off at the last minute, and it would have been his fault. Liam remembered leaving the pub with his own conquest, passing Jenna astride Dan's knee, and barely stopping to give his friend a warning.

He'd seen the woman again this morning. In the post office, this time on her own, taking some money out from the cashpoint. He had longed to go up to her and ask how she was. She looked fragile, tired. She didn't see him. He followed her outside to see a sleek Mercedes pull up – the driver gave an impatient pip on the horn and she scurried to get into the car. Had the driver been the source of her unhappiness? The reason why she had clung so tightly to him during sex – he couldn't call it making love; he didn't even know her name. He hated not knowing the end of the story, but he couldn't muster up the courage to approach her.

The wedding, the one-night stand – they had both left him feeling that someone had pulled the plug and he had been left with the scum clinging to him. And so he had resolved to turn over a new leaf and leave behind the hedonistic love-them-and-leave-them lifestyle he'd indulged in for so long. It had suited him to be footloose and fancy free, but when it left you feeling grubby and guilty, it was time to change. That kind of behaviour was OK in your twenties, but not in your mid-thirties. He had looked at Dan waiting for his beautiful bride and had felt a mixture of shame and envy. As the two of them had spoken their vows, he had vowed himself to make some drastic changes.

Only here he was again. Old habits die hard, he thought ruefully as the barman handed him the replenished glasses.

You don't have to jump her bones, he reminded himself. You can just have a perfectly pleasant conversation and leave it at that.

He took the glasses, turned and walked outside. For a moment, he thought she'd got bored of waiting and had gone, and he felt a twinge of disappointment but no – she was still there. She'd sat down at one of the tables. She smiled at him as he approached and he was struck by how attractive she was. Attractive and quite a bit older than him, he thought. Just like the last one. A bit more together than the last one, though. Not quite so much baggage.

Just a friendly chat, he told himself, wondering if he'd be able to override his instinct. It would be easy, he knew it would. At his time of life, you learnt to read the signals.

They chatted for hours. They were very different, but they found things in common. A love of Indian food – she swore by Madhur Jaffrey, he swore by making it up as he went along. A love of Dan Brown – a guilty pleasure for both of them. They both wanted to go to Machu Picchu, preferably at Christmas time; they both hated Christmas. And as the pub started emptying, she looked at him.

'I'm never going to sleep, if I go to bed now,' she said. 'I had a huge nap this afternoon. I'm going to take a walk along the beach.'

This was the time for Liam to say goodbye. The cue to say, 'It's been nice meeting you,' and to go back to the hotel.

'I'll come with you.'

The moon shone brightly on the sand as they walked, the lights of Everdene twinkling behind them. Helena had taken off her boots and rolled up her jeans. She looked less intimidating without the extra height. Softer somehow. Liam found himself intrigued by her – she seemed a curious mixture of hyper-confident and strangely reticent. He wondered what her history was – a woman like her didn't get through life without romantic entanglement, and she'd mentioned coming here because she'd had a tough time. A traumatic break-up?

He wasn't going to ask. He didn't want to get too familiar. Keep it casual.

'Oh look,' he said, pointing at the sky. 'Orion's Belt, as clear as you like.' And felt like an absolute idiot.

She was as certain as she could ever be. After all, she'd given Neal eight years before she realised he was not the one, so why shouldn't she make up her mind after a few hours? And if she'd gone down the donor route, she would have had no inkling. At least she knew Liam had a work ethic, a sense of humour and a zest for life. And he knew his constellations . . .

She shivered in the moonlight. It was chilly in just a T-shirt, and her feet were freezing.

'I need to get back inside. I need a hot chocolate to warm me up.' She paused. 'Would you like one? I can stick a slug of brandy in it, or marshmallows. Whichever . . .'

She trailed off, suddenly losing confidence in her plan.

It's OK, she told herself. You don't *have* to sleep with him.

'Can I just have the brandy?' he asked.

In the end, she had brandy too, that spread its fiery warmth right through her body and gave her the courage to put her arms around his neck and look into his eyes. Their lips met for a moment, for the most fleeting of kisses, before he put his hands on her arms and pushed her away gently.

'I can't do this,' he said.

Helena wasn't sure she had heard him correctly.

'Sorry?'

'This – one-night stand thing. It's not right.'

She gave a little laugh.

'Come on. We're both grown-ups.'

Liam peeled himself away from her. He stared up at the ceiling.

'It's not you,' he said. 'It's—'

'Oh, for fuck's sake.' Helena turned away and walked over to the kitchen area. She squirted some Fairy Liquid savagely into the sink and turned on the taps. 'Just bugger off if you want to. I can handle it.'

'Hang on a minute,' said Liam. 'I really like you. I want it to . . . matter. I don't want to just get my leg over

264

and walk off.' He gave her a rueful smile. 'I've done that once too often.'

Helena nodded sagely.

'I'm guessing there's history behind this?'

'Like I said,' he replied. 'It's not you . . .'

Helena rolled her eyes.

'Goodnight.'

She plunged their brandy glasses into the sink full of warm water. She heard the door of the beach hut click softly as he left.

Trust her to pick the one guy on the planet who had sworn a vow of celibacy to father her child.

The next morning, she heard a bang on her beach-hut door. She looked at her watch, bleary eyed. It was only just after seven. What was going on? She rolled out of bed and staggered across the room. Mornings were not her strong point. Not until she'd had two mugs of Earl Grey at least.

He was standing at the top of the step, dressed in a wetsuit, holding up another. On the sand behind him lay two boards.

'Surf's up,' he announced cheerfully. 'Let's get the best waves before you get an audience.'

She stood in the doorway, speechless.

'Come on. Chop-chop.'

No one did this to Helena Dickinson. Took her by surprise. Told her what to do. Set her a challenge she wasn't sure she could meet.

He held out the wetsuit.

'I reckon you're about a size twelve? Stick it on. Let's get going.'

*

Three hours later and she was exhausted. She didn't know what ached more, her arms, her legs or her stomach muscles. She was battered from falling off – wiping out, as they called it – but she'd finally done it. She'd stood up on her board and rode in on a wave. Not very elegantly, granted, but she felt as if she was flying. When she finally fell, he came and gave her a hand to stand up.

'I did it!' she cried, triumphant. 'I totally did it. It was fantastic!'

'That's it now,' he grinned. 'You'll be hooked.'

Without thinking, she threw her arms around his neck. Their lips met, salty. It was a brief kiss, but a kiss full of promise, full of meaning, before a wave came up behind her and knocked her off her feet.

She came up laughing. He was right. She was hooked.

She managed to drag herself back to the hut on trembling legs. He teased her all the way. It was a new experience for her, a man who tested her, who wasn't afraid to make fun. No one at the hospital ever did, and Neal certainly wasn't one for light-hearted japes.

She made them pancakes, with sliced banana, Devon clotted cream and drizzles of maple syrup. They lay on a rug in the sun afterwards, in a carbohydrate slump.

'There's something I need to tell you,' said Helena.

'Shit,' Liam sat up. 'You're not married. Tell me you're not married.'

'I'm not married,' she assured him. 'But I'm not a drug rep either.'

And so she told him the truth. About her job, and about Neal doing a runner. And he wasn't fazed, or freaked out, or pissed off that she'd lied to him. He lay there listening to her unburden herself, and when she'd finished he just stretched out a hand and took hers.

They fell asleep together in the sun.

10

PERFECT STORM

Sirens screeched. Bells rang. Somewhere in the background, Dizzee Rascal begged for someone to come and dance with him. Despite the cacophony, Serena was gripping the steering wheel with total concentration. She eased off the throttle as she took the corner, then put her foot down as she drove hell for leather down the straight before slowing down again for the hairpin bend. She could see the finishing line, the audience cheering either side of the road, as she maxed the car for the last half-mile, then swept under the flags to tumultuous applause two seconds before her rival.

'Yesss!' She jumped off her seat, arms in the air in a gesture of triumph.

Next to her, Adrian slid off his seat with a wry grin of defeat.

'I never knew you could drive like that.'

'I'll let you into a secret.' She leant in close to him, and he breathed in her scent. He should be used to it by now, but it still made him light-headed. 'I used to come in here with Harry. When he was about thirteen. We played all the games, but that was his favourite. I bet our initials are still in the computer.'

They walked away from the Grand Prix simulator. All around them, people were hypnotised by the games on offer, even though the odds were stacked against them. Fruit machines, roulette wheels, Kentucky Derbys: they pumped coins in endlessly, the thumping cascade of occasional winnings spurring them on.

'Of course, Philip would have flipped if he knew. He hates this place.' She made a face, imitating her husband. '*It's for drongoes.*'

She didn't have to explain to Adrian. He knew his own brother only too well. He could just imagine his reaction if he found out his wife and son had been sneaking into the arcade for a bit of harmless fun. Sneeringly condescending vitriol. And some sort of sadistic punishment for Serena when she was least expecting it – a cruel put-down in front of guests, probably, or his refusal to attend some social occasion she was looking forward to. Petty punishments, because Philip was a coward and a bully. Adrian had been at the mercy of his brother's tongue more times than he cared to remember when they were young, and because of his placid nature he had never retaliated.

He was getting his own back now, however.

Not that this was motivated by revenge. Not at all. Adrian genuinely adored Serena. He had done since the day Philip had brought her home with him to meet the family, nearly twenty years ago. Adrian had only been sixteen then, and at the time thought it was probably a rite of passage to fancy your brother's girlfriend and that he would get over it one day. But he hadn't. Gradually, over the summers at Everdene, they had become closer. And closer. Until now . . .

He grabbed her to him, suddenly overwhelmed by his strength of feeling. The slightly surreal surroundings had brought it home even more. It was nearly the end of the summer; The Shack would be handed over to someone else come the autumn. If they didn't come clean, she would slip away, back to Warwickshire, and maybe the strength of *her* feelings would fade. The summers were the only time they had together – snatched, stolen moments, always cautious not to arouse anyone's suspicion. The rest of the time they communicated by mobile via an elaborate system of codes. He thought back on those phone calls; they sometimes spoke for hours, lying on their respective beds, the miles stretching interminably between them. Even when they spoke about the mundane it was intimate, and when they spoke about the intimate . . .

'We have to tell everyone,' he told her. 'We have to tell them now. Or we never will.'

He pushed her back against the fruit machine. He could feel the bass through her body. He wanted her so badly it hurt.

They still hadn't had sex. Something was holding them back. When it happened, they both wanted it to be right, not a sin. They'd only ever kissed. He couldn't imagine anything better than kissing her, but no doubt it would be.

'I know.' She looked into his eyes, her gaze unfaltering. Behind her head the machine flashed and winked. 'I'll tell Philip tonight.'

'And I'll tell my mother.' Adrian didn't relish the

prospect. Jane had had her fair share of bad news this year, and she was very protective of her family. He didn't know how kindly she would take to someone trying to destroy it from within. Serena would be the scapegoat, he knew that already. Not him. And not Philip.

They held each other tightly. Around them, chaos reigned – neon flashed, machines beeped and squawked, the carpet swirled in a tangle of electric blue and acid yellow. The air was thick with the scent of burgers and candy floss from the snack bar in the corner, and kids wandered around with cups full of luminous flavoured ice. It was hell or heaven, depending where you stood on amusement arcades.

'Dad?' To six-year-old Spike, blinking up at them, it was absolute paradise. But he looked confused. Why were the two of them hugging like that?

They peeled away from each other quickly. It had been one of the strictest rules of their affair, not to compromise Spike in any way.

'Hey.' Adrian ruffled his son's hair, the little tuft that still stood up in the front, the tuft that had given him his name. 'Serena just beat me hands down.'

'I've run out of money.' Spike held out his hands to prove he wasn't lying.

'Two pounds. That was your limit.'

'I wanted to win the Bart toy. I nearly got it.'

Adrian sighed. That was the problem with the arcade. It taunted you and teased you, made you believe you were about to come away with one of its crummy prizes. Spike had been longing for a Bart Simpson cuddly toy from the grabber.

'Let's give it one more go,' said Serena, taking Spike's hand. 'You never know.'

'I do know,' said Adrian, but he followed them anyway.

Serena slotted another fifty pence into the machine. She bent down next to Spike and told him which buttons to press to manipulate the grabber. Adrian knew what would happen. It would hover tentatively over Bart, then reach down with its claws and clutch helplessly at the prize, an ineffectual grasp of maybe an arm or a leg, before raising itself up again to its starting position, empty-handed.

But to Adrian's amazement, under Serena's guidance and encouragement, Spike managed to position the grabber in just the right spot. He squealed in excitement as Bart was born aloft. Moments later, he had him in his arms, a fluorescent-yellow toy made of cheap synthetic fibre that undoubtedly did not bear the approval of the programme-makers.

Seeing the incredible pleasure on his son's face made Adrian feel warm inside. It was what life was all about. And he knew that a future with Serena would make sure his life would be filled with these moments. It was one of the things – one of the many things – that he loved about her, the way she treated Spike. She always had time for him, had time to make things special. She always thought about what he might like, and bought him little presents. Nothing expensive – a windmill on a stick, a set of paper flags to stick in his sandcastles, his favourite magazine. Or a delicious oyster, the ice cream packed inside the wafer shell – a sweet treat that wouldn't spoil his lunch.

He shut his eyes so he could savour this precious

moment. Tomorrow, all hell would have broken loose. She might be his, or she might not. He prayed she had the strength to fight for what they had talked about incessantly for over a year now, but he knew she had a lot more to lose than he did. Serena had a marriage, and two children, and a family home. Adrian just had Spike. And Spike was only ever on loan to him as and when his mother thought fit. So he had nothing to lose, and everything to gain.

Adrian waited until Spike was tucked up in his bunk with Bart firmly under his arm, then poured his mother a glass of Bourgogne Aligote and flipped the lid on a Peroni for himself before he took the plunge. He, Jane and Spike were alone at The Shack; Philip, Serena, Harry and Amelia had rented a hut a few doors down, and David and Chrissie and their three were coming down the next afternoon, all in readiness for the annual end-of-season party at the weekend. That seemed a lifetime away at the moment. Adrian knew he had to strike now, before arrangements took over and everyone descended into pre-party hysteria and catering crises, which they did every year.

His mother, he thought, looked well. She had seemed very relaxed this summer, despite, or perhaps because of, her bereavement. In the past, she had always been on tenterhooks, having to second-guess Graham's mood, pussyfoot around him.

Adrian didn't need a therapist to tell him that it was probably his relationship with his mother that had fuelled his relationship with Serena. They were both in the thrall of powerful but selfish men who treated them like dirt. Adrian had always tried to protect his mother from his father, but what could he do when the cruelty was more mental than physical, when he couldn't put his finger on what his father had ever done, only knew that it made his mother desperately unhappy? At least with Serena, who suffered in much the same way, he could do something to help her, by taking her away from the source of her unhappiness.

He remembered the first day he realised that she felt for him too. Just over three years ago. He had found her crying round the back of the hut where they hung the wetsuits to dry.

'What's the matter?' he asked, astonished at the emotion that rose up inside him. The urge to protect her, and the urge to thump Philip, whom he guessed was behind her misery.

'Just a silly argument,' she tried to assure him, but the tears flowed thicker and faster. He put an arm round her, and she buried her face in his chest. He could have stood like that for ever.

She didn't confide in him that time. He knew he would have to build up trust. So he didn't probe, he was just there. And when, finally, the tears stopped because there couldn't possibly be any more, he told her he was going out in the RIB, the lightweight speedboat the family had bought a few years before and kept in a unit further down the estuary.

'Fancy coming?' he asked. 'It'll blow away the cobwebs. Mum's looking after Spike for a while. I said I'd go and check the boat out, give it an overhaul.'

She sniffed, and nodded, balling her hanky up and

shoving it in her pocket. 'That would be lovely.' She paused, frowned. 'I better check with Philip.'

'Why?' asked Adrian. 'You're a grown woman. Harry and Amelia are old enough to look after themselves. What's the problem?'

She thought about it for a moment, then nodded.

'You're right,' she replied, and followed him to his beaten-up old Mitsubishi Warrior. He took Spike's child seat out of the front to make room for her. Once she was inside, he couldn't believe he had captured her. The smell of her scent filled the cab, overpowering the roll-up butts in the ashtray (though he never smoked when Spike was in the car) and the open packet of Cheesy Wotsits on the dash.

'What are you wearing?' he asked, and she looked at him a little askance. 'I mean your perfume . . .'

She laughed. 'Coco. By Chanel.'

'Coco . . .' he murmured. A few days later, when he got back home, he went into Bath, to House of Fraser, and begged a sample off the woman at the Chanel counter. He wondered if it was really pervy, to breathe in the essence of Serena before he went to bed at night. He found it comforting.

They hooked the boat trailer to the back of the truck, then drove to a slipway on the estuary where they could launch it easily, just the two of them. Adrian loved the boat – it was so light and so powerful, gliding across the water. He opened the throttle and they flew over the waves. It was immensely exhilarating and, Adrian knew, dangerous – they only had to hit a wave at the wrong angle and the boat would flip – but he was a good judge of what he was doing. Besides, he wanted adrenalin. He wanted something to cover up the real reason his heart was racing.

He pulled the boat onto a tiny beach along the coast where the family often came for picnics. They clambered out, falling onto the sand, laughing. And then they stopped laughing and looked at each other.

'Shit,' said Adrian.

'Oh,' said Serena, surprised.

They hadn't looked back since. They had tried to resist it, but it was bigger than both of them. It felt so, so right when they were together. But of course, it was dynamite. You couldn't have an affair with your brother's wife and not expect fireworks. And Serena was riddled with guilt, almost paralysed. He would hold her in his arms while she sobbed, distraught.

'This is so wrong,' she would wail.

'But we haven't done anything,' Adrian would assure her.

'But we want to,' she'd reply, clinging on and making his shirt wet with her tears.

'I know . . .'

Now, Adrian took a swig of his beer. His mouth was dry with nerves. Every time he went to speak, his nerve failed him and he found something to do instead. Open a packet of peanuts. Tidy away Spike's Lego. Then he pictured Serena having to tell Philip, and it spurred him on. His was by far the easier option.

'Mum . . .'

Jane looked up from reading *The Times* with a half-smile. Adrian hesitated again. She seemed so much happier lately, looking so much younger than her years, a sparkle in her eye. He didn't want to be responsible for bringing her down again, but he couldn't keep quiet for ever.

'I've got something to tell you. Something important. I think it might be a bit of a shock.'

Jane dropped the paper.

'It's not Donna?' she asked. 'She's not taking Spike to Australia? Please, no . . .'

'No. No – nothing like that.'

'Thank God.'

It hadn't occurred to Adrian that his mother would jump to the wrong conclusion, but it wasn't that surprising. Donna was for ever making empty threats she didn't keep.

Donna had been what he thought was the antidote to Serena. He had fallen for her seven years ago, a stunning raven-haired vixen who ran a vintage dress shop in Frome, where he was living. He had thought her exotic, ethereal, intriguing. By the time he realised she was highly strung, self-centred and delusional, she was pregnant. He couldn't stand to spend another minute in her company, but he wasn't going to turn his back on the baby. For months she tormented him, pretending she was going to have an abortion, pretending she'd already had one, denying he was the father. By the time Spike was born, Adrian realised she was borderline insane, and he was determined to do as much as he could to protect his son. Donna, however, didn't make it easy for him. She didn't make anything easy for anyone, not even herself. And that was why his parents had bought him his tiny flat, so that he would have a permanent base for Spike whenever he had access. Ever since, the Miltons had all lived in fear that the little boy they loved so much would come to some harm at Donna's hands, or that she would run off with someone and they would never see her again. The only weapon they had was money – Jane and Graham had continually forked out for things, and it was only because Spike was so adorable that it didn't cause more resentment.

'It's not about Donna,' Adrian repeated. 'It's about Serena. Me and Serena.'

His mother gave him The Look. The Look that made you admit to pinching the last custard cream from the biscuit jar. He swallowed.

'I don't know how it's happened, but it has. We're . . . in love. And she's going to leave Philip.'

Jane gave a little laugh.

'Adrian. Don't be ridiculous. That's . . . impossible.'

'No, it's not.' He had to be firm. 'We've been talking about it for nearly a year, and we've finally decided.'

'A year . . . ?'

Jane paled as the realisation dawned that her son was speaking the truth.

'It's not what we both wanted,' Adrian told her. 'The last thing I wanted to do was to break up my brother's marriage.'

'Oh, Adrian,' his mother sighed. She wasn't angry, Adrian realised. She just looked incredibly sad.

'Listen, Mum. We love each other. We can't live without each other. And Serena can't live with Philip any longer.'

'But she's his *wife*.'

Adrian sighed. His mother belonged to a generation who still believed in for better for worse, no matter how bad it got.

'Mum, you know Philip's a bastard to her . . .' He felt guilty hitting her with this one, but it was true. Serena had put up with Philip's callous bullying for years. Just like his own mother had. 'He's just like Dad.'

Jane looked up sharply.

'What do you mean?'

'Please, Mum. I don't want to drag it all up. But I know you didn't have an easy time.'

Jane didn't contradict him. She put her face in her hands for a moment while she took in the implications.

Adrian looked around, at the walls that were more familiar to him than the home he had grown up in, or the house where he lived now. He knew every knot in the wood, every crack in the floorboards. He remembered as if it was yesterday sleeping in the bunk where Spike was now, the ceiling as low as a ship's cabin, the mattress lumpy – but why would you care when you had a whole summer by the sea?

He could also remember waking there in what felt like the middle of the night, but was probably only about ten o'clock, and hearing his father berate his mother in that low but insistent voice that went on and on and on. He could never quite make out the words, but he knew they were nasty, because his mother would cry. And he would lie there clutching the ears of his velvet Eeyore, wishing he was brave enough to scramble down and tell his father to stop, but he never had the courage.

They must have loved each other once, just as Serena and Philip must have done. When did love turn to hate, passion to disdain, tenderness to cruelty?

'She's going to come and live with me in Frome,' he went on. 'She's going to help me run my business. She's going to do all the stuff I'm rubbish at. Paperwork, sending out bills, doing quotes. Chasing customers. She's got loads of ideas how I can expand, and how to market the business. She's what I need. We're going to be as poor as church mice to start with, but we'll have each other. Plus having her there means I can have Spike with me a bit more – she's happy to pick him up from school while I'm working, instead of him having to go to that bloody aftercare club Donna insists on when she's at the shop . . .'

He trailed off. The emotion was getting to him, the thought of how different his future was going to be.

Jane finally looked up again. Her eyes were brimming with tears.

'I understand,' she said simply. 'I can't give you my blessing, because Philip is my son too, and I have to be impartial. But I do understand. What it's like to love someone.' She tried to smile. 'I like Serena very much. And I know she will be good to Spike. Which is, after all, what really matters in all of this.'

Adrian nodded. He found he had a lump in his throat too.

'I promise you, Mum. This wasn't some sordid affair. We haven't even . . .' He attempted a grin. 'I won't go into details, but this is about love, not sex, or obsession. She's good for me, and I know she's been unhappy. For a very long time.'

Pain fluttered over Jane's face. It pains every mother to know that their child has inflicted misery on someone else.

'Philip?' she asked. 'Does he know?'

Adrian took a deep breath in. He didn't like to think about it.

'She's telling him right now.'

Serena had given Harry and Amelia twenty quid to go to the Ship Aground for the evening.

'I need to speak to your father.'

Harry looked at his mother anxiously.

'Will you be all right, Mum?'

'Of course.' Serena smiled brightly, but the fact that Harry even had to ask convinced her she was doing the right thing. She knew both the children had picked up on her unhappiness, and that they both suffered at the hands of their father's short fuse, his unreasonably high standards, his ability to undermine their confidence. There was always tension in the house. No one ever knew when Philip might strike. He could, after all, be so very, very nice. But the flip-side . . .

Serena no longer thought that breaking up her marriage was going to be a sign of failure. It would be a relief for all of them, and although it would mean upheaval of a different nature, how wonderful to be able to sit at a table and not wait for the acerbic diatribe, the lectures, the grilling. She hugged them both as they left, her beautiful children. Harry, who despite his father's best attempts to belittle him had done so well, about to start medicine at Bristol. And quirky little Amelia, who found her refuge in her art and was off to do a foundation course instead of A levels, much to Philip's disgust. They'd be all right; they could come and live with her and Adrian in the holidays, though there wouldn't be much room. And of course there wouldn't be The Shack any more, their summer refuge.

It was definitely a time for change.

'Millie Taplow. Lucy Bartlett. Nicola Morley-Webb.'

Serena kept her voice low and calm as she recited the list of names to her husband. It wasn't a definitive list, just the few she could be absolutely sure of, given the gossip and the evidence of her own eyes, and the way the girls reacted when they saw her at a social event – none of them was a particularly good actress, none of them could look her in the eye. And none of them, for some reason, could take their eyes off Philip while he was in the room. They were completely transparent. But then, they were very, very young and totally in his thrall.

He just stared back at her, frowning slightly, shaking his head.

'What about them?'

'When I go up to speak to a girl at one of your little cocktail parties, and she jumps as if she's been scalded, and spills her drink, and can't get away from me fast enough, and spends the rest of the time following you round the room with puppy-dog eyes, what am I supposed to think?'

'A crush. Hardly proof of anything.'

'I don't need proof,' said Serena calmly. 'I know and you know what happened. Time and time and time again. I'm not putting up with it any more.'

'Who's been speaking to you?' demanded Philip. 'That bloody Eleanor Tripp, I bet. Filling your head with all sorts of rubbish, and you know why? Because she's a frustrated dyke, Serena, and she probably wants to get her hand in your knickers.'

'Eleanor's been a very loyal friend.' Eleanor was another professor on the English course, specialising in medieval literature, and she had provided a very welcome shoulder for Serena to cry on, on more than one occasion. But she had only listened, never judged. 'And actually, Philip, I'm afraid it's a bit more serious than that. It's Adrian.'

Philip blinked.

'What's Adrian? What does he know about my life?'

'I mean . . . it's Adrian that's brought this all about. I'm leaving you, Philip, and I'm going to live with him.'

Philip stared at her for a good five seconds, then burst out laughing.

'Going to live with Adrian? In that squalid little flat in that bloody hippy dippy Hicksville town? With that mad, bipolar witch breathing down your neck? And what are you going to live *on*, exactly? He manages to bash out about one coffee table every other month. Hardly enough to keep you in the manner to which you've become accustomed.'

'You talk as if you've been keeping me in the lap of luxury, Philip.' Serena's eyes were cold as they bored into him. 'When did I last have a new dress? Or a new pair of shoes that weren't for everyday? Not that money is what it's about.' She held up her hand to stop him interrupting. 'Money's never been the issue for me.'

'So what is the issue?' Philip sneered. 'Sex?'

'No. Sex has got nothing to do with it either. It's about having a chance to be happy.'

'Happy?'

As an English professor, he seemed to be struggling unduly with the definition of a very simple word. He was completely flummoxed. A combination of shock and not really having a leg to stand on, supposed Serena.

'What about the kids? What about their,' he paused for effect, '*happiness*?' he finished sarcastically.

'I'm sure they'll be upset,' replied Serena. 'But I think they'll understand. They've known I've been miserable for a long time.'

Something dark flickered across Philip's face. He was totally on his back foot. And he didn't like the thought that his children had been somehow complicit in this. He stepped forwards.

'You bitch,' he said. 'You've been very clever, haven't you? Manipulating everything to make yourself look whiter than white, when all the time you've been fucking my *brother*, you filthy slut—'

'Let me stop you there. I have never *fucked* anyone else while I've been married to you.'

'You must have been doing something. It wasn't just something you dreamt up on the spur of the moment.'

'No,' admitted Serena. 'It was just something that happened. I suppose you could say we fell in love.'

Philip's eyes were like slits. No man likes being made a fool of, and especially a philanderer.

'You'll get nothing,' he declared. 'And you won't see the children.'

'Actually, that's entirely up to them. They're both over sixteen. And I'm entitled to half of everything.'

'I'll fight you every inch of the way.'

'Fine,' said Serena. 'To be honest, that's exactly what I expected.'

284

She picked up a cardigan and slung it round her shoulders.

'Where are you going?'

'Out,' she replied.

'You can't just drop a bombshell like that and walk off.'

'I was going to give you some time. To think. Before we discuss the details. I don't want to get embroiled in an argument. I want to make this as painless as possible.'

'You want me to make this easy for you, you mean?'

She gave him a twisted smile, a smile that was covering up the fact she was trying hard not to cry.

'You've never made anything easy for me, Philip.'

Moments later, he was left alone in the middle of the hut as the door swung shut behind her.

He felt his chest tighten. He put a fist to his heart, to ascertain how steady the beat was. Wow, that would be a cliché, wouldn't it, if he keeled over with a heart attack? But after a few seconds of deep breathing, the tightness passed and Philip was able to relax, before he thought about his next move.

Shit. He was well and truly stitched up like a kipper. Those names Serena had trotted out – they were just the tip of an iceberg, though he thought she probably knew that. Which meant he didn't have a leg to stand on. All the time he thought he'd been so clever, she had known all along. Bloody Eleanor Tripp. She saw too much, with those cold, hooded eyes of hers. She'd probably put a stopwatch on all of his tutorials, making notes if they ran over, running back to Serena to report back. Man-hating witch.

It had been like a drug over the years. A new intake every year, of stunning, intelligent, nubile young creatures, all hanging on his every word. He loved selecting his next lover, as mouth-watering as picking from a box of handmade chocolates. Then betting with himself how long it would take to make her succumb. He had perfected his methodology. A little extra attention. A few glowing comments to make her feel good. An extra tutorial, to go over something. A glass of wine. A finger along the curve of a cheek – they were putty in his hands by that stage. Philip knew he was an attractive man, that his knowledge was an aphrodisiac to those hungry to learn. That they were flattered when he made them feel special. Once he had captured them, he would keep them going for about six months, having enjoyed their wide eyes as he taught them things about their bodies they'd had no idea of, then gently dropped them.

'My wife suspects,' he would murmur, stroking the inside of a softer than soft thigh. 'I don't want a scandal.'

They always wept bitterly, but in the end went without demur. Somehow he had managed to escape detection. None of them had ever compared notes, because he made them promise.

'This has never happened to me before,' he would say. 'This has been very special. I will always treasure it. But it can't go on.'

The irony of all this, however, was he had slowed down of late. He no longer felt so ardent. He didn't salivate as the first years trooped in for freshers' week. And last term he had heard two girls, quite distinctly, discussing him.

'Ewww, no way. I couldn't,' one of them squealed. 'He must be at least fifty.'

Which he wasn't. Not for quite a while. And he had thought his greying sweep of hair lent him a distinguished air.

The exchange had dented his confidence. He couldn't bear the thought of rejection, of some ravishing girl pushing him away in distaste. And so this year, he hadn't sought out new prey. Instead, he had actually started to enjoy his own wife's company. He had noticed how radiant she looked lately, how she was growing into her looks rather than fading. She seemed to be bursting with vitality, bubbling over with a new-found confidence. It had rather intrigued him. Next to her, undergraduates seemed raw, unformed, naive, while Serena was womanly, mysterious . . .

And now he knew why.

He was suddenly overcome with the humiliation. A hot flush spread over him; breathing seemed difficult again. How on earth could he face the rest of the family after this? His own children, for heaven's sake? And his mother – what would his mother say? Would Serena be using her list of his indiscretions as part of her defence? And the annual party? When everyone on the beach gathered at The Shack to celebrate the end of the summer? How could he face them all?

He sat down heavily on the end of the bed he and Serena had been sharing and put his face in his hands. He knew, absolutely, that he had the ending he deserved. He could taste the bile of regret in the back of his throat, but it was too late to be sorry now. Or was it? Was there any way he could get her back? A holiday? A diamond? An apology? A promise . . . ? Philip suspected not. He had never seen Serena so calm, so sure of herself. He'd blown it, by being selfish, and smug, and arrogant, and thinking he was immortal, untouchable . . .

Philip stood up smartly. He wasn't one for navel-gazing and beating himself up, he reminded himself. He was a man of positive action – the grass didn't grow under his feet. He pulled the suitcase out from under the bed and started throwing his clothes back in. Serena would have nothing to put hers in at the end of the week, but that was her problem. He was going home. He was going to leave her to explain her decision to all and sundry. If he wasn't there, he didn't have to face it.

Besides, it was the start of a new academic year in a couple of weeks. He'd get back to the faculty, sort his study out. Order some wine from Majestic, plan a cocktail party for the new intake – he'd do blinis and smoked salmon. Immediately, his mind went to lustrous long hair, innocent eyes and pearlescent skin. He swept up the car keys. He'd take the car too. He wasn't going to worry about how Serena and the children would get back. It was her bloody problem.

Adrian sat on the sand with his arms around his knees. How many times had he sat here over the years, looking out to sea? He would miss it, for sure. The view had an instantly calming effect. It enabled you to see things for what they were, and to realise that other things didn't really matter.

He saw her walking up the beach towards him. Her blond curls were ruffling in the breeze. She wore cut-off jeans and a red gingham shirt knotted at the waist, a cardigan round her shoulders, her feet bare.

'OK?'

She sat down next to him. She sighed.

'I'm sure it will get nastier before it gets better. Philip won't let this go without a fight.'

They sat in silence side by side for a moment, each enjoying the warmth from the other's body, the closeness, the lack of any need to say anything. Then Adrian put his hand up to her face, turning it to his, and kissed her.

At last, she was his.

And he was hers.

Inside The Shack, Jane went to cover Spike over with his duvet. Bart had rolled out of his arms and she tucked the pair of them back in again. She felt drained by what Adrian had told her. It threw up so many questions. Not just practical ones, but questions about her role as a mother.

What could she have done to prevent this ghastly situation? She knew deep down it was Philip's failings that were the root cause. He was so like Graham, it was spooky – they had the same defence mechanisms, the same superior attitude, the same ability to blame other people for their own shortcomings. She should have worked harder when he was little to delete these character traits, but looking back now she didn't think they had been so apparent when he was small.

Her mobile rang. Her heart leapt into her mouth, as it always did when her phone rang at a peculiar time.

It was her solicitor, Norman.

'Jane? I'm so sorry to disturb you so late, but I've just had rather a strange phone call. From Terence Shaw's agent. The writer? He wanted me to let you know – he passed away yesterday.'

'Oh my goodness.' She made her way across the room and sank into a chair. She had absolutely no idea what to think or feel. 'Oh my goodness,' she repeated, feeling rather confused.

'The funeral will be on Thursday. In London. He thought you might like to go. And, of course, I'll come with you if you'd like. It is invitation only, but he seemed to think it might be important to you . . . ?'

That Norman was dying of curiosity there was no doubt. Jane knew she had to give him some sort of explanation.

'I worked for him when I was young. I . . . typed out one of his books. He was . . . quite a character.'

She wasn't going to start spilling the beans about her misspent youth to her solicitor over the telephone. Norman was the soul of discretion, which was why she had employed him for so long, but she didn't want to shock him.

'I'll come up on the train,' she decided straight away. 'I'll come to your office first.'

She hung up, her hand shaking.

The love of her life. Dead.

There was no hope any longer. Nothing to dream about.

Yet somehow she felt the most immense sense of relief, and liberation. And in that moment, she felt glad that Adrian had stuck out for what he believed in. And hoped that one day, maybe Philip would find the same happiness with someone else. It might be too late for her, but if she could teach her children, and her grand-children, the value of true love, then she wouldn't have suffered in vain.

11
HARBOUR LIGHTS

It was a pearl-grey morning just after dawn as Roy drove his ancient Volvo estate down the steep, winding lane that led from his house to Everdene beach. He must have done the journey a thousand, a million times, but he never tired of the dramatic view. The waves this morning reared up like rampant stags and hurled themselves against the craggy rocks, spume billowing. Further out to sea, the water was calm, a sheet of silver steel waiting to be brought to life by the rising sun. It was going to be a hot one, he could tell that by the haze. In a few hours this road would be bumper-to-bumper, filled with impatient motorists eager to get to the beach. There would be road rage before the day was out.

As he drove towards the beach-hut car park he saw Jane waiting by the entrance. She looked pale and anxious, as if she hadn't slept, and was wearing jeans and a light mac. She'd come to ask him the day before if he would give her a lift to the station – she knew he was always up early, and the chances of any of her family emerging willingly at that time were fairly slim.

He had been only too pleased to oblige.

'Thank you so much,' she said as she slipped into the passenger seat. 'I'm going to have to do a mercy dash into the shops at Paddington – I didn't bring any suitable clothes with me. I didn't think I'd be going to another funeral quite so quickly.'

Her tone was dry and she managed a fleeting smile.

'Terence Shaw, eh?' replied Roy, keeping his tone neutral. He remembered her working for Everdene's infamous author that summer. Roy had always wondered what had gone on between Jane and Terence. Something, he was certain.

But Jane obviously didn't want to talk about it. She pulled down the passenger mirror to check her appearance, gave a little shudder of distaste – 'I look like a corpse myself' – then snapped the mirror back into place and turned to him with a bright smile.

'Terribly inconvenient, really, having to go up to town just before the party. I've left it all in the capable hands of Chrissie and Serena.'

Roy chuckled.

'Should be fine, then.'

'Well, I don't know.' Jane coughed, slightly embarrassed. 'Serena's just left Philip.' There was another pause. 'For Adrian.'

Although he was driving, Roy turned to look at her in amazement, just for one second, then wrenched his gaze back to the road. He digested the information quietly, as was his wont, then whistled.

'Fireworks?'

'Actually, no. It's all rather calm. Philip just upped and left. He went back home. I haven't managed to speak to him yet. But I think the general consensus is . . .' She

293

trailed off with a small sigh as she thought about the soap opera that was her family. 'Serena was bound to leave Philip anyway, in the end, and better the devil we know. And I think it will be a good thing for Spike if it all works out – he and Serena have always been close.'

Roy shook his head in disbelief.

'I know,' Jane laughed shakily. 'You couldn't make it up, as they say. Anyway, I'm going to try not to let it spoil the party. The Last Party.'

She leant her head back against the headrest. Why did those three words sound so melancholy? It wouldn't be the last party, either, just the last one that she would organise. She was sure the other beach-hut owners would carry on the tradition. Everyone looked forward to it – it was the highlight of the summer. Always held on the Saturday night of the August bank holiday, it started at three o'clock in the afternoon and had been known to carry on until three the next morning. It had been instigated by Jane's mother, and when Jane came back as Mrs Milton she reinstated it. Entry was by a bottle of champagne per head and a contribution to the food – either salad to accompany the pig roast or a pudding. The dress code was 'Black Tie or Beach Beautiful', with the older generation opting for the former and the young the latter, though there had been a fashion of late for the options to be mixed, with men turning up in dinner jackets and surfing shorts. This tongue-in-cheek inter- pretation pretty much summed up the tone of the affair, which inevitably ended in girls in ball gowns being chucked into the sea amidst much shrieking and laughter.

'I've arranged to borrow the trestle tables again from

the village hall.' Roy decided he would stick to talking about arrangements. It seemed safer. 'I'll drive them down first thing Saturday morning so you can set up. Then drop the beer barrels over just after lunchtime – we don't want them getting too hot in the sun. The pig roast bloke will be there about then too.'

'Fantastic.' Jane laid a hand on his arm. 'Where would I be without you?'

Roy didn't reply. It wasn't the sort of question that required an answer.

Ten minutes later he drove onto the forecourt of the station and pulled up outside the ticket office. Jane jumped out, and stuck her head back in through the door to say goodbye.

'You're an absolute star.'

'Give me a call when you get on the train home. I'll come and pick you up.'

'Really?'

'Of course.'

She smiled her thanks at him and slammed the door shut. He watched as she walked towards the entrance, her head held high, and he wondered what was really going through her mind. He sighed.

Even now, half a lifetime later, the longing was still there.

Roy had woken up on the morning of the first Everdene beach party with butterflies.

He hadn't had butterflies for years, not even on Christmas Eve or his birthday. He was eighteen now, and he supposed that after the age of thirteen or fourteen you grew out of it, that nothing excited you so much once you were firmly on the trail to adulthood, but his stomach that morning belied that assumption. His mum was frying bacon in the kitchen, and the smell made him feel quite nauseous.

Why did he feel like this? He told himself he was being stupid, behaving like a girl. But in the back of his mind, he couldn't forget Jane flinging her arms round his neck in delight the afternoon before, when her mother had said, 'I hope you're coming to the party, Roy? You can't miss it after all your hard work.'

'You must come!' Jane had insisted. 'It's going to be such fun. Say you will.'

He'd been shocked to be invited. He thought he was just Mrs Lowe's dogsbody. The party had been a much smaller event in those days – there had only been twelve beach huts altogether – but Prue was still flapping, getting as many people embroiled as possible, because that was her way, and she'd homed in on Roy as a willing slave.

Roy had spent the week running around obeying her elaborate instructions, even though he was pretty certain he wasn't going to get paid for the privilege. But he didn't mind, because it meant he could be near to Jane, and wouldn't need to think up excuses to speak to her. All summer he hadn't been able to get her out of his head. Every song that came on the radio reminded him of her. 'Summer Holiday' by Cliff Richard, which never failed to make him smile. 'She Loves You' by The Beatles – well, he could dream, couldn't he? Although actually he didn't know why he was even giving it a thought. She was totally out of his reach and besides, wasn't he already spoken for?

But nothing ever stopped a teenage boy from fantasising. And fantasise he did, all day and all night. He thought about her yellow hair, and how it might feel between his fingers. He thought about her golden skin, those laughing eyes. He thought about kissing her, and it made his heart feel as if it might explode, burst right out of his chest. He thought about her slightly husky, posh voice, clipped and impatient, and the preposterous things she sometimes said – always followed by that laugh that made him tingle from head to toe.

Marie never made him tingle, or made his heart feel like exploding. He liked her, a lot. But he wasn't enthralled by her. Nothing about her made him wonder. He didn't lie awake dreaming of simply holding her in his arms. He'd kissed Marie. Done more than kissed her, though he hadn't gone all the way yet. He'd touched her breasts, which were pleasingly round and soft. He'd touched her between her legs, and she'd looked at him, thrilled and horrified, before pushing his hand away and murmuring 'Not yet'. And being a chivalrous sort of boy, he'd obliged. It wouldn't be long before he'd be allowed to do it again, because she hadn't pushed him away that quickly, and he could tell by the way she'd taken a sharp breath in that she'd liked it. They'd been going together for nearly a year, and she didn't deserve his treacherous daydreams. She'd be horribly upset if she knew that Jane was the one who occupied his waking hours. And his sleeping ones. Although he thought she suspected something. She'd been very stroppy whenever she found Jane in the ice-cream kiosk with him.

He hated seeing them together. It highlighted the difference in them too much. Marie was buxom, a proper

Devon maid, with dark hair. Pretty, but you only had to look at her mother to see which way she would go. She was blunt, straightforward. She didn't take any messing about. Roy could tell that by the way she treated her customers – she soon gave them short shrift if they became difficult. And he knew everything about Marie that there was to know. They were both born in the village, they'd been to the same schools – she couldn't possibly have a secret from him. He knew what she wanted from life: to carry on working in her parents' café, get married, probably to him, and have a couple of children. Why would she do anything else?

Jane, by contrast, was slender, elegant, exotic, fascinating. She told him about another world that was out there – he listened, rapt, to her tales of London. Of the music that spilled from cafés and clubs night and day, of the famous people she'd glimpsed, of the shops filled with wondrous clothes and the buzz, the continual buzz.

'Nothing like boring old Everdene. There's always something going on.'

Roy wanted to protest. He was never bored in Everdene. As far as he was concerned there was always something to do, something to look at, but he had to admit that the city did sound exciting. Different, anyway. Whether he'd ever be able to experience it was another matter. Probably not. For a start, he wouldn't have a clue how to get there, or what to do when he arrived. And he'd be bound to stick out like a sore thumb – a country bumpkin. He imagined himself the target of thieves and pickpockets, fleeced, like Oliver Twist.

'You should come up one day.' She looked at him with a mischievous little smile. 'I could show you the sights.

Take you to a night club.' She reached up and fingered his shirt. 'We'd have to take you shopping first. But I think we could transform you.'

Roy could feel himself blushing as she glanced him up and down and nodded approvingly. What did she have in mind, he wondered?

She was just toying with him, he told himself that morning, as he pulled on his scruffy clothes. Mrs Lowe had a list of tasks as long as his arm. He should have time to come home before the party and have a bath, put on something smart. Or at least clean – he didn't really have anything that smart. He was a Devon boy, an outside boy, whose family didn't even go to church. Why would he have anything smart? He didn't have time to go into Bamford and get something, either. If Mrs Lowe had invited him earlier in the week, he might have had a chance . . .

His mum handed him a bacon sandwich as he went into the kitchen.

'No, thanks,' he told her, and she looked at him, frowning.

'What's up?'

'Nothing. I'm just not hungry. I'll have a cup of tea, though.'

She pursed her lips.

'Don't you go getting any ideas from that lot,' she told him.

'Don't be daft, Mum.'

She handed him a cup of tea, dark brown and steaming hot. He spooned two sugars in.

'Is Marie going to the party?' His mother always came straight to the point.

Roy stirred his tea.

'No. And they've only asked me so I can run round after them. Not because they want me there.'

'As long as you realise that.'

Roy smiled to himself. He was never going to have any delusions of grandeur as long as his mother was around. But he did feel bad about Marie. He'd told her about being invited, because Roy suspected it was better to be honest on the surface, especially if you were harbouring dishonest thoughts. She hadn't been happy, but there would have been merry hell to pay if she'd found out afterwards.

'And that Jane Lowe isn't half as good as she thinks she is.'

Was he going red? He felt hot at the mention of her name. He buried his face in his cup so he could blame the steam from the tea.

'And there's been rumours,' his mother told him.

'What sort of rumours?'

'About her and that writer.'

Roy shrugged. 'There's always rumours in Everdene,' he replied. He put down his cup. 'I'm off now, Mum. OK?'

He gave her a kiss on the cheek and she responded with a nod. She wasn't overly affectionate, his mother. But she cared about him, he knew she did. That was a warning shot she'd just given him, and he knew she was right to fire it. But he didn't care if he got hurt. That's how bad he'd got it.

Jane's train arrived at Paddington just after half past nine. She hurried along the platform to the small arcade of shops at the back of the station, and went into Monsoon. There was a summer sale on, and her heart sank – the racks were crammed. There was too much to choose from. This was insane, she thought. Panic-buying an outfit for the funeral of a man she'd had a silly affair with nearly fifty years ago? Why was she even going? Maybe she'd forget it. Maybe she'd just take a taxi over to the Wallace Collection, spend the morning browsing the Rembrandts and the Fragonards and the Canalettos and go into their wonderful café for a slice of coffee cake . . .

'Can I help you?'

She turned to the assistant with a smile.

'I need a dress. For a funeral. Something plainish – it doesn't have to be black. Sorry, I know it's a bit of a macabre request . . .'

The girl didn't seem fazed.

'We get all sorts of people coming in here in a panic,' she assured her. 'It's what you get for being in a train station. We've got a nice dress in navy silk,' she went on, assessing Jane for her size with expert eyes. 'I'll see if we've got a twelve.'

Jane looked half-heartedly through the jewellery whilst the girl went off to see what she could find. She was going to go to the funeral. Of course she was. Apart from anything, she wanted to say goodbye to the man who had played such an important part in shaping her life, even though he didn't know it. She sighed. Even now, she could remember how she used to feel every morning as she climbed the dunes up to his house. The thrill, the frisson, the heavenly bliss as he opened the door and she looked into those eyes.

She imagined those eyes now, shut for ever. Terence in his coffin. Something terrible welled up inside her, and for a moment she thought she was going to faint.

'Are you all right?' The assistant was standing next to her, a selection of dresses in one hand.

'Yes, yes – I'm fine. Thank you.' Jane gathered herself together. 'Is there somewhere I can try these on?'

As she followed the girl to the changing room, she made a mental checklist. She needed to go to Boots, for tissues and Bach's Rescue Remedy, and paracetamol for the stress headache that was bound to kick in later. She wondered if there would be time for Norman to take her for a swift gin and tonic before the funeral.

The party, of course, was a huge success. How could it not be, in such a glorious setting, on an afternoon in late August, with the sun shining at the perfect temperature? With children and dogs scampering happily, endless supplies of sausages cooked on an open fire, plenty to drink, everyone feeling relaxed and lazy and the real world seeming millions of miles away. Friendships that had begun tentatively over the summer as the beach-hut owners got to know each other became cemented as the huge vat of fruit punch gradually emptied. Roy was surprised he was enjoying himself as much as he was. He had thought he would feel out of place, and might be treated liked the hired help, but not a bit of it. He was quickly recruited to play French cricket, where he proved to be a formidable batsman, gaining instant respect from the men and admiration from the girls – he couldn't help noticing a small gaggle of them giving him sly glances, then looking away, then giggling with each other. He wasn't interested in any of them, of course – they were only about fourteen – but it went some way towards boosting his confidence. Roy knew he was considered good-looking, with his dark eyes and hair and burnished skin from working outdoors, but he wasn't cocky about it. He'd always been . . . well, not shy, but reserved. He wasn't a great talker. He was an observer. And a doer. He was getting admiring glances from the older women as well, he noticed as the afternoon wore on. After much deliberation, he had decided to wear a pair of white cricket trousers and an Aertex shirt, but eventually he took off his top, showing his tanned and well-defined torso.

Jane ran a finger teasingly down his sternum.

'Look at you,' she said, and he looked down at her finger, where she held it just at the bottom of his ribcage for a moment. Then he looked up and held her gaze. She blushed, her lips curled up in a tiny, secretive smile, and she turned away.

Roy was left standing, unsure what this meant. He took in a deep breath to calm his racing pulse, then went to find a cool drink. It was all too much. The heat. The beer. The anticipation. He wasn't sure what Jane was thinking at all. She'd paid him plenty of attention. She sat and ate her food with him. She'd poured too much salad cream onto her plate, and insisted on scooping some up and giving it to him, even though he didn't much care for it. And she'd brought him a beer while he was playing French cricket. And now this . . . intimate gesture. He thought she might be a bit drunk. He'd seen her fill her glass up several times from the punch bowl, and he knew it was strong. He'd seen Prue Lowe chuck a whole bottle of brandy in.

Yet although she'd paid him plenty of attention, she'd spoken to other blokes too. Roy hated the feeling he had inside when he saw her doing it, even though she was probably just being polite. They were mostly her neighbours on the beach, after all. But he couldn't help the burning sensation in his chest. Jealousy, he supposed.

Probably the same feeling Marie had when she found him with Jane.

Every now and then, he watched her drift away from the crowds, lost in thought, clearly in another world, and he wondered what was on her mind.

By seven o'clock, the younger children had all been bunged in the scout tent which had been erected as their den. They burrowed down with their blankets and pillows, giggling and kicking and whispering. Someone had brought down a portable record player and plugged it into The Shack's electricity supply. A rangy boy sat in the doorway and played a selection of the latest 45s from the hit parade whilst everyone danced. Jane grabbed Roy's hand.

'Come on.'

At first, Roy really wasn't sure. He'd only ever danced with Marie in public before, whenever someone local had a party or a wedding. And not the way people seemed to be dancing here – wild gesticulating and hip-wiggling. He felt horribly self-conscious. He stood in front of her, shuffling slightly awkwardly from side to side, not wanting to draw attention to himself, as she shimmied in front of him.

'Hey, you,' she poked him playfully in the stomach. 'Relax a bit.'

As the tempo of the music increased, he did. It got into your bloodstream, somehow. Plus nobody seemed to care what anyone else was doing. He grinned. It was madness – all these slightly tipsy people on the beach, dancing as if their lives depended upon it. The lanky boy put on another record. As the opening riffs sounded, Jane jumped up and down with excitement.

'Have you heard this?' she gasped. 'It's brilliant.'

It was 'You Really Got Me', by The Kinks. With its grinding guitar and manic drumbeat, it had everyone going, waving their arms in the air and singing along to the chorus. Over and over again it was played, and as Roy listened, it filled him with bravado, made him believe that he really was capable of getting the girl he wanted. He moved in closer to her, and she grabbed both of his hands, holding them high as she twisted her hips in time to the music. He imitated her movements. Gradually she inched in closer until they were touching.

'Girl, you really got me going . . .'

As the sun started to fall and the light dimmed, Prue lit candles and lanterns, and the tempo of the music dropped. Jane moved in even closer, put her hands on his shoulders, pressed herself up against him. He could barely breathe, certainly couldn't speak, as he gently put his hands on her waist. He felt as if he was touching the most precious china; felt slightly self-conscious of his work-roughened hands, but she didn't seem to mind. His throat tightened as she snuggled into him, and the most extraordinary feeling rose up inside him. It wasn't just lust, although that was raging inside him, there was no doubt about that. It was the incredible sensation that his wildest dream had just come true.

As the music swirled round them, she closed her eyes and rested her head on his shoulder. He didn't want to move, in case he broke the dream. He didn't think about Marie, and what she would think if she could see them. He didn't want anything to spoil the moment, in case this was all he ever had.

Her eyes opened and she looked at him dreamily.

'Come with me,' she whispered, and she took him by the hand. As the sun finally slipped over the horizon, she led him around to the back of the beach huts. No one noticed them going. Things were getting quite raucous now; there were shrieks and guffaws.

They stood together in the dark.

'Hold me,' she whispered.

As he put his arms around her, Roy's throat felt tight, his body felt hot. Blood pounded in his ears. He almost, almost didn't think he could cope, as she brought her lips to meet his.

It was everything he'd ever dreamt of. He wanted it to last for ever. Nothing could be better than holding her in his arms. He breathed in the lemony-soapy smell of her hair. She was so warm, so soft. He ran his fingers over her back, caressing her gently as he kissed her. He didn't feel nervous any more. It felt so natural, as if they were made for each other.

Suddenly she jerked away. She looked distressed. There were tears in her eyes.

'I'm sorry,' she whispered.

'What is it?' he asked, alarmed that he had gone too

far, that he had taken some liberty that had frightened her.

She just shook her head and walked off.

Roy stood stock-still, fists clenched, dumbfounded. What had he done? It had felt so right. Surely she'd felt it too, that wonderful glow – it had seemed as if they were in a bubble, just the two of them, bathed in warmth. But no. Obviously she hadn't felt the same at all. She couldn't get away from him fast enough. Suddenly he shivered as the damp night air wrapped itself round him, any hint of that warmth now gone. He couldn't face going back to join the party. He didn't want to look at her, searching for an explanation. He felt ashamed, but he hadn't forced himself upon her, had he? She was the one who had led him behind the huts, she'd asked him to hold her; she'd held her face up to be kissed. He would never, ever have tried to take advantage. Had he misread the signs? What had he done that was so repellent? He realised with horror that he was going to cry, and clenched his jaw to stop himself.

He turned to face the wind that had picked up and was now sweeping in across the sea, and trudged along the back of the huts, hiding in the shadows so that no one would notice he was making his escape, wrapping his arms around himself to keep out the cold and trying to forget the feeling of her velvet skin on his.

Jane arrived at her solicitors in Fitzrovia at ten past eleven. She was dressed in her new dress, and had also bought some low-heeled pumps. She was conscious that her legs were bare, which didn't feel right for a funeral, but she hadn't had time to get tights, and at least her legs

307

were brown from the summer on the beach. She'd bought a double strand of faux pearls too, big, chunky ones that added a touch of Chanel glamour to the outfit. She'd decided against a hat, although her upbringing told her she should wear one. It was summer. It was Terence, for heaven's sake. He'd always eschewed convention. She'd been surprised the funeral was in a church, but maybe he had found God in his final days. Though she doubted it. He'd considered *himself* to be God.

She entered the cool of the foyer, with its black and white marble floor and comfortable chairs. Moments later, Norman greeted her with a kiss on both cheeks in his immaculate dark grey pinstripe suit.

'We should go,' he said, flicking a glance at the grandfather clock that quietly ticked away the minutes. 'Though there are a few things I need to talk to you about . . .'

'Not now,' said Jane. 'Please let me get this over with first. I don't think I can take any more bad news.'

Norman looked at her.

'My daughter-in-law has left Philip. For Adrian.' She gave a wry smile.

Norman raised one eyebrow just two millimetres. He was rarely rattled by anything. 'Nothing like keeping it in the family.' He put a hand on her elbow to escort her out onto the street, where he looked for a taxi. 'And actually, you needn't worry. There's no bad news this time.'

He put up his arm to hail a black cab that was cruising towards them.

'Well, that makes a change.' Jane climbed inside as Norman held the door open, and settled herself on the back seat. She gave the driver the name of the church.

Smack bang in the middle of Soho. Typical Terence. Never knowingly far from the nearest drink, even in death. She shut her eyes as the cab sped through the squares and side streets, avoiding the chaos of Tottenham Court Road and Oxford Street. Next to her, Norman maintained a discreet silence. He always knew exactly what to do. Why couldn't she have found someone like Norman? A stalwart, a gentleman? Did his wife know how lucky she was, she wondered?

The church was packed. The congregation ranged from shifty-looking Irishmen in bad suits to an elegant woman in black and white houndstooth and an ostrich-feather hat. Jane ran her eye over them all, assessing who they might be and what their association to Terence was. Bookies, lovers, landlords, a generous sprinkling of publishing types, drinking companions, other writers, more lovers, a traumatised girl with mousy, shoulder-length hair in an ill-fitting grey dress who couldn't stop crying, family at the front – there were two men who must be brothers – a couple of nurses, perhaps from the hospice. He had clearly inspired loyalty throughout his life, even if he had never showed any.

After all, she was here, wasn't she?

She knew he'd married twice, or was it three times, because there were always articles in the weekend papers about what a bastard he was to live with – torrid tales of his selfish, narcissistic, womanising, drinking ways, and none of it had surprised her, only that the women always seemed to go back for more and professed to love him. She tried to figure out which of the many women in the front rows were his wives, but it was difficult – they all looked equally upset. She recognised Barbara with a jolt –

a shadow of that vibrant creature who had jumped out of the Mini that day. She was hollow-cheeked and sunken-eyed, her hair so thin you could see her scalp, but she was still as chic as she had been then, in a crêpe coatdress and spindly heels, clutching a pair of leather gloves.

Jane and Norman took a seat in a pew near the back. She didn't feel entitled to be any nearer the front – what had she been in his life, after all? And she didn't want anybody wondering who she was. She opened the order of service – again, surprised that it was so conventional, but maybe he hadn't had any input. She felt Norman, reassuringly solid and calm next to her, and as the vicar began, she took just one breath in. She was going to be able to handle it. She had to.

The final address was given by an extraordinary creature of about thirty-two. She was tall, with endless legs, a mass of wild hair that had been dyed fuchsia but was fading, and burning green eyes. She wore a brocade mini-dress, and her bare legs sported crocodile cowboy boots that matched her hair. Around her neck was slung an assortment of necklaces that she might have picked up in one handful from a jumble sale.

Terence's daughter. By whom, Jane didn't know, but she could feel the force of her personality ten rows back. The girl clutched the edges of the lectern fiercely with her fingers as she spoke, using no notes, with warmth and passion about her father. It was entirely unsentimental, but almost unbearably moving, as she recounted being lifted onto the bar of a Soho club by him at two o'clock in the morning to sing for the customers, then being made boiled eggs and soldiers when they finally stumbled home – she was six years old and she'd had the time of her life.

There was hardly a dry eye in the church as she finished her reminiscence, because she had captured Terence's spirit so perfectly.

'Dad was never one to be predictable,' she wound up. 'He always liked to surprise. And he managed to surprise us right up to the end. The family went to hear the will read this morning – some of us have flights to catch and we couldn't wait till after the funeral.' She laid her disapproving gaze on some poor unfortunate in the front row. 'And it proved to be quite a revelation.' She paused for a moment, clearly enjoying having the entire congregation in her thrall. She smiled a menacing smile.

'To misquote the immortal words of Shirley Conran,' she raked the audience with those hawk-like eyes which, Jane realised now, were carbon copies of her father's, 'which one of you bitches is Jane Milton?'

The congregation gave a collective gasp, and there was only a momentary pause before they began to look at each other for an explanation. The girl just stood there, a smile on her lips.

'Whoever you are,' she went on, 'just let it be known that we shall be contesting the will.'

Jane froze. Her heart was pounding, but she understood immediately the importance of not giving anything away. She felt Norman's hand on her arm giving her the same message. And although her instinct was to flee, she summoned up all her acting ability to put on an expression of innocent curiosity, exchanging a shrug and a smile with her immediate neighbours, as if to say 'Jane Milton? I've never heard of her.'

By now, the vicar had hurried up to the pulpit and ushered the girl away. She went quite willingly; clearly happy she had made her point, leaving chaos and consternation in her wake.

Ten minutes later, as a pianist played Liszt's 'Funérailles' and the congregation began to disperse, Jane felt as if she was in a film. She moved through the throngs with an impassive face, the music filling the air with its melancholic drama, Norman shadowing her closely as he led her swiftly out of the church, not loitering on the pavement to hail a cab as before, but walking her down the road, then left down a side street, and then right again, before finally calling a halt.

'My God,' breathed Jane. 'Norman – what do you know of all this? What's it all about?'

He summoned a taxi from thin air and gestured her inside. Once they were seated, he told her.

'Terence's solicitor called me this morning. He's left you the rights to *Exorcising Demons*. The family are furious. And, needless to say, curious.' He gave her a wry smile. 'As am I, I have to confess.'

She stared at him, astonished.

'The rights? I don't understand . . .'

Norman flicked a look at the taxi driver. They were always earwigging.

'Let's get ourselves settled somewhere quiet and I'll explain it to you. It's pretty significant, Jane.'

The taxi drew up outside Browns Hotel in Mayfair. Jane followed Norman in a daze as he led her through to the English Tea Room and settled her on a velvet sofa in a corner, then crisply ordered champagne tea for two. Norman always knew exactly what to do on any occasion, and Jane was grateful for the discreet anonymity of the location and the imminent arrival of a drink.

'He's left you the rights to the book,' Norman began explaining. 'Which means you get the royalties. And they,' he gave her a meaningful look, 'are going to be pretty substantial. There's going to be a huge furore over the rediscovery of the manuscript, which I gather was missing for nearly half a century. The publishers have organised a print run of two hundred thousand. Not only do they consider it to be a work of genius, his absolute best, but the fact that it was missing will add to the media attention it garners.'

Jane's throat was dry. She nodded as she took in the implications. This was Terence finally salving his conscience. As the waiter arrived with the tea, and presented the three-tier cake stand with a flourish, then poured a glass of champagne for them each, she was overcome with a desire to laugh. Which she did, then put a hand over her mouth.

'I'm so sorry, Norman. It's just . . .'

Norman's eyes were twinkling. He was so used to dishing out bad news, and wrangling with dry and dusty legal loopholes, that this was a novelty for him. And Jane was one of his favourite clients. He had been outraged on her behalf at the mess Graham had left her in. This was a delightful postscript as far as he was concerned. Although not without its caveats, as he was going to go on to explain.

'There's no doubt this will go quite some way to solving your financial problems. But it carries with it its own thorny issues, not least the question of publicity. The publishers know there is a story behind this, Jane, and they'll be pushing for it.' He looked at her perspicaciously. 'Apparently Terence made it quite clear in his will that the story is yours, and yours alone, to tell if you want to. It's pretty valuable in itself – you could get a substantial sum from one of the Saturday broadsheets, depending on the . . . subject matter. How . . . revealing it is. Of course, the juicier it is, the more copies the book will sell.'

Jane nodded. She could see that only too clearly. The story was dynamite. She didn't need Max Clifford to tell her that. She took a sip of champagne, quite shaken, and not sure what to think.

'As I said, the family are not happy – particularly his most recent wife and the daughter you saw at the funeral. They're talking about contesting the will, but they haven't got a leg to stand on. Terence was quite lucid when he changed it, wrapped it up good and proper, thankfully, so it's watertight. Which makes you potentially very wealthy, Jane. Even more so, depending on how you decide to play it. You might well decide that anonymity is worth more to you than the extra cash would be. But bear in mind that the press will probably now have your name, after that debacle at the funeral' – Norman's withering tone made it quite clear he thought the daughter's behaviour out of order – 'and although Terence wasn't exactly . . .' he groped for a suitable analogy, 'David Beckham in terms of popular appeal, he had a certain cult status, so there will be interest in tracking you down and getting your side of the story.'

After several more sips of deliciously crisp Taittinger, Jane thought it was about time she spoke. She could see that Norman, despite his professional discretion, was itching for the truth. More than once, his eyebrows had risen more than their usual minuscule amount.

'It's a short and rather pathetic story,' she told him. 'It finally ended earlier this summer. But it began in 1964 . . .'

The day after the party the heavens opened and it rained solidly for three days, which suited Roy perfectly. It meant he could keep his head low, and it also meant that all the beach-hut owners, including the Lowes, hastily began to shut up for the summer and leave Everdene. By the time he went back down to the huts, The Shack was firmly locked. It was as if the party had never happened. A fine mist came in from the sea and heavy clouds hung over the horizon, as if his mood was dictating the weather. The beach was deserted. It was as desolate as he was.

Nothing could have prepared him for the way he felt. Bereft. Abandoned. As if Jane had hacked a piece of his heart out and taken it back home with her. And he had no one to talk to. His friends would only take the mickey. His mother would say 'I told you so'. He only talked to his dad about drill bits and fishing, not affairs of the heart.

And he certainly couldn't talk to Marie.

He avoided her for as long as he possibly could. He had his hands full making the huts good for the winter, ensuring they were totally weatherproof and secure before the really bad weather set in. Twice she came down to see him while he was working, and he pretended to be busier than he really was. He'd taken the sandwiches and cake she'd brought him and turned away, climbing back onto the roof he was mending. He couldn't bear to see the hurt on her face. She didn't deserve his hostility. It wasn't her fault he didn't want the consolation prize. And he didn't think it was fair on Marie to be the consolation prize either. No one wants to be second best.

But he didn't have the courage to tell her how he felt, because then he really would be left with nothing. After all, Jane wasn't going to come knocking on his door, telling him she had made a mistake and declaring undying love. She was gone, back to London and the bright lights, probably, and chances are he wouldn't see her again, at least not until next summer, by which time she would probably be in love with some impossibly sophisticated man she had met in one of the nightclubs she kept talking about. He had just been someone to chat to while she was bored, a minor distraction.

The thought depressed him profoundly, but Roy was nothing if not a realist, and he had plenty of time to ponder his predicament as he hammered and sawed and oiled and painted. By the time the following weekend came around, he had arrived at the conclusion that he would just have to make the most of what he had got. He would take Marie out for dinner, get dressed up, try and see if he could spark something up between them. He did *like* her, after all. She'd been good enough for him once. He wasn't going to let Jane's rejection ruin his life.

He booked a table for two at Captain Jack's, the tiny restaurant at the top of the town. Marie's eyes had lit up when he told her, and she almost seemed to go into a panic, flustering about what to wear. He told her she'd look lovely in anything, but he could tell this wasn't what she wanted to hear. And by the time the Saturday came around and he went to pick her up from the flat above the café where she lived with her parents, he could tell she had somehow, in the intervening days, gone into Bamford and bought a new dress. A yellow dress, not unlike one Jane had worn.

Only on Jane it had looked simple, elegant, fresh. It didn't really suit Marie. It was too tight around the bust, and the colour did nothing for her. But he admired her anyway, because that was what you had to do. They walked through the early-evening sun, through the streets, his arm in hers. She was chattering, excited. He could feel her body brush up against his as they walked. She wanted to be close to him. He wanted to be a million miles away.

At the restaurant, they were treated like a king and queen. Most of the summer visitors had left, and so there were only a few diners. Nothing was too much trouble. They had a gin and bitter lemon at the bar before they sat down, and Roy ordered a bottle of wine – the maître d' had guided him kindly, not condescendingly, towards his choice.

After two glasses, a flushed Marie finally brought the party up.

'It went on till gone midnight,' she told him.

'Did it?' he replied. 'I left at about eight. Everyone was getting a bit . . .'

'Yes,' she told him, then leant in, her eyes gleaming. 'And do you know what else? Apparently Jane Lowe's been having a thing with that writer. You know, the one in the big house.'

Roy felt himself go hot, and his blood start to foment.

'You shouldn't listen to gossip.'

'It's not gossip. Catherine Lammas heard them . . . doing it when she went there to clean.' She sat back with a smile of satisfaction. 'So there.'

Roy looked down at his steak. He thought he might be sick. He took another swig of wine.

'Imagine – carrying on with a man old enough to be her father. And he's got another woman in there now. Some glamour-puss from London. I bet she sent Jane packing . . .'

Marie's words washed over him. Roy emptied his glass, then nodded as the maître d' indicated he would bring another bottle. It was the only way he was going to get through the evening. He couldn't listen to another word of her prattle – malicious gossip that was totally unfounded.

Although, deep down, he knew it probably wasn't.

Marie went into raptures over the dessert trolley. Roy couldn't face his rum baba, so she had that too. Then the maître d' brought them over two Irish coffees. On the house.

Marie's eyes were brighter than ever and her cheeks were flushed as Roy paid the bill and escorted her out of the restaurant. It was dark, and the stars were twinkling.

'Let's go down to the beach,' said Marie, tugging at his hand. 'Come on!'

He didn't want to go to the beach. He wanted to go home and slide into bed, alone with his thoughts, so he could mull over what he'd just been told. Was what Marie told him true – that Jane had had an affair with Terence Shaw? Had she been toying with Roy because she had been rejected, passed over for a better model? He shook his head, as if to banish all the questions that were whirling round. He held Marie's hand, followed her onto the beach, steadying her as she stumbled slightly in the sand, unused to her high heels.

'Let's go into one of the huts,' she was saying, entirely intent on mischief. He didn't protest; he knew they were all locked. He'd follow her down to the end, then walk her back up the beach, take her home . . .

The third one she tried was open.

She pulled him inside.

Suddenly Marie's hands were everywhere. All over him. And her lips. She tasted of Irish coffee and wine and the pale pink lipstick she had touched up before they left the restaurant. He felt the softness of her body against his, the swell of her breasts. She took his hand and guided it under her skirt and then up, up, up – to the tops of her stockings, where he could feel the flesh of her thighs. He stroked them, and she moaned, pushing herself against his hand. He took it a little higher, to the cotton of her knickers, sliding his fingers inside . . .

He was hard now. His body didn't seem to listen to what his mind was saying – that this was wrong. That he shouldn't go any further if he didn't really love her. But something else took over, some primal urge that clearly she was feeling too. She was fumbling with the zip of her dress. Suddenly she was in front of him, nearly naked, and he groaned, half in despair, half in desire. She tugged at his waistband. He needed no encouragement. Soon they were on the floor, stripped of their clothing, lying on a rug he had grabbed and flung over the rough floorboards.

Was he crazy? This was the worst possible thing he could do. But he just couldn't resist. And maybe this was what they needed to do. Maybe this would bring them together. She was pulling him on top of her. He just had to be careful . . .

Roy woke the next morning with a thick head and a terrible sense of dread. Images of the night before flashed before him as he stumbled out of bed and down to the kitchen. He needed tea. The large brown pot was on the side, still half full. He poured himself a cup, sat down at the kitchen table. He could hear his mother dragging the Hoover around the front room. Last night's meal suddenly repeated on him. It had all been too much. His blood felt thick.

And he felt ashamed. He should never, ever have done it with Marie like that. OK, so she had encouraged him. She'd been all over him. There was no denying that. But knowing what he felt about her, knowing that only twenty minutes earlier he had wanted to get away from her, didn't want to hear another word, he should have resisted. He could have done it without hurting her feelings. He could have told her he wanted the first time to be special, maybe in a hotel.

Instead of animal. He'd been a bloody animal, giving in to his urges like that. And what would she think now? Having sex would definitely give her the idea that they were a proper, serious couple. That things had somehow moved on. And she'd want to do it again. She'd enjoyed it enough, that much he could tell.

Roy swallowed the sugary sludge at the bottom of his cup. He had to get out. He had to get away. Otherwise he would be trapped for ever. He knew he'd never have the prize he really wanted, but there must be other girls out there like Jane – exciting, beguiling, who could show him a new world. He was ready to experience something else, taste the things Jane had told him about. The things he heard about on the radio and read in the papers. The things he would never get in Everdene, not in a million years. It was so far away from everything, so far behind everything, it would never catch up.

He rinsed his cup in the sink. His next lot of wages from the estate were due at the end of September, and he still had most of August's packet left. He had some money saved up in his Post Office Savings Account. He could sell his bicycle. He had enough for the train to London, and a roof over his head somewhere cheap for a while. He'd give himself four weeks, and if nothing happened he could come back. It wasn't as if he would miss anything. Only the seasons changed in Everdene. And maybe he would find himself a new life. There'd be work, surely? Building sites were always crying out for labour, strong young men like him, and he was handier than most.

His mother wouldn't be happy, he knew that, but it was his life, and he was ready for her objections. His father wouldn't judge him either way. And Marie? She would, he knew, be devastated, but she would get over it eventually. And he couldn't stop himself from doing the things he wanted, just so he didn't hurt her.

His mother came in, dragging the Hoover behind her like a recalcitrant toddler.

'You were in late.' Her eyes asked a million questions.

'Yep,' answered Roy, giving nothing away.

His mother smiled. 'She's a good girl, Marie.'

You wouldn't say that if you'd seen her last night, thought Roy, but he said nothing. In fact, saying nothing was going to be his policy from now on. He wasn't going to tell anyone his plans. That would make it so much easier. He would just head for the station on his day of escape, and leave a note for each of them. Cowardly? Maybe, but so much easier than steeling himself for the hysteria and the opposition he knew he would face. They would try every trick in the book between them to make him stay, and he was having none of it. In the meantime, he would keep his head down and stay out of everyone's way.

Three weeks later, Marie came down to the house to see him. Her eyes were swollen and puffy. She looked terrible. Roy's heart sank. How could she have got wind of him going? He'd managed to avoid her by taking on extra work labouring on a house that was being built in the next village, getting up at dawn and not returning until after dusk. And he hadn't breathed a word of his plans to a soul. Perhaps they had told her in the post office that he had drawn his money out. People in Everdene were very good at putting two and two together. He would have to think of something. A motorcycle – could he say he was buying a motorcycle?

'What is it?' he asked her.

Marie looked at him, and in that second every plan he had made over the past few weeks crumbled to nothing.

'I think I'm pregnant.'

As predicted, Jane had a thundering headache by the time she got on the six o'clock train at Paddington, though possibly thanks more to the three glasses of champagne Norman had poured down her than anything. She downed two tablets with some Evian water, then leant her head against the window pane as the train slid out of the station and through the insalubrious tower blocks that leered over the sidings.

She was still reeling from the shock of the afternoon's revelation. She had travelled up this morning a virtual bankrupt, with no real idea of how she was going to finance herself for the rest of her life. Now, she was almost certainly solvent again, although the money wasn't in the bank just yet and would take some time to materialise. Publication for *Exorcising Demons* was scheduled for November. And in the meantime, she had to decide if she was going to play ball with the press.

Was she prepared to spill her guts for money? She had always rather despised people who did so, but now she was facing the prospect of thousands of pounds for revealing the details of something that had happened years ago, and affected no one but herself now that Terence was dead, it was rather tempting. She could see for herself it was rather a wonderful story – even the phlegmatic Norman had nearly choked on his Taittinger when she told him the details.

Why not, she finally decided. As long as she made sure that her story was told in a reputable paper, like *The Times* or the *Independent* (and Terence Shaw was hardly red-top fodder) then what could go wrong? She wasn't ashamed of what she had done. And anyway, she could arrange to be away when the story broke. She didn't really fancy being trailed by reporters asking for the more salacious details. Norman had even mentioned talk of the film rights, which in turn would send sales of the book escalating. So really it was up to her to make as much of the story as she could. She smiled – what was that game the kids played? Who would play you in the film of your life?

Never mind that, she told herself. Before she started casting her teenage self, there were so many decisions. Not least what she was now going to do with the house. And The Shack. Once she had informed the bank of this latest development, they would hold fire, she was certain. As the train picked up speed and rolled past the fields of Berkshire in the encroaching dusk, she decided she would continue with the sale of her house – it was far too large, and she rather fancied a completely new beginning. A nice mansion flat in Chelsea or Kensington, perhaps.

And The Shack? If you had asked her at the beginning of the summer, she would have done anything to save it and keep it in the family. But now, as her family began to fracture, she wondered what the point was. They had certainly got a great deal of pleasure and enjoyment out of it over the years, but maybe it was time for them all to move on, her included. Perhaps the best thing would be to sell it and split the cash up between the three boys. She had no doubt it would come in useful. Yes, she decided. She would go ahead with the sale. Norman had a pile of offers in his office – they had already been through them and agreed which one to accept.

It was definitely the right thing to do. Once she had sold The Shack, and her story, she would have a clean slate. She had buried her husband, and her lover. It was time for her own story to begin.

They had been surprisingly content, Roy and Marie. They had got married before Marie had started to show too much, a quiet December wedding, just both sets of parents and a few friends. Roy used the money he had taken out of his post office account to buy her a ring, and a beautiful Silver Cross pram for the baby girl that had been their saving grace. At first they had lived with Marie's parents, in her bedroom in the flat over the café, because that way it was easy for Marie to carry on working. Then when the second daughter came along two years later, they had moved up the road to a flat of their own.

Eventually, Marie's parents had retired, and she had taken over the running of the café. By the time the two girls were at school, she had turned it around. With Roy's help, she had knocked through into the courtyard at the back and made a little tea garden, filled with pots of flowers. She opened later and did fish suppers, which proved a roaring success. It became a little goldmine, and Roy was proud of her. In the back of his mind, he could never imagine Jane getting stuck in like this and making a success of herself. She would have needed looking after, pampering, and he would never have made her happy.

With him working for the estate, putting up the rest of the beach huts, and the 'foreigners' he took in season, when people wanted help with their holiday homes, soon Roy and Marie had enough cash to buy a little house of their own, one of the old coastguard cottages on the road out of Everdene. They loved the house, with its low beams and wonky walls, and the tiny garden overlooking the sea. Roy woke up every morning and was glad. There was still a bit of him that wondered what he had missed out on, but how could you not be content with your lot when you looked out of your bedroom window to crashing waves and Lundy Island in the distance?

They were pillars of Everdene society. Marie was on the Parish Council and helped run the playgroup even after the girls left and went to school. They helped organise the summer fete and the Christmas Fayre. Although the visitors outnumbered the residents for many months of the year, there was still a strong community. Roy belonged here, he realised. And it was a wonderful place to bring up the girls. Marie might not have been the love of his life, but perhaps he was happier for it. Perhaps a companion made you more content than a grand passion.

He was certainly devastated when she had died. It had been mercifully swift, four months from diagnosis to death, but he had been shocked by the emptiness he felt when she had gone. It was five years ago now. For eighteen months he had gone into a decline. Not quite a depression, because he had still functioned, but his daughters had been worried. Then one day he had told himself that moping was never going to bring her back. He had gutted the house from top to bottom. Thrown out all her stuff – her 'bits', the silly china ornaments, her clothes. He'd ripped up all the carpets, thrown out all the curtains, stripped the walls of the heavy floral paper she had favoured. Then he'd painted the house brilliant white from top to bottom, sanded and oiled the floorboards, and put up simple wooden venetian blinds. The girls had been upset at first – it didn't feel like home any more – but Roy had explained that's what he needed. He didn't want to live with Marie's ghost. He wanted a blank slate. Relieved that at least their father was no longer pining, the girls eventually agreed that the house was better for it – brighter – as was he.

He went to the local college and learnt photography. He bought himself a computer and spent hours fiddling about, eventually printing out exquisite photos he had taken of the area – close-ups of the local wildlife that only someone like he knew where to find: puffins, seals, jelly-fish, crabs. He framed them and sold them through a local gallery. Life had a simple rhythm. Work, pint in the Ship Aground, home for dinner – he'd taught himself to cook as well, working his way through a Jamie Oliver cookbook from beginning to end.

He knew Jane Milton had been surprised when he invited her for supper, and even more surprised when he'd presented the sea bass cooked in spring onion and ginger, served with watercress and orange salad, followed by pineapple granita. She had admired his photographs, exclaimed over the view, tapped her foot to the jazz that came out of the hidden speakers he had installed. He sensed she had been expecting some poky pensioners' cottage and an indifferent meal. She had enjoyed their evening, telling him that it was the first time she had relaxed since Graham's funeral, and he took this as a compliment.

He realised now, as he drove to the station – she had phoned just after she left Paddington to say she was on the train – that the chances of their friendship developing into something deeper were slim. The Shack was as good as sold – he knew there had been any number of enquiries, and several good offers. He felt a twinge of sadness – not that he harboured any delusions about late-blossoming romance, but in spite of, or perhaps because of, his initial obsession with Jane, he had become very fond of her over the years. By the time she had re-appeared with Graham Milton, he already had two children, and then she quickly became pregnant with hers, which inoculated them both from the memory of that night at the party. They had become firm friends, Roy almost a surrogate husband at times when she was down at Everdene without Graham and needed male assistance – though only ever of the practical kind. He had changed tyres for her, put her children's feet in buckets of hot water when they had stepped on weaver fish, had taken them out over the rocks around the cove to see the seals when they were in . . . And even now, here he was, collecting her from the station. Did she use him? he wondered. Maybe. But he didn't actually mind.

He watched her coming out of the station. She was in a dark blue dress – her funeral attire, he realised, and wondered how it had gone. Again he remembered the rumour – Marie's gleaming eyes as she told him about the supposed affair. He had never found out if it was true.

She opened the door and got in, leaning over to kiss him on the cheek in gratitude.

'What a day!' she exclaimed. 'You wouldn't believe. You won't believe.' She put her hands up to her face and pushed back her hair. 'Will there be a shop open? Can I get something to eat? The train had run out of sandwiches . . .'

'Why don't I make you an omelette?' suggested Roy. 'Saves stopping. Then I can drop you back.'

'Would you? Oh, that sounds wonderful. I'm sure none of the others will have thought to save me anything,

328

and I'm not sure I can face them yet.' She kicked off her shoes and wiggled her toes. 'And I can tell you my news. But you must promise not to say a word.'

Roy just smiled. She knew as well as he did that he was hardly likely to breathe a single syllable. Roy had always known how to keep his counsel.

Jane sat back comfortably on the sofa in Roy's living room and stretched out her legs. She was exhausted, but very grateful for his offer. She couldn't quite face going back to her family yet – she would be hit with a barrage of questions, and problems that had arisen over the party, and no doubt there would have been some drama over the Adrian/Philip/Serena triangle. Roy's house was a little haven from all of that. Delicious smells wafted from the kitchen. She ran her eye around the room, admiring the simplicity – his black and white photos on the wall, a shelf of books, another shelf of CDs. On the coffee table next to her was an open brochure for a world cruise. She picked it up – a luxury cruise, by the looks of it, and her mouth watered as she leafed through it. Enticing locations, top-notch accommodation, wonderful food. How heavenly . . .

'Are you going on a cruise, then?' she asked teasingly, as Roy came through with her supper on a tray.

'I thought I might. Thought it was about time I saw something of the world. Nothing much happens in Everdene in November. It would make a change.'

He put the omelette in front of her. A perfect yellow crescent, flecked with parsley and chives picked from the garden. A handful of cherry tomatoes from the greenhouse. And a glass of crisp white wine.

'Thank you so much,' said Jane, and picked up her knife and fork thoughtfully. A cruise in November. It sounded ideal. She could be miles from home when her story hit the newsstands. Soaking up the sun while tongues wagged.

She looked up at Roy. He was watching her rather intently. Waiting for her verdict on the omelette, she supposed, but he blushed and looked away when she caught his eye. Strange, she thought, but maybe he was self-conscious about his cooking.

'Roy – be honest with me,' she said. 'I'll totally understand if you say no. But this cruise you're thinking about . . . how would you like a travelling companion?'

12

THE ROCKPOOL

Alison hadn't been at all convinced when Mike had suggested a week in Everdene for Chayenne's first holiday. Even less so when he had proudly announced he had booked a beach hut for them to stay in. The British seaside on a bank holiday? She pictured kiss-me-quick hats and men with fat stomachs slumbering in deck-chairs. She wanted to go to Majorca, but Mike had insisted it would be too traumatic for Chayenne to go abroad – she might not like flying, or the heat, or the food. Alison thought longingly of the villa they had rented once or twice in Puerto Pollensa, and held her tongue. He was probably right. He seemed to be right on all matters concerning Chayenne so far. He had an instinct for what she needed. Which was probably why the two of them had bonded so well.

And Alison had been left feeling like a spare part.

She had known it would be difficult. After all, they'd had to jump through enough hoops, and it had been made clear at every stage of the process that adoption was no picnic. Applications, assessments, preparation classes, counselling. References. Endless meetings with the social workers. Forms and more forms. Until finally, two years after they had come to the conclusion that they were never going to have children of their own and that this was the right thing to do, Alison and Mike became Chayenne's mum and dad.

She was seven years old. She had lived for all of her short life with a bipolar mother, in a house that was stinkingly filthy, piled up to the rafters with junk her mother had accumulated obsessively. Even now Chayenne freaked out when Alison tried to get her into a shower. She could, eventually, coax her into a bath, but only a very shallow one. Alison didn't think that swimming about in your own dirty water made you properly clean, but she knew she had to be patient.

Only she'd never found it easy to be patient. She did her best to look calm and serene, but inwardly she spent half her life screaming. She wasn't used to coaxing and cajoling and murmuring gentle words of encouragement. As a busy estate agent who ran her own office, she expected people to ask how high when she said jump.

Well, an erstwhile estate agent. She and Mike had agreed that she would take some time off when Chayenne arrived. The same amount of time she would have had off if she'd had a baby. Three of the months had already gone, and the remaining six stretched interminably in front of her.

She hadn't expected to feel like this. She hated – *hated* – herself for finding it all so difficult. She had been so sure she would rise to the occasion, even though there had been no shortage of people telling her it would be more testing than anything she had ever faced – but Alison had never been afraid of a challenge. Now, however, she was finding her confidence waning on a daily basis. She was starting to doubt her own judgement. She was almost frightened of Chayenne, of how she was going to respond to her, of what her reaction was going to be.

And as Alison's confidence shrivelled, Mike's seemed to grow. He sensed Chayenne's needs and could elicit a positive response from her. They were becoming quite the twosome, partners in crime, and were growing even closer on this holiday.

When Alison had taken Chayenne down to the water's edge to paddle, the child had screamed blue murder. Everyone had turned to see what she could possibly be doing to her. Alison had been mortified, and had hurried Chayenne back to the hut as quickly as possible. Mike had reprimanded her quietly, insisted that she had pushed the girl too far too quickly. Alison had felt totally undermined and thoroughly guilty as she listened to Chayenne's shuddering sobs, and had shed a few tears herself in the privacy of the loo.

Two days later, under Mike's expert and intuitive tutelage, Chayenne was running in and out of the water giggling, and had demanded a bodyboard. Mike had of course given in to her demand immediately. Today, they were spending the morning in the sea, complete with new wetsuit, goggles and armbands, while Alison sat on the veranda of the hut with her binoculars, watching their progress and wondering where it was she was going wrong.

She understood it was going to take a long time for the little girl to adapt. That her behaviour patterns were ingrained in her. That she wouldn't go from abused, neglected and traumatised to happy and carefree overnight. Alison had thought that it would be easy to love. She had wished for so long for someone to nurture and care for. But she felt cold inside, and resentful – of both her daughter and her husband – and she loathed herself for it.

The social worker had warned her that it would be difficult for Chayenne to bond. She had, after all, only known maltreatment from her mother, so it was going to take a long time to earn her trust. Alison knew that she was the grown-up, that she was the one in the position of strength, but still it hurt when the little girl turned away from her and stretched out her arms to Mike. Chayenne never smiled at her, just seemed to specialise in sullen glares or wary glances that made Alison feel like dirt. She had tried every trick in the book: firm jollity, loving kindness, trying to treat her like a baby, a grown-up, a friend, an ally. She'd tried buying her love, with shopping trips when they had come back with carrier bags bulging with clothes and games and DVDs. She'd tried activities – taking her for a bike ride, to the bowling alley. She'd tried reading to her, but Chayenne didn't seem to have any concept of being read to and immediately got bored. Except when Mike read her a bedtime story, when she snuggled up and listened, rapt, eyes round with wonder. Alison had learnt to keep away. It hurt too much. It was all she'd ever wanted, a dear little girl in a brushed cotton nightdress, all ready to be tucked up in bed with cuddles and kisses. Instead, she had a hostile monster who pushed her away time and again.

'Give her time,' Mike kept saying, but it was all right for him. He was reaping the rewards, after all. And sometimes Alison wondered if he enjoyed the way things had turned out. If he was secretly trying to turn Chayenne against her, as some sort of punishment for the fact that she couldn't bear him any children of her own. She knew that was crazy – that wasn't the sort of man Mike was, not at all – but the continual stress was making her lose her judgement. She was becoming paranoid. To the point where she was starting to feel that Mike and Chayenne would be better off without her.

Maybe the whole thing had been a mistake. Maybe she should have pulled out long before the adoption went through, when she had first started having nagging doubts. Doubts she had successfully managed to cover up throughout the entire process, because she had persuaded herself that it would all be all right in the end, that once Chayenne was officially theirs they could concentrate on becoming a family, and that she would eventually come to love her as her own.

Now, as she sat outside the beach hut, this eventuality seemed entirely unlikely, and she was powerless to do anything. She couldn't send her back – she wasn't a dress she'd ordered on the internet that hadn't lived up to her expectations. She was a living, breathing human being, and she was certainly better off with Alison and Mike than she had been with her mother. So Alison was going to have to find a way to deal with it.

She watched the pair of them come up the beach in their wetsuits. They looked to any outsider like a normal father and daughter, chasing each other across the sand and laughing. Eventually they reached the hut.

'Did you have a lovely time?' asked Alison. Every time

she spoke to Chayenne she felt she sounded false, her voice ringing with an enthusiasm she didn't feel.

'Awesome,' said Mike, but Chayenne didn't respond. 'Go and get yourself dry, sweetheart. Then get dressed for lunch.'

'I'll give you a hand.' Alison stood up. Chayenne still struggled with simple tasks, and couldn't manage her buttons.

'I'm fine.' Chayenne spoke flatly, and didn't look her in the eye. 'I can do it myself.'

The two of them watched her go into the hut.

'Quite the Miss Independent now,' noted Mike.

'She hates me.' Alison knew she sounded like a child. 'Why doesn't she want me to help?'

'Because she wants to prove to us that she can manage.' Mike couldn't hide his exasperation. 'It's not about you, Alison. It's about her.'

'I know it's about her.' Alison clenched her fists tightly to stop herself from crying. 'Everything's about her.'

'Of course it is,' replied Mike. 'She's seven years old and she's had a shit life.'

'I'll go and get the lunch.' She stood up. There was no point in having the conversation. She was wrong and she knew it. Which made it even worse.

David bent over with his hands on his knees, trying to regain his breath. It was three miles from one end of the beach to the other, and he had run non-stop. He was badly out of condition, and now he had to run back. He was determined to do it, though. He'd been a complete slob lately, and he'd forgotten how good running was for clearing your head and giving you a chance to think about things.

He certainly had a lot to think about. When Adrian had told him about him and Serena the night before, he had been shocked, deeply shocked. He could see how it had happened – of course he could. Philip was a tricky customer, Serena was a very attractive girl, and Adrian . . . well, Adrian was Adrian and always managed to leave a trail of disruption wherever he went, although until now he had kept his destructive tendencies away from his own family. It was almost as if he had been saving it up to cause maximum damage, blowing apart the fabric of the Miltons with one treacherous move.

David couldn't help feeling that it wasn't just about the fact that Adrian and Serena had fallen in love and couldn't help themselves. He was very fond of his brother, but he wasn't taken in by Adrian the Victim. He knew very well that Adrian wasn't a victim at all, but an arch manipulator who knew exactly how to get what he wanted, whether it was a flat bought and paid for by his parents, or his brother's wife. But he was charming nonetheless.

As the eldest brother, David wondered if perhaps he should step in and take control of the situation. He supposed with the death of his father he was now the head of the family, but it wasn't a role that sat comfortably with him. Besides, what on earth could he do? He had visions of a family conference, all of them sitting round a table like the Ewings at Southfork, and immediately dismissed the idea. What good would it do? Philip certainly wouldn't attend. And it would only upset his mother. She'd had enough to deal with this summer.

He leant against a rock and stretched out his calves, hoping it would ease the burning sensation on the way back. Running on the sand was surprisingly tough, but he could already feel it doing him good, and he resolved he would go for a run every morning for the remainder of the holiday. His last holiday at Everdene.

He couldn't believe that he wouldn't be coming back. Because he wouldn't – there would be no point once The Shack had gone. He turned and started his way back along the beach, memories crowded into his mind. It had been such a huge part of their life for so long, he wasn't sure how they would all manage without it. Coming to Everdene had provided a rhythm that would no longer be there. Life wasn't going to be the same without the annual jaunts: the winter trips to paint the exterior, the ceremonial opening, the birthday barbecues, the infamous bank holiday party which was even now being prepared . . .

But life wasn't going to be the same anyway. With Adrian and Serena's revelation, the family was fractured. It was going to be a long time before they all felt comfortable with the new arrangement – if indeed it went ahead. David wouldn't put it past Philip to fight for his wife, if only so it meant that Adrian couldn't have her. He had been like that all through their childhood – possessive and unable to share – while Adrian had always been able to engineer things to get what he wanted. David always had to be the referee, trying to keep the peace between his two younger brothers. And now, thirty or so years later, he felt he should be doing the same. He should know what to do now, but he didn't. After all, this wasn't beach balls and cricket bats being fought over, it was people, and the fallout affected more than just Adrian and Philip. There were Spike and Harry and Amelia to consider. It was beyond his remit. He realised he didn't want to get involved. He would be there for any of them if they wanted support or advice, but he wasn't going to go wading in and dictating terms, like he might have done when they were small.

As he pounded back up the beach, he pondered that if it wasn't for The Shack, the affair would probably never have happened. There wouldn't have been long, hot, lazy summers for Adrian and Serena to get closer and closer. They might have seen each other once, maybe twice a year at some family event, but there would have been no opportunity for their relationship to turn into something significant. Maybe this affair marked the end of an era. Maybe it was going to make it easier for them all to move on.

He slowed down as he reached the halfway point. He was determined not to let the way things turned out sour his memories. He looked out over the ocean, remembering the three of them learning to swim, then bodyboard, then surf in its cerulean depths. And their own children doing the same. They were all waterbabies. He looked at the dunes, and remembered rolling down them, getting giddier and giddier as he reached the bottom, then standing drunkenly, only to do it all over again.

He remembered the three of them ruling the Ship Aground as teenagers, only a few years between them, total babe magnets with their sun-streaked hair and tans, the infamous Milton brothers. And it was always Adrian and Philip who competed over women. It had often been the source of tension, although of course the outcome hadn't mattered so much then. They were transient holiday romances. Only now history was repeating itself, and a family was going to be broken up. Bloody Adrian, thought David. Though in fact, bloody Philip too. If he had been a more attentive husband, and not such a sleazy Lothario, Serena wouldn't have been tempted to stray.

Alison laid out what she thought was the perfect lunch on the picnic table in front of the hut. Soft white bread rolls with ham, crisps, carrot sticks, hummus, and a big bowl of strawberries. She had already learnt not to present Chayenne with granary bread. The child had been brought up on a diet of McDonald's and sugary cereal, which she used to eat in handfuls from the box. Alison was gradually trying to wean her onto healthier foods, but it was an uphill struggle.

Chayenne refused to eat anything but the crisps.

'Don't stress,' said Mike. 'She'll eat when she's hungry.'

'But she must be starving! She's been in the water all morning.'

Mike put up his hand to calm her.

'It's fine. Just leave her a plate with some food on for later.'

Alison pursed her lips, then caught Chayenne looking at her with what she was sure was a triumphant gleam in her eye. She cleared the table and walked back inside quickly. She could feel the tears coming. She didn't want to be the enemy. She didn't want to be this person – the disapproving bad cop. All she wanted was the best for Chayenne, but it was so difficult. She felt a wave of exhaustion. Living in a state of tension was completely draining her.

She tensed even more as Mike came in behind her.

'I'm going to wander up to the village for a paper,' he said. 'Can you keep an eye on her for half an hour?'

'Of course I can!' she replied. 'She probably needs a rest, anyway.'

He came up and gave her a hug.

'Listen,' he said. 'I know it's tough, but it will be fine in the end. She's got seven years of hell to get out of her system. Don't blame yourself.'

Alison felt herself soften. He was right, of course he was. Mike wasn't her enemy, he was her husband and her best friend. And they had to get through this together.

'I'm sorry,' she told him. 'I'm just finding it hard. I'm . . . jealous, I suppose.'

'She doesn't know how to show she loves you yet.' Mike squeezed her in his arms even tighter. 'But she will. Because how could she not love you?'

For some reason, this made Alison want to cry even more than the frustration of earlier. She laughed as she wiped away the couple of tears that escaped despite her best efforts.

'Come on,' said Mike. 'Forget about clearing up. Come and sit outside under the parasol with Chayenne. I'll bring you both back an ice cream.'

David's lungs were screaming and his calves were burning as he reached the first of the beach huts. He didn't want an audience, so he slowed down to a brisk walk. He'd cool down by walking as far as the rocks at the top of the beach, get his breath back. Then he supposed he'd better get back to the hut, and get his instructions from Serena and Chrissie. Thank God everyone had preparations for the party to focus on. It helped the awkwardness.

His heart rate slowed as he reached the top of the beach, and he started to get his breath back. There was a time when he could have done that run without even breaking into a sweat. He resolved to hit the gym when he got home and get himself match-fit again. He didn't want Chrissie thinking he'd run to seed and going off with a younger model . . . though he didn't think she would. They were pretty solid, he and Chrissie, even if they did have their ups and downs. But no one had a totally smooth ride. That would make life boring. You had to earn the high points by having low ones as well.

He kicked off his trainers and socks, stuffing the one into the other, and walked through one of the rock pools to cool off his feet. The air smelt different here, and he breathed it in – the briny scent of the seaweed always made him nostalgic. The three boys had spent hours scrambling over these rocks with their nets, bringing home buckets of unfortunate creatures for inspection and identification with their *Observer's Book of Sea and Seashore*. It had been idyllic, and David was grateful that he had been able to give his own children the same pleasures.

The tide was coming in now, filling up all the dips and nooks with flurries of water. He remembered Adrian wandering away from them one day, and then becoming trapped on a rock as the water rose. The little boy was too terrified to climb down into its swirling depths, and too frightened to jump. Philip had refused to do anything to help, and David remembered now seeing a look of what he suspected was pleasure on his brother's face, evidence of Philip's sadistic streak. In the end, David had skirted around the rocks, leaping over the chasms until he had reached Adrian, and had guided him back, holding his hand as he jumped. He remembered Adrian dropping his hand as soon as they had reached safety, not wanting to look like a cissy in front of his brothers. Philip had just smirked.

As he replayed the scene that was now so telling, David looked over the rocks and picked out the one that Adrian had been stranded on. The landscape hadn't changed in all those years – he thought he could imagine the frightened figure on there even now. And then he realised that there *was* a figure on there. He took off his sunglasses, peered even closer. It was a little girl. A little girl who was sitting, perched on top of the rocks, her arms around her knees, clearly frozen in fear. The water was getting higher and higher as each wave came in with the tide. Unless she knew the rocks well, she was going to be completely stranded in a matter of minutes.

David ran into her eye-line and gave her a wave.

'Hey!' he shouted. 'Hang on. I'll come and get you.'

The child didn't reply. Either she hadn't heard him, or she was too scared to respond. David began clambering over the rocks, swearing as a sharp barnacle dug into his foot. He didn't have time to put his shoes back on.

'Alison!'

Alison's eyes snapped open. Mike's tone was sharp. What had happened? She sat up, sure she'd only shut her eyes for a moment. It had been so warm in the afternoon sun, and she was exhausted. Chayenne had been happy on the rug next to her, messing about with the Nintendo DS that Alison had resisted buying at first, though she was glad she had now she realised that it brought considerable respite.

The DS was lying on the blanket, still emitting squawks and beeps.

'Where's Chayenne?'

Mike was standing over her, a Magnum in one hand and a Fab in the other.

Alison's heart rate doubled.

'She was here a second ago. She must have gone to the loo.'

The bitter taste of fear swam up into her mouth. Mike ran into the hut and appeared moments later.

'She's not here. Where the hell has she gone? What happened? You fell asleep!' He glared at her accusingly.

'I shut my eyes for two minutes. She was right next to me.'

'Well, she's not now.'

Alison put a hand to her brow to shade her eyes from the sun and scanned the beach. A yellow T-shirt and denim shorts, that's what she'd been wearing. Hadn't she? She couldn't be sure now. Shit – the beach had filled up since lunchtime. The sunny weather had brought the grockles out in droves. They were sitting in clusters, spreading out their blankets and putting up their windbreaks. It was almost impossible to pick out an individual child.

'I'll start looking. I'll go and find the lifeguard.'

'No.' Mike's tone was firm. 'Stay here in case she comes back. How long do you think she's been gone?'

Alison had no idea. She couldn't answer. She couldn't

look Mike in the eye. He gave her one hard look of reproach, then set off down the beach.

Alison felt her knees go weak and she sank back down onto the rug. Dear God, she pleaded silently, please let her be safe. She thought of all the terrible things that could happen to a little girl in such a short space of time. She cupped her hands round her face and scanned the beach again. It was hopeless.

'Put your arms around my neck,' David instructed. The little girl stared blankly at him. 'Come on. We haven't got long. This rock will be covered completely in a minute. You'll be fine. I'll carry you. I've done it hundreds of times with my daughter.'

The girl obeyed eventually, and David scooped her up. She barely weighed anything. She was painfully thin, just a scrap. He could feel the tension in her body as he held her, taut as a piano wire.

'Hey,' he said jovially. 'This is an adventure. This happened to my brother when we were little. But I know the secret escape route. Three rocks this way, then two rocks that, and we'll be able to get back onto the sand. Ready?'

She nodded dumbly, then buried her face in his neck as he began to negotiate the journey – never easy, but even more difficult when you were holding someone. It could have been Adrian he was holding, he thought, as he scrambled over the eddying incoming tide. Where had all that time gone? And were they so very different from the three boys who had spent their childhood on these slippery rocks?

He slipped once, grazing his knee badly, but he

scrambled to his feet again, then made the last leap to freedom and safety.

The little girl didn't want to let him go. She was whispering something.

'Eh?' he said, leaning in closer to her.

'I want my mum.'

'OK,' he said. 'Let's see if we can find her. Are you just here for the day?'

She shook her head.

'Are you staying here?'

She looked very confused.

'I don't know.'

'What's your mummy's name? We can go and find the lifeguard. He's got a special loudspeaker.'

The child seemed to be thinking very hard.

'What's your mummy's name?' he prompted again.

Again, silence.

'Alison,' she managed eventually. 'Alison,' she repeated more definitely, as if this time she was quite sure.

'Okey-doke.' David thought about putting the child down, but she didn't seem to want to let him go, so he decided he would carry her. She barely weighed anything, so she was hardly a burden. He scanned the beach for the lifeguard's truck, positioned in between the safety flags, and started heading for it.

'There.' The child pointed to the row of huts. 'There. That's where we live.'

'In the huts?'

'The green one.'

'You're very lucky. Those huts are very special.'

She didn't respond. Maybe she was in shock? David

strode out across the sand, the searing heat of the afternoon sun burning his feet.

'Your mummy's going to be very pleased to see you.'

Alison had never known terror like it. At one point she thought she was going to pass out. How could she ever forgive herself if anything had happened? And Mike would never forgive her, she knew that. She searched the beach to see if she could see him, to see if he was walking back up with that familiar little figure, but there was no sign.

'Hey!'

An assertive voice made her turn. A tall man was striding towards her, a child in his arms.

Chayenne.

Alison swayed for a moment, dizzy with the relief, her mouth dry, as the man came nearer.

'I found her on the rocks,' he was saying. 'She had a bit of an adventure.'

Thank God he wasn't going to chastise her. She didn't think she could cope. She held out her arms.

Chayenne looked at her. She was ready for the stony stare, for the child to recoil, and she prayed she wouldn't. Her rescuer would think it strange.

But to her amazement, Chayenne held out her arms. Alison stumbled forward in disbelief, reaching out for her, her heart nearly bursting with joy as she took the little body and pulled it into her.

'Mummy.'

Just one little word. Just one little word, but it meant so much. Alison felt a lump in her throat and an overwhelming sense of elation that she knew she had never felt before, and would probably never feel again.

'I love you,' she murmured, burying her face in Chayenne's neck. 'I love you . . .'

There was no answer, but a pair of thin arms squeezed her just a little bit more tightly round the neck.

'Thank you,' she said to the man, and he stuck up his thumb in a gesture of goodwill.

'No worries,' he replied, and jogged his way back along the beach.

13
FLOTSAM AND JETSAM

Whichever deity it was that controlled the weather could not have failed to notice that there was a party being planned on Everdene beach that bank holiday. And it must have heard the silent and not so silent prayers that were sent up by the organisers, for the day dawned as warm and balmy as a holiday brochure, and all the reports confirmed that the weather was set fair for the entire weekend.

A large section of the beach in front of the first five huts, starting with The Shack, had been roped off to designate the official party area, and a cluster of gazebos and tents had been erected. There was a drinks tent, centred around a mighty bucket of punch made by Jane Milton from a recipe handed down to her by her mother, which had been served at the very first party in 1964. It was said to be deadly but delicious. There were also barrels of beer, and tubs full of ice on which rested cans of fizzy pop for the children and bottles of water. Two more tubs filled with ice waited for the bottles of champagne which were the entry ticket – these would be drunk as the sun went down. Gaily coloured bunting abounded, as did inflatable palm trees and flamingos and parrots. Cardboard cut-outs of hula girls and Hawaiian tiki gods were dotted around amongst the tables and chairs. The pig roast was already turning, and the gazebo next to it contained a long trestle table where the salads, bread and plates were waiting. Another table stood by ready for puddings. There was a bouncy castle for the children, and, as had long been the tradition, a huge tent had been put up and filled with rugs and cushions, to protect the smaller guests from the sun during the afternoon, and to provide somewhere for them to crash out as the evening went on. Miraculously, they always seemed to conk out at about nine, sleeping through all the noise and allowing the adults to really let their hair down.

Jane ran through her checklist yet again, though she had organised this party so many times she could do it standing on her head. She kept the thought that this was the last time to the back of her mind. She wanted to enjoy tonight, not get emotional.

She had phoned Norman the day before, and told him which offer to accept. The potential buyer had, apparently, been delighted. She had wanted the deal under way before the party, for some reason, so she could say her farewells and then make a clean break of it. Besides, she could always come and visit if she wanted to. She looked over at Roy, who was unloading some extra chairs from the back of his Volvo. She felt a squeeze of pleasure inside. She realised now how much she had come to depend on him over the years. He had been a true friend – more than a friend – and the more she got to know him, the more intrigued she was. It was funny, she had never got to know anything about his private life when

Graham was alive – or maybe it wasn't funny at all. Maybe she had held back for a reason. Her mind flashed back suddenly, to a girl in a yellow dress, and a boy in white cricket trousers. How different their lives might have been . . .

She couldn't spend the afternoon reminiscing. She dragged her mind back to the here and now. She couldn't help feeling a bit sad that all her family weren't around her – Philip had gone home and was refusing to speak to anyone, although he had texted to assure her he was basically all right. It was hard being the mother of someone who had behaved so badly throughout their marriage – your instinct was to protect them, and yet you had to face up to the truth: that he pretty much deserved what he had got. Although being cuckolded by your own brother was probably a punishment too far.

And Adrian and Serena did look happy. They had come clean to the whole family – Serena had told Harry and Amelia, and Adrian had told his brother David, then they had told Spike together. Jane was worried about Harry more than anyone – he had been very quiet since the news, whereas Amelia, in typical fashion, had looked at the situation to see what she could get out of it and had already decided she wanted to move in with them in Frome and go to college in Bath. Amelia was a survivor, like her father, but Harry was more sensitive. Still, he'd be near enough to his mother when he went to medical school in Bristol.

She checked her watch – just half an hour before the party began. There was nothing else she could do until it started. She smiled at the sun, asking it silently to hang in there, and went back into the hut to get ready.

Harry was setting up an elaborate sound system for the party, hoping that the music he had downloaded was catholic enough to keep everyone happy. He'd gone for compilation albums of the last four decades, as well as a comprehensive selection of up-to-date hits for the younger generation. If history was anything to go by, the dancing would go on until the small hours.

He was glad he had something to keep him occupied. He was still reeling from his mother's revelation – about the prospect of having his uncle as a stepfather, although they hadn't intimated they were getting married. The whole thing had made him feel a bit sick, if he was honest. OK, so he knew his father was no angel. No one had ever said it out loud before, but he knew in his gut Philip played away. He could tell by the way his mother sighed when he phoned to say he would be home late; by the way his father was so robustly cheerful the next day. Almost smug. He didn't do anything as pat as try and be extra nice when he returned from one of his liaisons: Philip never apologised for anything, let alone something he hadn't admitted to. So Harry always felt it was his duty to be extra nice to his mother – when he was home from school, at least. The rest of the time he didn't like to think of her alone and miserable, knowing her husband was out flirting with first-year students, and worse. So the bottom line was he didn't blame her for leaving, though he was shocked about Adrian. Very shocked. He wasn't sure about the nasty feeling it gave him in his stomach, though he thought it might be jealousy. Jealousy that Spike was going to get his mum's attention, while he was off in his first year at uni and supposed to be grown up and independent when actually he felt very small and a bit like crying.

What a wuss. No wonder Florence had run a mile from him. That was the other thing that was giving him a nasty feeling – the knowledge that she would be there at the party tonight. After that disastrous episode with her in June, just after he'd finished his exams, he had fled back home and got a job at Warwick Castle, showing tourists around. But he'd had to come back for the bank holiday party. It was a family tradition, and the last one. So here he was, nearly two months later, hoping and praying that when he set eyes on her he would feel nothing.

Sarah was trying to suppress her inner control freak while the girls helped her ice the beach-hut biscuits. She had baked a hundred – tricky given the facilities, but she had managed – and now they were all spread out on the table while she mixed up icing in shades of pink, blue, green and yellow. She decided the best plan was to give the girls ten to do between them, which they could mess up as much as they liked, and do the others herself. She'd cut out a dinky little template, and was going to decorate them with stripes and a little lifebuoy. They'd be popular with the kids at the party, at least. Everyone who came had to contribute something towards the food, and Sarah had wanted to do something special.

Something that would take her mind off the fact that Ian was refusing to come.

It had, quite frankly, been the worst summer of her life. Ian was not taking being made redundant very well. He had had a spurt of optimism at first, done some networking, applied for jobs he'd seen in the paper or on the internet, but gradually his enthusiasm had waned. He had become bitter, and bad-tempered, snapping at her and the children. Eventually he had stopped making any sort of an effort at all, claiming that it was humiliating to be continually rejected. Sarah had tried to be sympathetic, but inside she was panicking – what if he didn't get another job? What would they do? She tried to build up her own business, pitching for as many jobs as she could, but it was difficult when the girls were at home, and even though Ian wasn't working he didn't seem to think it was his place to look after them. Plus she'd sent her book ideas off to her agent and had heard nothing, which was very dispiriting.

Added to that was the huge difficulty of trying to resist phoning Oliver. He had said to call any time. But she knew absolutely that was not the answer to any of her problems. She relived over and over again in her mind the incredible night they had shared together. It made her feel both guilty and thrilled. What wouldn't she give to experience that again? She could set it up in a trice, she knew she could, but how could she contemplate cheating on her husband again when he was so depressed?

Gradually, however, she was running out of sympathy. Ian had become so negative, so unpleasant, that life was pretty unbearable. It had got to the point where he had stopped shaving, stopped showering, often didn't bother getting dressed until gone midday. When she remonstrated, he snarled at her. What was the point? She began to spend as much time out of the house as she could with the girls, which of course meant she couldn't work, which in turn meant they didn't even have her money coming in. They couldn't go on like this for ever, but she didn't know where to find a solution. When she had suggested he go back to college to retrain, she thought he was going to hit her.

And he wouldn't go out. They had any number of invitations to parties and barbecues, but he quite simply refused to socialise, because he didn't want to face the questions. Everyone knew he had been made redundant, because news like that travelled fast.

'I'm a fucking failure,' he shouted at her, when she had tried to persuade him to join some friends at a dinner party. 'I don't want everyone asking me what I'm up to because I'm up to fuck all.'

She had slunk away, unable to argue, because he didn't want to hear anyone else's side of the story.

The beach hut had been the only thing to bring in a reliable sum that summer. He had wanted to rent it out for the bank holiday week too – six hundred quid would go a long way towards paying the mortgage – but she had put her foot down. The bank holiday week was always their week. They needed a holiday. The girls needed a holiday. He had backed down, but he had refused to come. He didn't want to have to admit his situation over and over again to the rest of the beach-hut owners.

It had been a huge relief to spend the week away from him. The girls, who had become increasingly subdued in the light of Ian's behaviour, had come out of their shells again. And they were all excited about the party. They had been every year since they'd bought the hut, and it was the highlight of the summer for all of them. Despite the lack of funds, Sarah had been into Bamford and bought them a new dress each. In the sales, so she didn't feel too guilty. And while she was there, she had seen the most beautiful white beaded chiffon dress for herself, at a quarter of its original price. It was low cut, and almost backless, but if she wore it with flip-flops, it wouldn't look tarty . . . She wrestled with her conscience, decided against it, took the girls into a café for cake, then just as they were on their way back to the car, she turned around and ran back to the shop, getting there just as it closed.

Once they'd finished the biscuits, she laid them in the cool of the cupboard to dry. It was time to get ready. She kept checking her phone to see if Ian had called to say he'd had a change of heart and was on his way. She knew she should hope that he would, but in her heart of hearts she was relieved when the phone remained determinedly silent.

She looked at her dress on the hanger. It was going to look amazing. She'd got some plain silver hoop earrings to wear with it. Then her heart sank. What was the point of putting on a gorgeous dress when your husband refused to have anything to do with you, and the man you really wanted to wear it for was firmly out of bounds?

Fiona hid in the tiny bathroom of the beach hut, trembling.

This was it. This was her first real test. She could do it. She really could. At least she hoped so. She had to. For herself, for the children, but most of all, for Tim.

He had been absolutely brilliant. After she'd finally plucked up the courage to tell him the truth, he had driven straight down to Everdene to collect her. He had swept her up in her arms while she cried, and for the first time in her married life, she had felt safe. He had been mortified that she had kept her terrible secret for so long, and hadn't judged her. He had promised to stick by her, whatever she decided to do. He'd found her a wonderful counsellor, who had unravelled everything and put it all into perspective and worked out a plan to help her face life without the crutch she had relied on for so, so long. And once it was out in the open – in her marriage, at least – she found the courage to face her demons.

It was tough. Hideously tough. Every day was a challenge, and a battle, but she was absolutely determined. She had come so close to destroying everything she had. It made her feel hot and shivery when she thought back over it. The years of drunken oblivion, the accident. The one-night stand . . .

She had seen him once. In the Spar. He had smiled at her, tentatively, across the shop. She remembered feeling an overwhelming sense of relief that he looked so normal, so nice. When she had tried to remember him the next day, she couldn't visualise him properly, and she had been terrified that she had picked up some complete thug, but he looked perfectly respectable – especially now he was wearing normal clothes and not a fairy outfit. She didn't speak to him, though. She couldn't face that. And he'd been sensitive enough to respect that. What would she have done if he'd barrelled up to her and said, 'Hello, darlin'? She had confessed her night of shame to her counsellor, who hadn't been judgemental, hadn't said anything really, but she had felt better for getting it off her chest.

Four weeks. She had managed four weeks without a drink. The days were long, the nights even longer, and there were days when her body screamed for the relief.

There was nothing to replace it with. Even sleep didn't bring respite, because she found herself troubled by images of the things she had done over the years, waking up in a sweat as she pictured herself lurching through yet another party, tottering on her heels, making a fool of herself even though at the time she had told herself she was fine, absolutely fine. But she'd done it. Tim had been kind – he had got rid of every drop of alcohol in the house, and didn't drink either. She didn't think she could have coped if he had pulled the cork on a bottle of cool Sauvignon each night and expected her to go without. And they had avoided social functions, which hadn't been too difficult as a lot of people had been away on holiday, and you could always decline an invitation by saying you were away too, or had visitors coming.

But the Everdene beach party couldn't be avoided. They went every year, without fail. Tim had asked her kindly if she wanted them to duck out, but Fiona didn't want to. She had to face reality sometime. She had to learn to operate without alcohol in the real world, not in a cushioned, protected pseudo-reality. And at least she felt comfortable here. People in Everdene didn't seem to judge you, not like at home where you had to watch your every step.

She looked in the mirror. She had to admit, she looked better. She had filled out slightly and looked less gaunt, because when she had been drinking, food had never been a priority. Her eyes looked brighter. She held out both hands flat in front of her. Steady. Usually she would have got ready for a party while drinking two or three glasses of champagne. But not tonight.

She touched up her lipgloss one more time and left the

bathroom. Tim was sprawled in a chair reading the paper – he looked handsome in his dinner jacket. He glanced up at her and smiled.

'The kids have gone already. They couldn't wait – they wanted to get on the bouncy castle.'

He stood up.

'You look gorgeous.' He came over to her and kissed her.

'Mmmm.' To her surprise, she found herself kissing him back. And a little flicker of something sparked deep down in her belly. She had felt dead inside for so long. She couldn't remember the last time they had made love, not really. She was always comatose by bedtime – why would Tim want to have sex with a corpse?

But now, suddenly, the feeling was flooding back. He was trailing his fingers down her back, and it made her shiver with desire. She pushed herself against him, and she could tell he was aroused too.

'Do you think,' she murmured between kisses, 'it would matter awfully if we were just a tiny bit late?'

It was half past eight. The party was in full swing. The pig roast had been devoured, totally stripped. There was nothing left but bone. As the sun set, the smaller children were ushered into the scout tent to settle down, and bottles of champagne were cracked open. Jane had wondered about giving a little farewell speech, proposing a toast, but decided that it was a bit hammy, and she didn't want to break the carefree mood of the party. It was, she decided, the best one yet. In which case, it was definitely time to move on. Chrissie had talked to her about the possibility of funding a rescue package for The

Shack, but they had agreed in the end that so much had changed, it was best to let it go. Chrissie was talking about getting a place somewhere hot instead, so her three would be all right.

Jane felt a tiny bit guilty about the rest of the grand-children. They'd had such fun here over the years. But if she was honest, they were all growing up themselves. Harry was off to university – he'd have his own plans for the summer from now on. Amelia had hundreds of friends she was always making plans with. And Spike – well, things were going to be different for him In a good way, she thought. She had always thought Serena an excellent mother – far better than Spike's own mother. She hoped Donna wouldn't give them any trouble, but she thought not. At the end of the day, all Donna was really after was an easy life, and Serena being around would definitely mean that.

Adrian was panicking. He couldn't find Serena. She had been rather quiet this afternoon. She didn't seem to be looking forward to the party, although she had denied it when he questioned her.

He searched through the crowds, in the drinks tent. Went back into the hut to see if she had gone to lie down or something. But she was nowhere to be seen. His heart lurched. Had she decided on some mercy dash back home to see Philip? Had she changed her mind?

He saw Chrissie, and grabbed her.

'Have you seen Serena?'

Chrissie had been very disapproving, when they had told her. But Adrian had drawn her aside and had a heart-to-heart, explaining how unhappy Serena had been for a long time, how they had started out as friends, and it had grown into something else. Chrissie hadn't looked convinced, but then she'd always been a bit chippy, thought Adrian.

'I think she went into the children's tent with Spike,' she told him.

He turned to go, but Chrissie stopped him.

'Wait,' she said. 'I just want to say . . . good luck. I thought you were both selfish idiots looking for a cheap thrill at first. And I was a bit pissed off that you tried to con me into buying The Shack. But . . . I can see it's something deeper than that.' She paused. 'I hope you'll be happy.'

Stunned, Adrian managed a smile. 'Thank you. It means a lot.'

Chrissie touched him on the arm and walked away. Adrian watched her go and felt filled with emotion. Shit, he wasn't going to cry, was he? It had been a rollercoaster of a few days. A new life ahead of him, the old one coming to an end with the last beach party. He needed to pull himself together.

He walked over to the scout tent and pulled back the flap. He felt relief as he saw Serena, sitting next to Spike who was curled up in his sleeping bag with Bart under his arm. She was stroking his hair, sending him off to sleep.

This time, Adrian didn't try and stop the little tear that rolled down his cheek.

Sarah had sneaked off back to her hut to sit on the step and have a cigarette. She had just finished rolling it and put it in her mouth when the flare from a lighter appeared in front of her.

A Zippo lighter.

'Shit!' She dropped the cigarette in alarm. 'Oliver. What the fuck are you doing here?'

'Well, that's a nice greeting,' he replied, leaning down to pick up her roll-up. He put it back between her lips and she felt heat zip through her from head to foot. She pulled the cigarette out angrily.

'What are you doing here?' she repeated.

'I couldn't live without you a minute longer.' He looked straight into her eyes.

She swallowed. There was none of his usual teasing tone. He seemed deadly serious.

'Don't be ridiculous. We hardly know each other.'

'I know enough.' He leaned into her. She could smell his cologne. Him. 'I think about you every second of every minute of every hour of every day.'

'Right . . .' She didn't know how to respond. This was quite a confession. And ironic, though she wasn't going to admit that.

'This doesn't happen to me, Sarah. I don't do obsession. I do casual, meaningless shags and move on. But this is different.'

'It's probably only because I told you no. I don't imagine you're a man who likes rejection.' She tried to keep her voice light, but it was shaking. 'I've told you. I'm married. I can't deal with it.'

'Sarah – your husband's a twat.' She looked at him, startled. 'I saw him last night at the Johnsons'.'

'What?' This made her sit up. What the hell was Ian doing at the Johnsons'? This was the man who couldn't face going out in public, who had point-blank refused to come to the beach party.

362

'Oh yes. He was letting his hair right down. Drunk as a skunk and twice as obnoxious. They had to kick him out in the end, before he started throwing punches.'

'He's very unhappy. He's going through a tough time.'

'Why do you defend him when he's a total knob?'

Sarah felt indignant.

'Because he's my husband and I love him and he isn't always a knob and don't you remember those words "for better or for worse"? The whole point of marriage is you're supposed to stick by the one you love—'

He kissed her. And she let him. Oh God.

He drew back.

'That's why I love you,' he said softly.

'Don't,' she pleaded.

'I want you in my life. I just want to be able to see you. Even if it doesn't involve sex . . .'

She rolled her eyes. 'Yeah, right.'

'Honestly. I think you could make me a better person.'

'You're full of shit.' She stared him out. 'You just want a shag.'

He shook his head. 'I think you deserve someone who cares about you. He's taking the piss, Sarah. I know exactly what's going on. He's bullying you and undermining you because he's unhappy, and you're running round like a headless chicken trying to keep everything afloat, but no one thinks about you.' He paused. 'Do they?'

She looked down. 'No.'

He put his hands on her shoulders, ran his thumbs up her neck. Oh God . . .

'I'm not playing your game, Oliver,' she insisted,

though her body was betraying her. Liquid gold was oozing into her stomach.

'Let me just be with you tonight. You can introduce me as a family friend.'

She hesitated.

'You can't stay. I've got the girls.'

'Of course not. I've booked a room.'

She looked at him. Was he fibbing?

He was running the back of his fingers along her jaw.

She would have to be superhuman to resist.

'What about your wife?' she gasped, remembering the intimidating woman at the Johnsons' party. The divorce lawyer, for heaven's sake.

'I don't care,' Oliver told her. 'I've had long enough to think about it to know that. I want to be with you, Sarah.'

'OK. But no funny stuff. Not here,' she managed to reply, finding it difficult to breathe.

'No funny stuff.'

'Just tonight? Then you'll leave me alone. I can't handle it, Oliver . . .'

'Just tonight. I promise.'

She was here. She'd turned up late, but Florence was finally here. Harry sensed her before he even saw her. The hairs on the back of his neck had tingled, then he had spotted her in the crowd, making her way towards him with a cigarette in one hand and a bottle of beer in the other.

She was coming over to talk to him. Harry felt his heart hammering. What should he say? Was she still going out with Marky Burns? He wanted to walk off, but he was drawn to her magnetically.

'Hi,' he said. Genius.

'Hey,' she replied, and lit another cigarette with the end of the one she had just finished. She chucked the stub on the ground carelessly. Harry felt the urge to cover it with sand, but he didn't want her to think he was making some kind of point.

'Have you . . . had a good summer?' God, he was doing a perfect impersonation of Harry Enfield's Tory Boy. He cringed inside.

'I've been doing the festivals. Totally amazing. But I'm knackered. I can't remember the last time I had a proper night's sleep.'

Actually, now he looked closer, it showed. In just four weeks she had changed dramatically. Her face was puffy, and her skin had broken out in spots. Her hair seemed matt and dull, scraped back into a high ponytail. Her nails were chewed. Her clothes were rumpled and grubby. She looked . . . skanky, he decided. He took a step back. The cigarette she was smoking was cheap, harsh, and it mixed in with some rank perfume she had doused herself in. Probably to cover up the fact she hadn't had a shower.

He couldn't think of a thing to say to her. Then he fell back on the tried-and-tested boring question of the late summer.

'How were your results?'

There was a flicker in her eyes, as if she was deciding what to tell him.

'I . . . um . . . didn't get in. I didn't get the grades. Just one grade off, but that's all it needs to be.' She looked a bit shamefaced. 'Going to have to reapply next year.'

'Shit. Sorry about that.' Harry didn't say he'd got straight As. He was never one to gloat.

'So – are you off to Bristol?'

'Yeah. Another month yet.'

'Should be cool.'

'Definitely. Probably. I don't know . . .'

She took another drag of her cigarette. She looked awkward.

'Listen . . . Harry . . . I'm sorry I was such a bitch earlier in the summer.'

He shrugged.

'Hey, it's fine. No worries.'

'Seriously. I was out of order. And he was such a jerk.'

Harry grinned.

'Yeah, well – I could have told you that.'

She thumped him on the shoulder.

'Shut – up.'

He pretended to rub the spot where she'd hit him. 'That was a bit harsh.'

Then he looked at her and realised she was crying. Real tears, in those eyes he had once found mesmerising.

'You OK?'

She nodded, then shook her head. 'Yes. No. No! I've screwed up everything. Why am I such a . . . waste of space?'

Because you're selfish? And you think you're something you're not? And you don't give a toss how anyone else feels? All of these things ran through Harry's head, but he didn't say any of them, because he was basically a kind boy. He patted her on the shoulder. This was the cue she needed, and she threw herself against him. He recoiled slightly, amazed. Wasn't this secretly what he had been dreaming of all summer? Only now he didn't want her anywhere near him. He felt a slight revulsion.

'Listen, I've got to go and change the music. We don't want a Beatles medley *all* night.'

He extricated himself from her embrace as politely as he could. She looked at him dully. Her make-up had streaked down her face. Some women could carry that off, Harry knew, but on Florence, it wasn't a good look.

'Catch you later,' he said, and strode off towards the sound system.

Jane stood on the steps of The Shack and looked at the scene around her.

It was magical. The moon threw its light over the sea and the sand, immersing the guests in a silvery glow. Everyone was dancing – men in dinner jackets, women in sparkling, shimmering dresses. Lanterns flickered all around them. As the song that was playing came to an end, everyone stopped for a moment, laughing, chattering, reaching for a much-needed drink. Then the chords of the next song struck up.

It was The Kinks, 'You Really Got Me'. Everyone leapt back into action, galvanised by the tune that was familiar to all generations.

Jane was immediately transported back in time. Everything was almost the same. There were more people now, and the music was louder, the bass pounding out, but it could have been that same night. She looked over to the house at the top of the dunes and remembered how she had been feeling – a young girl whose life had just been turned upside down, and who had no idea where to go next. And for all of her life she never quite managed to get rid of that feeling, until today. All that had been laid to rest. She felt at one with herself.

She turned, and saw Roy was standing next to her, smiling, holding out his hand.

'Come on,' he said. 'Let's show them how it's done.'

She walked down the steps with a smile. She took Roy's hand, and put the other on his shoulder.

Tomorrow she would start to clear out a lifetime of belongings from The Shack, in readiness for its new owner. But tonight . . . tonight she would dance on the sands by the light of the moon.

14
THE LOVE SHACK

Kirsty could hear Dan tooting the car horn impatiently in the drive outside. She zipped up her weekend case and picked up her handbag. She really didn't need this. She would have given anything for a lie-in this morning; she felt so tired. But Dan had insisted. The forecast was great for the weekend, and they always spent her birthday at Everdene. It was a tradition. Liam was coming down the next day with his new girlfriend. Helena – a cardiothoracic consultant, apparently, and quite a bit older than him. They were madly in love, which was great, thought Kirsty, because that's what Liam needed. Someone constant in his life. It was definitely time he settled down too. They were all growing up at last, she realised.

She ran down the stairs and got into the car.

'You OK?' asked Dan, concerned. 'You look a bit pale.'

'Haven't had time to put any make-up on.' Kirsty settled into the seat and fastened her belt.

Dan switched on the engine.

'You can have a sleep,' he said. 'We'll be there by lunchtime.'

'Great,' said Kirsty, shutting her eyes. She didn't need any encouragement. By the time they reached the motorway, she was asleep.

She woke up as they pulled into the car park at Everdene just after midday. As was often the case in October, the weather was dazzling: a bright sun, low in the sky, that gave off a gentle warmth. A delicious breeze that was perfect for kite-flying – the skyline was filled with fluttering colours. Seagulls swooped, cawing triumphantly. The occasional cloud skipped across the periwinkle blue.

'Let's take a walk on the beach,' said Dan. 'Then go to the Ship Aground for some lunch.'

Kirsty nodded. A bit of exercise wouldn't do her any harm. She hadn't done as much as usual this week. She pulled her wellies out of the boot and tugged them on.

'I thought you'd want to get straight in the surf. The waves are great.'

Dan shook his head. 'I'll wait till Liam gets here. You and Helena can get to know each other then. Sit and drink hot chocolate.'

'Sounds perfect.' Kirsty's mouth was watering at the prospect already. The café on the front did amazing hot chocolate, with whipped cream and marshmallows and a Flake stuck in it . . .

Dan took her hand and they walked down the slipway, turning left to follow the beach past the huts.

'Oh my God,' said Kirsty. 'Look, they've painted the first one pink. It's been blue for as long as I can remember.'

'They sold it, didn't they?' said Dan. 'The new owners must have had it painted.'

'It looks amazing.'

They walked towards it. It was a perfect pink. Not brash, but soft. Slightly dusty.

'Lucky things,' sighed Kirsty.

'Let's go and say hello to them,' said Dan. 'Welcome them to Everdene.'

'We can't do that.'

'Why not?'

'Well, I don't know. It just seems a bit . . .'

They were at the bottom of the steps. Kirsty looked at the sign.

'Look! It used to be called The Shack. They've changed it to The Love Shack.'

Dan grinned. It was one of their favourite songs. A summer anthem.

'B52s fans. They've obviously got good taste.'

He started up the stairs.

'Dan – don't. It's embarrassing.'

'Why not? They're obviously like-minded people.'

He had his hand on the doorknob. Kirsty sighed and followed him.

'They're not even in.'

She looked down, puzzled. He had a key. He was opening the lock.

'What are you doing?'

He opened the door. He ushered her inside.

'Happy birthday.'

Kirsty stared at him.

'What?'

'Happy birthday!'

She hesitated.

'We're staying here for the weekend? I thought we'd booked into a B and B?'

She stepped inside, and her breath was taken away.

The whole hut had been completely redone. It was mostly white, with Nantucket-style kitchen units, a huge ponyskin rug on the floor, leather bean bags, a modular sofa covered in crushed white velvet. A vase of white freesias sat on a low coffee table, filling the air with their scent.

'It's totally stunning,' breathed Kirsty.

'Thank you,' said Dan, modestly.

She frowned. He smiled.

'You still don't get it, do you?'

'What?'

'Happy birthday. This is your present. This is your hut.' He rolled his eyes in exasperation. 'I bought it for you.'

Kirsty's hands flew to her mouth.

'Oh my God . . . Dan . . .'

'I figured we spend so much time down here, wasting money on hotels and B and Bs, we might as well make the investment.'

'It's so beautiful.'

She wandered through the hut, touching everything in wonder. He'd thought of every detail, from the Bose iPod dock to the outsize French coffee cups. Not that she would be drinking much coffee over the next few months.

'Dan. I need to tell you something.'

He frowned.

'Don't you like it?'

'Of course I like it. I absolutely love it. I wasn't going to tell you till later, until I'd done another test, just to make sure . . .'

She trailed off, looking a bit bashful.

He could barely get the words out.

'You're having a baby,' he croaked.

She nodded, big fat tears of joy flooding her eyes. And the next moment she found his arms around her, and he was swinging her round, giving great shouts of joy.

'Careful. Careful!' she pleaded, laughing.

'I'm so happy,' he told her. 'I'm so, so happy.'

Later, they sat on the top step outside The Love Shack wrapped up in their warmest jumpers and scarves, Dan with a beer, and Kirsty with elderflower cordial. They watched the waves inching up the beach in the afternoon sun, and imagined the future: small hands in theirs, chubby little legs toddling down to the water's edge. Tiny fingers patting sandcastles into shape; pudgy feet dabbling in rock pools. Kirsty's eyes closed and she leant against Dan. He put his arm around her as she fell asleep again.

A lifetime of sunshine and laughter lay in front of them.

Behind

THE BEACH HUT

I've always been fascinated by beach huts. With their bright colours and their quirky names, they seem to have an optimistic outlook on life – a seaside idyll where nothing can go wrong.

But, of course, it can. As I watched the inhabitants of a row of beach huts last summer, I wondered what really went on behind the gaily painted doors. We all know how quickly a holiday can turn into hell. The pressure to have fun during that precious week away is enormous. And being away from the daily routine, supposedly relaxing, soon becomes a chance to focus on what is really wrong in one's life. Irritating habits become a source of friction, the need for a drink creeps up earlier and earlier: playing happy families is not as easy as it seems.

I wanted to dig a little deeper behind the façade, and reveal the truth behind the picture-postcard perfection. Here was a mini-community – a place where long-established friendships flourished, transient relationships were struck up and holiday romances began. Inside each hut I was going to find a unique story. For one person, their hut is a haven. For another, it is a prison. And with a long tradition of beach huts being handed down in the family, there would also be secrets, grudges, skeletons and rivalries. It was a writer's dream watching the dramas unfold behind the weather-beaten walls – the only problem was going to be where to stop . . .

The British beach hut began as a nod towards modesty, as huts on wheels were trundled down to the sea in order for ladies to change discreetly and slip into the water without fear of losing their reputation. Even Queen Victoria had one, ceremoniously wheeled out on to the beach at Osbourne on the Isle of Wight. Gradually, as bathing became more popular, the huts became more substantial and more permanent, often being constructed from old railway carriages or driftwood, which has given them the iconic appearance we love today.

The south coast in particular is peppered with these eccentric and endearing reminders of a happier age. They don't seem to move with the times, but remain pretty basic, harking back to an era of make-do and mend, peculiarly British in their lack of glamour and creature comforts.

Yet due to a combination of their scarcity and their charm, they have become something of a status symbol these days, as parents hope to recapture the innocence of their youth for their children: all deck chairs, thermos flasks and French cricket. They are also proving to be a sound investment as they hold their price. Huts in particularly desirable areas can invite spirited bidding as potential buyers battle for ownership.

Celebrity beach hut owners include Tracy Emin, who sold her hut at Whitstable to art dealer Charles Saatchi, only for it to be burned in a fire at his warehouse, Keith Richards, who has a hut at West Wittering near Chichester, and of course there is the royal hut at Holkham in Norfolk.

The rules for anyone owning a beach hut can be draconian. Some councils forbid owners to stay in their huts after dark, others restrict occupation to the summer months. And there are often strict guidelines on appearance – one council insists their huts are painted white, another prefers them to be multi-coloured – and woe betide the owner who flouts the regulations.

Prime spots include Southwold in Suffolk and Mudeford in Dorset, where huts can go for over £100,000. Southend and Whitstable become more affordable, with the real bargains to be found up in the northeast. And if you're not quite sure that a beach hut is for you, but you'd like a taste of the experience, then why not rent one for a week?

orget surfing, splashing about in rockpools or building sandcastles. For me, a week on the beach means the opportunity to get stuck into a really good book – or three. The ideal beach read is entirely engrossing yet at the same time undemanding. Here are my recommendations:

Scruples – Judith Krantz

Fingersmith – Sarah Waters

Dark Angel – Sally Beauman

Valley of the Dolls – Jacqueline Susann

The Group – Mary McCarthy

Doctor Zhivago – Boris Pasternak

Madame Bovary – Gustave Flaubert

Rebecca – Daphne du Maurier

Cold Comfort Farm – Stella Gibbons

The Pop Larkin Chronicles – H. E. Bates

The Jeeves Omnibus – P. G. Woodhouse

Miss Marple Omnibus – Agatha Christie

Labyrinth – Kate Mosse

Although kitchen equipment is likely to be limited in a beach hut, food is an essential part of the British summer holiday. Here are a few recipes which mean summer to me:

Banana Pancakes

These are great at any time of day, and are particularly good as a hangover cure!

> 1 250g tub ricotta cheese
>   [which I then use as the cup]
> ¾ cup flour
> ¾ cup milk
> ½ tsp baking powder
> 1 tbsp sugar
> 3 large eggs, separated
>
> 1 tbsp butter
> 3 tbsp brown sugar
> 3 bananas

∾ Combine the dry ingredients in one bowl, and the ricotta, milk and egg yolks in another.

∾ Beat the egg whites until stiff. Combine the wet and dry ingredients, then fold in the egg whites.

7

- Melt some butter in a small frying pan and ladle in just enough mix to cover the surface. Cook for two minutes then toss – if you dare! – and cook the other side.

- Meanwhile, melt remaining butter and the brown sugar in another pan. Halve the bananas lengthways and cook gently till soft.

- Serve each pancake with half a banana, some clotted cream and a generous serving of Jack Johnson.

Crab and Sweetcorn Chowder

This is great brought down to the beach in a flask, especially if the weather is proving a little brisk, and is great for warming through children who have been in the water all day:

1 onion
2 sticks celery
2 large leeks
2 large potatoes – diced
1 pint chicken stock
1 fresh crab
1 tin sweetcorn

∾ Slice the onion, celery and leeks and soften in olive oil. Add the diced potato and cook gently for several minutes, then add the stock and leave to simmer until the potato is soft but still has a little bite. You can add a pinch of celery salt or dry English mustard at this point. Flake the white and brown crabmeat together and add to the chowder. Heat through, then add the sweetcorn. Finish with a swirl of cream if you like.

Pizzaladiere

This is my own hybrid of pizza and the Provençal pissaladière made famous by Elizabeth David. Serve for lunch, or cut into smaller squares and have with an aperitif.

    1 pack ready rolled puff pastry
    1 tin chopped tomatoes
    1 200g bag grated cheddar and mozzarella
    1 tub fresh anchovies
    1 tub pitted black olives

∾ Strain the tomatoes of their excess juice then spread on to the sheet of pastry. Sprinkle over the cheese. Top with anchovies in an artful criss-cross pattern, then stud with the olives. Cook for twenty minutes in a hot-ish oven until the base is nice and crisp, then cut into slices or squares.

∾ If you're not an anchovy fan, then try it with slices of chorizo and chargrilled artichoke. In fact, pretty much anything from the deli counter goes!

White chocolate and raspberry cake

This cake is squidgy and gooey and will keep for ages wrapped in foil. Although it won't last two minutes once you've started it . . .

250g butter
150g white chocolate
250ml milk
1 tsp good vanilla essence
300g caster sugar
250g self-raising flour
1 tsp baking powder
2 large eggs
1 punnet raspberries

∾ Melt the butter, chocolate, milk, vanilla and sugar in a pan carefully and stir until thoroughly mixed and smooth. Sift the flour and baking powder into a bowl, then pour the chocolate mix in and stir thoroughly. Add the two beaten eggs, then mix the raspberries in until they are evenly spread.

∾ Pour into a greased and lined 23-inch tin, and bake at gas mark 3, 160 degrees for about an hour. Check towards the end and cover with foil if the top is browning. The cake is supposed to be squidgy but it might need a little longer if it's still runny – mine have never turned out the same twice, but always good!

∾ Serve with extra raspberries and lashings of clotted cream. Then go for a run.

COCKTAILS

Cocktails are an essential part of beach hut life.
I always keep a bottle of vodka, a bag of limes, some
sprigs of mint and an assortment of juices – orange,
cranberry, grapefruit, tropical – as well as a couple
of bottles of ginger beer, for making up a jug of
something cool and refreshing if guests drop in.
But if you fancy something a bit more sophisticated,
here are some ideas:

Cointreau Caipirinha

This is perfect to sip as the sun goes down, and takes
the edge off nicely.

2 shots Cointreau
fresh lime
crushed ice

❧ Squeeze two lime quarters into a glass.
Add crushed ice, then pour over Cointreau
and add a fresh lime quarter for garnish.

Campari Crush

I love Campari for its glorious incarnadine colour and sophisticated, Côte d'Azur-ishness. This is ideal if you find it a little bitter on its own.

> 2 shots Campari
> 1 shot Limoncello
> 2 lemon wedges

∾ Muddle the lemon wedges slightly in a glass. Pour over Campari and Limoncello.

Bikini Martini

This should break the ice at any beach party.

> 1 shot gin
> 1 shot Blue Curaçao
> 1 shot peach schnapps

∾ Add measures to a cocktail shaker with crushed ice and shake. Strain into a martini glass with a slice of orange.

Michelada

This was introduced to me by my friends Simon and Alice, who discovered it in Mexico.

You will need:

> *your favourite Mexican beer*
> *limes*
> *Tabasco*
> *ice*
> *salt*

∾ Salt the rim of your glass. Half fill with crushed ice. Add a smidgeon of Tabasco, then squeeze half a lime over. Fill the glass with beer. Relax!